New Mexico Weddings

Janet Lee Barton

ISBN 978-1-60260-107-9

Scripture quotations are taken from the King James Version of the Bible.

Cover image: Owaki/Kulla/Corbis

Published by Barbour Publishing, Inc., P.O. Box 719, Uhrichsville, Ohio 44683, www.barbourbooks.com

Our mission is to publish and distribute inspirational products offering exceptional value and biblical encouragement to the masses.

Printed in the United States of America.

Dear Readers,

I've lived in states all over the south, and I now reside in Oklahoma, but having been born and raised in New Mexico, it will always be home to me. When I began this series, the only place that seemed natural to set it in—even in the fictional town of Sweet Springs—was New Mexico. Just as I love my home state, so do the characters in all the stories in *New Mexico Weddings*. It's their home. The Brelands and Tanners make up a big, loving family and because these stories are so connected, it does my heart good to see them all in one book. Their love for the Lord is strengthened through each story and becomes strong and steadfast. Their love for each other is constant, and their loving, meddling, and matchmaking is something they just can't seem to help.

I hope you enjoy Jake and Sara's story in *Family Circle* as they struggle to put the past behind them and find a future together; Luke and Rae in *Family Ties* as they fall in love—in spite of the family complications with his aunt and her father; and Eric and Lacy in *Family Reunion*, who find love with the help of a young boy who needs a whole family. With a few more romances thrown in for good measure, these families find that falling in love isn't just for the young. And while life-changing events bring them home to family, it's love that makes them stay and the Lord who guides them to true happiness.

Thank you for choosing to read *New Mexico Weddings*,
Janet Lee Barton

Family Circle

Dedication

To my Lord and Savior for showing me the way.
To my family for their love and encouragement always.
To my church family for rejoicing with me, and
To the real "Teddy Bear Brigade" for your inspiration.
I love you all.

Chapter 1

Jake Breland pulled himself out of the nightmare, drenched with sweat and shaking all over. His heart beat so hard he could hear it. That meant he was alive, didn't it?

Slinging the tangled covers aside, he stumbled down the hall to Meggie's room. The night-light cast a warm glow over the room, and as soon as he heard her soft, even breathing coming from the crib, he let go of the breath he'd been holding. Meggie was all right and he *was* alive. It was just the nightmare. Again. The nightmare was coming so often now, he dreaded going to bed.

Jake bent over and inhaled the sweet baby scent of his daughter. He forced himself not to pick her up and hold her. There was no sense ruining her peaceful sleep. As he watched her, his own heartbeat returned to normal. He leaned over and placed a featherlight kiss on her forehead. Meggie stirred, and afraid she'd sense his presence and wake up, Jake quietly backed out of the room. Pausing at the door to his bedroom, he shook his head and made his way down the darkened hall to the kitchen. He wouldn't be able to sleep after that dream. Besides, he had some thinking to do.

Flipping the light switch on, he looked at the clock and sighed. He might as well call it a night and put the coffee on. Leaning against the cabinet, he waited for the coffee to finish brewing and shivered as the cool night air hit his still-damp back.

He rubbed his temples and closed his eyes. All he could see was a replay of the nightmare, Meggie crying and crying and crawling all over the apartment while he lay unconscious or dead in his bed. It always ended the same—with Meggie crying out, and no one there to hear her cries. No one.

Jake shuddered. What if it were real? What if something did happen to him and no one was nearby to take care of Meggie?

He hadn't been able to find a suitable housekeeper since Mrs. Morrow broke her arm, so he'd had no choice but to put Meggie in day care. He doubted the staff would check on her if she missed a day. They'd just figure he'd kept her at home. It might be days or weeks before someone would find Meggie. By then what could happen to her?

Jake shook his head, pushing the horrible images from his mind. The thought of Meggie having no one to care for her was more than he could deal with. He poured his coffee and wandered into the living room. Picking up the remote, he turned the TV on, keeping the volume low, but he stared at the screen without seeing.

When had these nightmares started? Not in the first few weeks following Melissa's death. He'd been too busy trying to accept the loss of his wife and be both mother and father to his newborn baby to sleep much at all. In the following months he'd had the dreams sporadically, but not until recently, when there'd been talk of opening an office overseas and putting him in charge, had they started coming almost nightly.

Suddenly he knew that wasn't an option. He wasn't taking Meggie halfway around the world, and he wasn't leaving her. He didn't need a partnership in a prestigious law firm. He needed more time with his daughter.

Back home, he wouldn't have to set up his own practice. His cousin John had asked him to come into partnership with him more than once. With two of them to share the workload, there'd be more time for Meggie.

Jake sighed and ran his fingers through his tousled hair. He'd never planned or wanted to move back home. Now he had his daughter to think of. He couldn't put it off any longer.

He might not have family here in Albuquerque to make sure Meggie was all right, but he had them in southern New Mexico, in his small hometown of Sweet Springs. Family who'd offered over and over to help. He had to make sure that if anything happened to him, she'd have someone right there, right away. It was time. Time to go home.

Sara Tanner tied off the embroidery thread and looked at her work with a critical eye. She held it up for her grandfather's inspection. "How's it look, Grandpa? If you were two or three, would it appeal to you?"

William Oliver lowered the newspaper he'd been reading, looked over the top of his bifocals, and chuckled. "It appeals to me at seventy, darlin'. I'm sure it would appeal to me if I were a child." He got up from the kitchen table and brought the coffeepot over to refill their cups.

"They are cute, aren't they? I'm so glad we decided to do this." Sara slipped the finished teddy bear into a bag with the others she'd made that week.

"You ladies at church do some real good things. I bet those little bears will mean a lot to the small children brought into the emergency room."

Sara took a sip of coffee and nodded. "That's what we're hoping. The hospital thought it was a great idea. We'll know for sure soon. I'm going to pick up the rest and deliver them tomorrow afternoon."

"Tomorrow?" Her grandfather slapped his forehead. "I forgot to tell you—Nora called. You've been summoned to lunch tomorrow."

Sara sighed and shook her head. "That's an apt description of her invitations, if I ever heard one. I dread going. She's just going to try to convince me to move out to the ranch again."

"That's the last place you need to be."

"I know, Grandpa, and I've told her it's not going to happen. I'm running out of ways to say no, but she was Wade's mother. I can't just tell her to get lost."

Her grandfather grinned and nodded. "Even though that's exactly what you should do."

Sara chuckled. "No, I shouldn't, but I have to admit I'd certainly like to at times."

"Well, darlin', I don't like the way she wants to control your life. You've had enough of that."

Sara reached across the table to squeeze his hand. "I'm not going to let her control me, Grandpa. I promise." She made the promise to herself, too. Her mother-in-law could be overpowering at times. She changed the subject. "What are you going to do tomorrow?"

"I'm not sure. I have my garden planted. Ben and Lydia are away at a livestock auction, so we won't be having our regular chess game. Got plenty of time on my hands. Want me to go with you to Nora's?"

Sara chuckled. Bless his heart. "That's a great idea, Grandpa. Do you think you can put up with her for that long?"

"Nora's no problem for me. I'll be fine. Besides, that cook of hers is worth it."

Sara laughed, circling the table to hug him. "I don't know what I'd do without you."

He hugged her back. "Nope, it's the other way around, Sara. I was just rambling around this old house 'til you moved in. You take real good care of me."

Tears pooled in Sara's eyes. They were a pair, the two of them. She knew who'd been taking care of whom. Until a few months ago, she'd been the one on the receiving end of all the care from her grandfather, her husband's family, and her church family. "Thank you, Grandpa. I love you."

"Guess I'll be calling it a night," he said after clearing his throat. "I love you, honey. I'm proud of the way you're getting on with things." He nodded his head and pushed away from the table. "Real proud. Just don't let Nora tell you how to live your life."

"I won't. You sleep well." She gave him another hug and took their cups to the sink.

It took only a few minutes to clean up the kitchen. Not yet ready for bed, Sara slipped out to sit in the front-porch swing. Putting it in motion, she caught the delicate smell of the lilac bush behind her.

It felt so good to notice small things again: the sweet smell of the honeysuckle climbing the trellis, the soft feel of the gentle breeze. How bright the stars shone down. Spring was here. Everything was coming to life, and for the first time in a long time, Sara felt alive.

Bowing her head, she said a silent prayer of thanksgiving for Grandpa, all of the Tanners and Brelands, and her church family. It'd taken them all to get her through the past year. She wouldn't have made it without them. Most of all, she thanked the Lord for seeing to it that she'd had them to help her.

She couldn't wait until fall, when she'd be returning to her teaching job at the high school. She'd just have to keep herself busy until then—and convince Nora that she was not moving to the ranch. Period. Easier said than done. Her mother-in-law did not like to take no for an answer. Sara could just picture the two of them living together. Two widows growing old together. The thought drew a shudder from her. Maybe she would cancel tomorrow's lunch with Nora, after all. There would be other lunches. There always were.

Sara kept the swing in motion until her eyes grew heavy. She hadn't had trouble sleeping for several months, but still, she didn't like to go to bed until she was almost asleep on her feet. Entering the house quietly, she locked the door and went upstairs. She'd sleep well tonight. She was sure of it.

Sara felt she'd taken the coward's way out by canceling her lunch with Nora, but her excuse of having to pick up those adorable teddy bears was a valid one. Besides, she didn't want lunch with Nora to put a damper on her good mood.

One more stop and she'd have the last of the teddy bears gathered up. She was excited about taking them to the hospital. All of the ladies had been so eager to help make them, and the hospital was thrilled with the offer. If having a teddy bear to cuddle while receiving medical attention could ease the fear of just one child, their work would be well worth the hours spent.

She pulled to a stop at the curb in front of Ellie Tanner's house and hurried down the walk and up the porch steps. "Gram?" Sara called, opening the screen door. "You here?"

"Back here, Sara. In the kitchen," came the reply.

Bypassing the living room, Sara hurried through the dining room into the sunny kitchen at the back of the house. The sight of Gram sitting at the table watching an adorable baby girl attempt to feed herself stopped Sara in her tracks. Her heart twisted and turned, and she forgot to breathe until Gram turned in her seat and said, "Sara?"

Sara forced the air out of her lungs and tried to smile.

Gram quickly got up and led her to a chair. "Oh, my dear Sara. I'm so sorry. I didn't even think to warn you."

Sara blinked quickly to hide the tears that threatened and shook her head. "No, Gram. It's fine. I. . .I just didn't expect to see a baby at your table." She forced her gaze off the child.

Sara patted the older woman's hand that still rested on her shoulder. "I'm fine, Gram. Really. But who is this little beauty? Who are you doing a favor for now?"

Gram gave Sara a warm hug and took her seat once more, handing the baby another chicken stick and being rewarded with a huge grin.

"This is my great-granddaughter Meggie, Jake's daughter. This is Sara, Meggie." She turned back to face Sara. "He finally came to his senses and decided to move back home. He's going to join John's firm as a partner." Gram handed the baby a cup of milk as she continued her explanation. "They're discussing it all over lunch."

Jake. Back here. Sara's heart seemed to screech to a stop before it jumped into high gear. Her gaze snapped back to the baby. *Jake's baby.* The little girl had his dark hair, his eyes, and his coloring. Meggie grinned at her, and Sara saw a miniature dimple—exactly like the one Jake had. Like the one she used to tease him about, just so he'd grin at her. She'd stand on tiptoe and plant a quick kiss on the dimple before it disappeared. She shook her head to clear the vision she'd conjured in her mind.

Sara wasn't sure she was ready to see her first love after all these years and all that had happened. She started to her feet just as Gram set a cup of tea in front of her. When had Gram made it? How long had she been sitting there staring at the baby?

She tried to sound calm. "I just came by to pick up the teddy bears, Gram. I really need to get to the hospital."

"After you drink that tea, child. You aren't driving anywhere right now. Not until I know you're all right."

Realizing she was not in any shape to drive, Sara nodded her head and took a sip of the hot, sweet liquid. *Lord, please get me through this. You've helped me with everything else, please help me over this new hurdle.*

"Sara."

Sara pulled her gaze from the baby, who shyly glanced from Gram to Sara and back again.

"Yes, ma'am?"

"Is it seeing a baby or the fact that Jake is moving back that's upsetting you?"

Gram always did have a way of zeroing in on a problem. Sara was saved from answering when the baby suddenly let out a wail and banged the tray, sending her food flying and milk splashing. The wail quickly turned to giggles, and the baby started bouncing up and down in her seat.

Sara couldn't help but laugh. Milk was dripping off the tray and running down the baby's face, and Gram's lap held an assortment of finger food.

"Why, you little minx!" Gram laughed and looked around as if unsure what to do next.

"I'll clean up the mess, Gram. It won't take a minute."

Sara grabbed the washcloth the older woman had handy and started to wipe off the baby's face while Gram emptied her lap, still chuckling.

Sara's heart turned over as Meggie reached out and clung to her blouse, trying to climb out of the high chair. The baby's grip tightened as Gram tried to take her.

In that moment, Sara's heart melted. "It's okay. I'll take her."

Gram chuckled. "I don't think she's giving you much choice. This one has a mind of her own." She took the cloth from Sara to finish cleaning up the mess.

Sara managed to unhook the safety belt keeping the baby in place, and Meggie lunged, climbing into Sara's arms. The baby held on for dear life and hid her face in the curve of Sara's neck. Sara's arms tightened around Meggie, and she murmured soothing noises to the baby, finding that the one thing she'd been avoiding for months was exactly what she needed. The feel of a baby in her arms. Closing her eyes, she cuddled Meggie close and sighed deeply. *Lord, thank You. You always seem to know what I need, when I need it.*

Finished with the cleanup, Gram turned to Sara. "I can take her now." She held her arms out to Meggie, but the baby clung to Sara.

"If you don't mind, I'll just hold her a little longer."

"You're sure?" Gram asked, concern etching her face.

Sara nodded and took her seat again. "I'm sure. I think this is just what we both need."

Gram looked closely at the two and nodded. "I think you may be right." She freshened up their tea and peeked at Meggie. "Her eyes are closed. I wonder if she's asleep or just playing possum."

Sara gently tightened her hold on the baby. "Doesn't matter to me. I'll just enjoy holding her close as long as she'll let me."

Gram nodded and tears gathered in her eyes. "Sara, you will have another one of your own, one day. The Lord will see to that."

Sara rubbed Meggie's back lightly, enjoying the feel of the warm little body in her arms. "I hope so, Gram. He brought me here today, and He knew how badly I needed the feel of a baby in my arms, even before I did." She closed her eyes and inhaled the sweet, powder scent of Meggie.

"I guess we all thought it would be too painful for you. Maybe we've been a bit overprotective."

"No, Gram. You've all been wonderful. I don't know what I would have done without you."

"I'm just glad Jake has realized he can use some help."

Not wanting to be rude, Sara forced herself to respond to the change of subject. "Will he be staying with you or at the ranch with Luke?"

"He's going to stay here with me." Gram's smile showed her pleasure at having her grandson back in town. "He says he wants to find a house in town or build one, since his office will be here. He doesn't want to commute back and forth from the ranch."

Although unsure of how she felt about seeing Jake again, Sara still felt curious about his reasons for coming back. He'd said once that he couldn't wait to get out of Sweet Springs. "What made him decide to move back? Did he say?"

"Just that Meggie needed to know her family, and he knows someone will be here for her if something should happen to him." Gram sighed. "He's not the same Jake. He seems bitter, angry."

"That's not so unusual, Gram. I had to get over a lot of that, too."

"But that's just it, Sara. You have gotten on with your life. You are dealing with it. Jake hasn't."

"I had all of you to help me."

Gram nodded her head. "And you let the Lord heal you. I don't think Jake is on speaking terms with Him. And without that, I'm not sure how much help the rest of us can be to him."

Sara pushed thoughts of how much Jake had hurt her to the back of her mind. That was the past and had nothing to do with the present. She could relate to the pain he was going through now and felt only sorrow that he might be at odds with the Lord. "We'll just have to pray. You know the Lord doesn't let go of His children."

The older woman patted Sara's hand. "I do know that, but I seemed to have forgotten for the moment. Thank you for reminding me." She reached over and brushed her fingers through the fine hair of the now gently snoring baby and smiled at Sara. "She's certainly taken up with you. You'll be all right while I gather up the teddy bears?"

Sara glanced down at the sleeping baby and smiled. "We'll be fine. I'm in no hurry to let her go."

As Gram left the room, Sara took in every detail of the sweet-smelling infant. Little hands with the tiny indentations where knuckles would one day be. She rubbed a finger over a soft, pudgy hand, and Meggie smiled in her sleep. Fine, dark hair curled softly around the cherubic face. Thick, dark eyelashes hid midnight blue eyes that Sara knew she'd inherited from Jake. She really was a beauty.

Sara's sigh was ragged. A baby with no mother. A mother with no baby. Each receiving comfort from one another. She brushed her lips gently over Meggie's velvety cheek, and try as she might, she couldn't stop the tear that escaped and slid down her face.

Hearing footsteps in the hall, Sara quickly brushed her hand across her cheek, not wanting Gram to catch her crying. She forced a smile and looked up as the footsteps came to a stop just inside the kitchen door.

The breath caught in her throat as she looked up into the eyes of Jake Breland.

Jake returned to his grandmother's house feeling better than he had in months. He was surprised at how good it felt to be home. He was looking forward to the partnership he and his cousin John were forming. Meggie was with Gram. There would always be someone in Sweet Springs to care for her if he couldn't. A huge weight had been lifted, and he found himself whistling as he entered the house. He heard a noise coming from the kitchen and headed there. Just inside the door, he stopped in his tracks.

Jake had known this moment would come. He'd tried to prepare himself for seeing her again. But no way had he prepared himself for the sight of Sara holding his child. The woman he'd loved so long ago cradling the child of the woman who'd come between them. How could something that seemed so wrong look so right? What was she doing here, holding his daughter so close?

"Sara." His stomach did a nosedive and he clenched his fists. "Is something wrong with Meggie? Where's Gram? Is she all right?"

Jake watched the color drain from Sara's face as she quickly shook her head. "Everything is fine. Gram went upstairs to get some things I have to deliver to the hospital. That's what I stopped by for," she quickly assured him.

Jake nodded and relaxed his fingers, relieved that nothing was wrong. "I see you've met my Meggie."

Sara nodded and looked down at his sleeping daughter. "She's beautiful, Jake. I'm. . .sorry about Melissa. I should have written, called. . . ."

Jake shook his head as he crossed the room. "Don't worry about it." He knew his words sounded gruff. He couldn't help it. He wasn't sure what to say to Sara after all this time. "I'm sorry about Wade."

He watched Sara swallow and saw his pain mirrored in her eyes. She nodded. "I know." She bit her bottom lip before continuing. "I didn't know you were moving back to Sweet Springs. Gram just told me."

Jake rubbed the back of his neck, feeling more uncomfortable by the minute. "I didn't know I was moving back until a few weeks ago, and I didn't tell anyone until I got here," he said, wondering why he felt the need to explain his presence.

Seeing Sara again made him wonder if he'd made the right decision. But one glance at Meggie, and he knew he'd had no choice. It was for her sake he'd decided to come home.

Seeing more questions in Sara's eyes, questions he knew he might never be able to answer, Jake turned away to pour himself a cup of coffee. "She wasn't too much for Gram, was she?"

"No, I don't think so." Sara chuckled. "She got a little exuberant with her lunch and dumped most of it onto Gram's lap, but that was nothing."

Jake smiled, even as he noted the hint of nervousness in Sara's voice. "That's my Meggie. Mealtime is an adventure for her."

Turning back to Sara, he leaned against the cabinet. The years had been good to her. She didn't look much older than the last time he'd seen her. Auburn hair was pulled back into a clasp at the base of her neck, instead of up into a ponytail as she'd once worn it. Her deep green eyes were still as large and inviting as the creek on a hot summer day. Her smile seemed strained, yet her presence was calmer, more serene than he remembered, despite the pain in her eyes.

He looked away and cleared his throat. "I didn't give Gram much notice that I was moving back. I hope it won't be too much for her to help me out with Meggie for a little while, until I can get settled and find a housekeeper." Was Gram all he could talk about? He could remember a time when he'd had no trouble finding things to say to Sara. If there had been a lull in the conversation, he certainly hadn't stood around wondering what to say next. He'd have pulled her into his arms and kissed her. His gaze strayed to her full lips. Yes, that's what he would have done. But he couldn't do that now.

"I don't think there's much that Gram isn't willing or able to take on," Sara said, breaking into his thoughts. "She's delighted to have a baby to make over." She motioned toward the hallway. "She should be back down soon."

Jake knew she was as anxious for Gram's presence as he was. When he'd come into the kitchen to find Sara holding Meggie, it'd been obvious that she felt completely at home. Now she seemed as uncomfortable as he felt. He should know that nothing stayed the same. The easy relationship he and Sara had once shared was a thing of the past. Like it or not, he was going to have to deal with it. Just like he'd dealt with everything else. Alone.

When he glanced at Sara again, he saw that her attention was on Meggie, and the tenderness with which she looked down at his daughter was so compelling, it reached out to him. Suddenly, he felt threatened. Without knowing why, he was filled with a compulsion to hold Meggie in his arms.

He crossed the distance between them in two strides and held out his arms. "I'll take her now," he said abruptly.

Trying not to wake Meggie, Sara stood and quickly shifted the baby into Jake's arms. The flood of longing she felt in relinquishing the little girl didn't surprise her. She knew it was natural. But she was totally unprepared for the flash of awareness shooting up her arm when she brushed against Jake's arm during the transfer. Stepping back, she hoped he wouldn't notice her shaking. She wished she could just leave without the teddy bears she'd come to collect, but that would raise all kinds of questions with Gram—questions she wasn't ready to face. Sara forced herself to sit back down at the table and take a sip of her now lukewarm tea.

"I'll just put her in her crib," Jake said, his voice sounding husky. "I'll see what's holding up Gram while I'm up there." He turned and started out of the room. "Good-bye, Sara."

"Good-bye, Jake."

Only it wasn't good-bye, Sara thought as she watched him leave, his back stiff and straight. She and Jake both lived here now. Sweet Springs was a small town. There was no way they could avoid seeing each other. Obviously he was as uncomfortable around her as she was near him. Wishing things could be different didn't make them so, and she was going to have to get used to running into Jake and Meggie.

Sara took a deep breath. She could handle it. But only with the Lord's help. She knew she didn't have the strength to do it on her own.

"Sara, I'm sorry I took so long. I had to finish up one little bear's face." Gram bustled into the kitchen. She took one look at Sara and plunked down in a chair next to her. "I ran into Jake upstairs. Did he say something to upset you?"

Sara shook her head. Jake hadn't said much of anything. But neither had she. "No, Gram. I think we were both just a little uncomfortable with each other."

Gram nodded in agreement. "That's to be expected. You were both young and in love once. Then you went your separate ways."

"How did you know—"

"You young people. You think we old ones don't have eyes?" Gram chuckled. "It was obvious. The whole family thought an engagement was imminent. Then Jake went off to college and ended up marrying Melissa, and you married Wade a year later. I always wondered if you married him on the rebound," she stated bluntly.

"Gram! I loved Wade. He was a wonderful husband." Sara's insides churned. She just couldn't deal with this now, not after seeing Jake again. She had to get out of here.

"I know you loved him, dear. And you were a wonderful wife to him, but. . . I also know you once loved Jake. . .and that he loved you." Gram reached over and patted Sara's hand. "I'm not trying to meddle. I'm just saying that the uncomfortable feelings won't last forever. You and Jake care too much about each other."

Sara stood and gathered up her purse and the bag of teddy bears, shaking her head. "I don't know. I think we've both changed too much." She bent and kissed the top of the older woman's head. "But don't you worry about it. Okay?"

"I'll walk you out." Gram rose from the chair. "You be sure and let me know how they like those little bears, you hear?"

They made their way back to the front door, and Gram gave Sara a hug. "Don't you let the fact that Jake is here keep you away, Sara. You're family too, you know."

Only by marriage. And since Wade's death, not even that. But she loved Gram and didn't want to cause her any pain by reminding her. "Thanks. I'll let you know how our bears go over." After a quick good-bye, Sara forced herself to step sedately down the walk rather than running away like she wanted to.

Starting her car, she took off and tried to shake the sudden feeling of loss that invaded her. She loved Gram and her extended family, but it wasn't going to be the same now. It couldn't be—not with Jake back in town.

Jake stepped back from the hall window and started down the stairs, relieved that Sara was leaving yet feeling like a heel. He'd been rude to her. He knew that. It'd just been such a shock to see her sitting in the kitchen, completely at home, holding his child in her arms. The aura of peace surrounding them had pulled a yearning from him so strong, so unexpected that he'd felt lost, alone, on the outside looking in.

Only holding Meggie close and rocking her for a few minutes before he put her to bed had helped. He was just now beginning to realize that he needed Meggie as much as she needed him. She was the only thing in his life that made it worth living.

He entered the kitchen to find his grandmother sipping a cup of tea. He poured himself a fresh cup of coffee and joined her at the table.

"Is Meggie still sleeping?" she asked.

Jake leaned back in his chair and nodded. "I guess the trip wore her out."

"Changes do that to children, sometimes. She sure took a liking to Sara."

Knowing his grandmother, Jake sensed there was more coming. "Seemed like it. Sara certainly seems to feel at home here."

Gram looked him in the eye. "Why shouldn't she? She was married to your cousin. She's family."

Jake felt defensive. "Only by marriage."

"Jake Breland!" Gram set her cup down so hard, tea sloshed over the side. "When did that ever make a difference in this family?"

Jake knew it never had. He wouldn't have wanted it to. But the bad feelings he'd had for Wade colored his judgment and made him continue. "Well, Wade's gone now."

"Yes. He is. And if it'd been you instead of Melissa who'd died, she would still be a part of this family. Jake, I can't believe how insensitive you've become."

"You're right, Gram. I'm sorry." And he was. But he still couldn't come to terms with the past. Not after seeing Sara again.

"Well, that's something. Maybe there is still enough of the old Jake left to feel some compassion. After all, Sara has gone through as much pain as you have. More."

"How could that be?"

Gram closed her eyes and shook her head. "You lost your wife in childbirth, and I know it was devastating." When she opened her eyes, tears filled them. She reached over and covered one of his hands with hers. "I know it still is, Jake. But you have your child. Sara not only lost Wade in that car accident, she lost the baby she was carrying."

Chapter 2

Jake's stomach clenched. Lowering his head, he willed himself to swallow past the knot in his throat and breathe normally. Sara had lost a baby. He hadn't known she was pregnant. No wonder she'd looked so bereft when he'd taken Meggie from her. Tears stung the back of his eyes, and he blinked rapidly to hold them back. Once he thought he had control, he looked at his grandmother. "Why didn't someone tell me?"

Gram ran her hand over her own teary eyes. "You were dealing with your own pain, away from us all. We didn't think you needed anything more to deal with."

Jake propped his elbows on the table and cradled his head with his hands. He thought about Meggie sleeping peacefully upstairs, and for the first time in a long time, he thanked the Lord for sparing him the pain Sara must feel.

"Did she lose it in the wreck?" Jake realized how little he knew about Wade's death. He didn't even know if Sara was with him.

"Because of it, yes." Gram got up to refill his coffee cup. When she sat back down, she clasped her hands together. "Wade was killed instantly, but Sara was put in intensive care. There were internal injuries. I know they did the best they could, but she lost the baby the next day."

She wiped her eyes with her apron. "We thought we were going to lose Sara too. Only the Lord and prayer brought her through."

Jake cleared his throat. "She seems to be dealing with it all very well." Except for when he'd taken Meggie from her.

Gram nodded. "She's come a long way, Jake. A long way. Today was the first time she's held a baby since she lost her own. I didn't think to warn her Meggie was here before she came to get the teddy bears. But they took to each other right off, and she said she'd been needing to hold a baby for so long."

Jake walked over to the open back door. Leaning against the doorframe, he looked out on the backyard and shook his head. "I wish I'd known, Gram."

Maybe he'd have thought before he practically yanked Meggie away from Sara. What must she be thinking? He hadn't even mentioned being sorry about her losing the baby. He was going to have to talk to her, try to explain.

The front screen door slammed, and they heard footsteps and voices heading for the kitchen. His brother Luke and cousin John were arguing over the pros and cons of their favorite baseball teams as they reached the kitchen doorway.

"Shh." Gram put her finger to her mouth. "We have a sleeping baby upstairs and you two sound as though you're trying to be heard over the crowd at that game you're talking about."

The two men looked at each other and shrugged, tiptoeing the rest of the way into the kitchen.

"Sorry, Gram." Luke bent down and gave her a kiss and a hug. He grinned at Jake. "Hi, big brother. When's the little darlin' due to wake up? I sure would like to see her."

"So would I," John added. "We came over just to see her." He pulled two cups out of the cabinet and filled them for himself and Luke. "And to see if Gram would take pity on us bachelors and invite us to supper."

She got up from the table and thumped him on the shoulder. "When have you ever had to ask?"

John chuckled and gave Gram a kiss on the cheek, being careful not to slosh coffee on her. "It's so good to know we're always welcome at your table."

"You are. As long as you remember I just cook. You three have cleanup duty."

Luke saluted her. "Yes, ma'am!" He kissed her other cheek.

Gram shook her head and went about getting supper started.

"You're awful quiet, Jake. Not regretting moving back already, are you?" John asked.

Jake shook his head in response to his cousin's question, although he was wondering if he'd made a major mistake. It'd been much harder than he'd realized it would be to see Sara again. And now he was going to have to see her sooner than he'd like so he could apologize for this afternoon.

"Gram just told me about Sara. About her losing the baby. I didn't know." Jake looked pointedly at his brother.

"Yeah, well, you had a lot to deal with about that time," Luke replied.

"Still, someone should have told me. I didn't even tell her I was sorry about the baby when I saw her today." Jake saw Luke and John exchange a look.

"I'm sorry, Jake. We just didn't know how to go about it," Luke said. "There was so much grief in the family around that time. Sara will understand."

Would she? Jake hoped so. But he was going to have to explain soon. He couldn't let her think he was totally unfeeling.

A cry from the second floor signaled Meggie was awake. All three men jumped to their feet. Jake was first up the stairs with Luke right behind him. John tried to overtake Luke but was pushed back.

"Hey, John, I'm the uncle," Luke protested. "You're just a cousin. You have to wait your turn."

The conversation drifted down to the kitchen where Gram was busy pulling out a skillet. She rolled her eyes and chuckled. Boys would be boys. Luke and John would be good for Jake. He needed the bantering, teasing love of his family. They'd do all they could to help him adjust to moving back. With the Lord's help, he'd heal.

Sara felt a little better as she left the hospital. At least for a short while she'd been able to push Jake to the back of her mind. The bears had been a big hit with the nurses on duty. She'd even seen how well they would go over with the children when little Ricky Monroe was brought in with a gash on his head. He'd been climbing up to his tree house when his foot slipped and he fell, scraping his head in the process. He'd been really frightened of being sewn up until the nurse handed him the little bear to hold on to. He was so busy checking it out, the stitches were finished before he knew it.

The ladies would be so pleased. She reminded herself to call Gram later, hoping Jake wouldn't answer the phone. *Jake.*

She still couldn't believe he was back in town. Gram was right; he'd changed. He seemed older than his years, aloof and lonely. He was very protective of Meggie; that was obvious. Or maybe she was misreading him. Maybe he just hadn't wanted *her* to hold his child.

Sara sighed. So much had changed. Neither of them were the same people they'd been all those years ago. She didn't know this Jake at all. Still, her heart went out to him. She could understand having to carve a new life out for yourself when all you really wanted was your old one. It wasn't easy, but it had to be done. She knew she'd never be able to do it without the help of the Lord and Grandpa and Wade's family—Jake's family, too. Would he be willing to share them now that he was home?

Sara pulled in the drive and hurried into the house. It was time to start supper, and she couldn't worry about it now. She'd leave it all in the Lord's hands.

The mouth-watering smell of homemade stew greeted her as she entered the kitchen. Her grandfather turned from checking on a pan of corn bread in the oven.

"Grandpa, I'm sorry I'm late getting home."

"No problem, darlin'. I was just waiting until you drove up to finish it up. Gave me something to do."

Sara hugged him and started setting the table. "I appreciate it, Grandpa. I would have been finished sooner, but I was at Gram's longer than I expected."

He nodded. "Ellie called a little while ago to see if you were back yet. She told me Jake and his baby girl are moving back." Grandpa took a seat at the table. "Said you two took to each other right off."

"Oh, Grandpa, she's adorable." Sara chuckled and told him about Meggie's lunch as she joined him at the table. "She grabbed hold of me and wouldn't let go. It felt so good to hold her. You know?"

Grandpa patted her hand. "Hindsight is always better than foresight. We erred on the side of caution, I guess, keeping babies and little ones away from you. We were just afraid it would be too painful, Sara."

"I know. But it was just what I needed."

Grandpa cleared his throat. "What about Jake? How does he seem?"

The timer went off, and Sara got up to take the corn bread out of the oven, glad for a minute or two to regroup. She placed the pan on a pad in the center of the table. "He's still struggling, I think."

"I guess he's been trying to deal with it all on his own. Maybe now he's home, we can help," Grandpa suggested.

Sara ladled the stew into bowls and brought them to the table while Grandpa cut the corn bread. Once they were seated again, he offered the blessing and asked the Lord to help them to help Jake in whatever way was needed.

"I hope he lets his family help him now that he's home," Sara said. "I can't imagine how hard the last year would have been on my own." She shook her head.

"Ellie said he's going to look for a house or build one in town."

"That's what she told me. He'll be staying with her for now. He seems a little concerned that Gram might not be up to keeping Meggie all day."

"Ellie? I don't think there's much that woman isn't up to."

"She's something, isn't she?"

"She sure is."

Something about the way he spoke made Sara look at her grandfather more closely. Could it be he was interested in Gram? They both went to the seniors class at church on Tuesday mornings and served on several committees together. Was there romance in the air? Sara tried to stifle a small chuckle.

"What? Did you say something, darlin'?"

She shook her head. "I was just agreeing with you."

The phone rang and Sara went to answer it, moaning inwardly at the sound of her mother-in-law's voice on the other end.

"Sara dear, did you get the teddy bears delivered safe and sound?" Nora asked.

Sara knew that wasn't the reason her mother-in-law had called, but she went along with it. "I did. They were a big hit, too."

"That's good, dear. I heard something today."

"Oh? What did you hear?" Nora was always on top of anything new that happened around town. She made it her business to know everyone else's. Sara admonished herself for her unkind thoughts, but they were true. Nora seemed to keep up with everyone and everything without having to leave the ranch.

"Jake is back in town."

"Yes, I know."

"Oh?"

"He came in while I was at Gram's picking up the bears she made."

"Humph. I guess he decided he needed some help with that child."

"That child's name is Meggie, Nora, and she's adorable. I'm sure Jake could use some help. He's had a great loss to deal with, as well as trying to be both mother and father to a baby." Sara was surprised at how defensive she sounded, but sometimes Nora's attitude really got to her.

"Well, yes, I guess it has been hard on him. But you've gotten through worse, dear."

Sara looked up to see her grandfather watching her. She rolled her eyes, signaling that Nora was giving her opinion as always. "Was there anything else, Nora? We were eating dinner."

"Oh. Well, I wanted to see if you were free for lunch tomorrow."

The teddy bears were delivered. Sara couldn't come up with another excuse. She sighed silently. "Of course, Nora."

"Good. I'll meet you at Deana's at noon then. Unless you'd like me to pick you up?"

"No, I have some errands to run afterward. I'll just meet you there."

"All right, dear. You have a good evening."

"You, too, Nora."

Sara hung up and sat back down at the table. "I do care about Nora, Grandpa, I really do. And I know she's lonely. But sometimes she just makes me feel. . . smothered."

"Honey, you're a sweet and giving woman. But you're going to have to be careful that you don't let Nora try to run your life."

"She's already trying to do that, but I'm not going to let her. I just don't want to hurt her."

Grandpa got up to refill his bowl. "I know you don't, Sara, but she can't cling to you forever. You have your own life to get on with."

"I know." Somehow getting on with that life had seemed easier last night than it did right this minute.

Meggie entertained everyone at supper that night. She grinned and cooed at her uncle Luke and cousin John. Jake held his breath, waiting for her to throw something at one of them, but she was on her best behavior.

"Look, look, did you see that grin she gave me?" Luke asked.

"She's a beauty, Jake," John said. "You'll have to beat the guys off with a stick when she gets to be a teenager."

"Hey, now. Let's not rush things." Jake watched as his daughter soaked up the attention like a sponge in water and knew he'd made the right decision in moving back. Meggie needed to know her family. Luke and John had fought over who got to hold her, feed her, and wipe her face ever since they'd gone upstairs with him to get her.

She'd been crying at the strange surroundings until Jake walked into the room. Then she'd given him that smile that always made his heart turn to mush, held out her arms to him, and said the most beautiful word in the world: "Dada." He'd lifted her out of her bed and gathered her close before turning to introduce her to her uncle and cousin.

When she'd seen Luke and John, she'd plopped her thumb in her mouth and laid her head on his shoulder, shy at first. But after they'd acted like a couple of two-year-olds trying to get her attention, she'd finally rewarded them each with a smile.

When Luke held out his hands to her and she went right to him, Jake felt much the same as he had when he saw her in Sara's arms. Abandoned. He shook the feeling off as he saw Luke's joy in holding his niece and Meggie's obvious love of the attention. That was why he had come back. For Meggie to have the family connections he'd grown up with. Now as he watched Luke, John, and Gram try to win his little girl's heart, he realized how much he'd missed being around his family. Resentment toward Wade flared up, and Jake worked to smother it. Wade was gone. What kind of person resented a dead man?

"All right!" John's exclamation brought Jake out of his thoughts.

After checking her cousin out all through supper, Meggie had finally lifted her arms to John. Jake cleaned her face and hands, unbuckled her highchair belt, and watched closely as John picked her up.

"I have held a baby before, Jake," John said, lifting Meggie out of the chair. "I know how to do this."

"Guess I'm a little overprotective," Jake admitted.

"Maybe just a little," John teased. "Now let me enjoy her. It took me long enough to get her to come to me."

"None of you have Sara's touch," Gram said. "Meggie took to her right off."

And they'd looked so natural and content; it'd made him almost jerk Meggie out of her arms. Jake couldn't shake the look in Sara's eyes out of his mind. He had to talk to her, try to explain that he hadn't known she'd lost her baby.

"We may not have a woman's touch, but we got Meggie to take to us, just the same," Luke said. "Let's take her into the living room and give her those toys we brought, John."

Jake followed them, glad for the diversion. "Going to spoil her already, are you?"

"That's what uncles and cousins are for, right, Gram?"

Chuckling, she joined them in the living room. "That's right, but Grammies get to spoil them most of all."

"Uh-oh, I can see I have a whole new set of problems moving back here."

Luke slapped him on the back. "You haven't seen anything yet, brother."

Sara remembered to call Gram before she started cleaning the kitchen. Her heart thudded with each ring. *Please, please don't let Jake answer the phone.* When Gram answered, Sara hoped her sigh of relief wasn't audible. She quickly told the older woman how well the teddy bears had gone over and asked how Meggie was settling in.

"She's having a great time, Sara. Luke and John came over and brought her some toys. I wish you could see all these grown men falling all over themselves trying to get that baby just to smile at them."

Sara laughed. "I bet that is a sight." She could hear exuberant noises in the background and wished she could see them all playing with Meggie.

"I think it's just what they both need. To be around family."

"I'm sure it is, Gram." It was a wonderful family and one she was proud to be part of, if only by marriage. She hoped she could stay close to them all with Jake back.

"Sara dear, I. . ."

"What is it, Gram?"

"Well, I told Jake about you losing the baby. We hadn't told him because of all he was going through at the time."

"It's all right, Gram. I understand."

"I think he feels real bad that he didn't know."

"There's no need for him to. Don't you worry about it."

"Well, you stop by anytime you need a baby to hold, you hear? And don't forget about Sunday night supper."

"Thanks, Gram. I will, and I won't forget. Grandpa wouldn't let me."

The older woman chuckled. "He'd better not. Good night, dear."

"Night, Gram." Sara placed the receiver back on the phone and began cleaning the kitchen on autopilot. She was sure Gram was right that being around family would help Jake and Meggie. Melissa had had no living relatives, and the only family Meggie had was Jake's. That little girl needed to grow up being close to them. Everyone should know they had a family. Sara didn't know what she would have done after her parents died if it hadn't been for her grandparents taking her in and loving her.

She hoped being back with his family would take that haunted look from Jake's eyes. He looked so lost and alone. She did the only thing she could do for him. She prayed. *Dear Lord, I don't pretend to know Jake's relationship with You, but please help him heal. Please let him and Meggie make a good life here. In Jesus' name, amen.*

Sara put a pot of coffee on and sat down to call the rest of the women who had made teddy bears. Everyone was thrilled that the bears had gone over so well and promised to have more ready in a month.

She took coffee to Grandpa and joined him in watching a rerun of *Happy Days*.

"Did you remember to call Ellie?" Grandpa asked during a commercial.

"I did. She reminded me about Sunday night supper."

"Did you tell her we wouldn't miss it?"

"I didn't think I had to. I just told her *you* wouldn't let me forget it."

Grandpa chuckled. "You were right. I do look forward to her supper all week."

Was it the suppers or Gram's company that Grandpa looked forward to?

Sara admitted to herself that she might worry if Grandpa showed signs of being sweet on any other woman. But she would only rejoice if those two dear people cared for one another. She was going to have to watch the two of them closely Sunday night.

When the sitcom was over, she went into the kitchen and made a batch of Grandpa's favorite cookies. He'd fixed supper for the two of them; the least she could do was keep the cookie jar filled. She wasn't surprised to see him enter the kitchen just as she took out the first sheet of chocolate chip cookies.

"Mmm, those sure smell good." He got a glass and poured them both a glass of milk. "You spoil me, honey."

He took a bite of warm cookie. "You make them just like your grandmother did. That woman sure could cook."

"Yes, she could. Gram's a pretty good cook, too."

Grandpa nodded. "She sure is. Good woman, Ellie."

Sara smiled. "She's one of the best."

"Watching a toddler is going to keep her hopping, that's for sure." Grandpa changed the subject. "But I know she's thrilled to have that baby close."

"She was glowing this afternoon. But I think this must have been a fairly sudden decision. Jake said he didn't give much notice. I'm sure if he'd been planning it for any length of time, he would have let the family know."

"Ellie would have said something if she'd known."

"Oh, I'm sure she would have. Having a baby around is going to be good for the whole family. You should have heard the laughter coming over the phone lines earlier. From what Gram said, I think Meggie's uncle Luke and cousin John are already in love with her."

"I'll have to get over there to see her soon." He paused. "You're all right, aren't you, honey? I mean with Jake coming back and all. . . ."

"Why wouldn't I be?"

"Well now, darlin', I seem to remember you doing your share of crying over him years ago."

"That was a long time ago, Grandpa." Sara didn't want to tell him that since seeing Jake, those days seemed closer somehow. The night Jake had been late coming home to celebrate her birthday and had caught Wade trying to comfort her with a kiss had suddenly become very vivid. She could remember Jake yelling and accusing her and Wade of seeing each other behind his back. She'd tried to explain, but Jake wouldn't listen. He'd turned on his heel and walked out of her life.

She got up to take the next tray of cookies out of the oven and bent to kiss the top of Grandpa's head. "Don't worry about me. That was all a lifetime ago."

"I'm not going to worry. With all that you've come through this last year, I don't think there's much you can't handle now."

"Thank you, Grandpa." His vote of confidence buoyed her spirits. It was the way she'd felt when she'd left home this morning. Somehow with all that'd happened during the day, she'd lost the joy she'd started out with.

Grandpa ate one more cookie and got to his feet. "I think I'll go up and read awhile. Don't you stay up too late, you hear? You'll need all your wits about you for that lunch with Nora tomorrow." He chuckled as he headed out of the room.

Sara couldn't stop herself from joining in. He was right. Tomorrow would definitely be a challenge. "Night, Grandpa. I love you."

"Love you, too, darlin'."

Sara took the last batch of cookies from the oven, washed the baking dishes, and put everything away. She was still too keyed up to call it a night and decided to enjoy the early spring weather once more. As she opened the front door, her feet suddenly froze in place. Her hand flew to her throat.

Jake was standing there, his Stetson in one hand and the other raised to knock at the door. "Sara, I'm sorry. I didn't mean to frighten you. I saw your lights on and. . .um, could we talk a minute?"

Sara released the breath she'd been holding. "Of course. Would you like to come in?" Her heart did a tap dance. What did he want to talk about?

"No, that's all right. I won't take much of your time." He took a step back and leaned against the porch rail, crossing his booted feet.

Sara slipped outside and leaned back against the screen door. Did he feel as tense around her as she did near him? The silence thickened until she could stand it no longer. "Are Gram and Meggie all right? Nothing is wrong, is it?"

"They're fine. Gram was watching the news when I left, and Meggie is asleep. For the night, I hope. Meggie loves all the attention she's been getting, but everything is new to her."

"Your family will help her adjust to the move in no time, Jake. They're wonderful—I don't know what I would have done without them." Something inside her whispered it was Jake who needed them badly now.

"Yeah, they are. Except they didn't tell me. . ." He looked down at his feet and back up again before his brown gaze settled on her face. "Sara, I'm sorry for appearing so unfeeling this afternoon. I didn't know about the baby you lost. I'm so very sorry. . . ."

"Jake, it's all right," she said softly. "You had your own pain to deal with. This evening Gram told me that they hadn't told you."

"I wish I'd known."

Sara nodded. She could hear the sincerity in his voice. "I know."

"Wishing doesn't change much, does it?"

She knew he was talking about more than the fact that no one had told him about her baby. "No, it doesn't."

Jake looked as though he was going to reach out to her, but then he straightened and turned to go. He cleared his throat and turned back to face her once more. "Guess I'd better get back. Meggie may wake up and be frightened in a new place and all."

"Okay." The awkwardness between them squeezed at Sara's heart. "Thank you, Jake."

He put his hat back on and tipped it slightly before he turned and headed down the steps.

Sara watched him walk to his car, and something about his slumped shoulders reached out to her. The sorrow surrounding him was almost tangible. Her heart went out to him, for she knew the feeling well. But she knew where to turn when those moments of utter misery threatened to drown her. Tears gathered in her eyes. *Dear Lord, please help Jake the way You've helped me.*

She turned to go back inside. Sitting out in the cool night air no longer held any appeal. She'd only think about other times she'd sat on this same porch, in that same porch swing. . .with Jake.

She wasn't going to let herself think about the past. Not about the bad times—or the good. No, she wasn't ready to dredge it all up. Jake was right: Wishing wouldn't change a thing.

Chapter 3

Jake looked down at his sleeping daughter. Dark hair curled around her little face. Every few seconds, she sucked the tiny thumb in her mouth. The other hand clutched a stuffed toy. Her soft, even breathing was music to his ears. He could not imagine life without Meggie. How did Sara find the strength to go on day after day? She seemed to have come to terms with it all, but he didn't know how.

He covered Meggie up and quietly left the room, leaving a night-light glowing and keeping the door cracked. Making his way downstairs, he let himself out the front door. Gram had gone up to bed shortly after he'd returned from Sara's. He didn't tell her where he'd gone, but he suspected she knew.

Jake lowered himself onto the porch steps and leaned back to look at the starry sky. He thought he'd feel better after apologizing to Sara, but he'd been wrong. Seeing her on the same front porch where they'd spent so much time only brought back memories best left buried.

But how was he going to keep such thoughts at bay now that they lived in the same town again? He hoped they didn't run into each other at every turn. How could he have forgotten that she was now a part of his extended family? Jake ran his fingers through his hair. Had he just blocked out all thoughts of Sara? Had that made it all easier on him?

A deep sigh escaped him. He shook his head and groaned. She'd looked wonderful tonight. Tendrils of hair had escaped from her french braid, making him want to reach out and curl a wisp around his finger the way he used to. He'd had to catch himself to keep from doing just that. And her eyes. How could eyes reflect such deep sadness and serenity at the same time?

There was a quiet peace about Sara that he wished he could find for himself. He would have liked to ask her about how she'd reached that point in her life, but he couldn't. There was a time he could have asked her anything, but not now. He'd felt so awkward around her; he could barely get out the few sentences he'd gone there to say.

Jake got to his feet. Maybe he should have waited for another day to talk to her, but he wouldn't have been able to sleep. He knew he'd changed a lot, but he couldn't live with the idea that she thought him totally insensitive after this afternoon.

Making sure the door was locked, he turned out the lights and headed for bed. Tomorrow he was going to call a Realtor. The sooner he decided whether to buy or build, the sooner he and Meggie would be in their own home. And the less likely he'd be to run into Sara.

Sara glanced at her watch as she parked her car on Main Street. She'd gotten off to a slow start that morning and was going to be late for her lunch with Nora. Her mother-in-law hated tardiness, but it couldn't be helped.

She'd tossed and turned most of the night. Jake's return had shaken her, no doubt about it. There'd been a time when they could talk about anything. But that was then, and this was now, and nothing was going to change that fact. Still, she wished she didn't feel so on edge around him.

The tinkling bell above the door announced her arrival at the diner. Sara spotted Nora sitting in a booth and checking the time on her watch. She hurried over and quickly slipped into the seat across from her mother-in-law.

"I'm sorry I'm late, Nora. I didn't sleep well last night, and I just couldn't get going this morning."

She was rewarded with a half smile. "It's all right, dear. Was there any particular reason you had trouble sleeping? You aren't coming down with a cold, are you?"

"No, I don't think so. I guess I was just too tired." Or too keyed up after Jake's visit. But she wasn't going to tell Nora that. She grabbed a menu and scanned the lunch specials.

"Well, you do keep yourself quite busy these days. You haven't been out to the ranch in several weeks."

Sara took a deep breath and smiled at her mother-in-law. "I'm sorry I haven't made it out there lately, Nora."

Sara was relieved when the waitress came to take their order, but she realized it was only a short reprieve.

The waitress had no more than turned her back when Nora got to the heart of the matter. "I really do wish you would move back to the ranch, Sara."

"And I wish you'd just move into town." Sara caught her breath as soon as the words left her mouth. She couldn't believe she'd actually said them out loud. She was just so weary of this conversation.

Nora sat up straighter and inhaled sharply. "Why would I want to do that? I have a perfectly beautiful home at the ranch. I can come into town whenever I feel like it, but the ranch is my home."

Sara nodded, knowing she should have kept quiet. "I just thought you might be happier here. There's more to do, you could see more of your friends—"

"I'm perfectly happy at the ranch. It's where I raised Wade. I don't want to move."

Sara reached over and patted Nora's hand. "My point exactly. I can understand that, Nora. I don't want to move, either," she said softly.

Nora jerked her hand from underneath Sara's. She took a sip of coffee and brushed at crumbs only she could see. "I see."

"I hope you do. Nora, you know you'll always be family to me. You've been wonderful to me, and I love you. But Grandpa isn't getting any younger, and I want to be close by. It will be much easier on me when I resume teaching in the fall if I'm living in town. I—"

"There is no need for you to teach. Wade never wanted you to work, Sara. If you invest what he left you, you shouldn't need to work."

"Nora, I want to teach. When Wade was alive, I loved being his wife, but I never felt I had enough to do then, and I need to keep busy. I can't just sit around—"

"Like I do. Is that what you're saying?"

"Nora, no! I—"

A look from Nora silenced her as the waitress approached with their lunch. Sara was torn between relief and frustration when Nora changed the subject as soon as the waitress left the table.

"What are you bringing to Ellie's Sunday night?" Nora asked.

Caught off guard, Sara didn't want to tell her that she was trying to think of a way to avoid going to the regular Sunday night supper at Gram's. For as long as she could remember, Gram had invited family and friends to her home for supper after church on Sunday nights. But now, with Jake back in town, Sara felt the need to bow out. "I'm not sure."

"I think I'll have Cook bake one of her famous chile casseroles." Nora took a bite of her chicken-salad sandwich and chewed delicately.

Sara's appetite was diminishing rapidly as she thought about not being able to spend as much time with family as she liked. But the only way to avoid seeing Jake would be to distance herself from the whole family. It was his family, after all. She picked at the salad she'd ordered and tried not to think about it.

The bell over the door of the diner jingled several times, but it wasn't until she saw Nora's face flush that Sara took notice of who'd entered.

Luke Breland was striding over to the booth, with Jake slowly coming up behind him. Sara's heart started hammering in her chest.

"Aunt Nora, Sara! It's good to see you both." Luke gave them each a kiss on the cheek and motioned to Jake. "Look who showed up on Gram's doorstep yesterday."

The smile Nora gave Luke disappeared when she looked at Jake. "Jacob, I heard you were back in town with your daughter."

Jake looked irritated but bent to brush his lips across his aunt's cheek. "It's good to see you, too, Aunt Nora."

Nora's face flushed at his slight admonition. "You decided you needed help, did you, Jacob?"

Sara was appalled at Nora's rudeness. "We all need help from time to time, Nora. I've had to have a lot of that myself."

"I decided it was time Meggie got to know her family," Jake said gruffly.

"Well, I just hope watching her isn't too much for Ellie. She's not getting any younger, you know." Nora calmly took a sip of her iced tea.

Sara couldn't believe Nora was treating Jake so badly. "Nora, you know Gram loves babies. And there are plenty of people around to help out if she needs it."

"Including you, I suppose?"

"Of course, including me." Sara couldn't resist adding, "And you, too, Nora. After all, Meggie is your great-niece. I'm sure you'd be willing to step in if Gram needed you."

Nora coughed, almost choking on her tea, and Luke patted her on the back.

"Don't worry, Aunt Nora," Jake said. "I don't think you or Sara will be needed. I'm fully capable of taking care of my own daughter. And I'm sure John would understand if I worked at home."

He clapped Luke on the shoulder. "Speaking of work, we'd better get those sandwiches we ordered and get back to it. I'll go see if Deana has them ready."

Sara watched him walk away and willed her heartbeat to return to normal. She looked up to see Luke smiling down at her.

"Thanks for the offer to help Gram with Meggie, Sara. I know it wasn't easy for Jake to realize he needed to come home. I sure don't want him feeling like he's putting Gram out."

"I'm sure Gram's loving every minute of it." Sara smiled back at Luke. "But I'll check on her later to make sure she's all right."

Luke bent and kissed her cheek once more. "Thanks, Sara. Good-bye, Aunt Nora." He joined Jake at the door, and they left without so much as a backward glance from Jake.

"Humph! That boy has a lot of nerve coming back here," Nora said as soon as the two men were outside.

"Nora! What is your problem with Jake? He's your nephew!" Sara might not be happy that she was going to run into him at every turn, but he had a right to make his home here as much as she or anyone else did.

"How can you defend his coming back home and just dumping his daughter on Ellie?" Nora asked stiffly.

"Nora, Sweet Springs is his hometown. And I saw Gram with Meggie yesterday. I can assure you, she doesn't feel dumped upon!" Sara looked up in time to catch Nora dabbing at her eyes with a tissue and immediately felt bad for upsetting her.

"I'm sorry, Nora. But it's not like you to be rude to people." At least not to their face, Sara thought. Nora's technique was usually much more subtle.

"I just think he's made a mistake. He's going to let everyone get used to having the baby around and then he'll decide he wants to move back to Albuquerque."

While Nora's reasoning sounded logical, Sara felt that the woman was reaching for any reason to excuse her attitude toward Jake.

"I'm sure they will just be glad for whatever time they have with Meggie. She's delightful."

"Yes. . .I'm sure she is," Nora said, sounding wistful.

Sara immediately felt ashamed of herself for being critical. Although Nora had never seemed that excited about the prospect of becoming a grandmother, Sara was sure her mother-in-law would have loved the baby had it lived. Her heart knotted in pain at the losses they'd both suffered. "Nora, I—"

"I'm sorry, dear, but I really have to leave. I have a doctor's appointment," Nora said, easing out of the booth.

"You aren't sick, are you?" Sara asked, feeling even worse.

"Just a checkup. Since Doc Edwards married Hilda and retired, I haven't bothered to find a new doctor. But several people have told me that the new doctor in town is good, and you never know when you might need medical care. So I made an appointment. If I think he's any good, I'll have Doc's office send my records to him," she explained, pulling a wad of bills from her purse and laying them on the table. "That should take care of lunch. If not, I'll pay you later."

Sara stood and gave Nora the quick, impersonal hug she seemed to expect but not like. So much for having a nice, calm lunch with Nora, she thought as she watched the woman hurry out the door. She sat back down and pushed what was left of her salad away. What little appetite she'd managed to hold on to was now totally gone.

"Sara, you look like you could use a friend and a fresh cup of coffee." Deana stood with the coffeepot in one hand, two cups in the other, and a smile on her face.

Sara summoned up a smile of her own. She and Deana had been good friends since high school, and Deana could read her all too well. "You couldn't be more right. Can you join me?"

Deana glanced around the diner and motioned to the waitress that she was taking a break. She slid into the side of the booth Nora had vacated, pushed aside the empty plate, and poured them both some coffee.

"Mmm. Feels good just to sit down. Some days I wish Mom hadn't given me this diner when she got married. I have a whole new respect for that woman, though. She raised us all by working really, really hard. I never realized just how tough it was to run this place until I took over." Deana took a sip of coffee.

"Have you heard from her and Doc lately?"

Deana nodded. "They're camping up in Colorado. She said they'd be coming home in a week or two. I'm ready. I miss them when they're gone months at a time."

Sara nodded and stirred her tea.

"But I didn't take this break to talk about Mom and Doc."

"No?"

"No. I came because you're looking a little forlorn. And I want you to tell

Aunty Deana what has you so down in the dumps."

Sara chuckled and shrugged. "A little of this, a little of that. I was curt with Nora because she was rude to Jake, and now I feel bad. I don't know why I felt I needed to take up for him anyway."

"Maybe because it was the right thing to do?" Deana propped her chin in her hand and waited for Sara to answer.

"He just looks so. . .adrift, you know? And I don't know why Nora seems to get so edgy when his name is brought up. But then I got to thinking that maybe it has something to do with his child being all right, while I lost her grandchild."

"Now that kind of thinking is bound to make you feel bad. Quit looking for excuses for Nora's rudeness, my friend. Far as I can tell, she's never needed a reason to be rude. She just is."

Sara tried but failed to contain the chuckle that erupted.

Deana laughed along with her. "Now that's more like it. Don't you let Nora make you feel bad, Sara."

Sara sighed. "I just don't like to upset her."

"Honey, anyone who doesn't think like Nora or agree with everything she says and isn't at her beck and call upsets that woman. You of all people should know that by now."

"But she's so lonely. And. . .I still feel it was—"

"Sara, the wreck was *not* your fault. You were pregnant. You had a craving for ice cream at ten o'clock at night. You and Wade went to get some. Thousands of expectant parents do the exact same thing every night."

"I know, Deana. I really do know that. It's just that Wade was Nora's only son, and now that he's gone, I feel responsible for her. But she wants me to move back out to the ranch, and I just can't do that."

"Nor should you. Nora can't live your life for you, or hers through you. You are here for her, you care about her, but you have to get on with your life. Personally I never knew how you stood living out there with her when Wade was alive. I don't think I could have done it."

Sara was relieved when the bell on the door jangled, announcing more customers. She didn't want to lie and say it'd been easy living at the ranch, but she didn't want to sound disloyal to her husband's mother, either.

Deana sighed and slid out of the booth. "Break's over. Got to get back to the kitchen."

Sara gathered her purse and prepared to leave. "You take it easy, Deana. I'll talk to you later." She paid the waitress and headed out the door to her car.

So far the day wasn't going as planned. The lunch with Nora had been anything but calming. . .especially after Jake and Luke came into the diner. Sara still couldn't believe how protective of Jake she'd felt. Nora had no reason to be so rude to him. He was her nephew, and he'd suffered a loss in the past year, too.

How could she have acted so unfeeling toward him?

And why do I feel I have to take up for him at every turn? He's a grown man and perfectly capable of fighting his own battles. He could probably hold his own with Nora better than I could, anyway.

Sara pulled out of the parking space and headed for the grocery store. It was just that he seemed so unlike the Jake she used to know. He was so serious and aloof. And there was a look in his eyes that Sara couldn't name or forget. *O Lord, he needs You so much. Please ease his pain. Little Meggie needs him to be the happy, loving person he used to be.*

Sara sighed as she pulled into the parking lot of the grocery store. She wanted to help Jake, she really did. But all she could do was pray for him, knowing the Lord would listen.

Jake took the last bite of his cheeseburger and crumpled up the sack it'd come in. He aimed and threw, hitting the trash can at the side of John's desk.

"Good shot!" Luke whistled. "You been practicing trash ball a lot, brother?"

Jake chuckled and shook his head. "I was aiming for Aunt Nora's backside. That woman never has liked me."

John laughed. "Aunt Nora? What did she do now?"

"She was in Deana's when we went to pick up lunch." Luke crumpled his own bag and threw it away. "Wasn't too nice to Jake. Downright mean, if you ask me." He leaned back in one of two leather chairs facing John's desk.

"Nora never has been known for her sweetness."

"I shouldn't let her bother me," Jake explained, "but she made it sound like I just dumped Meggie in Gram's lap." He sat down in the empty chair and raked his fingers through his hair.

"Sara took up for you, though," Luke said. "And we all know Gram can speak for herself. She'll let you know if it's too much for her."

"Sara took up for you?" John whistled. "She rarely takes up for herself around Nora."

"Good thing she moved back in with her granddad after Wade died," Luke added. "Nora would love to call all the shots in Sara's life now." He stood and stretched. "I've got to get back to the ranch, boys. Uncle Ben should be calling me to let me know about the new livestock he bought. Let me know if there's anything I can do to help you get settled in, Jake. It's good to have you home, no matter how Aunt Nora feels about you." He chuckled on his way out the door.

John turned to Jake. "It is good to have you back. Don't you let Nora bother you."

"No, I won't," Jake assured his cousin. "I do want to make sure taking care of Meggie isn't too much for Gram, though. Mind if I take off early? I need to pick up some things at the store for Meggie, and—"

"Jake, you can take all the time you need. I'm just glad you finally agreed to come into practice with me. But there's no hurry. Get your bearings; get sweet Meggie settled in. If you feel you have to, you can take some files home to familiarize yourself with our clients, but you'll get to know them all soon enough. If you hadn't agreed to move back, I'd still be handling it all myself, anyway."

Jake nodded. Maybe he had been in too big a hurry to start working with John. There was no reason he couldn't get Meggie settled in a little better before he started working. "Thanks, John. I think I could use a little time to adjust to being back. And I don't want anyone thinking I can't take care of my own child."

John joined him at the door of the office and slapped him on the back. "Jake, no one is going to think that. After all, you've been taking care of her real well since Melissa's death. You turned down all kinds of help then. Don't let Aunt Nora get to you."

"Thanks, cousin." Jake felt his tension begin to ease. "It's good to be home."

"And even better to have you here. Kiss Meggie for me."

Jake nodded and grinned. "Now that I can do."

Sara pulled out the list she'd made that morning and grabbed a buggy. She wanted to make Grandpa his favorite meal as a way of thanking him for just being there. If he hadn't owned a home in this town, would she still be out at the ranch, living under Nora's thumbnail? Sara did care about Wade's mother, but there was no way she could live with her, and she hoped Nora would stop asking after today.

Sara's mood improved quickly once she was in the store and running into first one and then another smiling face. Mrs. Mead gushed about how happy she was the bears had been a hit and thanked Sara for coming up with the idea. Ida Connors hadn't helped with the bears the first time around, but after hearing how well they went over, she offered to help with the next batch.

Sara had put the lunchtime episode out of her mind by the time she'd picked up the ingredients for the meatloaf. Smiling, she turned down the next aisle and headed to the checkout lane, picturing the smile on Grandpa's face when he saw what was for supper. She would have plowed right into Jake's buggy if he hadn't swerved to the other side of the aisle.

Sara's hand flew to her mouth as she realized she'd almost hit him. "Jake! I'm sorry. Obviously I wasn't looking where I was going."

"It's all right, Sara. I looked up just in time. We seem to be running into each other today."

Sara noticed the buggy was full of disposable diapers and an assortment of baby food and snacks. There was something endearing about such a masculine man shopping for a baby with ease. "Is Meggie settling in all right? I was going to check on her and Gram this afternoon."

"She's settling in fine. And there's no need for you to check on them. John and I decided to slow down my return to work for a little while, so you can assure Nora that I won't be taking advantage of Gram."

"Jake, I—"

"I'm sorry, Sara. That was uncalled for. I guess I'm still stinging from Nora's remarks. Thank you for. . .coming to my defense earlier."

Sara nodded and tried to hide the sudden hurt she felt that he obviously didn't want her helping Gram with Meggie. It was probably for the best, but it still stung. "It's all right, Jake. I'm sorry Nora was so rude."

"It's not your fault. I hope she didn't give you too hard a time about taking up for me."

"She'll get over it." Sara saw the first hint of a smile from Jake.

"That's what I figured," he said. "But I don't want to give her anything to fuel that tongue of hers. I'm going to make this my home again whether she's happy about it or not."

"I know the family is glad to have you home, Jake. Gram is thrilled." She just wished she didn't feel so unsure of herself around him. It was a feeling that seemed to deepen each time she saw him.

"I want Meggie to know her family," Jake continued.

"She should. It's a good family to know."

Jake nodded. "Yes, it is."

Sara didn't know what to say next.

Jake found his voice first. "I'd better get going and let you finish your shopping."

Sara was almost relieved to be able to put her cart in motion. "I do need to get supper started. Tell Gram I said hi and give Meggie an extra hug for me."

"I will."

"Bye, Jake."

"Bye, Sara," Jake said as he rounded the corner.

Sara paid for her purchases and headed for her car. No, life wasn't going to get any easier with Jake back in town.

Chapter 4

Sara crumbled crackers, chopped onion and bell pepper, and grated carrots, while trying to banish thoughts of Jake from her mind. Adding some of each ingredient a little at a time, she mixed them with a combination of ground beef and bulk sausage before adding the seasonings, eggs, and tomato soup. She was concentrating so hard on keeping her thoughts off Jake, she didn't hear Grandpa slip up behind her.

"Smells good in here already." He looked over her shoulder. "Meatloaf! How did you know that's what I've been hungry for?"

She had to chuckle. "It was a pretty good guess. You're always hungry for meatloaf, Grandpa."

"Just yours, honey. You make it just like your grandmother did. But I have to admit, I like yours even better with that cheese you tuck inside."

"Thanks. That's quite a compliment." Sara continued to mold the mixture into a loaf, leaving some to the side and hollowing out the center. She then filled it with grated cheese and covered it with the remaining meat mixture. Grandpa was right. It did smell good even before it was cooked.

Sara slid the loaf pan into the oven and added two foil-wrapped potatoes alongside the pan, before turning to her grandfather. "Should be ready in about an hour. Want a glass of iced tea? We could sit out on the porch for a while."

"Sounds good to me," Grandpa said. But he turned her toward the door. "You go on out and I'll bring the tea. You look a little frazzled."

"Am I that obvious?" At her grandfather's grin, she shrugged and chuckled. "Okay, I'll meet you out front."

Setting the swing in motion, Sara closed her eyes and tried to relax as she swung back and forth. She was going to have to learn how to deal with an unhappy Nora *and* with running into Jake again. She simply had no choice in the matter.

She prayed silently, asking the Lord to help her deal with the changes that Jake's return would cause. Sara knew the Lord would help her through it all. She just had to give it over to Him. With the acknowledgment that He still was in control, the tension she'd felt all afternoon began to drain away.

"You had lunch with Nora, didn't you? Is that what had you uptight?" Grandpa asked as he let the screen door slam behind him. He handed her a glass of tea and sat down in the wicker rocker across from the swing.

Sara nodded. "It sure contributed to it. I upset her, and I didn't want to." She took a sip of tea.

"Oh? Want to tell me about it?" He settled back in the rocker.

"Jake and Luke came in while we were there, and Nora was just plain rude to Jake. She practically accused him of dumping Meggie on Gram, and I found myself taking up for him."

"No!" Grandpa shook his head and chuckled. "Nora probably wasn't too happy about that."

"Especially not after I'd told her I didn't want to move to the ranch."

"Well, darlin', you did the right thing on both counts. You don't want to move back to the ranch, and she shouldn't have been rude to Jake."

"I even found myself offering to help, if Meggie got to be too much for Gram."

"I'm glad to hear it, darlin'. I went to see Ellie today. You were right. Meggie is adorable. And she's a handful." He smiled. "She kept us both busy until Jake showed up."

"I think he's afraid she might be too much for Gram."

Grandpa leaned back and started rocking. "Well, Ellie isn't going to admit that she might be, but I'm sure relieved that Jake isn't going to work full-time, just yet. I'm afraid keeping Meggie on an everyday basis might just be a little too hard for her."

He shook his head and grinned. "She's pulling up to everything, trying to walk. Ellie says she can say a few words, too. She's something, that Meggie is."

"Yes, she certainly is." Remembering how wonderful it felt to hold Meggie in her arms, Sara almost wished Jake hadn't decided to take his time settling into the law practice. She'd have loved to help with the baby. But it wouldn't matter. Jake had made it perfectly clear that he didn't want her help.

"Jake, don't you take anything Nora says to heart," Gram declared. "Meggie and I will be just fine. And there are plenty of people around to help me, if I need them to." She poured them both some coffee and sat down at the table, where they watched Meggie stack blocks in a playpen set up by the back door. "That woman just doesn't know how to mind her own business."

Jake had to chuckle. "Gram, that woman is your daughter-in-law."

"I know. She wasn't always this way. Nora's turned bitter over the years since Mark was killed in Vietnam." Gram sighed and shook her head. "It's sad. The Nora he married was a kind and caring woman. Just don't you let her get to you."

"Don't worry. I'm determined not to let her bother me. I just don't want anyone else thinking that I've come home to dump Meggie on my family."

"Did Will make you feel that way before he left here?"

"No, he didn't." In fact, Sara's grandfather had been very nice, welcoming him back to Sweet Springs.

"And no one else, except Nora, is going to, either. Jake, you're being too hard on yourself. The whole town knows you've been taking care of Meggie ever since Melissa's death—and that you turned down repeated offers of help."

Jake leaned back in his chair and rubbed the back of his neck. "Actually, I think taking a break and getting settled will help both me and Meggie. The move is bound to unsettle her, and I'd like to make it as easy as I can on her."

"Jake, as long as you are in her life, that baby doesn't care where she lives. Children adjust much easier than we adults do. Take the break if you think it will do you some good. Just don't do it on my account."

Jake tried not to smile. His grandmother would never change. She wasn't about to admit that watching Meggie might be too much for her. But looking closely at her, there was no denying the fact that she looked plumb tuckered out.

"I thought I'd bring some of the files home and go over them here so that I'm familiar with our clients when I do start working full-time with John. And I can contact a Realtor. If I don't find a house I like, I'll just look into building one."

"You know you are welcome to live here as long as you need to."

"I know that, Gram. And I thank you. But the sooner I find Meggie and me a place of our own, the easier it will be to make Sweet Springs home again." He knew he'd made the right decision in coming back, but there were some things he was going to have to work at getting used to. Like running into Sara when he least expected it. And he hadn't expected it today. Not at the diner and especially not at the grocery store.

"Sara offered to help if you needed her. I think that upset Nora even more than my presence did. She looked like she'd sucked on a sour lemon."

Ellie shook her head. "You know, she's going to have to start living her own life one of these days."

"Sara?"

"No, Nora. Sara will get on with hers in time. She's young. But Nora seems to delight in trying to run everyone's life but her own."

"Luke and John said it took a lot for Sara to stand up to her today. Why is that? She's Wade's widow. She doesn't owe Nora anything."

"No, she doesn't. But Sara doesn't want to hurt her, either, Jake. Nora has clung to her since Wade's death, and Sara feels she's all Nora has left of Wade."

Wade. Jake wondered if he'd ever get over resenting the man who won Sara's heart. Chair legs scraped the kitchen floor as Jake got to his feet and tried to bury the past once more. He bent to pick Meggie up and cuddle her.

"Jake?"

He turned his attention back to his grandmother. "Yes, ma'am?"

"Wade's gone. You're going to have to come to terms with the past. You know things aren't always what they seem."

"I don't have time to think about the past, Gram." He blew kisses on the back of Meggie's neck to hear her giggle. "Making a new life for myself and Meggie is about all I can handle right now. We're going to go play in the backyard. Why don't you take a nap before supper? I'll cook tonight. I can cook, you know."

"Humph! Jake Breland, I've never been a nap taker and I'm not about to take one at five thirty in the afternoon. I wouldn't sleep a wink tonight. And I'm not ready to turn my kitchen over to anyone, either." Gram got up from the table and walked over to the refrigerator. "I'll call you when supper is ready."

Jake hoisted Meggie onto his hip and headed outside. "Come on, sugar. I think we've been dismissed."

Sara had just been congratulating herself for managing not to run into Jake for the last several days—until Lydia, John's mother, called inviting her to a welcome home cookout for Jake.

"I'm not sure, Lydia, I—"

"You don't have a thing that's pressing, and you know it, Sara. Now be a good girl and say you'll come. You don't get out enough, and besides, I'm not taking no for an answer."

Sara sighed. She knew Lydia meant what she said. She'd been after Sara to get out more for months. Besides, there'd be too many questions from the family if she didn't go. "I'll be there. Can I bring anything?"

"Just yourself and Will. We're just having hamburgers and hot dogs. And dessert, of course."

"Grandpa will love that."

"You'll both have a good time, you'll see."

Sure we will, Sara thought as she said good-bye and hung up the phone. She'd spent the last few days helping Grandpa with weeding and watering his garden. And she'd done some serious spring cleaning. . .anything to keep from going out and possibly running into Jake again. Seeing him only confused her.

This was the man who'd hurt her all those years ago by dumping her and then marrying Melissa several months later. Why did she feel this strong need to reach out to him now? He just looked so lost and alone the few times she'd seen him. He should be the last person she was thinking of, but she'd thought of little else since his return.

She'd wanted to call Gram and see how Meggie was doing several times during the day, but she'd been afraid Jake would answer the phone. Part of her resented the fact that she no longer felt she could just pick up the phone and call whenever she wanted to, and the other part of her wanted to take the easy way out by staying away. Seeing Jake wasn't easy; it wasn't easy at all.

Well, Lydia had taken care of all her good intentions. Now she'd have to show up or have everyone upset that she didn't.

Sara poured a glass of iced tea and took it outside. She'd asked Grandpa to take a pot of soup and a batch of cookies she'd made over to Gram's for her. She felt she was helping in some way by seeing to it that Gram had a break from cooking a meal here and there. And this way she'd get news of Meggie when he got home.

She just wished she'd get past this overwhelming urge to hold Meggie again. Tears threatened to well up, and Sara forced them back down. She wasn't going to cry. She wasn't going to let herself. She'd spent the better part of a year crying over her loss, and she wasn't about to start crying over what might have been.

She had to get up and get busy doing something, anything to get her mind off the past. She'd get dressed and go shopping, that's what she'd do. Maybe buying something new to wear to Lydia's party would get her out of her doldrums. It'd be fun, and surely Jake wouldn't be shopping in a ladies' dress shop.

Half an hour later, Sara came out of the dressing room wearing a colorful sundress. Catching a glimpse of someone, she sighed. This day wasn't getting any better. While Jake wasn't in the shop, Nora was.

"Sara dear. I thought that was your car outside. If I'd known you were going shopping, I'd have asked you to come with me. We could have had lunch together." Nora's gaze took in the long dress Sara had on. "That's a little bright for you, don't you think?"

It was better to laugh than cry, Sara thought as she chuckled. "I like it, Nora. It feels cool and summery."

"Are you buying it for anything special?"

"Lydia is throwing a party—"

"Yes, for Jake. I was invited, too."

"Oh? And you're shopping for something new, too. That's nice, Nora."

"No. I am not buying anything new for that party. I really hadn't planned on going. I just saw your car outside and thought I'd stop in and see you."

"That was nice of you, Nora. The shopping trip was just spur of the moment. I haven't bought anything new in a long time." Not since she'd bought her maternity clothes. Nora had been with her that day and insisted on buying several outfits for her. They'd had a very good time. Sara had forgotten how excited about the baby Nora had been. Now she wondered if the sadness in Nora's eyes was reflected in her own.

Sara forced herself to put thoughts of the past away. She couldn't let herself start thinking about the pain of the last year. She'd come too far. But still, she felt some of the weight of Nora's sadness. "Why don't you come have supper with me and Grandpa?"

"No, dear. I have some errands to run. I'll leave you to your shopping." Nora pulled the shoulder strap of her handbag higher up and turned to leave. "I'll see you tomorrow night, though."

"Oh, good. You've changed your mind? You're going to go? Lydia will be so—"

Nora was out the door before Sara finished the sentence. Sara sighed and headed back to the dressing room. She wasn't making Nora very happy these days.

By the time the next evening rolled around, Sara wanted nothing more than to get out of going to the party for Jake, but Grandpa was excited about it. She dressed in the colorful dress she'd bought the day before and joined him downstairs.

"You look beautiful, darlin'. It's time we had a party around here. You need a change of scenery."

Sara forced herself to smile. Grandpa loved parties, and she wasn't about to spoil his fun. "Thank you. You don't look too bad yourself. And you smell really good. You trying to impress anyone I know, Grandpa?"

"Just Meggie." He chuckled. "You know that little tyke has been playing hard to get. Won't let me hold her at all."

Mention of the baby's name made Sara realize how she was hoping to see her tonight.

Jake took a deep breath as he followed Ellie up the walk. "Be a sweetie tonight, Meggie, and help me through this," he whispered in the baby's ear.

He hadn't wanted a fuss made over his coming home, but he didn't want to hurt Aunt Lydia and Uncle Ben, so here he was. He'd dreaded it all day. But there was no getting out of it. He just hoped that everyone was so enthralled with his daughter that he could blend into the background.

John answered the door and took Meggie and her diaper bag. Meggie was quite happy with all the attention, and Jake had to force himself not to take her back. Luke came up and led him away before he could protest.

"Meggie will be just fine, Jake. If she starts crying, you can rest assured John will find you."

By the time they'd made their way outside, Jake felt like he'd greeted most of Sweet Springs. Everyone was very nice and seemed genuinely pleased that he was back. He spotted Nora holding court, seated in a chaise across the yard, and was thankful that he didn't have to speak to her just yet. What was she doing here anyway? He knew she wasn't here to welcome him home. Run him out on the rails would be more like it.

Just then Aunt Lydia and Uncle Ben rushed up to him and welcomed him home. Lydia wanted to know where Meggie was and immediately went inside to look for her.

Luke helped to nudge Jake's memory by putting names to faces of old classmates and friends who came up to him, and after a while, Jake began to relax and have a good time. But it wasn't until he spotted Will and Sara coming out the back door that he knew in spite of the past, in spite of trying to block thoughts of her out of his mind, in spite of the fact that she should be the last person he wanted to see, he'd been waiting to see if she would be here, all along. She looked out across the yard and her eyes met his. Sara smiled, and he was struck once more by the peaceful serenity in her eyes. She'd come to terms with the pain she'd suffered, but he didn't know how.

She looked wonderful. Her auburn hair was caught up on top of her head, and she was in an aqua and yellow sundress that looked wonderful on her. He knew from the way family and friends alike greeted her that Sara was special to everyone here. There was no getting around it. As much as he felt he needed to stay away from her, she was a part of his family and this town. Oh yes, he was going to have to find a way to deal with the fact that he was drawn to Sara as much now as he ever had been in the past.

Sara was glad so many people turned out for Jake's party, especially after the way Nora had treated him in the diner. When she glanced up and caught Jake looking at her, she smiled and her heart seemed to somersault all the way to her stomach when he smiled back. For a moment she wished she could change the past and go back to the time when they'd been best friends and shared everything—

"You look lovely, dear," Nora said, appearing from nowhere. "I wish Wade were here to see you."

Looking into the cool blue eyes of her mother-in-law, Sara was reminded that there would be no going back to being friends with Jake. "Thank you, Nora. You look wonderful, too. I meant to ask you about your doctor's appointment. How did it go? Did you like the new doctor?"

"Humph! Dr. Richard Wellington is just a little too full of himself. I don't think I'll be going back after I get the results from my blood work."

"Oh, I'm sorry you didn't like him, Nora."

Meggie was brought outside just then, and she claimed the spotlight without even trying. Luke took her from John but wasn't allowed to keep her for long. Sara and Grandpa chuckled as Meggie reached out to first one and then another family member until she got to Gram. She was settling into this family life really quickly.

But when Gram sat down between Sara and Grandpa, still holding Meggie in her arms, Sara's fingers itched to take the baby and hold her once more. She barely noticed Nora's quick departure from her side.

"I think she's getting just a little tired," Gram said. The baby was looking around with almost a glazed look in her eyes. "Meggie, do you remember Sara?" Gram asked as she turned the baby toward Sara.

"Hi, sweetness. Do you remember me?" Sara smiled at the baby.

Immediately, Meggie reached out to her. "Sawa."

Delighted that Meggie said her name, Sara wasn't sure if Meggie dove for her, or if she grabbed the baby. The next thing she knew, the baby was in her arms and had her head on Sara's shoulder.

"Oh, how sweet," Gram said. "She certainly does remember you, Sara."

Sara rocked the baby back and forth, loving the feel of her in her arms. She couldn't resist planting tiny kisses on her silky soft hair. Meggie was quickly claiming a piece of her heart.

"Well, would you look at that?" Grandpa asked moments later.

Gram smiled. "It seems as though Meggie was just waiting for your arms to fall asleep in, Sara."

Sara chuckled and tightened her hold on the baby. "I'll take that as a compliment."

"Oh, you should," Gram said. "I have to rock her for a long time before she goes to sleep. She'll fall right to sleep in Jake's arms, but not mine."

The bond Sara had felt that first day in Gram's kitchen grew even stronger as she sat and watched the party with Meggie in her arms. She knew she should lay the baby down, but she didn't want to let her go. Not yet.

Jake was beginning to tire of trying to keep names and faces straight. He wanted to find Meggie and make sure she was all right. He wasn't used to letting others take care of her, and he'd made himself stand and make conversation for over an hour now. It was time to find his daughter.

He started across the yard, but seeing Meggie in Sara's arms once more stopped him in his tracks. Sara was rocking back and forth, staring down at the baby. From the looks of it, Meggie was sound asleep. Gram and Will were looking on and talking to her.

His first instinct was to do what he'd done that first day in Gram's kitchen. Just take her from Sara and make a quick run for it. But he couldn't do that. Not here. He wasn't about to make a scene in front of his family and friends.

An invisible link seemed to be forming between Sara and his daughter, and he wasn't sure he liked it. Nor did he understand it. And he didn't have a clue what to do about it. He forced himself to walk casually up to the small group and smile. "She couldn't take any more attention, huh?"

Gram chuckled. "I guess not. She recognized Sara and reached out to her. It took her all of about a minute to crash."

"Doesn't take her long some nights. I guess I should be getting her home," Jake said, hoping his grandmother would agree, but knowing she wouldn't.

"It's early yet, Jake. We haven't even eaten yet. I'm sure Lydia will have a bed Meggie can sleep in for a while," Gram said. "Let me go ask." She was up and gone before Jake could stop her.

"Do you want to take her, Jake?" Sara asked softly.

Yes, he wanted to take her from Sara. There was something about the two of them so close together that pulled at his heart and created a longing within himself that he neither welcomed nor understood. But he was reminded of the look on Sara's face when he'd taken Meggie from her before, and he knew he wasn't going to let himself react that way again. The least he could do was let her hold his child for a few minutes.

"I don't want to jostle her too much. No need to wake her up," Jake said, although he was pretty sure nothing would wake Meggie up, as tired as she'd been lately.

Lydia came back outside with Gram. "I turned down the guest bed. I even have one of those bed rails to keep her from rolling off. She should be fine there. You know which room it is, Sara?"

Sara nodded and looked at Jake.

"Lead the way." He put his hand on her elbow to help her up from the bench she was sitting on and motioned for her to go first.

He followed Sara through the kitchen and up the stairs as she held his child in her arms. She turned to the right in the hall and they entered a small room with a twin bed that had indeed been turned down. A soft light lent a cozy glow to the scene.

Sara laid Meggie down, but the baby had a firm grip on her dress. She gently dislodged the little fingers, rolled the baby on her side, and rubbed her back. Meggie smiled in her sleep and plopped her thumb back into her mouth. Sara looked up at Jake and whispered, "Should I take her shoes off?"

Watching her with his child, Jake suddenly realized how very much Sara had lost and his heart twisted for her. He cleared his throat but still couldn't find his voice, so he just nodded.

He watched her fumble with one small shoe and then the other. Sara seemed to have forgotten he was there as she covered Meggie up with the sheet and caressed her cheek. "Sweet dreams, little Meggie."

She kissed her brow, stood, and backed away while he put the guardrail in place.

Jake bent over and kissed his daughter's cheek before turning back to Sara.

"Thank you, Jake." Her smile was real, but so was the sheen of tears in her eyes. Jake reached out and pulled her into his arms, wanting only to comfort her. Sara's head was on his shoulder, and they rocked back and forth for several minutes.

He wasn't sure what to say, he just wanted to make her feel better somehow. "Sara—"

Sara lifted her eyes to his and smiled through her tears. "Jake, I'm all right. Truly I am." Her voice broke for a moment before she continued. "It's just so good to hold a child."

Knowing he could never fully understand what Sara was feeling, Jake simply nodded, while he marveled that there was no bitterness in her eyes. "I'm sorry I took her away from you the other day."

Sara shook her head. "There's no need to apologize. I've seen you looking for her all evening. I think you're having a hard time trying to share her, and that's understandable. After all, it's just been the two of you since she was born."

That she read him so well came as no surprise to Jake. Sara had always understood him. But it was disconcerting that she still did after all these years.

His eyes strayed to her lips, and he found himself wondering if they tasted the same. Feeling the need to know, his head dipped and his lips lightly brushed hers.

Sara responded. Her lips clung for a second, for two, before she pulled away.

Jake wanted to kiss her again, but his eyes met hers and he saw the confusion in them. What could he possibly be thinking? Sara was not in his future. She'd opted out of his past. Hadn't he learned anything over the years?

Chapter 5

Sara's heart charged into triple time as she stood there looking at Jake. What just happened here? She'd wanted Jake to kiss her. Wanted him to hold her. The touch of his lips on hers felt familiar and comforting.

What was wrong with her? How could it feel so right to be in his arms? It'd been over between them long ago. She'd loved Wade. How could she be so disloyal to his memory?

The look in Jake's eyes mirrored her own confusion. She wanted both to reach out to him and to flee. She chose to run. "I'd better check on Grandpa," she said, backing out of the room.

Jake cleared his throat and nodded. He turned back to Meggie. Sara saw him bend down and kiss his daughter again before she turned and hurried back downstairs.

Sara didn't realize she was holding her breath until she entered the kitchen and saw that in reality, only a few minutes had passed since she and Jake had taken Meggie upstairs.

Ben was on his way out the door with more hamburger patties to put on the grill. Lydia was slicing onions and tomatoes. She'd commandeered Nora into tearing lettuce leaves and placing them on a big tray. Other family members were busy with the small jobs that always made huge gatherings somehow work. No one seemed to have missed them, or so Sara thought until she met her mother-in-law's chilly glance.

"There you are," Nora said. "I came in the house looking for you, and Lydia put me to work."

Sara hurried over and began helping Nora. "I'll do that for you."

Lydia chuckled. "I thought you came in to help out, Nora. If you'd asked, I could have told you Sara was upstairs putting the baby to bed."

The sound of Jake's heavy footsteps came down the stairs. When he entered the kitchen, Sara willed herself not to look at him, concentrating instead on tearing lettuce.

"Thanks for the loan of the room, Aunt Lydia," Jake said. "If you hear her wake up, please call me in."

"Of course, Jake. She'll be fine," Lydia reassured him. "You go on outside and enjoy your party. We'll listen for her."

"Thanks for getting her to sleep, Sara." Jake stood in the middle of the room, appearing to be waiting for her to say something.

Looking up and meeting his eyes, she said, "You're welcome. It was a pleasure to have her in my arms."

Jake gave a brief nod before heading outside, and Sara watched him go, remembering the feel of being in his arms just minutes ago. It'd felt like coming home, like—

"Sara, are you going to stand there staring into space, or help me with this lettuce?" Nora arched an eyebrow at her.

Sara ducked her head and continued tearing lettuce. She tried unsuccessfully to keep the color from stealing into her face. She'd been reliving Jake's kiss, and now the guilt that she'd enjoyed it washed over her. Wade had been gone over a year now, but it didn't seem right to be attracted to another man—especially when that man was his cousin. Yet right or wrong, she was drawn to Jake.

One glance at Nora told her that her mother-in-law wasn't happy about the short time Sara and Jake had spent together upstairs. The woman's lips were pursed together. Frown lines gathered between her eyebrows. Suddenly, Nora's hand pressed against her chest and she closed her eyes.

Sara reached out and touched Nora's shoulder. "Are you all right?"

Nora shook her head. "I'll be fine."

"You're sure? You look a little pale."

"I think I may be coming down with something. I do have a headache and feel nauseated. I think I'll just get my purse and go on home."

"I'll go up and get your things, Nora," Lydia said, washing her hands at the sink.

"No, no! I can get them myself. I'll see myself out. You see to your guests." She hurried upstairs, leaving Lydia and Sara to stare at one another.

"I'm a little worried about her, Lydia. She hasn't seemed herself lately," Sara said.

"Maybe it's just stress. It's been a hard year for Nora," Lydia said. "I think I tend to forget that sometimes, she's just so. . .Nora." She shook her head. "I doubt I'd have been anywhere near as strong as she's been had I lost my only son."

"I think I'll go up and make sure she is all right," Sara said, wiping her hands. She ran lightly up the stairs and turned to the right to peek into Lydia's room where guests had been instructed to leave the items they didn't want to carry around all evening.

Nora wasn't in the bedroom. The bathroom door was ajar, and Sara could see she wasn't there, either. She came out of the room and glanced down the hall. Nora must have turned on the landing and gone out the front door. She'd call in a little while and make sure she made it home safely.

The door to the room Meggie was napping in was slightly ajar, and Sara quietly peeked inside. Surprise took her breath away. There, on her knees beside the bed, was Nora. Tears flooded Sara's eyes as she watched her mother-in-law reach out and gently smooth back the hair on Meggie's forehead. But when she saw Nora bend over to kiss the baby's cheek, Sara's hand quickly covered her mouth to quiet the sob that formed in her throat.

Knowing Nora thought she was alone, Sara quickly backed out of the room and tried to calm herself. She must have made some kind of noise, though, because Nora's head turned sharply and she swiftly got to her feet and joined Sara in the hall. Sara's first instinct was to give Nora a hug, but her mother-in-law had never been comfortable with genuine demonstrations of affection or comfort.

"You might ask Lydia if she has one of those gates to put up at the door so that the baby doesn't fall down the stairs," Nora said brusquely as she started down the hall.

"Yes, yes, I'll ask her," Sara answered.

"She could crawl to the end of bed and get down," Nora continued. "If she got out of the room she could get hurt."

On the landing leading to both the front and the back of the house, Nora stopped Sara from turning to go back to the kitchen. "Meggie is a beautiful child. But Jake only came home to find a mother for her," Nora whispered.

"Nora, we don't know that. He just wants Meggie to be raised around his family."

Nora shook her head and whispered more urgently, "Mark my words. He hurt you once before, he'll hurt you again. Only this time there'll be no Wade to pick up the pieces." She pulled her purse strap over her shoulder and took the flight of stairs leading to the front door, leaving Sara standing on the landing, speechless and feeling the weight of her loss all over again.

Nora didn't need to remind her that Wade was no longer here. She lived with that knowledge every day of her life, always wishing she hadn't wanted that ice cream. Oh, she knew that the wreck wasn't her fault. A drunk driver had plowed into Wade's car. Still, she'd been the one craving ice cream, and that was the only reason they were in the car at ten o'clock that night.

Nora had never implied that she was to blame. But in the back of her mind, Sara could never quiet the voice that kept telling her that if she hadn't wanted that ice cream so bad, Wade and her baby might still be here. *O Lord, please help me. I thought I was doing so well.*

"Sara? Nora?" Lydia called from the bottom of the stairs.

"It's me, Lydia." Sara brushed away the tears that'd fallen and hoped Lydia wouldn't be able to tell she'd been crying in the dim light. "Nora just left. She was checking on Meggie and told me to ask if you have one of those gates for the door."

"Oh my. I certainly do. I totally forgot about that." Lydia bustled up the stairs, passed Sara, and led the way to the storage closet at the end of the hall. By the time she'd pulled out the gate, Sara had herself under control.

They both peeked in at the sleeping child while making sure the gate was snug against the door frame.

"Look at that. A thumb sucker. If I remember right, Jake used to suck his thumb, too," Lydia whispered. They started back to the kitchen.

Downstairs, Lydia poured them both a glass of iced tea and led Sara out onto the deck where Ben was grilling burgers and wieners. She handed her a plate. "You eat and go enjoy yourself, darlin'. Enjoy life a little."

Sara forced herself to fix a plate and eat. She managed to mingle with friends and family for the rest of the evening, taking care not to join any groups standing around Jake.

Jake renewed acquaintances and rebonded with family throughout the evening, all the while trying not to think of holding Sara in his arms and the kiss they had shared. Brief though it had been, it'd shaken him far more than he wanted to admit. He told himself he wasn't interested in starting up with Sara again, even if he could imagine that she might still care about him. All he wanted was to be able to raise Meggie in the same loving atmosphere he'd grown up in and make sure family was close by if anything should ever happen to him. That's all.

Yet when Sara came back outside with his aunt Lydia, Jake found his gaze seeking her out, in spite of the fact that he'd resolved to avoid her as much as possible. She'd looked so vulnerable putting Meggie down for her nap. And when he saw the tears in her eyes, he'd wanted to console her somehow. That's all. Just help her past that moment of sadness.

Now as their eyes met across the yard and Sara glanced away, he knew he'd only succeeded in making them both feel more uncomfortable with each other than they already had. When he realized she was trying to avoid him by joining only the clusters of people he wasn't part of, he tried to make things easier by leaving whatever group she headed toward. It was a cat-and-mouse game in reverse. The last thing either of them seemed to want was to catch up with the other.

Jake wondered which of them was more relieved when the party started to break up.

Sara had never been so glad for a party to end in her life. Trying to avoid Jake at his own welcome-home party had been draining enough, but once they were home, Grandpa wanted to rehash the whole evening over hot chocolate. Thankfully, he did most of the talking so all she had to do was add an agreeable murmur here and there.

"Nora left early, didn't she? I was a little surprised to see her there at all."

"She wasn't feeling well. I meant to call her to make sure she got home all right." Sara glanced at the clock and decided it was too late to call.

"More than likely, she just came for appearance's sake and left as soon as she could. We both know she isn't too happy about Jake coming back home." Grandpa leaned back in his chair and brought his cup to his mouth.

"I don't understand that, Grandpa. She used to ask about him and Melissa at every family gathering."

"That could have been more from curiosity than any kind of concern. Nora doesn't seem to care about many people these days. Just you. And I do worry that she's going to keep you from building a new life for yourself."

"I'm not going to let that happen. But she is Wade's mother, and I do feel a responsibility to her."

"I know you do." He drained his cup and took it to the sink to rinse out. He turned back to Sara. "You know, I think Nora needs to make a new life for herself. She's still a nice-looking woman. If she'd just soften up a bit, she could probably attract a man."

"That'd be wonderful, Grandpa, except I've heard her say she didn't want another man in her life too many times." Sara joined him at the sink and kissed him on the cheek. "But it's a great idea. We'll have to be on the lookout for someone."

The older man patted her on the back and nodded his head. "I'll talk to Ellie about it. If we put our heads together, we're bound to come up with someone."

Sara smiled to herself. *Looks like he's come up with one more reason to see Gram.* She really was going to have to watch those two a little closer from now on. "Let me know who you two come up with."

He crossed the room and started upstairs. "I'll do that, darlin'. I sure will do that."

Sara straightened up the kitchen and headed up to her own room. It'd been a very long evening. She did hope her mother-in-law was all right. If Nora wasn't in church tomorrow morning, she'd check on her first thing when she got home from the service. Maybe Grandpa was right. A man in Nora's life might perk her up. She'd been a widow a long time.

Sara prepared for bed, still wondering about the tenderness she'd witnessed Nora showing Meggie at the party. She would have made a good grandmother. *And I would have made a good mother.* But neither was to be and she wasn't going to let herself slide into a self-pitying mode again. She'd spent quite enough time there.

There might come a day when she could think of starting a family with another man, but it wasn't now. Yet knowing that fact didn't keep thoughts of Jake at bay. Being in his arms for those few short moments had taken her back to a time when she'd felt completely at home there.

It was probably good that Nora had reminded her of how Wade had picked up the pieces. She'd been shattered the night of her birthday when Jake had accused her and Wade of seeing each other behind his back. He had walked up when Wade was giving her a casual kiss, assuring her that Jake would be there to wish her happy birthday soon. That was all it'd been, but Jake hadn't stayed around to hear an explanation. Instead, he'd flown into a rage and taken off.

She'd cried herself sick for weeks and even tried calling to talk to him. He was never in. Finally, Wade had gone up to college to talk to Jake. When he came back, it was with the news that Jake was getting married to someone else. Sara couldn't remember much of the rest of that year, except that Wade had always been there for her. He'd taken her wherever she needed to go, escorted her to all kinds of events, and helped her get over his cousin.

She'd come to love Wade in a whole different way than she'd loved Jake, and when he'd asked her to marry him, she hadn't hesitated. She'd said yes. There might not have been bells and whistles, but they'd had a comfortable relationship and a good marriage, and she missed him dearly.

Now she felt guilty, angry, and confused for being comforted by the very man who'd hurt her all those years ago.

Jake tossed and turned all night. But it wasn't his old nightmare keeping him awake. He simply couldn't get Sara out of his mind. He threw off the covers and got out of bed. The sun was just coming up. He'd check on Meggie and go put the coffee on for Gram. It wasn't often anyone beat her up of a morning.

Meggie was already awake and playing with one of the stuffed animals in her bed. She looked up at him with that beautiful smile and reached out to him. "Dada!"

Nothing in this world felt as good as having his daughter in his arms. He changed her diaper and carried her downstairs to the playpen in the kitchen. After quickly putting the coffee on, he played hide-and-seek behind one of Meggie's big stuffed toys, while waiting for the coffee to brew. It'd just finished when Gram joined them.

"Well, this is a treat. Not often do I wake to the smell of coffee first thing in the morning." She crossed the room to give both Meggie and Jake a kiss on the cheek. "It's so nice to have you two here."

"I was hoping I'd beat you down." Jake kissed his grandmother on the cheek. "That's not easy to do."

Gram chuckled as she poured two cups of coffee and set his on the table. "I must have slept in this morning."

Jake sat down across from her and cradled the cup in both hands, savoring the rich aromatic smell before taking a sip.

"You haven't forgotten your promise, have you?"

"No, Gram, I haven't forgotten. I'll feed Meggie as soon as I get a cup of coffee in me and then go get her ready." It was Sunday, and he'd promised Gram that he and Meggie would go to Sunday school and church with her. As if he'd had a choice. Anyone who lived in Ellie Tanner's home went to church on Sunday.

He really didn't mind. Taking Meggie to church would be one less thing to feel guilty about, Jake realized as he prepared his daughter's oatmeal and juice, while Gram began working on their breakfast. He'd promised Melissa that if anything happened to her, he'd see to it that their child knew the Lord. And he wanted her to have a good relationship with God. Like he'd had before.

Watching Meggie try to feed herself took all of his attention. She did pretty well until he tried to help. Then she pulled back on the spoon, and oatmeal went flying. It kept him busy, just trying to keep everything from ending up on the floor.

Gram set a plate of bacon and eggs in front of him just as Meggie took her last bite.

"You eat your breakfast and I'll get Meggie dressed," Gram said, reaching to pick at his hair. "I think you'd better jump in the shower. Meggie got more oatmeal on you than on herself or the floor."

"Typical mealtime with my daughter. Most of it ends up anywhere but inside her," Jake said, chuckling. He took Meggie from her high chair and handed her to Gram. "Thanks for your help, Gram. You'll know better what to dress her in than I would."

"You do fine, Jake. Meggie always looks adorable, don't you, sweetie? Let's see. Do we need to wash your hair this morning?" She chuckled and checked Meggie's hair. "No, looks like Daddy got all the mess today."

Jake joined her laughter and watched as she and his daughter left the room. He quickly ate his meal and rinsed off his plate before hurrying upstairs to get in the shower. You had to act fast with oatmeal. It acted like cement if it sat in one place too long.

When Sara and her grandfather took their seats in church that morning, she knew something was up. A bevy of females was clustered in the middle of the aisle.

The last person she expected to see in church that Sunday was Jake Breland. But he was sitting beside Gram, looking very ill at ease with all the attention he and Meggie were getting. Meggie, however, seemed to be eating it all up as she sat in her daddy's lap. She looked adorable dressed in pink and white gingham. Luke came in late, took one look at the crowd around his brother, grinned, and then backtracked to enter the pew from the other side. Aunt Lydia, Uncle Ben, and John seated themselves in the pew behind them.

It appeared as if most of the young single women were busy welcoming Jake and his daughter home. If Nora was right in her assumption that he'd come home only to find a mother for Meggie, Sara figured he'd have several to choose from. For some reason that thought didn't set well with her, but she told herself it wasn't jealousy.

Too bad Nora wasn't here to see how many women seemed to be interested in exploring that very subject. Sara made a mental note to be sure to check on her as soon as she got home from church.

Finally, one of the deacons stood at the podium and cleared his throat, trying to get everyone's attention. Sara halfway expected to hear an announcement about an eligible bachelor being back in town. She was glad Jake had come to church, though. She hoped Gram was wrong in thinking that Jake's relationship with the Lord wasn't what it should be.

Sara tried to keep her mind on the service. She joined in the singing and heard Jake's baritone joining in. She'd forgotten what a beautiful voice he had. Meggie kept looking at her daddy's lips move, as if she'd never seen him sing before. She clapped when the first song was over, bringing chuckles from those around her.

More than once during the service, Sara had to force her attention away from Meggie and back to the sermon. The regular minister and his wife, David and Gina Morgan, were away on a missionary trip and were scheduled to return later in the week. Gina was one of Sara's best friends, and the couple had been a source of great strength for Sara over the past year. She really missed them. Gina's father, Tom Edwards, filled in for David, giving a good message on turning one's life over to God each and every day.

When the worship service came to an end, Sara hoped Grandpa wouldn't stand around talking for too long. She hurried out to the foyer ahead of him. Much as she wanted to reach out to Meggie, she didn't want to deal with Jake.

Looking back into the sanctuary, she recognized there was no need to worry about running into Jake. He and Meggie appeared to be held captive once more. Sara hadn't had any idea there were that many single women attending church, and she tried to tamp down the flash of jealousy she felt seeing Jake be the focus of all of their attention. Fortunately she didn't have to sort out her feelings, because just then she was approached by one of the deacons, who asked about the teddy bear project.

As soon as she and Gramps got home, Sara kicked off her heels and sat down to call Nora. But Nora didn't appear to be in the mood to talk. No, she wasn't sick. No, she didn't want company. Sara sighed as she hung up. She just wished Nora would move into town. Uncle Ben ran the ranch from his place. There was really no need for Nora to stay out there. It would make it so much easier for her to check on her from time to time.

Sara finished up the roast she'd put on before leaving for church that morning, but her thoughts kept returning to Meggie and how adorable she'd looked sitting in Jake's lap.

Grandpa said the prayer before the meal and then filled his plate. "What did you think of the reception Jake got at church this morning?"

Sara had been trying *not* to think of it. "Nora told me he'd only come home to find a mother for Meggie. If that's the case, it looks like he'll have his pick."

Grandpa chuckled. "Just 'cause he's got a lot to choose from, doesn't mean any of them would be his pick, darlin'."

"Well, I'm sure it's none of my business." Sara passed the mashed potatoes to her grandfather.

"None of Nora's, that's for sure." He took a bite of roast and sighed appreciatively.

Sara's appetite had disappeared. She just pushed the food around on her plate. Why did it bother her so much to see all those women converging on Jake and Meggie this morning? She was going to have to get a grip on the situation. Jake was a handsome man, and he was bound to start dating sooner or later.

"This is really good, Sara," Grandpa said.

"Thank you." Sara smiled across the table at her grandfather. He was always so careful to compliment her on her cooking. Grandma had trained him well.

"What are you going to make for Sunday supper at Ellie's?"

Sara moaned inwardly. She didn't want to go to the supper at Gram's tonight. She wouldn't be able to avoid Jake, and she wasn't ready to deal with making small talk with him.

"I'm not sure I'm going tonight, Grandpa. I haven't spent much time with Deana lately, and I thought I'd see if she wanted to do something." Deana loved Gram's suppers, too. Sara hoped she could talk her into taking in a movie instead.

"And miss Sunday night supper?"

His face looked so crestfallen, Sara had to chuckle. "You can go, Grandpa. I'll make that blueberry pie you like so well for you to take."

"Well, all right, but I wish you'd change your mind and go. You love those suppers with the family."

And she did. But they weren't going to be the same now that Jake was back. It wouldn't be long before the whole family picked up on how uncomfortable they both felt around each other. Then everyone would start to feel uncomfortable too. Sara wanted to avoid that as long as possible.

Her heart tightened at the thought of spending less time with the family she loved. She didn't feel she could call Gram just to chat anymore, and now she wasn't sure she'd ever feel comfortable at Sunday supper again. With Jake's return, changes were occurring much faster than she'd anticipated. Part of her wished he'd stayed in Albuquerque, and the other part wanted nothing more than a repeat of last night. A repeat of that moment of feeling she was where she'd always been meant to be. Held securely in Jake Breland's arms.

Chapter 6

With Meggie napping in her playpen close by, Jake sat at the kitchen table shelling pecans for Gram to make pies for her Sunday supper. He wondered how he'd forgotten about Gram's suppers. As a child and young man it'd been one of his favorite things about Sundays.

He'd probably blocked it out during his period of self-exile. He'd been so unhappy ten years ago. Crushed by Sara and Wade's betrayal, marrying Melissa and trying to make their marriage work despite the way it began—it had all been much easier to handle from Albuquerque.

For years, he'd avoided family gatherings, telling his grandmother they were going to Melissa's parents for all the holidays. They had spent some time with her family, but then her parents had been killed in an airplane crash. By that time, he was so used to not being in Sweet Springs, he had felt no desire to come home for the holidays. On those rare occasions when he'd made plans to come back, he had made sure word got out early. It seemed that Wade wasn't anxious to see him, either. He and Sara were either gone or busy with something else, and the result was that they'd never had to deal with seeing each other.

Now Jake sat at his grandmother's kitchen table, wondering if Sara and her grandfather would be there for supper and feeling disloyal to the mother of his child for even thinking about Sara. The familiar guilt that he'd never loved Melissa as much as she loved him washed over him. He'd tried. He had learned to love her, and he truly did miss her, but he'd always been suspicious about the way their marriage started. When Melissa came to him and told him she was pregnant, he did what he knew he should. He took responsibility for his actions and asked her to marry him. And when she'd lost the baby a few weeks after their wedding, he'd kept his vows and promised Melissa they'd stay married and work to make it a good one, but in the back of his mind, there'd always been that question. Did Melissa trick him into marrying her? Had she ever been pregnant?

In spite of his suspicions, they had turned their marriage into a good one. Only Melissa had done most of the work that built their relationship, and Jake knew it. She'd been a good wife, and she would have been a wonderful mother to Meggie. He wished he could have loved her more. Now she was gone, and he could never go back and say the things she would have loved to hear from him.

Jake cracked another pecan, but his mind wasn't on what he was doing. He'd made so many mistakes. Oh, he'd tried to make things right. He'd taken responsibility for his actions and he'd asked the Lord for forgiveness. But he'd always felt he should do more to earn it, and now with Melissa gone, he never would be able to. All he could do was be the best father to Meggie that he could be. That he was determined to do. *Please, God. Let me do that right.*

"Tom had a good lesson today," Gram said, bringing him back to the present.

Jake nodded in agreement. "I didn't know Tom was the minister here."

"Oh, he's not. His son-in-law, David Morgan, is. He and Gina are due back from Guatemala this week some time."

"David Morgan? He's a preacher?" Jake remembered David Morgan from high school, but he'd never have thought his friend would become a minister.

Gram came over to the table and patted his shoulder. "He is. One of the best I've ever heard, too. I'm sorry, Jake. We really didn't keep you up-to-date very well, did we?"

"Well, Gram, it's not all your fault. I didn't show much interest in what went on in Sweet Springs." He reached up and patted the hand that rested on his shoulder. "I'm sorry."

"You're home now, though. You'll catch up in no time." She looked into the bowl of freshly shelled pecans. "That's probably enough for now."

"You sure? I haven't had a piece of your pecan pie in years. I could probably eat a whole one by myself." Jake grinned at her.

"No way, big brother," Luke said, coming in the back door.

Both Gram and Jake shushed him, and Luke took care that the door didn't slam behind him. He crossed the room to kiss his grandmother's cheek. "If you get a pie to yourself, so do I," he said to his brother.

"Help Jake shell a few more pecans, and I'll make an extra pie for you both to share."

The brothers grinned at each other and started working on the pecans. "Meggie sleeping?"

Jake nodded toward the playpen over in the corner and glanced at the clock. "She should be waking up any minute now."

"All that attention at church must have worn her out," Luke teased and then dodged the pecan Jake threw at him.

"I know it wore me out," Jake admitted. "I didn't know there were that many single women in all of Sweet Springs."

He had noticed that Sara hadn't approached him and Meggie. She seemed to be avoiding him, which he knew was for the best. Still, it rankled. He hadn't been able to sort through his feelings from the night before, and right this minute, he wasn't in a hurry to figure them out.

"I know what you mean," Luke said. "And I sure didn't know they were all so hard up they'd be fighting over my brother."

Even Gram joined in the laughter that time. "There were quite a few young women around our pew today."

"Well, if you'd like a clear field, Luke, you can get the word out that I'm not interested."

"Nah, you can let them down all by yourself, big brother."

"I didn't know we'd raised you two to think so highly of yourselves." Gram stood facing the two men with her hands on her hips. "There were some fine young women in that group—some of whom might not want either of you, if they could hear the way you are talking right now."

"Aw, I'm just teasing Jake, Gram. You know how we are."

"Too bad some of those nice young ladies don't," she said, then shook her head and went back to her piecrusts, chuckling to herself every now and then.

Jake wasn't aware he was looking for Sara until Will showed up that night after church without her. He heard his grandmother ask Will why Sara hadn't come, but he couldn't quite make out the answer from across the room.

He didn't welcome the sharp pang of disappointment he felt. What was wrong with him? His mind warned him to stay as far away from Sara as possible, but the rest of him ignored the signals and looked for her at every opportunity.

"What's with you, Jake?" John joined him in a corner of the large wrap-around porch. "You look like you've lost your best friend."

He had, Jake thought, a long time ago. For that's what he and Sara had started out as. Best friends. Both orphaned at early ages, they'd found they had much in common, and they'd formed a close friendship. There was nothing he hadn't been able to talk to her about, until the night he'd found her and Wade kissing. He shook his head. "No, I was just thinking back to when we were all young and how so much has changed."

"We had some great times, didn't we? This is a great family to be raised in. And Sweet Springs is a good town to grow up in. I can't imagine living anywhere else," John said. "I don't know how you stayed away as long as you did."

Jake shrugged. What could he say? That he was too immature to handle seeing Wade and Sara build a life together? He couldn't do that to Melissa's memory.

But he did have some questions he'd like answers to. "John, why didn't you and Luke—anyone in the family for that matter—tell me Sara and Wade were seeing each other behind my back?"

Luke walked up just in time to hear the question and spoke up before John could say anything. "What are you talking about, man? Sara was heartbroken when you married Melissa."

Jake shook his head. "No, she wasn't. She and Wade were seeing each other long before that."

"I think you're mistaken, Jake," Luke said.

"I saw them kissing!"

Luke and John looked at each other and shook their heads. "When was this?" John asked.

"On her birthday. I was late getting home. I'd had a flat tire."

Luke nodded. "I remember Sara was upset because you never showed up."

"But I did show up. And Wade and she were kissing."

Both Luke and John shook their heads. "I never even knew you were here," Luke said. "You went on back to school?"

"Yeah, I went back. I saw no reason to stay." Not then. But now, he knew he should have stayed to hear Sara out.

"Maybe Wade was just trying to comfort her."

Jake met John's eyes. "Yeah, right."

"Did you ask them about it?" John asked.

Jake turned away. He should have. But would that have changed anything? He shook his head. "From where I stood, there was no reason to ask. I saw them kissing."

"But you married Melissa just a couple of months after that." Luke looked closely at his brother. "We all thought you broke up with Sara because of Melissa."

"You thought wrong," Jake said. He wasn't going to tell them just why he'd married Melissa—there was no reason to now. But was it possible he'd been wrong about Wade and Sara? *Oh, dear Lord, could I have read everything wrong that night?*

"If there was anything going on between Sara and Wade before you married Melissa, we didn't know about it, Jake. We'd have said something if we did," Luke insisted. "You know we would have."

More family and church members began to arrive, and the conversation came to a halt. But Jake did feel closer to his family than he had in years. Until he felt the anger fading away, he hadn't even realized he'd been holding a grudge, thinking they'd covered up for Wade and Sara. At least if Wade and Sara had been seeing each other, his family hadn't been trying to keep it from him.

He managed to enjoy the Sunday supper. The only glitch in the night was hearing so many people ask about Sara, especially when he had a feeling that he was the reason she was staying away.

It'd taken some talking, but Deana did agree to go to the movies with Sara after church that night. Sara knew Deana was curious about why she was so determined not to go to Gram's, but Sara was given a reprieve from talking when, as they took their seats, the lights dimmed and the coming attractions started.

After the movie, they made their way out to the parking lot. "Well, the movie was okay, but I'm not sure it was worth missing one of Ellie's suppers. You going to tell me why we had to go tonight?" Deana asked as they walked to their cars.

Sara shrugged. "You never know how long a movie will be here."

"You know I'm not buying that answer, don't you? I think we need to talk."

Sara sighed. Deana knew her too well. "I'm not ready to talk about it yet."

Deana nodded. "Okay. You know where I am."

"Thanks, Deanie. For going with me tonight and for letting me off the hook."

"Oh, I'm just letting you off for the time being. Don't count on my forgetting."

"I know you won't." Sara chuckled as she got into her car, but she knew she was in for a lengthy question-and-answer session one of these days.

She'd barely gotten the door unlocked when Grandpa pulled up. He'd brought her home a plate of sandwiches and various desserts, and she felt bad for not asking Deana over for coffee.

"Everyone asked about you, Sara. Said to tell you they missed you." He set the plate on the table.

"That's sweet. It's nice to know you're missed," Sara said, taking a seat at the table.

"Ellie said to tell you that she's taking no excuses next week. Said she expects you to be there."

Knowing Gram, she probably had already figured out why Sara hadn't made an appearance. Sara made a noncommittal sound before biting into a sandwich.

Grandpa poured himself a cup of coffee and sat down across from her while she ate.

"How was Meggie tonight?"

"The main attraction, of course. She laps up all that attention, but only to a point. Several of the women who were so attentive at church came to supper, but Meggie wouldn't have much to do with them. She's very selective about who she lets hold her." Grandpa laughed. "Linda Plunket tried to take her from Jake, and Meggie started crying. Jake had to take her upstairs to calm her down."

"Poor Linda. I'm sure that made her feel awkward."

"Ellie made her feel better by telling her that Meggie was just now getting used to the family holding her."

"She'll adjust to having new people around soon." Sara chuckled. "As a member of the Breland/Tanner family, she won't have much choice."

"They're a good bunch of people."

"Yes, they are." Sara bit into a chocolate brownie.

She loved the family she'd married into. She'd missed being there tonight. But the tension between her and Jake was so strong that everyone in the family would be picking up on it. Nora had certainly not kept it a secret that she didn't like Jake being home. Any time spent in his company was bound to cause more tension between her and Nora.

Nora was right about one thing, Jake had hurt her in the past. She couldn't chance letting him hurt her again, and the easiest way to keep that from happening would be to see as little of Jake Breland as possible.

"You all right, darlin'?" Grandpa nudged her hand.

"What? Oh, I'm fine, Grandpa." Or she would be—if she could just stop thinking about Jake.

Sara called Nora first thing the next morning, but it seemed she was feeling much better. So much so that she wanted Sara to meet her for lunch. Relieved that Nora wasn't feeling worse, Sara agreed.

Just as she hung up the phone, it rang again. "Sara dear," Gram said, "I missed you last night."

"I'm sorry, Gram. Deana and I went to the movies. Grandpa had a real good time, though."

Gram chuckled. "Your grandpa always manages to have a good time. Did he tell you that we're in cahoots together?"

"Oh?"

"We're trying to find a man we can introduce Nora to. Probably should be someone she's never met. You know, someone who hasn't been the victim of her sharp tongue?"

Sara couldn't contain her laughter. "Gram! You and Grandpa better watch yourselves. I don't think Nora will take kindly to you meddling in her life," she teased.

"Well, someone needs to. Maybe it'd stop her from meddling in everyone else's. Anyway, that's not what I called to talk to you about. It's time to start planning our annual family reunion, and I could use your help if it wouldn't be too much trouble."

Sara's newfound resolve to see less of the family melted. "Of course, I'll help you. What do you need me to do?"

"I thought maybe you could come over today, and we could map out a few things."

For once Sara was grateful for one of Nora's lunch dates. "Well, I am having lunch with Nora at noon."

"That will work out just fine. Meggie takes her nap around two o'clock. Would that work for you? Should give you plenty of time with Nora."

More time than she needed, actually. But she didn't want to run into Jake, either. She hesitated.

"Sara dear, Jake is going into the office this afternoon. You won't have to run into him."

Sara didn't know what to say. She didn't want to lie to Gram, but she knew the older woman would see through any excuse she could come up with. "I'll be there around two."

"Thank you, dear. I knew I could count on you."

Sara hung up the phone with a half smile on her face. Gram knew everything. Good thing one could trust her not to tell it all.

This time Sara beat Nora to the diner. It was crowded when Sara got there, and Deana was busy in the back. Sara sighed with relief. One more reprieve from a heart-to-heart.

"Hello, dear," Nora said, sliding into the booth opposite Sara. She picked up the menu and began to study it. "How was Sunday supper?"

"Grandpa said there was a good turnout. I didn't go." Her answer seemed to pique Nora's interest.

"Oh? Why not?"

Sara shrugged. She certainly wasn't going to tell Nora it was because Jake had held her in his arms and kissed her on Saturday night and she wasn't ready to try to look into his eyes and pretend it didn't happen. "Deana and I took in a movie."

Nora seemed pleased. "That's nice, dear. I'm glad you are getting out more with friends like Deana."

Yes, of course she was, thought Sara. *As long as it wasn't a man—especially one named Jake Breland.* She immediately regretted her attitude.

"What are you doing this afternoon?" Nora asked as soon as they'd given their order to the waitress.

"Gram called and asked if I'd help plan the family reunion."

When she saw Nora's face tighten up, her first instinct was to assure Nora that Jake wouldn't be there. Her second was to tell herself that she didn't have to explain her actions to Nora, and her third was to wonder if she'd imagined the tender scene between Nora and Meggie that she'd seen the other night. It certainly wasn't in evidence today.

"Is it that time again?" Nora frowned. "Seems like we just had a reunion."

"Actually, there wasn't one last year. There was too much grieving. But Gram doesn't want her family losing touch, and I'm glad she's going ahead with this one. I love the Breland/ Tanner reunions."

"Well, I'd think she'd have enough help with Jake home. He could help her plan."

"Nora, you know men don't really like to plan these kinds of things." Sara was relieved that their lunch was served just then. Her mother-in-law's tone was turning chillier by the minute. Sara sighed and wished she'd just kept quiet about helping Gram. But Nora wouldn't like it if she thought she was being kept in the dark. Sara was going to have to keep these lunches with Nora to a minimum. All she seemed to get out of them lately was a bad case of indigestion.

"Come in, dear. Thank you so much for offering to help me with this." Gram met her at the door and led the way to the kitchen, where she checked on the contents of a large pot simmering on the back of the stove. She poured two cups of coffee and brought them to the table, where a plate of chocolate chip cookies rested. "I put a roast on before Jake left for the office, Meggie just went down for her nap, so we should have several hours of uninterrupted time."

"Looks like you have everything under control, Gram. How are you doing? Remember my offer to help with Meggie if this all gets too much for you." She took a sip of coffee and watched the older woman gather tablets and pencils before joining her at the table.

"I do remember, and I'll keep it in mind," Gram said, sitting down. "Right now, with Jake here of a morning, and Meggie sleeping in the afternoon, it's working out pretty well."

She certainly looked none the worse for wear, but she always had seemed to have the energy of a woman half her age. Sara could only hope that she aged as well.

Gram pulled out the list of family members and handed it to Sara. "I'm really hoping Laci will be able to come home for this reunion. I haven't seen that child in two years, but she's promised to try."

Laci was John's sister, and she'd moved to Dallas several years back to study design. Now she owned her own interior design company. Starting a new business had kept her extra busy, and she hadn't been able to make it home in quite some time.

"What date are you targeting? It's the end of May now."

Ellie nodded her head and looked at the calendar. "I know I'm cutting it close, but I'd like to try for the Fourth of July. A lot of family may have already made plans, but I'd dearly love to have as much of my family together as I can this Independence Day."

"Well, let's go for it. What do you want me to do?"

"Sara, I don't know what I'd do without you. I guess the first thing is to call my sister and brother in Arkansas and see if they can come. Then, there's Bill's brother and family. . . ."

The next few hours flew by as they kept the phone busy. Almost everyone was as anxious to pick up with the family reunion as Gram was. She had plenty of room in her home, but there was no way she could put everyone up. Sara called both motels in town for information about reserving rooms. She'd just poured them both a fresh cup of coffee when the back door opened.

Luke entered and gave both his grandmother and Sara a kiss on the cheek. He turned to his grandmother with a wide grin. "It sure smells good in here. Think you could set a plate for one more?"

Gram grinned up at him. "Since when do you have to ask?"

Realizing that Jake would be coming in soon, Sara quickly gathered her things together and crossed the room to kiss the older woman on the cheek. "I didn't realize it was getting so late. I'd better check on Grandpa. You call me if you think of anything else you need me to do, okay?"

"I will, dear. Thank you for helping today."

"You're welcome," Sara said as she headed for the door.

"Hey, where's my kiss?" Luke asked.

Sara shook her head and turned to kiss him on the cheek. "Night, Luke."

He reached out and tousled her hair. "Night, Sara."

She pulled the door shut behind her and sighed with relief that she'd been able to leave without running into Jake again. If only she could feel as comfortable around him as she felt around Luke.

Chapter 7

After several days had passed without running into Jake, Sara began to relax. Since Gram had told her that Jake went to the office each afternoon, Sara timed her visits with the older woman when she was sure that he wouldn't be there.

Plans for the reunion were moving along. They'd contacted Laci, and she'd promised she'd try her best to come. A couple of Gram's great-nieces and nephews had let her know they were coming as well. Sara loved hearing the excitement in Gram's voice and was glad things were coming together so well.

Nora hadn't expressed much excitement about the reunion, but she didn't get excited about too much these days. Sara was beginning to think Grandpa and Gram were right: Maybe Nora did need a man in her life.

Sara had just finished making calls to remind the ladies of the church about the next teddy bear-making meeting and poured herself a glass of iced tea, when the phone rang.

"Hi, Sara," the voice on the other end said after Sara had answered the phone. "I hear you've been quite busy since we've been gone."

"Gina! You're back. When did you get in? Did you have a good trip? When can we get together?"

"We got in last night, the trip was really rewarding, and anytime is good for me. I missed you!"

"How about the diner?" Sara looked at the clock. The lunch crowd would have cleared out by now. "In about thirty minutes?"

"I'll be there. I can't wait to get caught up on what's been happening in Sweet Springs."

A short while later, Sara parked at the diner. Gina was already waiting in a booth but got to her feet as soon as she spotted Sara. The two friends hugged and grinned at each other before taking their seats.

"A month is just too long for you and David to be gone. I really have missed you."

"We're glad to be home. But the trip really was such an eye-opener for me. We take so many things for granted here, Sara. The orphanage is growing so fast, I'm just glad we've been able to help down there. The children will steal your heart."

"I'm glad you were able to do it. Tom did a real good job while y'all were gone."

"I'll tell him you said so. He and Mom are going down to Guatemala with the next work group."

The waitress came for their order, and they both settled for apple pie and coffee. As soon as they were left alone, Gina grinned over at Sara.

"I hear we have a couple of new faces in town—and that they caused quite a stir in church on Sunday."

Sara chuckled and nodded. "Jake and Meggie. He's going into practice with John. They're staying at Gram's for now."

"That's what I understood." Gina turned serious. "How is he doing as a single parent?"

"He's very good with Meggie. And she's adorable, Gina. I know exactly what you mean by stealing your heart. She stole mine the very first day."

"It hasn't been too hard on you, seeing her. . ."

Sara shook her head. "The first day at Gram's, she reached out to me, and it was as if God gave me what I needed, a child to hold, even if only for a few minutes. It was time."

Deana came out from the kitchen, bringing their pie and coffee, and joined them for a few minutes before the coffee-break crowd descended upon the diner. "What was time?" she asked Sara.

"For me to hold a baby."

"Ah, Meggie, right? Jake brought her in with him the other day, and she really is a cutie. It won't be long before she's walking. I hope she's not too much for Ellie then."

"So do I. Jake is only working part of the day now, but that can't last forever."

The bell above the door tinkled, and the three of them looked toward the door.

Deana grinned. In came David, Jake, and John. "Do you think they have radar and know when we're talking about them?"

She stood up and stretched. "The afternoon crowd arrives. It's back to the grindstone for me. One of these days, I'd like to sit down and have a real gab session."

"We'll have to get together soon and have a real hen party," Gina said.

Deana nodded on her way back to the kitchen. "Sounds good to me. Let me know when."

David slid in beside his wife and kissed her on the cheek, while John pulled a chair to the end of the table, leaving the space beside Sara for Jake.

Sara scooted over to give him more room, knowing she'd congratulated herself too soon for managing not to run into him. From Jake's quick shrug and half smile, she surmised he hadn't expected to run into her, either. She hoped the flurry of greetings everyone else was involved in would help keep them from noticing how uncomfortable she and Jake were.

"I thought you were catching up in the church office this afternoon," Gina quizzed her husband.

"He was," John said. "But word had it that you two were back, and Jake and I searched him out and convinced him to take a break with us."

"Jake, it's good to see you again." Gina smiled across the table at him. "But I'm really looking forward to meeting your daughter. I've heard she's really something."

Sara watched Jake's smile turn into a proud-papa grin.

"She is that. You come by anytime. I'm always happy to show her off."

"Oh, we'll be there for Sunday supper, if not before," David said. "Ellie is one of our favorite people."

"How's she making out, keeping up with Meggie?" Gina asked.

"So far, so good. But I'm hoping it won't be for too long. I know Gram isn't getting any younger. I've been in contact with a Realtor, and I'm going to look at a few places this weekend. But what I'm really going to need is a housekeeper to watch over Meggie for me. Any ideas on how to find one?"

"Have you tried the employment office?"

"Not yet. I was hoping to find someone through recommendations from people I know and trust."

"Let me think on it," David said. "Maybe I can come up with someone."

"In the meantime, if Ellie needs help, feel free to call," Gina offered.

Jake glanced at Sara and back to Gina. "Thanks. A lot of people are willing to help Gram, and John is letting me take my time getting settled."

"There's no hurry," John interjected. "I'm just thankful you've agreed to come in as a partner." He looked over at David and Gina. "Now, we want to know all about your trip. How is Guatemala?"

David and Gina didn't need any more coaxing to talk about their experiences in Guatemala. Sara tried to listen intently as they explained the ongoing work at the orphanage, but part of her was attuned to each and every breath Jake took. She was relieved when the impromptu gathering came to an end.

Jake had enjoyed the afternoon. He liked getting to know David and Gina all over again. From all he'd heard, David made a wonderful minister. He found himself looking forward to hearing him on Sunday.

The only rough spot in the afternoon had been when they'd first entered the diner and he'd found himself sitting next to Sara. He felt like a fumbling teenager as he drank coffee and ate his pie, trying very hard not to let her know how totally aware of her he was. Obviously they were going to be running into each other more often. They had family and friends in common, and Sweet Springs was not a large city where he could lose himself in the crowds. Hopefully he and Sara would soon get used to being around each other. He was back to stay, and he certainly couldn't see Sara moving away.

When Jake got back to the office, a message from Gram was waiting for him, and he quickly punched in the number. She answered on the fifth ring.

"Gram, is anything wrong?"

"I don't think it's serious, but Meggie's been a little fussy this afternoon. She doesn't have a fever, but I can't get her to eat a thing and she's been crying off and on. Do you think she might be cutting a new tooth?"

"Probably her first molar. I'll stop on the way home and get some of that stuff that numbs her gums. Maybe that will help."

"That's what I was going to ask you to do. Poor baby."

Jake could hear Meggie crying and Gram making soothing noises to her. "I'll be home as soon as I get it, Gram."

Jake hurried down the street to the drugstore. It hadn't changed much from when he was young. It was probably one of the few drugstores left that still boasted a real soda bar. Jake grinned, remembering all the fun he'd had here as a kid. It was nice to know that some things stayed the same. He'd have to bring Meggie in for a soda when she got a little older.

"Jake?" a soft voice inquired. "Is Meggie sick?"

He turned to see the concerned look in Sara's eyes. "Not sick, really. We think she's teething."

"Oh, that's good. Well, not good for Meggie, but I'm glad it's nothing more serious."

"Thank you, Sara." He motioned to the shelf in front of him. "I think one of these will help."

Sara nodded. "I'm sure it will."

"If I can only figure out which one to buy." He pulled two different brands off the shelf and turned to her. "Do you have any idea which one I should go with?"

Sara looked at both and shrugged. "I think either one will be all right. I'm sorry, Jake. I really don't know which brand to go with."

"Don't feel bad, Sara. Neither do I, and I've bought it before." He put one back on the shelf and turned to her again. He wanted to say more but didn't know what to say. "I guess I'd better get it home."

"Yes. I hope it works quickly. Give Meggie a hug for me?"

Jake nodded. "I will." He hurried to the checkout counter. It seemed to be the day for running into Sara. Maybe with time, it'd get easier. But somehow he knew that wasn't gong to happen until they'd confronted the past, and he wasn't looking forward to that conversation at all. Not one bit.

Sara had left the diner with the beginning of a headache and had stopped at the drugstore to pick up some aspirin. She left with a full-blown headache and started home wondering when and where she was going to run into Jake again.

She'd certainly made up for lost time today. She would have to try harder if she was going to manage to miss running into him at every turn. Was it even possible to avoid him? And was running into him, being in close proximity to him, ever going to get any easier?

That evening while fixing supper, Sara told Grandpa about David and Gina's trip as well as about running into Jake at the drugstore and learning of Meggie's teething difficulties. When they sat down to eat, he thanked the Lord for bringing David and Gina home safely and asked that Meggie feel better real soon.

Sara couldn't help but smile. She knew Grandpa was as taken with Meggie as she was.

All through supper, she told herself not to worry about the little girl, but she kept wondering if the problem involved more than teething. Could she have a cold or maybe a childhood disease?

After she'd cleaned the kitchen, Sara could stand it no longer. It didn't matter who answered the phone. She had to know how Meggie was. She picked up the phone and dialed Gram's number.

"Hello?" Gram answered.

"Gram? How is Meggie? I saw Jake in the drugstore—"

"She's fine now. That teething medicine worked like a charm. We even managed to get some supper down her. Jake's giving her a bath now. We think she'll be okay."

"Oh, good. I just wanted to make sure it was nothing more serious." Sara pictured Jake bathing Meggie and putting her to sleep. He really was a wonderful daddy.

"No, we're sure she's teething. Her little gum is real swollen. We'll doctor her good before she goes to sleep. Hopefully that tooth will come right on through."

"I'll pray it does. If you need anything, you call, okay?'

"I will, Sara. Thank you for checking."

Sara sighed with relief as she hung up the phone. Life was complicated enough without Meggie getting sick.

~

That Sunday morning, Jake listened closely to David's sermon. At first he listened mostly from curiosity about how someone he had known back in high school would preach. But soon the content of the sermon gripped his attention. It was on forgiveness—how we should forgive others as Jesus forgives us and forgive ourselves once we've been forgiven. David went on to describe the importance of going forward rather than dwelling in the past.

Jake wanted to move forward with his life. He was tired of living in the past. He wanted a better relationship with the Lord. He left church feeling for the first time as if maybe that would be possible. If Sara was at Gram's supper that night, he was going to talk to her. It was time to mend the past.

~

Sara knew she couldn't get out of going to Gram's Sunday supper, and she really didn't want to. It was a sort of welcome home for David and Gina, and she would never hurt them by staying away. She spent the afternoon baking a cake and making a platter of sandwiches to take. Wanting to help Gram as much as she could, she and Will took separate cars to church that evening so she could hurry over as soon as services were over.

Thankfully, others had already arrived when she got there, so Sara went straight to the kitchen to help Gram get things on the table. The turnout was large, as she knew it would be. Everyone wanted to welcome David and Gina home. Sara was hopeful that she and Jake could mingle without running into each other.

Somehow they managed to do just that. Or at least she did. By keeping a careful eye on which direction Jake was headed, she was able to move from one room to another just a step before or behind him.

She helped Gram keep the table full, took a turn washing up dishes, and still managed to visit. She even got to hold Meggie for a minute before Lydia claimed the little girl. All in all things were going better than she'd expected. Even Nora seemed to relax and enjoy herself.

Sara was headed back around the living room to pick up empty plates and cups when someone tapped her on the back. She turned to find Jake smiling down at her.

"Sara, can we talk?"

"Now? Here?" Sara hated sounding so breathless.

Jake looked around. "How about out on the porch?"

"All right," she said, doubt coloring her voice. She and Jake had been trying to stay out of each other's way ever since he came home. Now he wanted to talk?

Jake steered her to the side door, and when they got outside, he led her to a quiet corner. "I don't quite know how to go about this," he said, running his fingers through his hair. "But Gram says it's time."

"Time for what, Jake?"

"To try to call a truce or something so that we can coexist in this town without making everyone around us uncomfortable. And today, David's sermon was on forgiveness. I just—"

"Jake, is that what this is all about?" Sara smiled up at him. "Because if it is, I forgave you for dumping me, long ago."

Jake's dark eyes glittered in the dark. "Dumping you? You were the one who was seeing my cousin behind my back."

"What are you talking about, Jake?" Sara whispered hoarsely. "I wasn't seeing Wade behind your back."

"Well, tell me who it was you were kissing that night. It certainly looked like Wade."

Sara gasped and turned around. She headed down the steps and ran out to her car, but Jake caught up with her before she got the door open.

"Sara, answer me." Jake's hand kept her from opening the car door.

"You lost the right to ask that question when you turned and walked away without listening to me that night." Sara looked back at the house and was relieved that no one seemed to have noticed them.

"Then it wasn't you I saw kissing Wade that night?"

"There was nothing going on between us, Jake. Nothing."

"That's not the way it looked to me. Not after I'd received several anonymous notes telling me different, that very week. And especially not after I saw you in Wade's arms."

"What are you talking about? I don't know anything about any notes. And Wade was just comforting me when I got upset because you hadn't shown up."

"Yeah, right."

"I don't owe you any explanations, Jake. You wouldn't listen that night. It wouldn't make any difference now. But I did *not* cheat on you. Wade and I didn't even start dating until after you married Melissa. From where I stand, it looks like you were the one doing the cheating."

Jake turned Sara to face him. "I never dated Melissa until after I saw you and Wade kissing that night."

"But you married her just a few months later."

"Yes, I did. But I wasn't seeing her before that night." Jake couldn't bring himself to tell Sara the full story—that after he had returned to college he had gotten drunk for the first and only time in his life and that weeks later Melissa had told him that she was pregnant with his child from that night.

"Wade said you admitted dating her when he went up to college to tell you there was nothing going on between us."

"Then he lied to you. And he never told me there was nothing going on between you two. He said that you didn't want to hurt me, but that you and he were in love. That he'd been in love with you for years."

"No! Wade wouldn't lie to me. He went to talk to you because I was so upset and I could never get you on the phone. He said he'd straighten everything out. Then when he came home, he said you were getting married."

"That much was true," Jake admitted. "I was getting married." He could never betray his dead wife by telling Sara that he got engaged because of Melissa's pregnancy. Besides, it would probably seem like a lame excuse. No one else knew of the pregnancy; Melissa had lost the child shortly after their wedding. He shook his head. Nothing he could do or say was going to change the past. The only thing he and Sara had was the future.

"Sara. Please. Can we call a truce? Can we put the past to rest and start over?"

"You're telling me my husband lied to me. How can you expect me to just put that to rest, Jake? I don't know that I can." Sara pulled on the door to the car, and Jake moved his hand away.

"I'm sorry, Sara."

"So am I, Jake." She got in the car, started the engine, and pulled away.

Jake watched her leave, feeling a mixture of regret and relief. Regret that he'd brought her more pain, but relief that the past was finally in the open. His heart felt lighter in the knowledge that while his cousin had betrayed him, Sara hadn't—at least not knowingly. But that relief ended when he realized that while Sara was innocent, he and Wade had chosen to act in ways that damaged many lives. And the pain from those actions lived on.

Chapter 8

All Sara wanted to do was keep driving—east to Roswell, west to Las Cruces—anywhere away from Sweet Springs. But she knew Grandpa would worry if he came home and she wasn't there. He'd be worried enough already that she hadn't told him she was leaving Gram's.

So she drove home the long way, up and down one tree-lined street after another, until she thought she had herself under control. Then she went home and dialed Gram's number.

Thankfully, Luke answered the phone. It was easy to convince him she wasn't feeling well without raising too many questions. He promised to tell Gramps she went home early and told her he hoped she felt better real soon.

Sara hoped so, too, but somehow she doubted it. Jake had just told her that Wade had lied about them. How could she accept that her whole married life had been based on a lie? *Dear Lord, how could that be?* Wade had been a good husband, faithful and loving. He wouldn't have lied to her, would he?

She shook her head. No. He wouldn't. And it didn't matter, anyway. Wade wasn't here to defend himself, and she wasn't going to start doubting him now.

She put the water on to make some hot tea and paced the kitchen while she waited for the kettle to whistle.

No matter how hard she tried to suppress them, questions about the past kept surfacing. How could Jake have thought she was seeing Wade back then? She'd been crazy about Jake from their very first date. That was what had hurt so much. He hadn't trusted her. It'd taken so long for her to get over him. Wade had been there, that was true, but it didn't mean he'd been in love with her all that time or that he'd been trying to break her and Jake up.

No, Jake was mistaken. Or making excuses for his actions that night. Wade was her husband, and she knew him.

The kettle whistled and Sara quickly made a cup of tea and took it up to her room, but the drink sat untouched as she sat in the rocker by the window and looked out. How could she and Jake possibly bury the past when a whole new set of questions had just been raised?

Jake shook his head as he watched the taillights of Sara's car disappear. If he could manage to physically kick himself, he would. As it stood, he was seriously thinking of getting his brother to do it for him. Luke would oblige, but he would have questions Jake wasn't ready to answer. It seemed he'd made more of a mess of things than they were before he'd started.

He slowly walked back into the house and went up to check on his sleeping daughter. He'd just put Meggie to bed when he'd come back downstairs earlier and spotted Sara in the dining room. He'd been looking for a chance to talk to her all night, but she seemed to be in any room except the one he was in. So he'd quickly grabbed the chance presented to him and sought to clear the air between them. Oh, yeah, he'd cleared things up all right.

Fat chance of any truce being called now. He should have just asked that they start over, instead of actually going into the past with Sara. Now it looked like he was trying to excuse his actions by blaming a man who was no longer around to defend himself.

And wasn't that exactly what he had done? He was the one who hadn't given Sara a chance to explain anything that night. He was the one who'd gotten drunk and couldn't even remember what he'd done that night. All he knew was what Melissa had told him, and that had resulted in their marriage.

Oh, Wade may have used everything to his advantage, but it was Jake who'd given him that chance by not trusting Sara in the first place. Even if Wade had told him the truth, Jake knew the outcome wouldn't have changed. By then it was too late. Melissa had told him that she was pregnant.

Jake felt sickened by his behavior. He'd blamed everyone around him for his own mistakes. Oh, he thought he'd accepted responsibility for his actions by marrying Melissa. But he'd continued to blame Wade and Sara for his reactions to seeing them together that night.

He looked down on his daughter as she slept peacefully and marveled that the Lord had allowed him to be her father. To Meggie, he was just "dada," and she loved him unconditionally. Of course she didn't know what a mess he'd made of so many things. Jake hoped she'd never have to know.

He wished he could just stay upstairs by himself. But plenty of people were still visiting, and Gram could probably use his help. He bent down and kissed Meggie's softly scented cheek before heading back downstairs.

David looked up from refilling his coffee cup when Jake entered the dining room. "Been checking on Meggie?" he asked.

Jake nodded and chuckled. "She's sleeping soundly, thank goodness. She's been teething this week, and she's still not used to having quite so many people around."

"Changes can be tiring for a baby," David agreed. He took a sip of coffee. "I saw you walk Sara to her car a little while ago. Was she not feeling well?"

Surprised by the quick change of subject, Jake looked around and was relieved that they had the room to themselves. "I think she was fine before she talked to me. Sara and I have been finding it a little difficult, being part of the same family."

David nodded. "I noticed the two of you seemed a little uncomfortable the other day at Deana's. Anything you want to talk about?"

Jake saw only genuine concern in David's eyes. But he shook his head and nodded toward the doorway, where Gina and Lydia were entering. "Thanks for the offer. Maybe one of these days. Now's not a good time."

"Just so you know, I always have the time."

Jake smiled and nodded. "I'll remember that."

He greeted the two women and went through to the kitchen to see if Gram needed anything. It was the least he could do after running off her best helper.

Funny how when you didn't want to run into a person, you couldn't seem to miss them, but when you wanted to run into someone, they were nowhere to be found, Jake thought. He'd been to Deana's at lunchtime two days in a row. He'd made several grocery runs for Gram and even strolled Meggie to the ice cream parlor last night, but Sara was nowhere to be found. He'd even checked out the drugstore to no avail. He was beginning to wonder if she'd left the country.

His search for a house wasn't turning up anything, either. He wanted an older home in town, in good condition. So, it seemed, did everyone who owned one. The ones that were available were either too little or too big.

Several lots were for sale, however, and after an initial meeting with a local architect and builder, it looked like he'd be at Gram's until he could have plans drawn up and a home built. Now, if he could just convince her to let him hire a housekeeper to help her out.

He approached the subject again at supper, when he had Luke to support his efforts. "Gram, I think it's time we put an ad in the paper to see if we can find a housekeeper to help you out."

Gram looked up at him, her knife poised motionless above a half-buttered biscuit. "Jake, I told you, I don't want some strange woman taking care of my house or helping me with my great-grandchild."

"But I know Meggie is a handful." Jake cut the chicken-fried steak into bite-sized pieces for his daughter and handed her a child-sized fork. She loved spearing food and feeding herself. He looked back at his grandmother and continued, "She's going to be walking and climbing before long. I don't want her wearing you out."

"Jake's right," Luke chimed in. "Meggie will run you ragged in no time once she starts walking. You are going to need some help."

"Lydia has been coming over some."

Jake nodded. "Uh-huh, and John said she told him that you practically run her off every time she mentions helping out."

"She has a house of her own to run and a husband to take care of."

Jake spooned some mashed potatoes onto Meggie's plate, and she gave him a cheesy grin.

"Anyone want more tea?" Gram started to get up.

"You sit, Gram." Luke got up and brought the pitcher over to the table. "Jake and I can certainly wait on ourselves."

"You'd think I was an old invalid, the way you two talk," she grumbled, lifting her glass for a refill.

"No, we don't," Jake answered, "and I certainly don't want our being here to turn you into one. How about this?" he added as he handed Meggie her sippy cup. "Do you think there might be a teenager or two from church who would want a part-time job? One who could come in afternoons and on Saturdays to help out?"

Gram looked over at him and smiled. "Now that I might be willing to think about. It just might work. I think there are one or two who could use the money."

Jake breathed a sigh of relief, and he and Luke did a high-five. Their grandmother could be one stubborn lady.

Sara had been trying to keep busy. She'd helped Grandpa in the garden, she'd made ten more teddy bears, and she'd rearranged the living room. She'd stayed away from Deana's, the grocery store, and downtown in general.

But while she'd successfully avoided Jake, she hadn't been able to put him and what he'd said out of her mind. She kept going over the conversation with him. What bothered her the most was her reaction to the knowledge that Jake hadn't been seeing Melissa all along like she'd thought. He truly did seem to think that she and Wade had been seeing each other, and if that was true, then he had cared about her. Even though it shouldn't matter after all these years, she wanted to believe that Jake had loved her. And that's what troubled her most of all—the realization that she still felt something for Jake.

Recognizing that she had to talk to someone who might give her some insight into the past, she invited Gina and David to supper. Grandpa and David were out inspecting the garden before starting a game of horseshoes. Gina insisted on helping Sara do most of the dishes before they served dessert.

"Okay, my friend. Open up," Gina said, as she helped clear the table. "I know something is bothering you."

"You're right about that." Sara smiled at her friend. "What gave me away? The panic in my voice as I issued my last-minute invitation?"

Gina chuckled and shook her head. "No, I think it was last week at Deana's. The tension between you and Jake."

Sara sank her hands into the hot water and started washing a plate. "So much for thinking no one could tell."

Gina gave her a quick hug and took the plate from her. "I take it it's not been easy to adjust to him being back?"

"Loving his family so much doesn't make it any easier. They all mean so much to me, I don't want to have to give them up."

"As if they'd let you! Jake hasn't told you to stay away or anything like that, surely—"

"No." Sara shook her head. "In fact, he'd like us to call a truce. To get past our past, so to speak."

"Well, that's one way to put it. Can you do that?"

"Oh, Gina, I want to. I really do. Obviously we're making it hard on everyone around us. We have the same family and friends. It's not fair to you all."

"But?"

"But Jake told me something the other night that I find hard to believe."

"What was that?"

"Remember when Wade went up to college to talk to Jake? And he came back and said Jake was getting married?"

Gina leaned against the counter and nodded. "I remember."

Sara scrubbed another plate. "Jake says that Wade told him that we—Wade and I—were in love."

"Ah. . ."

"Jake said that Wade had been in love with me for a long time before that."

"Does that surprise you? Surely you knew that."

Sara closed her eyes and shook her head. "No, I didn't. I thought he was just my good friend."

"Oh. . ." Gina took the plate from Sara and dried it. Then she turned Sara around and led her back to the table. "And now you're wondering if Jake is telling the truth about what Wade said to him?"

Sara nodded. "I never knew Wade to lie to me."

"Did he ever tell you he didn't love you while you were dating Jake?"

"Well, no. He knew I was crazy about Jake. But if he told Jake that we were in love with each other, he lied to Jake."

Gina nodded. "That's true." She rubbed Sara's tense shoulders. "Sara honey, I don't know what to tell you. I can tell you that I always had the impression Wade was in love with you. Not that he was actively trying to break you and Jake up, but that he'd be there in the wings if you ever needed him."

"Why didn't I see that?"

"All you could see back then was Jake."

"Well, I'm not sure the same could be said about Jake. He said he didn't start seeing Melissa until he found Wade kissing me that night. But that's pretty hard to believe."

Gina shook her head and went back to the sink. This time she washed. "Not to me."

Sara took the plate she handed her and began to dry. "Why not?"

"Because I saw the way he looked at you, Sara. I think Jake was crazy about you."

Sara shook her head and continued drying dishes, mulling over what Gina had said.

"I'll never know for sure, will I?"

"I don't know, Sara. But I do know one thing from experience. None of us can redo what's in the past. All we can do is go forward."

Sara took the dishcloth from Gina and wiped down the counter. "I know you're right. It's just not easy."

"No, it's not." Gina drained the dishwater and turned to Sara. "You haven't asked for my advice, but I'm going to give it anyway."

"You know I always value your opinion."

"I'd say put the past to rest, call a truce with Jake, and go forward. Wherever that takes you."

Before Sara could answer, the screen door opened and Grandpa stuck his head in. "Sure is nice out here. You girls going to join us?"

"We'll be right there, Grandpa."

Jake watched his daughter staring at the room full of other children. Meggie didn't seem to be sure she wanted to stay with the other toddlers. The woman who cared for them on Wednesday evenings at church showed Meggie a toy and introduced her to another little girl. Jake stayed until his daughter seemed to relax and become curious about the other children. He started to ease out the door and felt his heartstrings tug when Meggie casually waved her little hand and said, "Bye, Dada." Pride in the fact that she was handling his departure so well warred with the ache in his heart from realizing that she seemed so unconcerned about where he was going.

He took a seat in the pew with Gram and Luke in the adult class. Quickly he became immersed in David's lesson. The minister encouraged everyone to ask questions, and the discussion went beyond surface issues.

When the bell rang to end class, Jake got up to bring Meggie in for the song service. His heart gave a sudden lurch when he spotted Sara and Will two pews behind him. He nodded in passing, but hurried on up the aisle when he noticed Meggie's teacher bringing out her class.

"How'd she do?" he asked, as Meggie threw herself into his arms.

"She did really well. I think she liked it. It takes them a little time to adjust, but she didn't cry at all. That's a good sign."

Meggie waved good-bye to the teacher and looked around as Jake carried her back to his seat. She liked the singing, and to Jake's surprise, she stayed quiet through the closing prayer.

Before the service ended, David invited everyone to adjourn to the fellowship hall to celebrate the eightieth birthday of one of their members. Gram offered to serve the cake and ice cream, so Jake had no choice but to stay.

"Meggie, want some cake and ice cream?" Luke asked, holding his arms out to her.

She reached for her uncle. "I-ceam!"

Jake laughed and handed her to his brother. "Yeah, you can go with Uncle

Luke. And he can clean you up afterwards."

Luke made a face at him, and Jake watched the two of them head up the aisle. Just inside the fellowship hall, Luke and Meggie caught up with Sara and Will. Their words drifted back to Jake.

"Hi, sweet Meggie," Will said. "You going to get ice cream? Can I go with you and Uncle Luke?"

Meggie nodded and looked at Sara. "Sawa comin'?"

Jake saw Sara smile at Meggie and look back at him. "I am. But first I'm going to talk to your daddy, okay?"

" 'Kay."

Jake stood at the doorway of the sanctuary, his heart hammering in his chest. Now was his chance to apologize. What better place than a church, he thought fleetingly, as he strode across the foyer to join Sara at the door to the fellowship hall.

He took a deep breath. "Sara. I was hoping for a chance to talk to you."

She arched an eyebrow and smiled. "Oh? So was I. Wanting to talk to you."

"I'm sorry for upsetting you the other night. I was wrong—"

"Jake." Sara held up her hand and shook her head. "Do you still want to call that truce?"

"If we're going to live in the same town, I think it would be a good idea." Could she really be considering a truce after the way he'd hurt her on Sunday night? "What do you want?"

"What do I want?" Sara repeated his question and paused. She looked around at all the friends and family they shared. She smiled, seeing Luke help Meggie with her ice cream. And she saw Gina glancing their way from across the room.

"I think it might be easier to tell you what I don't want."

Jake nodded. "All right."

"I don't want our friends and family, especially your sweet Meggie, to feel the tension we feel. I don't want them to be uncomfortable every time the two of us are around." Sara looked him straight in the eyes. "And I don't want to rehash the past to get to that point."

Jake couldn't believe she was willing to bury the past and what he'd said the other night. He'd accused her of being untrue to him, he'd called her husband a liar, yet here she was offering to forget it all and go on.

"Jake? What don't you want?"

He never wanted to forget this moment. "I don't want to go back. I'd like to go forward, but do you think we can?"

Sara tilted her head to the side. "We won't know until we try, will we?"

Jake was ready to try. More than ready. He was tired of the past. All it had ever done was pull him down. He nodded. "No, we won't."

"Truce?" Sara asked, sticking out her hand.

Jake covered her small hand with both of his. "Truce."

They smiled at each other for several seconds before Sara gently pulled her hand from his. The tension between them was by no means gone, but there was a subtle difference to it.

John walked up to them, a plate of cake and ice cream in his hand. "What are you two discussing so seriously over here? World peace?"

They both chuckled, and Jake shook his head. "No. Just our little corner of it."

"Cake looks good. I think I'll go try it myself," Sara said. "Catch you two later."

Jake watched her walk over to the cake table, then scanned the room for Luke and Meggie. He nudged his cousin, and they both laughed. Luke was letting Meggie feed him, and from the looks of it, he was the one who'd need his face cleaned when the evening was over.

Sara took her plate from Gram and turned to find Gina at her elbow.

"Come on. I have a spot all picked out for us."

Sara knew she was going to be quizzed on her and Jake's conversation, but at least Gina waited to bring up the topic until after they'd taken seats off in a corner where, hopefully, they wouldn't be disturbed.

"So. . .how'd it go?"

"Truce is called and hopefully we'll be able to coexist in the same town without all of you wishing we'd both move away." Sara grinned at Gina and took a large bite of cake.

"Nah, before we'd get to that point, we'd probably lock the two of you in a room together. Or knock your heads together."

Sara chuckled. "Well, maybe you won't have to resort to those tactics now."

"You look better all ready."

"I thought about what you said. You were right."

"Only because experience taught me a few things."

Sara knew Gina was referring to her own relationship with David and how the couple had been forced to deal with a past of their own before they found happiness together. "Well, just don't expect Jake and me to turn out the way you and David did."

"No?"

Sara wasn't happy about the way her heart sped up at the thought of a future with Jake. That was not what this truce was about. "No. You can't compare Jake and me to you and David."

"You think not?" Gina quirked an eyebrow and nodded across the room to where Jake was sitting.

Sara looked up to find Jake's gaze on her. Her breath caught in her throat as he smiled, and it felt like a hundred butterflies were let loose against her ribs. She smiled back before turning around to answer her grinning friend. "No."

Gina chuckled. "Okay. I won't compare. I'll just sit back and watch."

Chapter 9

"Would you look at that?" Luke paused in cleaning frosting off his mouth and nudged Jake's arm.

"What?" Jake was busy wiping cake off Meggie's face and hands. Evidently forks and spoons didn't work when feeding Uncle Luke. Only hands would do.

"Gram and Will," Luke said. "He's making her take a break from serving. I thought he was getting seconds, but he was fixing a plate for Gram."

Jake turned to look across the room at the older couple. He saw Will pull out a chair for Gram and place a plate of cake and ice cream in front of her. Then he took a seat beside her and patted her back. They were either the very best of friends, or—

"Have I missed something?" Jake asked his brother.

"I think maybe we both have. Is that our grandmother blushing?"

Jake chuckled and nudged him. "Well, don't gawk at them."

"Gwalk, dada? I walk."

"I know you do, sweetheart." Jake chuckled as he put Meggie on her feet and took her hands in his. "Let's go get you a drink."

Meggie hadn't quite gotten up the courage to let go yet, but her greatest joy was trying to walk. Jake led her past the table his grandmother was seated at, and a quick glance told him that the older woman's cheeks did appear to be a little rosier than usual.

Jake helped Meggie climb up the steps to the toddler fountain and held her while she drank. The thought that Gram and Will might be sweet on each other didn't really bother Jake. It did create one more reason that he and Sara needed to make their truce work. But just because they'd called a truce didn't mean everything would be smooth sailing from here on out. He was sure that he and Sara would go out of their way to keep from making the people they cared about feel uncomfortable in their presence. Who knew? Maybe one day they wouldn't feel so tense around each other. But it wasn't going to happen until he could find a way to curb the attraction he felt for her.

Watching Sara and Gina deep in conversation, Jake admitted to himself that past or no past, he was attracted to her. And he knew it wouldn't matter if he had never met Sara before—he'd still be drawn to her. Yes, she was beautiful, but there was more. There was a depth to her that hadn't always been there; a light that seemed to come from deep inside. Suddenly Jake knew that her relationship with the Lord set Sara apart and gave her the peace he so desperately wanted.

Sara watched Jake walk Meggie to the water fountain and help her get a drink.

"He is crazy about that baby, isn't he?" Gina asked.

"He certainly is." Sara nodded. She loved watching Jake with Meggie. The love shining from his eyes when he looked at his daughter was so strong it was almost tangible. "It was just the two of them until he moved back here, and I think he's had a little bit of trouble letting others help him with her. Not that you'd know it to hear Nora talk."

"Oh? Nora isn't happy about Jake being back?"

Sara shook her head. "She thinks he came back just so he could dump Meggie on Gram, to hear her tell it." Sara instantly felt sorry for gossiping about her mother-in-law. "I shouldn't have said that. I'm sure she is just concerned about Gram taking on too much."

"Maybe that's what all of that was about, earlier." Gina looked thoughtful as she scooped up a bite of cake.

"What are you talking about, Gina? What happened?"

"Well, Nora was serving earlier, and when she saw you and Jake talking, she said something to Ellie, and I heard Ellie tell her that it wasn't any of her business. Then Nora left in a huff."

"I'd wondered where she was. She probably won't be happy with me. I've upset her several times over Jake. I guess this is another one."

"Sara, you can't let Nora bother you. You and Jake are part of the same family, just as Nora is. Getting along is a good thing. It makes life easier on everyone."

"I know. I just don't like upsetting her." She chuckled. "Grandpa and Gram think she needs a man in her life."

"Ah, that explains what those two have their heads together about. They're hatching a plan to get Nora together with someone?"

"Well now, it might have something to do with Nora, and it might not. I've been wondering about the two of them." Sara shook her head and grinned. "Don't they make an adorable couple?"

Gina laughed and nodded her head. "They do. My word, David and I go away for a month and come back to all kinds of matchmaking."

"Don't hold your breath to see if any of it is successful. Far as I know, those two haven't come up with anyone for Nora."

"What's this about someone for Nora?" Lydia asked, coming up behind them. "What a good idea!"

Sara and Gina both laughed.

"Grandpa and Gram seem to think so," Sara said. "We think that may be what they are talking about over there." She unobtrusively motioned to the table where the older couple was seated.

"Oh." Lydia sounded disappointed. "I thought maybe there was a romance brewing between those two."

"I wouldn't rule that out yet, either." Sara gathered up her plate and cup and led the way toward the kitchen to help with cleanup. "We've been wondering the very same thing."

The next few days gave the tentative truce a chance to work. Jake and Sara smiled hesitantly at each other in the grocery store and waved at each other from across the street. It felt like progress when they graduated from trying not to make eye contact to actual conversation during the next few days.

On Thursday, Jake was just entering the diner as Sara began to leave. He held the door open for her. "Good morning, Sara," hc said. "Nice day we're having."

"Good morning, Jake," Sara answered. "Yes, it is."

The next afternoon Jake was leaving just as she and Gina entered Deana's.

"Good afternoon, ladies," Jake said. "How are you both today?"

"Doing well, Jake," Gina answered.

"That's great. Thank you for the names you gave Gram. She said she was sure she could pick one or two girls to help out from the list you gave her." He turned to Sara and grinned. "And you, Sara? Have you had a good day?"

"Hi, Jake. I'm just fine. How are you? And Meggie and Gram, how are they?" Sara couldn't help it. She chuckled at their exaggerated politeness.

"We're doing just fine, thank you." His deep chuckle joined hers as he walked out the door.

Sara was still smiling when she took her seat across from Gina.

"Looks like the truce is holding," Gina said.

"Well, I don't think it's been tested yet. We've only seen each other in passing."

"You're both laughing at the situation. That's always a good sign."

"A sign of what?"

"Oh, come on, Sara. You two genuinely like each other. You always have."

Sara couldn't argue with her friend on that one. She and Jake had always liked each other. They'd been relaxed around each other whether they were talking or silent, and she did miss that closeness. Sara was relieved when the waitress interrupted their conversation. She didn't want to talk about her present feelings about Jake. She wasn't quite ready to admit how strong they were—even to herself.

But she did want to know about these helpers for Gram, and after the waitress left with their order, Sara turned her attention to Gina. "What's this about a helper for Gram? Is she having problems keeping up with Meggie? I offered to help anytime." If they were looking into others lending a hand, apparently Jake didn't want to take her up on her offer.

"Now don't get all riled up, Sara. From what Ellie told me, she still doesn't think she needs help. But Jake insisted she get someone. They finally compromised on getting one or two of the teens from church to come in after school to help out, at least until Jake gets into his own place and can hire a housekeeper."

"I could help out easily," Sara said. Some truce they were going to have if Jake didn't even trust her with his daughter.

"Sara, you know how independent Ellie is. She only agreed to this plan because she knows there are several girls who could use the money. It's her way of helping out. You know if it was more than a few hours a day or if she was sick or something like that, you're probably the first person she'd call."

Sara nodded. Gina was right and she was sure that Gram would call her. What she wasn't sure about was that Jake would ask her to help.

That same afternoon, she'd agreed to meet with Gram again to firm up some of the plans for the reunion. Truce or no truce, she was a little apprehensive as she knocked on the door and breathed a sigh of relief when Gram answered.

"Come in, dear. Meggie is down for a nap, and I'm just putting a roast on for supper." She led the way back to the kitchen and poured Sara a cup of coffee.

Gram finished browning the large roast and slipped it into the oven before joining Sara at the table. She gathered her lists together, looked through her glasses at Sara, and smiled. "Let's see, where did we leave off?"

The rest of the afternoon flew by as they made more phone calls and went over menus and shopping lists. Gram was as excited as a child about the coming reunion. They worked steadily until male banter and laughter alerted them that Jake and Luke were entering the kitchen.

"Sara! It's nice to see you," Luke said, crossing the kitchen to give his grandmother and Sara a kiss on the cheek.

Jake barely had time to smile at her before a squeal was heard from upstairs and he rushed to check on Meggie.

"Oh my, it's later than I thought," Gram said, looking at the clock. "Sara, why don't you call Will and tell him to come on over? This roast is big enough for all of us, and I just didn't seem to know when to stop peeling potatoes."

Sara noticed several more pots on the stove and realized Gram must have finished her meal preparations while she had been tied up on the phone. "That's all right, Gram. I'll go home. Grandpa may have already started supper."

The older woman picked up the phone. "Well, there's only one way to find out." She dialed the number just as Jake came back down the stairs with Meggie on his hip.

"Will, it's Ellie. Darlin', I'm afraid I've kept Sara here too long today. I've asked her and you, of course, to eat with us, but she was afraid you might have started supper already."

Apparently both Luke and Jake caught the change in their grandmother's tone as she talked to Sara's grandfather. Luke raised an eyebrow in Sara's direction and motioned toward Gram. Jake looked on as Sara shrugged and grinned.

Luke raised and lowered both eyebrows as they heard Gram's side of the conversation continue.

"I'll tell her. We'll be eating in about a half hour. We'll be looking for you."

Sara quickly hid her smile as Gram turned to her. "Your grandpa said he hadn't started a thing and he'd be glad to give you a break from cooking. He'll be right over." She looked down at her apron and reached up to fluff her hair. "Sara dear, would you check the roast? I need to go freshen up just a bit."

Luke, Sara, and even Jake could barely contain their chuckles until they were sure Gram was out of earshot.

"Did you hear that? Gram sounded all of sixteen on the phone," Jake said.

"From the sound of it, we may have to ask your grandfather what his intentions are," Luke added.

"Don't you dare embarrass those two wonderful people!" Sara said; but her giggles increased.

Meggie looked from her daddy to her uncle Luke to Sara and back again. Finally she giggled and clapped her hands, not wanting to miss out on any of the fun.

All three adults struggled to get their laughter under control before Gram came back downstairs, but they were still chuckling when she returned.

"My, my, I haven't heard this much laughter in a long time," she said as she entered the kitchen. She'd changed into a dress, put on lipstick, and coaxed her hair into soft silver waves around her face. "What has everyone's tickle bone turned on?"

Jake seemed to recover first. "Oh, Meggie got tickled about something and it just snowballed. You know how that goes. One person giggles, then another, and pretty soon, you have a whole roomful of people laughing and no one can tell you why."

"You look awfully nice, Gram. You wouldn't be sprucing up for any reason we need to know about, would you?" Luke asked.

Sara shook her head at him. What was he doing? Trying to embarrass Gram? How she and Grandpa felt about each other was none of their business.

"Lucas, I do not feel that question deserves an answer other than the obvious one. We have company coming for supper." She turned from the stove and arched an eyebrow at her youngest grandson. "Do I need any other reason to comb my hair and put a clean dress on?"

Jake and Sara couldn't help chuckling again, only this time their amusement was brought on by the look on Luke's face as he realized his grandmother had just put him in his place.

"Uh, no, ma'am, you don't." He crossed the room and kissed her cheek to make amends. "You look quite lovely, too."

"Thank you. Now you can mash the potatoes."

Luke saluted and rolled up his sleeves. "Yes, ma'am. I'll get on that right away."

Gram grinned at him. "Good."

Her attention turned to Jake and Sara. "Jake, will you sharpen the carving knife for me?"

"Yes, ma'am," Jake said, plopping Meggie in her playpen until suppertime.

"And, Sara, would you be a dear and set the table in the dining room?"

The three exchanged glances and tried to hide their smiles as they went about the chores they'd been given, feeling properly disciplined.

A few minutes later, Sara stood back and looked at the table. It looked nice. The doorbell rang, and Gram called out, "Sara dear, please let your grandfather in."

Sara hurried to do just that, wondering if her grandpa had taken the time to spruce himself up as well. She opened the door and caught a strong whiff of his aftershave. She'd never seen him look so nice except for when he went to church. While he didn't have a suit on this evening, he'd dressed in a nice pair of slacks and a white shirt. His hair was slicked back, and his bushy white eyebrows actually looked tamed. He'd even trimmed his moustache. *Oh my, this does look serious.*

"Why, Grandpa, don't you look nice."

"Thank you, darlin'." He looked around. "Where's Ellie? In the back?" Not waiting for an answer, he headed for the kitchen. Sara followed, a half smile on her lips. Grandpa seemed to feel even more at home here than she did. She noticed Gram blush as Grandpa walked over to her and took her hand in his.

"Ellie," he said, "thank you so much for inviting Sara and myself to supper."

Gram reached up and patted his cheek with her free hand. "You're very welcome, William."

They stood looking into each other's eyes until Luke called from by the stove, "Mashed potatoes are ready, Gram."

"Oh." Gram turned her attention to getting the meal on the table. "Yes, well, Jake, you get Meggie set up in the dining room. Luke, carry those potatoes in, please. And Sara dear, please get the rolls from the oven."

They all jumped to do Gram's bidding, feeling a little like intruders waiting to see what the older couple was going to do next. It wasn't until they'd reached the dining room and taken their seats that the three realized their respective grandparents were still in the kitchen. They looked at one another. The silence was deafening.

Several minutes passed before Gram led Grandpa out to the dining room. He put the nicely sliced roast in the center of the table before pulling out Gram's chair for her.

The relief was almost tangible when Meggie broke the silence by clapping her hands. "I hungy, Gma!"

"Will, would you please say grace, so we can feed this baby?"

"Dear Father, we thank You for this food we are about to eat, for those who prepared it, for this family and these friends. We thank You for watching over us and seeing to our needs daily. In Jesus' name, amen."

Jake quickly dished up some mashed potatoes and watched as his daughter filled her spoon. She managed to take her first bite without spilling any. And her second. It looked like his daughter had finally conquered using a spoon. "Meggie, you did it!"

Meggie put down her spoon and clapped her hands. From then on the evening was hers. She flirted and giggled between each bite. But as soon as she finished eating, she reached out to Sara.

"Sawa, hode."

When Sarah looked at Jake for permission to hold his daughter, he knew he'd never be able to deny her. He unbuckled Meggie and started to hand her to Sara, but Meggie said, "I walk."

Jake put her on her feet and steadied her. Meggie held on to his hands for a second and then let go. Everyone at the table silently watched Sara get out of her chair and kneel on the floor, holding her hands out to Meggie. Then, hands outstretched, Meggie took one. . .two. . .three steps straight into Sara's arms.

Sara hugged her. "Meggie, you did it! What a big girl you are!"

Meggie had to walk back to her daddy and then take turns walking to everyone else at the table while Uncle Luke took pictures. But she ended right back with Sara when she tired of showing off.

"Sawa, hode now."

It was impossible for Jake to keep his eyes off Meggie and Sara. Like it or not, they'd bonded to each other. It didn't bother Jake as much as it had when he'd first returned to town. Sara was wonderful with his daughter. She finished the rest of her meal with Meggie sitting in her lap as if she belonged there. When she brushed the hair from Meggie's cheek and kissed her, Jake was reminded of the night she'd put Meggie to bed. The night he'd held her in his arms and kissed her. His gaze strayed to her mouth, and he looked up to see color stealing up her face as her eyes met his. Was she remembering too? He liked the thought that she might be.

Meggie seemed content to stay right where she was, and Jake couldn't blame her. When the meal was over, the only thing that got her out of Sara's lap was the promise of a horsy ride from Uncle Luke. Sara insisted on clearing the table and doing the dishes, leaving Gram and her grandfather to visit while Jake and Luke played with Meggie.

It wasn't until Sara and her grandfather had left and Jake was upstairs giving Meggie her bath that he realized he was no closer to knowing how serious his grandmother and Will were about each other than he'd been before supper. While he'd meant to pay special attention to how they reacted to each other during the meal, it seemed his focus had been elsewhere. His attention had been taken by his daughter. . .and by Will's granddaughter.

Sara was tired but still too keyed up for sleep. She made some hot chocolate and took it to the front porch. Setting the swing in motion, she smiled, thinking back on the evening. The truce had held and she was glad. She and Jake had done the right thing by agreeing to it.

Now if she could just find a way to keep her heart from going into overdrive every time she was around him. Sara sighed and closed her eyes, but all she could see was the look in Jake's eyes while she held Meggie. She hoped that hadn't been pity she'd seen, because pity was the last thing she wanted from him. She couldn't deny it anymore. She was falling in love with Jake all over again.

Chapter 10

Jake sat in Meggie's room, still rocking the baby long after she'd fallen asleep and thinking back over the evening. After the awkwardness before Gram and Will came into the dining room, the evening had been a true delight. Now that she had let go of his fingers and gone off by herself, his daughter was officially a toddler.

He was actually glad she'd taken those first steps to Sara. He'd been able to watch them both, and it'd been hard to tell who'd been more excited, Meggie or Sara.

The truce was holding, and he was pleased, even with the stipulation to stay away from the past. There were only two reasons he'd ever want to visit those days again—to find out if Sara had truly loved him and to explain about Melissa.

But as he looked down at his sleeping child, Jake wasn't sure he could do that. Melissa had given him Meggie. And telling Sara that he suspected Melissa's first pregnancy might not have been genuine—that it actually was a trick to get him to the altar—seemed disloyal to the mother of his child. Not to mention that it would seem that he was laying the blame for the end of his relationship with Sara at someone else's feet, when he knew it was the result of his own choices.

For years he'd blamed Sara, Wade, and Melissa for messing up his life. How wrong he'd been. He was the one who had been so hotheaded that night that he'd refused to listen to Sara. He was the one who'd gone against all he'd been taught when he got back to college that night. Jake groaned in disgust with himself and nearly woke his sleeping child.

He stood up and carried Meggie to her crib. Laying her down gently, he patted her on the back to keep her asleep.

He propped his elbow on Meggie's crib and buried his face in his hands. *Oh, God, please forgive me for blaming others for the mistakes I've made. Please help me to truly take responsibility for the pain I've caused them and to mend my relationship with You. I'm not even sure how to go about it, so I just ask You to show me the way. In Jesus' name, amen.*

Jake bent down to brush his lips over Meggie's brow, thanking the Lord for blessing him with this child.

Sara was enjoying her second cup of coffee when Nora called the next morning. Somehow she knew it would be her mother-in-law before she answered the phone.

"Sara dear, I called last night but you weren't at home."

"No, Grandpa and I were at Gram's. I'd been helping her with—"

"With that baby. I knew she would be too much for Ellie."

"No, Nora. It wasn't Meggie. We were working on the reunion. We lost track of time and Gram asked Grandpa and me to eat supper with them." Sara wished she didn't constantly feel the need to explain everything to Nora.

"Oh. I see. And I suppose Jake was there, too?"

"Yes, he and Luke were both there."

"I see."

Sara didn't like the condescending tone her mother-in-law was using. "No, Nora, I don't think—"

"Sara, remember, I warned you about Jake. I saw him seek you out Wednesday night. He's got his sights on you as a mother for Meggie."

"Nora, Jake does not have his sights set on me." Sara knew her voice sounded as irritated as she felt, but she couldn't help it. Sara trembled just at the thought of being married to Jake and becoming Meggie's mommy. But having to hide those feelings from Nora and everyone else wasn't easy. And Sara knew it wasn't going to get any easier.

As if she sensed Sara's mood, Nora quickly changed her tone. "I'm sorry, dear, I just don't want to see you hurt. I want the best for you, you know that."

"I do know that, Nora. But Jake has moved back here. He's part of the family. You can't pretend he doesn't exist."

"Yes, well, I don't have to condone his dumping his child on Ellie."

"Nora, Jake has not dumped Meggie on anyone. He's hiring several of the teens from church to come in and help out. And I think he had to talk Gram into agreeing on that. Has it ever occurred to you that she's enjoying keeping Meggie?"

"I'm sure she's a joy. But Ellie isn't getting any younger."

Remembering the tenderness Nora had shown with Meggie, Sara sighed and shook her head. Maybe Nora was truly concerned about everyone. If so, it was a shame that she never came across that way.

"You're right, she isn't. But she's enjoying herself right now, and that's a blessing." Sara changed the subject. "How are you feeling, Nora? Have you been back to the doctor to get the results from your tests?"

"I'm fine. Just under a lot of stress, as if I didn't already know that. You know what kind of year it's been. I don't know why everyone expects me to act as if life is just rosy and I have no cares."

"Nora, no one expects that from you."

"Yes, well, Dr. Wellington seems to think I've grieved quite long enough. He had the audacity to tell me to find another doctor so that he would feel free to ask me out."

"Oh my." Sara grinned. Maybe Gram and Grandpa weren't needed in the matchmaking department after all.

"Well, I have no intentions of going out with the man."

"I've heard he's very nice, Nora. Gina thinks the world of him. And it'd be nice for you to get out occasionally."

"I'm too old for all of that dating nonsense."

"Nora, you aren't too old at all."

"Well, when you've been a widow as long as I have, then we'll see how old you feel."

Suddenly Sara's life, as Nora painted it, loomed out in front of her. . .long and lonely. Just as suddenly, she knew she didn't want to settle for being alone the rest of her life. She wanted a home and family. She wanted someone to love and take care of.

But there was no way she could tell Nora that. No way at all.

David's sermon that Sunday focused once again on trusting the Lord to forgive and then demonstrating that trust by forgiving ourselves and going forward instead of dwelling on any past wrongdoings.

Jake wondered if David might be preaching straight at him, because he'd never thought about forgiveness in quite that way before. He knew that he'd had a hard time forgiving himself and forgetting the past. Sometimes he wondered how God could love him after he'd strayed from all he'd believed and been taught.

He sought David out the next morning, showing up at his office with coffee and donuts.

"Does that offer to talk still stand?" he asked, waving the bag of donuts across the desk.

David laughed. "Sure does. It'd stand even if you didn't have something delicious in that bag. Come on in and sit down."

After they'd downed a couple donuts and most of the coffee, David leaned back in his chair and got to the point. "What do you want to talk about, my friend?"

Jake leaned forward and clasped his hands together. "I liked your lesson yesterday. About forgiveness."

"I'm glad. Was there anything particular about it you'd like to discuss?" David pulled his Bible to the center of the desk.

"The part about forgiving ourselves, forgetting the past, being. . .an act of trust?"

David nodded. "Many of us have problems with that. Sometimes it's hard for us to believe we're truly forgiven even after we've asked for that very thing."

"That verse you quoted from Philippians—"

"Philippians 3:13–15," David said as he opened his Bible and flipped through the pages. "*'Brothers, I do not consider myself yet to have taken hold of it. But one thing I do: Forgetting what is behind and straining toward what is ahead, I press on toward the goal to win the prize for which God has called me heavenward in Christ Jesus. All of us who are mature should take such a view of things. And if on some point you think differently, that too God will make clear to you.'* Is that it?"

Jake nodded. "That's it. I know I've dwelt in the past way too much. I'm tired of it weighing me down."

"Sounds to me like you're just about there, Jake." David chuckled. "Maybe God's making it all clear to you."

"I certainly hope so. It's about time I figured it out, don't you think?"

"Well, I was a late bloomer myself," David said. "Sadly, it seems to take some of us longer than others."

He got up and refilled their Styrofoam cups from a coffeepot he had set up in the corner. "How are you and Sara doing? Gina mentioned something about a truce being called."

"Ah, well, we decided it was time to try to get along. This town isn't going to grow so large that we can keep from running into one another. And we have the same family and friends."

"Want to talk about why you two feel so uncomfortable around each other?"

"Nah, it's in that past I'm trying to get past." Jake grinned.

"Yeah, Gina and I had one of those kinds of pasts ourselves." David nodded. "We did have to visit it a time or two before we were able to forgive each other."

Jake shook his head. "One of the amendments of the truce was that we don't 'rehash the past.' "

"Your amendment or hers?"

"Hers."

"That might make it a little harder to put to rest."

Jake looked down into his coffee cup and sighed. "That's what I'm afraid of."

David shook his head. "My friend, notice I said harder. Not impossible. Take it to the Lord and let Him handle it."

Jake grinned and got to his feet. "I think I'll do just that. Thanks, old friend."

David stood up and the two men shook hands. "Any time."

The Teddy Bear Brigade, as they'd taken to calling themselves, had decided to meet each Tuesday at the church for lunch and an afternoon of bear making. With one of the teens keeping watch over Meggie, Gram was free to join the group. Everyone brought their favorite dish, and David found one excuse after another to come into the fellowship hall, until finally the ladies insisted he join them for lunch.

Sara laughed, overhearing Gina admonish her husband at the same time she set a plate in front of him. "You are pitiful, you know? Taking advantage of these wonderful ladies, just because you're the minister." The sting was removed from Gina's words by the smile she bestowed upon her husband.

"I know, my love, I know." David nodded. "But you weren't in my office trying to endure the tempting smells wafting in from all this food. Why, my stomach was growling so loud I couldn't concentrate on tomorrow night's lesson."

Sara and Gram burst out laughing, and Gina just shook her head.

"Well, since you're here, would you be so kind as to say the blessing for us?"

David smiled at his wife and looked at all the ladies. "I'd be delighted. Please pray with me."

He bowed his head. "Dear Father, we thank You for all this food and for each of those who prepared it. Thank You for letting these sisters invite me to join in this meal. And thank You for the response they've had from these little bears they're making. Please continue to bless their work and each of their lives, dear Lord. In Jesus' name, amen."

Everyone enjoyed the meal, and David even helped with the cleanup before going back to his office.

"You've got a good man there, Gina," Gram said as the ladies settled down to their sewing.

"Yes, ma'am, I do." Gina threaded her needle. "It took us a long time to get it all together, though."

"Well, good things are usually worth the wait." Gram pinned a bear pattern to a short length of material. "How's Nora doing?" she asked Sara, changing the subject. "I haven't heard from her in several days."

Sara shook her head. "I'm not real sure. She had an appointment with that new doctor in town—"

"Dr. Wellington?" Gina asked. "He's supposed to be a very good doctor."

Gram winked at Sara. "Is he married?"

"No. He's never been married, from what I hear," Nell Schneider offered from across the table.

Sara got up and went to the kitchen, just off the fellowship hall, to put on a fresh pot of coffee. It was hard to keep from telling everyone that this Dr. Wellington was interested in her mother-in-law.

Gram followed her into the kitchen and pulled some Styrofoam cups down from the cabinet. "Might be a nice match for Nora," she whispered to Sara.

"Not if she doesn't like him," Sara whispered back.

Gina joined them in the small room. "What are you two cooking up now?" She grinned, as it seemed to dawn on her. "Oh. . .now, that might be a good match. He's very plain spoken. Doesn't impress me as the type to take much guff from anyone. He could be just the kind of man Nora needs."

Sara sighed. She couldn't keep it in any longer. "Well, we're halfway there. It seems Dr. Wellington is interested enough in Nora that he told her to find another doctor. He wants to ask her out."

Gram chuckled. "Now that does sound promising."

"Not as much as we'd like," Sara admitted. "Nora says she isn't interested."

"You think that's so?"

Sara shook her head. "I don't know. We were talking on the phone so I couldn't see her face. She says she's too old for a relationship."

"Oh, hogwash," Gram said. She went to the refrigerator and brought out some cream.

Sara grinned over at Gina. She had a feeling that would be Gram's opinion. At least it should be, if she and Grandpa were starting to care for one another.

"Maybe I'll just have me a talk with Nora," Gram continued.

"I think that's a great idea," Sara said.

"So do I," Gina added.

"I'll try to get with her in the next few days, and we'll have us a good long talk." As if that settled everything, Gram raised the service window facing the fellowship hall. "Ladies, coffee's ready."

Sara gave Gram a ride home. When they arrived, they found Meggie outside with Maria Bellows, one of the teens Jake had hired to help out. Enjoying the warm afternoon sun, Maria and Meggie sat together in the tire swing hanging from the large cottonwood tree in the backyard.

"Hi, Meggie," Sara called as Gram went inside to take care of her teddy bear supplies. "Are you having a good time?"

Meggie nodded and reached out to her. Sara dropped her purse to the ground. "Want me to swing you?"

Maria vacated the swing, and they laughed as Sara clumsily tried to seat herself in the tire swing. Once she felt halfway secure, she reached for the toddler. "Let's see if I remember how to do this."

Meggie giggled and clapped as they swung back and forth. Sara heard the back door slam but kept her eyes on the child, for fear of dropping her. "Maybe Daddy needs to look into getting a regular swing set for you," she observed.

"Daddy has been thinking the very same thing."

Sara's heart skipped more than a few beats as she recognized Jake's voice.

"Afternoon, ladies," he said, his smile taking in all three women.

"Hi, Mr. Breland. Meggie's been a really good girl this afternoon," Maria said. "If she's like this all the time, babysitting her will be a piece of cake."

Jake laughed. "Well, I can't guarantee she won't give you fits some days."

"That's all right. She's a sweetie anyway. We'll get along just fine."

"Thank you, Maria. There's a check for you on the kitchen table."

"Thanks." Maria waved to Meggie. "Bye, Meggie. I'll see you on Monday."

"Bye-bye." Meggie waved back.

"Bye, Mrs. Tanner, Mr. Breland." The young girl hurried across the lawn to get what Sara was sure was her first paycheck.

Sara let the swing gradually slow and brought it to a halt.

"Dada, hode me."

Jake took his daughter from Sara and grinned. "So, you think I should get a regular swing set?"

Sara struggled out of the swing as gracefully as she could, feeling Jake's eyes on her. She tried to ignore whatever it was that had her heart hammering against her sides. "Well, it might make it a little easier to swing her, unless. . .you know, they have those baby swings that Meggie would fit in, and you could attach it to the tree until she got big enough to sit in this one."

Jake scratched the back of his head. "Oh, yeah. I think I've seen those at the toy store. That's a good idea, Sara. I kind of hate to have to put up a swing set here, just to take it down in a few months when we move to our house."

"How's that going?" She wondered what kind of house he was going to build. Long ago they'd talked about the house they'd build some day, and she could still remember the floor plan they'd decided on.

"I'm supposed to meet with the builder tomorrow to go over some plans. Another week or two and hopefully I'll have the plans nailed down and he'll have all the subcontractors lined up."

"Jake Breland, what is this you have in my kitchen?" Gram called from the back door.

"Oh, that's my surprise for Meggie." He handed his daughter back to Sara. "I'll be right back."

He ran across the yard and into the house. When he and Gram came back out seconds later, he was carrying a large box. Sara watched as Jake knelt down and pulled an adorable golden retriever puppy from the box. Then he reached up for Meggie.

"Doggie, doggie!" Meggie said, as Jake held her close to the puppy and let her pet it.

Sara and Gram looked at each other and laughed, trying to figure out who was the most excited, Meggie, the puppy, or Jake. Gram kneeled down to pet the dog. "Now I wonder just who you bought this for, Jake—Meggie or yourself?"

Sara laughed at the injured expression on Jake's face.

"Now, Gram, you know I put my daughter's interests first." He reached down and helped his grandmother to her feet.

"Yes, I do. I'm teasing, Jake. It's a pretty dog."

"He is, isn't he?" Jake reached down and picked up Meggie while they watched the puppy run around. "We can keep it then?"

Even Meggie looked at her great-grandmother, as if she knew who had the final say.

"It can sleep in the utility room. But it stays out here during the day."

Jake grinned and bent to kiss his grandmother's cheek. "Thank you, Gram."

"Now, I'm going in to start supper." Gram smiled at Sara. "Want to stay and eat with us, Sara?"

"Thanks, Gram, but Grandpa is making stew." She reached out and tweaked

Meggie's nose. "I'd better be going."

"Maybe another time," Gram said, heading for the house. "Thanks for bringing me home."

The puppy decided to run rings around the older woman, and Sara and Jake laughed as she made a game out of pretending to turn and chase it. The puppy would stop in its tracks and yap at her before running around her again.

But Gram made one move a little too quickly, the puppy tumbled between her feet, and Gram tripped. Jake handed Meggie to Sara and ran toward his grandmother, but he wasn't fast enough and his grandmother landed on her ankle. By the time Sara and Meggie got there, Jake was tenderly checking Gram's foot and leg.

"I'm so sorry," he said to the injured woman. "I should never have brought that puppy home. I should have waited until Meggie and I were in our own place."

Gram patted his hand, although she was in obvious pain. "It wasn't the dog's fault, Jake. I shouldn't have been teasing it. Every once in a while, I forget I'm nearing eighty instead of eighteen."

Jake nodded and looked at Sara. "Maybe we should call an ambulance."

"Jacob Breland, I do not need an ambulance. Just get me in the house."

"No, Gram." Jake lifted her into his arms and looked at Sara. "Would you mind watching Meggie, Sara? I think I'd better get Gram to the hospital."

"Of course I'll stay. We'll be here when you get back."

Their eyes met, sharing unspoken concerns.

Sara and Meggie watched Jake gently ease Gram into his car and take off. Sara took the baby into the house and went to the phone. She dialed her home number, all the while praying, *Dear Lord, please let there be no broken bones. Please let Gram be all right.*

Chapter 11

After telling Grandpa about Gram's accident, Sara called the rest of the family to let them know what had happened. She was surprised when there was no answer at Nora's, but she left a message on her answering machine and hoped to hear from her later.

Grandpa came right over, bringing his Crock-Pot stew with him. But he paced so badly he made Sara even more nervous than she already was, and she finally sent him to the hospital to check on Gram.

Sara tried not to watch the clock and kept herself busy by entertaining Meggie and making her a supper of macaroni and cheese. She made sure it was cool enough before setting the bowl in front of Meggie, but when she began to fill the fork with macaroni, Meggie reached for it.

Sara relinquished the small utensil to her and chuckled as Meggie slowly forked several pieces of the cheesy pasta and deftly plopped them into her mouth.

Remembering the first day she'd watched Meggie make such a mess with finger food and a sippy cup, Sara marveled at how fast the little girl had caught on to the intricacies of feeding herself.

Grandpa called from the hospital to let her know that Gram was still waiting to see a doctor. There'd been a wreck earlier, and the doctors were tied up. He promised to call and update her as he could.

Sara had bathed Meggie and rocked her to sleep before the phone rang again. Jake was calling to update her and check on Meggie.

"How is Gram?" Sara asked. "Is anything broken?"

"Can you believe she didn't break a thing? But she does have a nasty sprained ankle and will be down for a while," he answered.

"Bless her heart. She's not going to like that at all."

"No, she's not a happy camper. And it's all my fault. I should never have brought that puppy home."

"Oh, Jake, I'm sure she doesn't blame you."

"No, she doesn't. But I blame myself." He changed the subject. "How's my girl? Did she give you any problems?"

Sara chuckled. "Not one. She fed herself, had a ball in the tub, and went right to sleep."

"Well, I just wanted to let you know that we'll be on our way as soon as we can get Gram released."

"Okay. I'll have supper on the table."

"You don't have to do that, Sara."

"It's no problem, Jake. Grandpa brought over the stew he had cooking. All I have to do is heat up some rolls and set the table."

"All right. Thank you, Sara, for staying with Meggie—for everything. I really appreciate it."

"You're welcome. . .hurry home. With Gram," Sara added quickly before hanging up the phone.

She set the table and put on a fresh pot of coffee. She'd just finished placing the rolls in the oven when the phone rang again. Nora had returned home and wanted to know the latest. Sara was glad that she could at least give her an updated report on Gram.

"I just got back from town," Nora said. "I wish I'd known. I could have gone to the hospital with. . .ah, to see about her."

"Well, they'll be home any minute now. I'll be sure and tell her you called to check on her," Sara said, wondering who Nora might have gone to the hospital *with.*

"Yes, please do, dear." Nora's tone cooled slightly. "I suppose this means you'll be helping her with the baby."

"Of course I'll help, Nora."

"Yes, well, I figured as much."

Sara heard a car pull up outside. "Nora, I think they're home now. I'll be sure and give Gram your love."

"Please do."

"I'll talk to you tomorrow and let you know how she's doing. Night, Nora." Sara hung up and ran to the door.

Her heart ached at the sight of Gram struggling to get out of the car. But she had to smile, hearing Jake try to convince his grandmother to let him carry her inside. "Gram, you have plenty of time to get used to those crutches tomorrow. Let me carry you into the house."

"No, Jake. I want to do it myself."

"Won't you let me carry you, Ellie?" Grandpa asked.

"Will, you aren't any younger than I am. You'd drop me or trip over something, and we'd both end up back at that hospital. Now both of you move out of my way. I can do this."

Sara could tell Gram was tired and hurting from the abrupt way in which she talked to two of her favorite men. They'd probably been hounding her about what she could and couldn't do all the way home. She had to chuckle as she watched Gram make her way to the back porch, with Jake and Grandpa right beside her. But as she watched the injured woman maneuver the steps on crutches, Sara was sure she knew how the two men felt. Her fingers itched to reach out and help. They breathed a collective sigh of relief when Gram made it through the back door and into the kitchen.

"Are you hungry?" Sara asked as Gram took her seat at the table.

"I am starved, dear, thank you."

"Me, too," Jake said. "The cafeteria was closed, and all they had were those awful vending machines. After you told me Will's stew was waiting, I just got hungrier." Jake chuckled. "What can I do to help?"

"You can put ice in the glasses and get the tea," Sara answered, bringing the stew to the table.

She dipped out a bowl for everyone while Jake took care of the drinks. Grandpa was busy finding an extra chair for Gram to prop her foot up on.

Once they were all seated, Jake offered the blessing and thanked the Lord that his grandmother wasn't hurt any worse.

"My, this stew is tasty, Will. Thank you. I didn't realize just how hungry I was," Gram said.

They'd barely finished eating when Luke, John, Lydia, and Ben showed up to check on Gram. Amid hugs and kisses, she tried to assure everyone she was fine, but the telltale black and blue inching up from her ankle to her calf said otherwise.

"I think I should stay here tonight, just in case you need help," Lydia offered.

Gram shook her head. "I'm perfectly capable of getting myself to bed. I don't need anyone to look after me, but I'll have to admit, I'll need some help with that little tyke upstairs."

"Don't worry about a thing, Gram. I can stay home with Meggie," Jake said.

John nodded. "He can. Or he can bring her into the office."

"I. . .I'd be glad to come over and watch Meggie. I'm only a few blocks away, and I'd love to help out, if it's all right with everyone." Sara looked at Jake to gauge his response. She wasn't sure what his quick frown was saying.

Grandpa chimed in with his two cents. "That's a good idea. Lydia would have to come in from the ranch. We live much closer, and I can come over and help out, too. There's no need for Jake to stay home all day when he has all of us to lend a hand."

"This is true. No matter how we work it out, Jake, we're family and we're here to help," Lydia said.

"Well, if I have any say in all this planning, I'd like to take Sara up on her offer," Gram said. "We're in the middle of planning the reunion anyway, and Meggie has taken to her from the very first. I think she'll be happier if Sara is around."

Everyone seemed to be looking at Jake for his approval. He looked around the room and knew this was exactly why he'd come back to Sweet Springs—having family nearby to help with Meggie when he needed them. He smiled and nodded.

"Thank you all. I know Gram and Meggie will be in good hands no matter who is with them." He hadn't expected to be turning to Sara for help, but his family would never understand if he turned down her generous offer. "If you really don't mind, Sara, I think Gram is right. Meggie will be thrilled to have you here each day."

Their eyes met, and for a brief moment he wished he could retract what he'd just said. Not because he didn't want Sara around, but because he did. He knew having her close by on a daily basis could lead to more heartache. Yet he wanted to be able to see her every day. He held his breath, waiting for her answer.

"I'll be here first thing in the morning. Just tell me what time you need me."

Early the next morning Sara let herself into Gram's sunny kitchen with the key she'd been given the night before. Jake had told her she didn't need to be there before nine o'clock, but she'd awakened early and couldn't see any sense in sitting around waiting when Gram might need help with something.

She quietly put the coffee on and went upstairs to check on the patient.

"God bless you, Sara," Gram said as she entered the room. "I'm a little stiffer than I thought I'd be this morning. Could you help me get out of this bed, please?"

"Of course I can. I should have slept here last night," she said, feeling bad that she hadn't insisted on staying. She helped Gram slide her legs to the side of the bed and put an arm around her to steady her while she balanced on the crutches.

"There was no need for you to stay here last night," Gram insisted as she slowly made her way across the room. "I slept fine. That pain pill put me right out. But I've been awake for about an hour, and I didn't want to wake Meggie too early by yelling for Jake to come help me."

Sara stood outside the bathroom door in case Gram needed her, but the older woman managed just fine. She refused to get back in bed and took a seat in the easy chair beside the window.

"You know me, Sara. I can't stay in bed. In fact, once Jake is up and around, would you ask him to help me downstairs? I'll be much more comfortable there than up here."

"Gram, you really ought to rest that ankle for a few days."

"I'm going to rest it. Just not up here. I want to be down where you and Meggie are."

Sara tried to talk her into staying in bed, but Gram could be stubborn, and Sara finally gave in.

They heard a knock on the door and looked up to see Jake sticking his head around the corner. "Good morning. How are you feeling, Grams?"

Sara caught her breath at how handsome he looked first thing in the morning. He was dressed in a maroon robe, but his eyes still had that sleepy look and his jaw was dark with an overnight beard. His smile had her heart tripping over itself, and she was glad Gram answered him.

"I'll feel much better once I get downstairs," she insisted. "I'd like you to help me get there. I don't like feeling cut off from everything."

Jake raised a questioning eyebrow at Sara. She shrugged and found her voice. "I think she's going to get downstairs one way or another. The safest way would probably be for you to help her."

Jake nodded. "Can you wait until I shower, Gram?"

"Of course."

"Then I'll hurry." He looked at Sara. "I think I hear Meggie stirring. Would you mind bringing her down to her playpen in the kitchen? She's used to playing in it until I get her breakfast ready."

"I'll be glad to," Sara said. She turned back to Gram. "Do you need me to get you anything first?"

Gram shook her head. "No, I'm fine until Jake comes back to get me. You go see about our little darlin'."

Sara didn't have to be prodded to check on Meggie. She followed Jake down the hall to the baby's room and watched his grin turn into a full-fledged chuckle as Meggie looked up and greeted him. "Dada!"

Twin sets of dimples greeted each other as Jake picked up his daughter. "Mornin', precious."

Meggie looked over his shoulder and spotted Sara for the first time. "Sawa!"

"Hi, Meggie. Can I get you ready and take you downstairs while Daddy takes his shower?"

Meggie reached out to her. Jake chuckled and kissed his daughter before handing her to Sara. "Well, I guess that answers your question."

"I think we're going to get along just fine, Jake. Don't you worry about us." Sara took Meggie over to the changing table and set about getting the baby ready to go downstairs.

"No, I won't," Jake said. He turned to the hall. "I'll be down to get her breakfast ready as soon as I get cleaned up and get Gram down there so she can oversee everything."

But by the time he got downstairs with Gram, Sara had bacon and eggs on the table and Meggie was in her chair, nibbling on toast and bacon.

"Oh, this is nice, Sara," Gram said as she shifted to get comfortable in her chair and prop her foot up on a small footstool Jake had found.

"Yes, it is," he said, taking his seat next to Meggie.

"I wasn't sure what to feed Meggie," Sara said, pouring three cups of coffee and taking a seat across from Jake. "I thought she could probably handle this."

Jake spooned some scrambled eggs onto Meggie's plate and handed her the small fork she liked. "This is fine. She loves bacon."

Sara sat back with her cup of coffee and watched Jake lift four pieces of bacon onto his plate. "And I can see her daddy does, too."

Jake chuckled and nodded. "She comes by it honestly."

"Tomorrow, have Will come on over for breakfast," Gram said. "No sense in him having to cook for himself while we're all enjoying each other's company."

"Yes, do," Jake added. "We've taken his cook away from him, the least we can do is have him join us."

"Grandpa doesn't mind. He—"

"Is a good man. But there's no sense messing up two kitchens when one will do," Gram said with a tone of finality.

Sara grinned and looked at Jake. He shrugged and nodded. "I'll be sure and ask him to come with me tomorrow, Gram. I'm sure he'll be showing up anytime now, anyway."

"Oh, Jake," Gram said, changing the subject, "before you go to work, did you buy any dog food?"

"It's in the back of my car. I'll be sure and get it before I leave." He looked at his grandmother. "If you're sure about keeping him. I really do feel badly, Gram."

A small whine was heard, and they looked up to see the puppy looking through the screen door. Meggie clapped her hands. "Doggie, doggie!"

"Now, how could I tell you to get rid of that puppy after that?" Gram asked. She shook her head. "I told you it wasn't the puppy's fault. Of course he can stay."

"Thanks, Gram." He went outside and was back in just a few minutes. "I fed the dog and gave him water, too. Do you need anything brought back down from upstairs?"

"No, my medicine is in my pocket, the crutches are right here—"

"And I'm here if she thinks of anything she needs," Sara added.

"And you're the only reason I can even think of going to work today. Thank you, Sara." Jake smiled at her from across the room.

"You're welcome. I'm glad I can help. I've had a lot of it given to me from this family."

Jake nodded and headed upstairs. He came back down only minutes later with a jacket slung over his shoulder. He kissed the top of Gram's head, "You take it easy today, you hear?"

"I will."

He bent down and kissed Meggie on the cheek. "You be a good girl for Sara, okay?"

Meggie nodded. " 'Kay."

Jake straightened and looked over at Sara, wishing he could kiss her, too. "I'll see you this evening. If you need anything, just call the office."

"I will." Sara smiled and nodded, motioning toward the door. "Shoo, Jake. We'll be just fine. I promise."

And they were. Grandpa came over and entertained Gram for most of the day, making sure she took a nap both morning and afternoon. While she slept, he took Meggie out to play with the puppy so that Sara could straighten up the upstairs rooms and do some wash.

The phone rang on and off all day with relatives, church members, and townspeople wanting to know how Gram was and offering to help in any way they could. By noon, Sara knew not to start supper, because several of the ladies from church were arranging to bring over a series of meals. The outpouring of care and concern for Gram reminded Sara of how lucky she felt to be part of such a wonderful church family.

But the best part of the day was, without a doubt, Meggie. Sara loved interacting with the toddler. At nap time, Meggie came to Sara with her blankie and crawled into her lap. Holding the baby close and rocking her, Sara envisioned her own child being cuddled close and rocked to sleep in heaven. She gathered Meggie just a little closer as the pain she always carried eased.

Chapter 12

The next week flew by for Sara as she tried to see that Gram took it easy and worked to keep up with Meggie. Sara kept her camera close by so she could get snapshots of an adorable Meggie toddling around, falling, and picking herself up.

Gram's ankle seemed to turn a different color each day. It went through varying shades of black, blue, and green before settling into a yellowish gray. But as always, the older woman's attitude inspired Sara. Gram didn't let the pain or the awkward use of crutches keep her down. Sara could only hope she'd be as full of life and living when she neared eighty.

While Meggie napped, she and Gram either worked on the plans for the reunion, or sewed and stuffed more teddy bears. Meggie woke up early one afternoon, and Sara brought her down to her playpen in the kitchen while she finished up one of the bears.

"Wat dat?" Meggie asked, pointing to the little bear.

"It's a bear, sweetie." Sara made one last stitch, tied it off, and cut the thread. She carried the brightly checkered bear over and showed it to Meggie. "Do you like it?"

Meggie dropped the blanket she'd been holding and grabbed the little stuffed animal. "Thanky, Sawa."

Sara's heart melted and she wondered why she'd never given the child one before. "You're welcome, sweetie."

Sara drove home unsure of which time of day she liked best lately. The mornings when she let herself in the back door, brought Meggie down, and started breakfast while Jake showered, dressed, and helped Gram get downstairs. Or the evenings, when he came home from work and they all ate supper at the big table in the kitchen.

She had no doubts about which part she liked least. She hated leaving at night. She always felt as if she'd left a big chunk of herself back at Gram's. As she pulled into the driveway at home, she was pretty certain it was her heart she'd left behind.

The next morning, Sara was delighted to see both Jake and Meggie already downstairs when she let herself in the back door. Jake had the coffee on and was holding Meggie on his hip while he stirred something on the stove. The little girl grinned widely when Sara greeted her.

"Sawa!" She held up the little bear Sara had given her the day before. "Ted-bear seep wif me."

"He did?" Sara looked around for the child's blanket and, finding no evidence of it, looked questioningly at Jake.

"It appears Meggie has given up her blankie for Ted-bear. She slept with him all night and had him clasped in her arms when I went in to get her this morning."

"Oh, how sweet. I kind of hate to see the blanket go, though."

Jake chuckled. "I know. She didn't even ask for it last night when I rocked her to sleep. But thank you for giving her the bear. She loves it."

He turned back to the oatmeal he was cooking for his daughter and poured out a bowl. "This just needs to cool. Would you mind taking Meggie while I go up and help Gram down? I'm meeting with the builder to finalize the house plans this morning."

"Of course I don't mind." Sara reached out and took Meggie into her arms. "Hi, sweetie. You ready to eat?"

"Ted-bear eat, too?"

"Hmm," Sara said to herself as she settled Meggie into her high chair. "I can see that we might need a spare bear around here. I'll see if we have enough of that material left to make another one."

By the end of the day, Meggie had a spare bear in her room, but she still hadn't asked for her blanket.

Jake came home from work that night with the plans to his and Meggie's new home under his arm. The rest of the family had been invited over to take a look, but they all had to wait until after supper when the table was cleared to get a look at them.

Jake spread the plans out on the table, stood back, and waited for comments. He answered question after question about this room and that. Then he noticed Sara looking intently at the plans, color flooding her face. She bit her bottom lip. Suddenly he realized what he had done. His plans matched exactly the plans he and Sara had talked about when they were young. He hadn't even been aware that he'd duplicated them.

The house would be a large two-story with a wide wraparound porch. The kitchen stood along one end with windows on the front, side, and back of the house. He remembered how Sara had commented years ago that she wanted to be able to look out and see their children playing no matter where she was in the house.

This house would have nooks and crannies much like Gram's house—all the little touches that builders usually didn't bother with anymore but that gave a house character. The same touches he and Sara had decided they wanted when they were young and in love. Suddenly he remembered that years ago he and Sara had walked along the very block where he was now building and how he had commented that he'd like to build a house there some day.

"I like it, bro," Luke said, bringing Jake out of his reverie.

"So do I. It's going to look especially good on that block. It'll look as though it's been there forever," John said. "It'll blend right in."

"It's going to be a lovely home for you and Meggie, Jake," Lydia agreed.

Jake was glad they all liked it, but he knew there was truly only one opinion that mattered to him.

Sara turned to him with a smile. "Well, it goes without saying that I love it."

That was the only reference she made that came close to touching on its similarities to their dream house, but it was enough to make Jake realize that his dream home wouldn't be complete without Sara in it. He wanted them back together. Not just as friends. While he'd been crazy about the younger Sara, he was head over heels in love with this one.

He looked into her eyes. "I was hoping you'd like it," he said, but his mind skittered all over the place. How could he let Sara know that he'd loved her all his life, without feeling disloyal to Meggie's mother? Was it possible that he ever could? Jake didn't know how much he could reveal to Sara about his and Melissa's relationship, but he did know one thing. He was in love with Sara, he wanted her in his and Meggie's life, and he was going to do everything in his power to make her see they truly were meant for each other.

Jake went to bed that night with a new determination. He was going to try to get Sara to fall in love with him again. He knew he was putting his heart on the line, but he also knew that he had no choice. He loved Sara, plain and simple. Now he just had to do his best to convince her they were meant to be together.

The first phase of Jake's plan went into action the next morning. He didn't have to do much talking to convince his grandmother and Will that Sara needed a break. But he knew persuading Sara might be a different story. So he did the only thing he could think of. He called Gina and David and enlisted their aid.

Jake dawdled over breakfast that morning so long that finally Sara asked him if he was taking the day off.

"No. But I can if you need me here to do anything."

"No, Jake, we're coping very well. I'm just not used to you being here after nine o'clock. Are you feeling all right?"

"Sara, I'm fine. I just wasn't in a hurry today. Actually, I—"

The phone rang right on cue and Jake answered it. "Hi, Gina. Yes, she's right here."

"It's for you." He handed the phone to Sara and poured himself another cup of coffee, trying not to let on that he was listening to Sara's side of the conversation.

"Oh, Gina, that sounds nice, but I'm not sure how I could leave Gram."

She was quiet for a minute and then said, "Well, yes, Grandpa is here."

Jake had his back to Sara and grinned at Will and Gram.

"What is it, darlin'?" Will asked Sara. "Does Gina need me for something?"

Sara asked Gina to hold on and turned to her grandfather and Gram. "She wants me to go to lunch with her today. I just don't think I should leave—"

"Now there is no reason you have to be chained to this house, Sara," Gram interjected. "Will can stay with me while you go have lunch."

"Well, then, with Grandpa here, I could take Meggie with me—"

"There's no need to take that baby. I can take care of her and Gram just fine," Will said.

"Or I could get one of the teens in to help this afternoon." Jake offered. "You need some time off for good behavior, Sara."

She held the receiver back to her ear. "Gina, I can make it. You'd think they all wanted to get rid of me today."

She smiled and nodded. "Yes, I know they are trying to take care of me. What time do you want to meet at the diner?"

Jake gave Will and Gram a thumbs-up sign and hoped the rest of his plan went half as well.

"Thank you all," she said when she got off the phone. "I do want to stop into the drugstore and pick up some pictures I took of Meggie anyway."

Satisfied that the first part of his plan was working, Jake kissed his daughter good-bye and headed out the door. But he turned back to Sara. "You have a good lunch, Sara, okay?"

Sara promised him she would and found herself looking forward to lunch with Gina. By one o'clock, she'd fed Meggie her lunch and put her down for a nap. Gram and Grandpa should be able to handle things for a few hours, but she felt bad leaving them with no lunch fixed.

Grandpa shooed her out the door. "I'm perfectly capable of making us a grilled cheese sandwich or heating up leftovers in the fridge, honey."

"I know, Grandpa."

"You just have a good time."

Gina was waiting at the diner when Sara got there. She'd made Deana promise to take a break and have lunch with the two of them when Sara showed up. Deana cooked most of the daily specials herself, but she did have two short order cooks and several waitresses, working two different shifts, to help out.

Deana brought their lunch to the table herself and turned to her help. "It's all yours. At least for an hour."

They just laughed at her.

"They know you too well, Deana," Sara said. "They know that all they have to do is give you that pitiful 'we need help' look, and you'll be on your feet and behind the counter in two seconds."

"Yeah, well, that's how it is when you own the place," Deana said.

"How is business these days, Deana? It always looks busier than ever when I'm in here." Gina took a bite of her roast beef sandwich.

"A little too good, some days. But I enjoy it." Deana grinned at her. "Oh, guess who was in here yesterday for early coffee?"

"David?" Gina asked.

Deana shook her head. "Nope."

"Luke and Jake?"

"Oh, they came in. But they aren't who I'm talking about."

Sara shrugged. "Okay, I give up. Who came in?"

"Nora. And she wasn't alone."

"Oh? Who was she with?"

"Dr. Wellington. And they were in very deep conversation until Nora seemed to get angry and flounced out of here."

Gina raised an eyebrow. "Well, so much for getting the two of them together."

Deana looked from one to the other. "You're wanting to play matchmaker?"

"Well, we'd thought they might make a good couple."

"They seemed to be getting along real well until Jake and Luke came in. Don't know what happened then. But the next thing I knew, Nora was hightailing it out of here."

"And what did Dr. Wellington do?" Gina asked.

"He chuckled and shook his head. Then he asked for another cup of coffee."

"I am going to have to meet this man," Sara said. "If Nora doesn't run him off, he may be just the man for her."

"I don't think he'd take any of her guff," Gina said.

"Exactly. I think she needs someone who isn't intimidated by her." Sara shrugged. "You know, someone who could let her bad moods roll right off of his back."

"That's a pretty tall order, Sara," Deana said. "I'm not sure that kind of man exists."

They all laughed and Sara sighed. "Well, we can hope."

The afternoon passed quickly. Deana wouldn't let either of them pay for lunch, and Gina wouldn't let her go back to Gram's.

"Ellie called me right after you left the house and said to tell you to make an afternoon of it. She called Maria and asked her to come over this afternoon."

"Maybe I've been crabby lately and they wanted a break from me."

Gina laughed. "You know better. They just don't want to wear you out."

At Sara's forlorn look, she relented and let her call to make sure Gram and Meggie were all right.

Once Sara heard Gram's voice and was assured all was well, she was able to relax and enjoy the afternoon. She and Gina went window shopping and stopped to pick up the pictures she'd taken of Meggie earlier in the week, and of course they ended right back at the diner for afternoon coffee. They were poring over the pictures of Meggie when a shadow fell across the table. Two shadows. David and Jake stood next to them, grinning.

"Now why does it not surprise me to see the two of you here?" Gina asked.

"Probably because we planned to meet here this morning," David grinned and slid into the booth alongside his wife.

Jake smiled down at Sara, and she slid over to make room for him. "And were you in on this plan, Jake?"

He chuckled and joined her in the booth. "You could say that. It took everyone to get you to take a break. You've been putting in some long hours lately. I just wanted you to know how much we—I—appreciate you."

"I. . .thank you, Jake." Taken aback by the compliment, Sara didn't quite know what to say. She slid the packet of snapshots over to him. "Here are those pictures of Meggie."

Jake grinned and pulled the packet closer. "Oh, Sara, these are wonderful. I haven't been the best at taking pictures of Meggie. Now I wish I'd taken more."

Sara pointed to one with Meggie asleep, her thumb stuck in her mouth and the teddy bear held tight in her arms. Another was of her playing with the puppy outside with Grandpa, and yet another had her sidling up to Gram and trying to share a cookie.

Jake looked at each picture and handed them to David. When he'd gone through them all, he looked into Sara's eyes. "Thank you."

"You're welcome. Would you like me to buy a photo album for them?"

"Let me look in Meggie's dresser. I'm pretty sure there's one there or in a box somewhere."

Sara nodded. "Okay. If you can't find one, I'll pick one up."

"Pssst, Sara," Gina whispered.

Sara looked over and saw Gina motioning to the other side of the diner.

"That's Dr. Wellington."

Sara turned her head and saw a tall, silver-haired man, about six feet tall and nicely built, sitting at a small table. He looked up at the waitress, and Sara could see that he had a wonderful smile.

She looked back at Gina. "He and Nora would look stunning together, wouldn't they?"

"What are you two up to now?" David asked.

"We aren't up to anything. Just hoping."

"About what?" Jake looked across the room. "Oh, he was in here with Nora yesterday, I think it was. She didn't stay long, though. She left right after Luke and I came in."

"We're hoping there might be a little romance in the air for them."

"Then you'd better pray about it," Jake said. "From what I saw, Nora wasn't too happy when she left here."

"But then it's hard to tell when Nora is happy, isn't it?" Gina asked.

"Sure is for me," Jake replied.

Gina looked over at the doctor and sighed. "Still, they would make a stunning couple."

"Wife of mine," David said, "you know it takes more than looking good together to make a good couple."

"Oh, yes, that I know," Gina grinned. "It takes love and trust and faith and God's blessing to make a good couple."

"And sometimes it takes years to get there," David added.

Gina leaned into the arm that surrounded her and nodded. "Sometimes it does."

Sara and Jake chuckled, knowing their friends were talking about themselves.

"And sometimes it takes knocking some chips off shoulders and rehashing old hurts to get to real healing." David winked at his wife.

"Sometimes it does." Gina repeated softly. They both shot Sara and Jake pointed looks.

"What?" Sara and Jake asked at the same time.

David slid out of the booth with Gina right behind him. He looked at Jake and Sara and smiled. "Dear friends, I think maybe it's time to bury that past of yours so you both can get on with the future. To that end, Gina and I are providing supper for Ellie, Will, and Meggie. Take your time."

With that, they walked out of the diner, leaving Jake and Sara at a loss for words.

Jake found his voice first. "I think my plans have just been sped forward." He shook his head and laughed out loud, bringing curious glances from nearby tables.

"Jake? What's so funny? And what plans are you talking about?" Sara asked.

He met her eyes and his laughter stopped. He reached out and twirled a piece of Sara's hair around his finger and smiled at her.

"I wanted to have a chance to talk to you without Meggie interrupting us, without you having to see to Gram and Will, without any of the hundred and one things you keep busy with at the house. So I came up with the plan to let you have an afternoon off."

"You had me spend the afternoon with Gina so you could talk to me? Jake, that doesn't make much sense." Sara pulled back and the tendril of hair slid through Jake's fingers.

"You needed an afternoon off. And it seemed the easiest way to get you to the diner. My plan was just to have coffee and then maybe stay awhile after Gina and David left. I didn't know they were going to add clearing up our past into the mix."

"Why didn't you just tell me you wanted to talk to me?"

"I was afraid you'd find something you just had to see to. It seems every time we're alone together for more than a couple of minutes, you find something that needs to be taken care of."

He was right. Sara was afraid that if they were alone for more than a few minutes, Jake might become aware of the love she felt for him and tried so hard to hide. She sighed lightly.

"Well, here we are," Sara said softly. "What do you want to talk about?"

He stared down at his coffee cup.

"Jake?"

He took a deep breath and looked into Sara's eyes. "I was wondering, if we could, well, if you would go to dinner with me one night."

"To dinner with you?" Sara looked confused.

Jake nodded. "You know, as in a dinner date?"

"A dinner date," she repeated. "With you?"

"Yes."

"Oh." Sara's heart seemed to do a double somersault before she could speak again. "I'd like that."

"You would?" Jake grinned. "I mean, you will?"

She nodded, feeling the color steal up her cheeks. What was wrong with her? She felt like a teenager being asked out for her very first date. "When?"

"How about Saturday night? Anywhere you want to go."

Sara smiled. Jake was as nervous as she was. "Anywhere is fine. You plan it."

Jake nodded. "All right. I'll pick you up at six thirty if that's okay?"

"That'd be fine."

They were both silent for a minute.

"Jake?"

"Yeah?"

"I don't know if I'm supposed to go home now, or back to Gram's house to pick up Grandpa."

Jake smiled and shook his head. "Neither do I. I'm afraid my planning hadn't gotten much past asking you for a date."

Their eyes met and they burst into laughter, spontaneous, shared, and comfortable.

Chapter 13

Jake followed Sara back to his grandmother's house. True to their word, Gina and David were already there, and they asked Jake and Sara to join everyone for the pizza they'd had delivered.

Although Jake noticed several curious glances, no one asked why they'd returned early. And no one said a word when Jake asked Will if he was up to babysitting on Saturday night while he and Sara went out to eat.

Will just grinned and said, "You bet I am."

That was it. No teasing remarks or nosy questions. Just acceptance.

After everyone left and Jake put Meggie to bed, he remembered to look for the photo album he was sure he'd packed. Melissa had made it, and he'd like to at least get all of those first pictures of Meggie in the album her mother had created especially for her.

A quick look through Meggie's dresser drawers told him it wasn't there, so Jake took down the two boxes he'd put in the top of the closet when they'd first moved back. The first box held clothes Meggie had grown out of before they left Albuquerque, but the second one held the album. It was covered in baby print material, with a covered heart that a picture could be slipped inside of gracing the front.

Jake took the album downstairs to the kitchen where he'd left the photos of Meggie. He knew he hadn't put any pictures in the album, so he was surprised when he opened the album up and saw a photo of himself and Melissa on the very first page. He remembered when the photo had been taken—right before Meggie's birth. An envelope had been slipped in behind the photo.

Jake pulled it out and turned it over in his hands. It was addressed to him and Meggie in Melissa's handwriting and was dated only a month before she'd died. He opened the envelope and drew out a letter.

All the guilt he'd ever felt for not loving Melissa enough came to the surface as Jake unfolded the single page and read the very first line:

To my two loves, Jake and Meggie,

I pray you never have to read this, because it will mean I'm not with you. I've been told it's a normal thing to be afraid of childbirth, and I am. And no, Jake, there is nothing wrong that I know of. But just to put my mind at ease, I'm writing this in case something should happen to me during delivery and I don't have a chance to tell you both how very much I love you.

My dear sweet Meggie, how I looked forward to holding you in my arms and being the best mother I could be to you. But it's not to be, if this letter is being read, so I have to tell you and your daddy a truth.

Jake, my love, I'm sorry. For I did deceive you in the beginning. I was not pregnant when you married me. I took advantage of your honor because I wanted so much to be your wife. I'd loved you for so long, and yet I knew you didn't love me. You tried your best. I know that. And it's not your fault. I robbed you of your chance for happiness by grasping at my own. I'm sorry, Jake. I pray that you will forgive me and find that happiness with someone who will be a loving mother to our daughter.

Precious Meggie. Please listen and learn. Never try to trick someone into marrying you. Your daddy has been a wonderful husband and has tried to make me happy in every way possible. But the one thing I wanted, his love, is the one thing he couldn't completely give me. You see, it always belonged to another. Yet your daddy gave up the happiness he could have had for me. For what he thought was his responsibility. I lied to him to get him to marry me. And he stayed with me when there was no reason for him to do so, because of his beliefs and the faith that I took advantage of. So instead of one person being unhappy, there were three or more. I tell you this now, my sweet Meggie, so that you will be happy for your daddy when he finds his own happiness after all of these years. And to keep you from making the same mistakes I did.

I've asked God for His forgiveness, and I know that I have it. Now I ask your daddy to forgive me. He has promised to take you to church and teach you all the things I didn't learn until I was an adult. If we can show you how to always look to the Lord to lead your way, you'll be fine, my love. I could leave you in no better hands than those of the Lord above and your daddy. I love you both with all my heart,

Mommy Melissa

Jake pressed his eyes shut against the sudden sting of tears and took a deep steadying breath. Finally he knew the truth.

Sara tried to stay busy to keep from getting nervous about her date with Jake. But it didn't work. And Nora didn't help matters. She called bright and early the next morning, and Sara could tell from the tone in her mother-in-law's voice that she wasn't at all happy.

"Sara, just what kind of hold does that man have over you?"

"Pardon me? What are you talking about, Nora?"

"I heard about you and Jake cozying up at the diner yesterday. I told you he only wants a mother for Meggie. Are you honestly going to let yourself be hurt by that man once more?"

"Nora—"

"I just can't stand by and let you do that without warning you, Sara. You are going to be hurt badly." With that, Nora hung up.

Sara stood looking at the receiver, shaking her head, at a total loss for words. She hung up the phone and sighed deeply. She truly didn't want to upset her mother-in-law, but the only way to avoid that would be to move to the ranch and never come into town, thereby avoiding running into Jake and Meggie at all. Sara knew that never had been an option.

Still, Nora's warning repeated itself over and over in her mind. Was Jake's only interest in her as a possible mother for Meggie? While she would love to have that role, she didn't want it without Jake's love.

She lost count of how many times that day she picked up the phone to cancel the date with Jake only to change her mind and hang up before the call went through. The truth was that she wanted to go out with him. She wanted to see where they were headed. Wanted to see if what she thought was happening between them really was. She hoped she wasn't in for more heartbreak.

Grandpa left for Gram's about thirty minutes before Jake was due to pick Sara up. Gina had called earlier to let Sara know that she and David were providing supper again for the two older people and Meggie, so she wouldn't have to worry about anything.

When Jake arrived a few minutes early, Sara was relieved that she didn't have time to get nervous. But when she opened the door to him, she knew she'd only been faking her serenity.

She'd decided to wear the aqua-and-yellow sundress she'd bought for his welcome-home party. As his glance took in what she was wearing and zeroed in on her mouth, she knew she'd worn it because it reminded her of the night when Jake had held her in his arms and kissed her. Noticing his eyes darken as he pulled his gaze away from her lips to her eyes, Sara was pretty sure he was also remembering that night.

"You—" Jake cleared his throat. "You look lovely."

"Thank you." He seemed almost as nervous as she felt, but he certainly looked handsome in dress slacks and a crisp white shirt, with his hair still damp from the shower. "You look very nice yourself."

She grabbed her purse and the wrap that came with the dress and locked the door behind her. They headed for Jake's car, and she savored the feel of his hand at the small of her back. He made her feel protected and special. "Where are we going?"

"Well, the choice is still yours, but I've been told there's a new restaurant just outside of town, Los Hacienda, that's very good. We could still go into Roswell or Ruidoso, if you'd rather."

"No. No, Los Hacienda sounds wonderful. I haven't been there yet, and I've heard the food is excellent."

"Well, I have to admit, I'm a little nervous about going too far away from Gram's right now."

Sara laughed as Jake opened the passenger door and she seated herself. "You must have read my mind. I kept thinking that we might want to be close by. Although Gina and David will be there, I'd still feel better if we don't go too far."

Jake smiled as he went around and took the driver's seat. Sara was already so protective of Meggie. Melissa couldn't have handpicked a better mother for their child. But Jake knew Sara's mothering abilities had nothing to do with his asking her out. He wanted to be with Sara, the woman he'd come to love even more than the teenager he'd planned to marry.

Jake had been told to ask for a river table, and he'd done that when he'd made reservations the day before. Now he was impressed when they were led to the second floor and shown to a table set in its own little alcove, with a small balcony off to the side, overlooking the Hondo River below.

The waiter lit the candle on their table, filled their water glasses, told them of the day's specials, and left them with menus. He returned quickly with a basket of tortilla chips and salsa. They both decided on the special of the day and were left alone once more.

"Oh, Jake. This is really beautiful," Sara said, looking around at the warm interior and back out to the river.

"A fitting setting for a beautiful woman." Jake didn't take his eyes off her as she turned back to him. She was beautiful, her green eyes glowing, her auburn hair on fire in the candlelight. She took his breath away.

"Jake—"

"I mean it, Sara." Jake reached across the table and took her hand in his. "You are beautiful, inside and out. You always have been."

Jake could see the color rise in her face even in the dim candlelight. He felt the tremble of her fingers in his hand, but she didn't pull away. Feeling a hope he was almost afraid of, Jake reached over with his other hand and raised her chin so that her eyes met his. "I love you, Sara. I always have."

Sara's hand slid out of his and covered her heart. She shook her head and looked around as if she wanted to escape. She bolted from her chair and ran out to the private balcony.

Jake was right behind her. He turned her to face him. "Sara?"

"Jake, you don't mean what you are saying. You loved Melissa—"

"Sara, I know you didn't want to go into the past, but we have to. I was so wrong to lose my temper and leave so long ago. Can you ever truly forgive me?"

"You know that I already have forgiven you, Jake. There's no need for this—"

Jake's fingers gently touched her lips to quiet her. "Sara, please, hear me out. I need you to know that I understand I was the one who threw our relationship away. I was the one who didn't trust you, myself, or the Lord back then. And

I ruined it all. I don't even remember the drive back to the university that night, but I know there was a party going on when I got there. I remember taking one beer, then two. I don't remember much after that. I got drunk, Sara. For the first and last time, yes, but I got royally drunk."

"Jake, we all make mistakes. You really don't have to do this."

Jake looked out over the vista before him but saw nothing of its beauty. He rubbed the back of his neck and closed his eyes. He knew what he said next might end any chance he ever had with Sara, but he had to say it.

He opened his eyes and looked into hers. "By the time I came to my senses and realized I needed to apologize to you, it was too late."

"What do you mean, too late?" Sara asked.

"I know now that you didn't betray me that night. But I betrayed you. And that betrayal changed the course of my life." Jake reached into his pocket and pulled out the letter from Melissa.

"I didn't feel free to tell you this until I found this letter the other night." He handed it to Sara. "I'm not sure I'll ever give it to Meggie to read. Maybe the best thing to do is to leave it all behind. But I want you to read it, Sara. I want you to understand."

Sara unfolded the piece of paper Jake handed her, and he stood still, his heart pounding as he waited. When she looked back at him, her eyes were overflowing with tears.

"Oh, Jake." She handed the letter back to him and brushed at her wet cheeks. "I don't know what to say. I truly thought you'd broken up with me for Melissa. But I didn't know—"

Jake looked down into her shimmering eyes. "I'm so sorry, Sara. If I hadn't been so stubborn and jealous that night—"

"You wouldn't have Meggie now," Sara finished. "And neither of us would want that."

Jake never knew who reached out first, but suddenly, Sara was right where he wanted her to be—held tightly in his arms.

"I know you loved Wade and had a good life with him, Sara. I learned to love Melissa, and I will be eternally grateful to her for giving me my Meggie. But I've always felt we were meant to be together. I do love you, Sara. I know that I always will. Is there any way. . .do you think it is possible for us to start over and go on from here? Could there be a second chance for us?"

Sara released a sob and a joyful chuckle all at once. "Oh, Jake, I hope so. I truly hope so."

Jake crushed her in his embrace and claimed her lips. At her unhesitating response, he deepened the kiss with sweet promise. The past was buried and the future begun.

Chapter 14

Sara could never remember enjoying a meal more. She knew there were stars in her eyes and she didn't care who saw them. Jake loved her. Had always loved her. She was sure the joy she felt was obvious to anyone looking at her. It had to be.

If anyone asked her later what she'd eaten, she wasn't sure she would be able to tell them. All she knew for certain was that Jake loved her and she loved him. Nora had been wrong. Melissa's letter had put all her doubts to rest. Sara thanked the Lord for letting Jake find the letter and have her read it.

Jake paid the waiter and they were getting ready to leave when Sara turned to see Nora near the doorway, staring at them. Nora was with Dr. Wellington, but she pulled away from him and approached their table.

"I knew there was something going on between the two of you! I knew it!"

Dr. Wellington approached the table, looking apologetic, and put a hand through Nora's arm. "Nora, our table is ready. Please—"

Nora jerked her arm away. "Not until I've said what's needed to be said ever since Jake came back to town."

"Nora, please," Sara said. "You are creating a scene." She knew Nora would hate herself once she realized how she had behaved in public. Appearances meant everything to her.

"I don't care. I'm going to say this. Of all the people in the world for you to take up with, don't you know that Wade would turn over in his grave to know it was Jake? He worked so hard to win you. Even had me writing those anonymous notes to get Jake to doubt your love—"

"Nora!" Sara couldn't believe the woman's horrible rudeness or her awful admission.

Jake put his arm protectively around Sara.

"Nora, that's enough!" Dr. Wellington said. He pulled her to face him. "We are going to our table now. Or we are going home. Your choice."

Nora looked around as if she only now realized where she was and what she had done. Her hand grasped her chest, and she crumpled into a heap.

Sara knelt at the doctor's side as he checked Nora's vital signs. He picked her up.

"I'm taking her to the hospital now. I don't want to wait for an ambulance."

Jake pulled Sara to her feet and gathered her purse and wrap. "We're right behind you."

Hours later, Sara and Jake sat in the hospital waiting room, still uncertain of Nora's condition.

"Sara? Are you all right?" Jake asked. "Do you want me to get you some coffee, hot chocolate, anything?"

"No, Jake. Thank you, I'm fine. I just wish Dr. Wellington would let us know how she is. I knew she was stressed, I knew it. I should have spent more time with her."

"Sara, you can't blame yourself for this. Nora must have some kind of underlying problem. You are not to blame."

Sara sighed and lowered her head, rocking back and forth on the waiting room couch. "I don't want to take the blame, but I—"

"She's going to be fine, Sara." Dr. Wellington crossed the room and held out his hand. "I'm Michael Wellington. I wish we could be meeting under better circumstances."

"Nora? She's going to be all right? Did she have a heart attack? A stroke?"

The doctor shook his head. "No, she didn't. I am going to keep her in here at least overnight for observation, but it wasn't a heart attack or a stroke. She's put herself under a lot of stress in the last few years, but of course you know that."

Even though his arm encircled her, Jake felt Sara pulling away from him inch by inch.

"Do you think she has a heart problem, Doctor?" he asked.

"No. At least not now, and none of the tests we've run show anything wrong with her heart. I do want her to undergo a stress test to be certain, but stress can cause a lot of problems when it's not under control, and it's obvious that the last year has taken its toll on Nora. I do apologize to you both for the scene she caused tonight."

Sara shook her head. "No, I should have seen this coming. I should have checked in on her more often. I should have seen that she was struggling."

"Sara. None of this is your fault. Nora brings a lot of this on herself."

Sara shook her head. "I should have known she needed me."

Jake exchanged glances with the doctor. He shrugged and shook his head.

"Well, right now Nora needs rest," the doctor said, "and I'll see that she gets it. You two should go on home. You can see her tomorrow."

Sara nodded and Jake shook Dr. Wellington's hand.

They walked out to Jake's car silently, but when he'd settled Sara and taken his seat, he turned to her before starting the car.

"Sara, Dr. Wellington is right. This isn't your fault."

Sara nodded. "I know. And it wasn't my fault that Wade and my baby were killed in the wreck. But if I hadn't wanted that ice cream, they might still be alive."

She looked over at Jake with tears in her eyes. When he reached to take her in his arms, she pulled back and shook her head. She sniffed and brushed at her tears.

"Jake, I'm not sure we can see each other again. I cannot take feeling responsible for something happening to Nora. I can't."

He wanted to yell and tell her she couldn't throw away what they had. Not now. But a quiet voice stopped him. *Trust in Me always,* it said.

Jake listened and tried to stay calm. "Sara, I love you. I want to have a life with you."

Sara turned her face to the window. "I want that, too, Jake. But right now I'm not sure it's going to be possible."

Jake took a deep breath. He'd waited this long, surely he could wait longer. And this time he was going to put his trust in the Lord.

~

The next few days were some of the longest Sara had ever endured. Nora seemed to have slid into a deep depression, and she wasn't talking. At least not to Sara—even though Sara spent most of every day in Nora's room, reading to her, talking to her, anything to get her to respond.

Sara knew that Nora could talk if she wanted to. She'd heard her speaking to the nurses. But as soon as Sara walked into the room, she clammed up.

Dr. Wellington had ordered a battery of tests, but so far nothing unusual had shown up. Sara knew he cared for Nora, but at the same time he seemed frustrated with her.

Gram was getting around without the crutches now, and Lydia took over planning the family reunion, while Gina and the church family stepped in to help so that Sara could be with Nora.

But Sara missed being at Gram's. Her heart cried out for Meggie, and she was afraid the baby would feel she'd abandoned her. Her heart twisted each time she thought of what Jake must be feeling. He'd laid his soul bare for her, and she'd left him without an answer.

She'd never felt so torn in her life, Sara thought as she walked down the hospital corridor from Nora's room to the cafeteria. She and Jake had been on the verge of staking out a future for themselves and Meggie, but now, with Nora in the hospital and knowing how she felt about Jake, the future seemed bleaker than ever.

Sara wanted to be with Jake and Meggie, but how could she possibly start a new life when her mother-in-law refused to even talk to her about anything, much less her relationship with Jake?

Sara ran into Dr. Wellington in the cafeteria line, and he bought her lunch and himself a cup of coffee and asked if he could join her. Sara was glad to have a chance to talk to him. "Have any of the test results pointed to what is wrong with Nora, Dr. Wellington?"

"No. And they aren't going to tell us anything we don't already know. Nora is basically healthy. She's just let the stress in her life take over, instead of handing things over to the Lord."

"You're sure she didn't have a heart attack?"

"Yes, Sara, I'm sure. Her heart is healthy."

Sara tried to blink the tears of relief away. Dr. Wellington reached out and took her hand. "I know you care deeply for your mother-in-law. So do I. But we can't take on the blame for Nora's stress. She's gone through no more than you have in the last year, Sara. You can't let her health rule your life."

"But I don't want her to think she doesn't matter to me."

"Then tell her that she does and get on with your life. You have that right."

"I want Nora to be happy."

The doctor nodded. "So do I. And I'm going to do everything I can to see that she is. But in the end, Sara, I can't make her happy. You can't make her happy. She has to learn to let herself be happy."

"I know what you are saying is true. It's just so hard to walk away and start a new life, knowing I'm hurting her."

"And what she's done hasn't hurt you? And Jake?" He shook his head. "No wonder you're the one who has rings under her eyes. Look closely at Nora when you see her again."

"I think I know what you're telling me. I've been praying about it. I'm sure the Lord will let me know what to do."

Dr. Wellington looked at his watch and stood up. "I'm sure He will. I'm going to look in on Nora now. You relax and enjoy your lunch."

Sara tried to do just that. But mostly, she just prayed.

Jake headed down the hall to Nora's room. He didn't know what else to do. If he waited for Sara to tell Nora to go fly a kite, he'd have a long wait. Yet all of this was taking its toll on her. He knew she loved him and Meggie. He could hear it in her voice when she called at night to see how Meggie and Gram were doing. He reassured Sara, but he didn't tell her that Meggie asked for her at least ten times a day. He couldn't put that kind of pressure on her. Neither could he ask her to marry him, knowing that Nora would never give them her blessing and would try to make Sara as unhappy as she could.

He'd just realized how very important family was to his daughter and to himself. And Nora was family. He had to try. But he dreaded the confrontation he knew was coming, and he stopped outside her room to gather his thoughts.

A male voice Jake recognized as Dr. Wellington's could be heard coming from the half-opened door. "Nora, you have got to get past this. You have to for Sara's sake, for your own sake. For our sake."

"I know I do, Michael," Nora cried. "It's just that Sara is all I have left of Wade, and she has been a daughter to me. But she loved Jake before she ever loved my son. I don't want to lose her, but I can't help but feel pushed aside. And I'm jealous. I wanted a grandchild so badly, and now Sara will get to be a mother, but I'm never going to be a grandmother."

Jake could hear sobbing from the other side of the door. His heart went out to his aunt, while at the same time he was appalled at her petty jealousy.

Judge not. Trust Me. The small voice made itself heard. Jake nodded. "I hear You, Lord," he whispered.

He needed the reminder. His jealousy had been the cause of his and Sara's first breakup. Now Nora's threatened to do the same. But this time, he was going to trust the Lord to lead his way. He bowed his head and said a quick prayer and then walked into Nora's room.

Nora's hand flew to her throat. "Jake! What—"

"Good afternoon, Jake," Dr. Wellington said, interrupting Nora, but he reached out and touched her shoulder. "It's good to see you again."

"Aunt Nora, Dr. Wellington." Jake strode into the center of the room. "I couldn't help but overhear part of your conversation."

His aunt's face paled as she looked at the doctor, who smiled at her and took her hand.

Jake cleared his throat. "I have a little girl who has a great-grandmother, and I'm hoping the woman I love will become her mommy. But every little girl needs a grammy."

The color began to return to Nora's face. "How about it, Aunt Nora? Want to make a deal?"

~

Sara finished her lunch, thinking over what Dr. Wellington had said. Nora didn't have heart trouble. She was going to be fine. All Sara could do for Nora was let her know she cared about her and would always be part of her family no matter who she married. If Nora would think rationally about it, she'd realize that marrying Jake would keep her in the family.

Sara disposed of her dirty dishes and headed back to Nora's room. She was going to take the doctor's advice and reassure her mother-in-law. Then she was going to Jake and Meggie and get on with her own life.

When she turned onto the corridor that led to Nora's room, Sara was surprised to see Jake outside the woman's room. He bowed his head before opening the door and entering. What was he doing? He knew how Nora felt about him. She hurried her pace until she arrived outside the room.

She entered quietly behind Jake, and what she heard sent a warm wave of love flooding through her heart. Jake was declaring his love for her and asking Nora to be a part of that love by being a grandmother to Meggie. He'd put his heart on the line with Sara, and now he was trying to make peace with Nora so that they could have a future.

Sara broke the silence that fell on the room. "Nora, if I were you, I'd take

Jake up on his offer." She walked up to Jake and wrapped her arms around him. "I certainly plan to."

Jake's smile lit his face as he gathered Sara close. "Nora, I meant what I said. Meggie needs a grammy. Think about it."

Nora's mouth opened and shut, but for once, nothing came out. Dr. Wellington stood at her side, grinning.

Jake and Sara backed out of the room. "You can give us your answer later, Aunt Nora," Jake said. "Right now, we have a few things to settle." He pulled Sara into the hall and looked down into her eyes. "Did you mean it? Will you marry me and be a mommy for Meggie?"

"I will."

Jake picked her up and twirled her around right there in the hospital corridor. He bent his head and sealed her answer with a kiss that healed the past and promised a lifetime of love for the future.

Epilogue

Dressed in lace, with her auburn hair swept up into an elegant french twist, Sara waited in the fellowship hall to begin her walk down the aisle behind her attendants, Deana and Gina. More nervous and happy than she could ever remember, she clung to her grandfather's arm, thinking back over the past few weeks since she and Jake had announced their engagement. Her heart filled with love for Jake, Meggie, their extended family, and friends, and she thanked the Lord for the blessings He'd bestowed on her.

There hadn't been any debate over the wedding date. As Gram stated, "What better time to have a wedding than on the Fourth of July? Everyone will be here for the family reunion, and by then your new home will be ready to move into."

Sara and Jake weren't about to argue. They'd waited such a long time to start their life together.

Nora had wasted no time in taking Jake up on his offer. She'd come to realize that the guilt she'd felt about sending Jake those anonymous notes all those years ago had surfaced when he'd moved back home. The fear and worry that he and Sara would discover what she had done had taken its toll on her health, but with the truth revealed and having received Jake and Sara's forgiveness, Nora began to count her blessings. By the end of that week, she was out of the hospital, helping Gram and Sara take care of Meggie while everyone in the family helped plan the wedding.

Sara let the school know that she wouldn't be teaching that fall. She and Jake had talked it over, and because Meggie had gone through so many changes in her young life, they decided that making sure she felt secure and loved was one of their top priorities. There would be plenty of time to teach once the toddler started school. Besides, Sara could think of nothing she'd rather do than enjoy the blessing God was giving her—to be Jake's wife and Meggie's mommy.

But the blessings hadn't stopped there. Nora was a different person. She'd turned into the woman Sara had only been given a glimpse of the night of Jake's welcome-home party. She was absolutely crazy about Meggie, and Meggie had taken to her as well. Nora would stay with Gram and help take care of Meggie while Jake and Sara went on a brief honeymoon to Santa Fe. And much to the delight of the whole family, Nora and Dr. Wellington had become an item around town.

Gram and Grandpa kept everyone guessing about their relationship. They seemed to be inseparable—chuckling and whispering together any time they were around each other—and Sara and Jake were sure they must be plotting and planning on how to add Dr. Wellington to the family.

"We're going to have to do something about those two," Sara had whispered to Jake the night before, as they'd watched their grandparents during the wedding rehearsal.

Jake nodded. "As soon as we get back from Santa Fe, we're going to have to do a little matchmaking ourselves."

Sara took a deep breath when she and Grandpa were given their signal and began their walk down the aisle. Her smile was tremulous, but she kept the tears of joy at bay by focusing on Jake.

With Luke and John by his side, Jake tried to hide his nervousness. But when Sara started down the aisle, he was sure his sigh of relief was audible. He couldn't take his eyes off her as she made her way to him, and he barely heard David ask who gave Sara away, or Will's answer. Finally she was standing by his side, and the moment he'd spent a lifetime waiting for had arrived.

Jake and Sara turned to David and exchanged their wedding vows in front of family, friends, and what must have been half the town. They were pronounced husband and wife, and Jake's lips claimed Sara's in a sweet promise to love her for the rest of their lives.

David introduced them as Mr. and Mrs. Jake Breland, and the two turned to face the loved ones who had just witnessed their promises to love, honor, and cherish each other. Jake smiled at his Meggie sitting contentedly in her Grammy Nora's lap, saw his grandmother and Sara's grandfather sitting side by side and Aunt Lydia and Uncle Ben behind them. The smiles of his and Sara's family and friends reflected their shared joy.

Jake pulled Sara's hand through his arm and looked down at his new bride before starting up the aisle. The love shining from her eyes had him swallowing the sudden lump in his throat, and he thanked the Lord for bringing him home, for bringing him and Sara together again, and for their ever-widening family circle.

Will nudged Ellie and whispered in her ear as they watched their grandchildren walk back up the aisle together. "Look at those two. We finally did it, didn't we, El? We finally got those two together."

"Oh, I think we had a lot of help from above, Will. We can't take all the credit ourselves," Ellie said softly, leaning closer to Will so that he could hear.

"That's true, El. Very true," Will nodded. "But, now that they are together and it looks like Nora has found a man who can handle her, maybe it's time we concentrated on ourselves for a while. We aren't getting any younger, you know."

"I've been wondering when you were going to realize that, William Oliver. It's about time you made this courting you've been doing official," Ellie said, patting Will's cheek.

He quickly captured her hand and brought it to his lips. "Consider it done, my sweet Ellie. Consider it done."

The wedding party spilled out onto the church grounds just as the first fireworks from the Independence Day celebration began crackling in the night sky. Jake pulled Sara close to his side, and as he bent his head to kiss her once more, the fireworks surrounding them reflected the pure light of love bursting forth from their hearts.

Family Ties

Dedication

To my Lord and Savior for showing me the way,
to the wonderful family He's blessed me with,
and to the real Sunday night supper crew.
I love you all!

Chapter 1

Luke Breland didn't quite know what the problem was, but lately he just didn't like himself much. He did know that he couldn't face one more night of his own cooking and, most especially, not a night made up of only his own company. Grabbing his Stetson from the hook beside the door, he shoved it on his head and walked out onto his back porch, letting the screen door slam behind him.

He reached his pickup with long strides, started the truck, and headed for Sweet Springs, debating where to go. He had relatives all over the place and knew he would be welcomed by any one of them. But his brother, Jake, had only been married to Sara for a few months. . .and they were still considered newlyweds. More than likely Gram was being courted, as they called it, by her beau, Will Oliver, and Aunt Nora and her suitor, Michael Wellington, were probably out to dinner or at a movie.

Luke sighed deeply and shook his head. It seemed his whole family was romantically involved with someone, all except for him and his cousin, John—and he was in Santa Fe lining up support for his upcoming senatorial campaign. Like it or not, Luke was on his own.

He headed for Deana's Diner where he could get a good meal and hopefully not have to answer a lot of questions about his rotten mood.

Rae Wellington became more and more frustrated as she drove down the tree-lined streets of Sweet Springs. She couldn't find her dad anywhere. He wasn't at his house, his office had been closed for several hours, and she'd checked with the hospital to see if he was on call, only to find out he wasn't. She'd even called his cell phone number to no avail. She supposed she should have let him know she was coming, but these days most of what she did was not planned.

Planning did no good. She learned that the hard way, after having her fiancé break up with her on the eve of her wedding—for her best friend, no less. She'd been left to cancel everything, return all of the wedding presents, and answer the phone calls of friends who pitied her. All in all, she thought she'd been doing pretty well through the summer. Then school started, and she found that Laura had been transferred to Zia High School, and watching Paul and her former best friend—so obviously in love—at meetings and in the halls of the high school where they all taught just intensified the pain of betrayal. She'd managed to make it through September and October, but it had become more difficult with each passing day, and finally she could take no more. This afternoon she'd put in for an immediate leave of absence, packed her car, and driven the four hours to Sweet Springs. She felt she just had to get away, at least until she could decide whether she could continue teaching at Zia High or should ask for a transfer to another school when an opening came up. Until then, all she wanted was to run into the comforting arms of her dad. And the only place she could do that was in the small town he now called home.

He'd been trying to get her to move down to Sweet Springs ever since the breakup, but Rae liked living in Albuquerque. She loved the view of the mountains from her living room window and liked the fact that it was the largest city in New Mexico, even though it would be considered small by national standards. She had no interest in moving to a tiny town like Sweet Springs—no matter how quaint it might be—and she couldn't understand why her dad wanted to live here. She was hoping to convince him to move back.

In Albuquerque there were so many choices of places to eat, deciding on where to go was sometimes a problem; here she was having a hard time even finding a café. And she needed to eat soon; otherwise the headache that had been building for the last fifty miles was going to settle in for a long stay. She should have stopped at one of the fast-food restaurants she'd passed on the way into town, but she kept remembering her dad talking about a place called Deana's Diner, where he took a lot of his meals. He'd mentioned it being right downtown and having great food.

Rae turned down what she hoped was the main street in town and breathed a sigh of relief that she found the diner right across from the courthouse in the square. She eased her small car into a parking space next to a cranberry red pickup and took a minute to run a brush through her hair.

There were only a few people in the diner when she entered. An older couple sat in one booth, two teenaged couples in another, and a cowboy type sat by himself at the counter. Rae slid into a booth and began to search her handbag for some aspirin. Before she could get the purse-sized bottle open, the waitress was there with water and a menu.

"One of those days?" the waitress asked with a smile. Tall and slim, with blond hair and brown eyes, she seemed a little rushed. Her name tag read Deana, and Rae realized she must be the owner.

When Rae nodded, Deana continued. "I know the feeling. My regular waitress is on vacation; my extra help didn't show up this afternoon, and I'm left shorthanded this evening. Good thing it's been fairly slow tonight."

"Oh, I'm sorry." Rae couldn't help but sympathize with the friendly young woman.

"It happens when you own the place." Deana shrugged and smiled, pointing out the day's special on the menu. "You might think about trying the chicken and dumplings. It's my mom's recipe, and it's pure comfort food, especially when you aren't feeling up to par. I'll leave you to glance over the menu for yourself and be back to take your order in a few minutes."

"Thanks." Rae downed the aspirin quickly before studying the menu, but her mind was already made up. Those chicken and dumplings did sound awfully good.

Oblivious to his surroundings, Luke waited for his order to come. He stared into his iced tea and sighed deeply. He seemed to be sighing a lot lately. He wasn't sure when this mood he was in had started, but as he thought back over the past few months, it seemed to have begun around the time all this romancing in his family became obvious. Oh, he was happy for them all; he really was. But it'd made him realize something about himself that he'd been ignoring for years. He was plain old lonesome. He couldn't deny it any longer. He wanted a family of his own—longed for a love of his own.

Fat chance of that happening. He'd dated most of the eligible women in the county, and it just never worked out. Most of them were hoping to find someone to take them out of the area, and Luke's roots went deep. He wasn't moving anywhere.

The ranch he helped run had been in his family for several generations, and he couldn't imagine doing anything else. No, he was going to have to come to grips with the fact that he might be single the rest of his life—and a few months ago, he had never given it a thought. But now. . .now, he was a pitiful excuse of a cowboy, crying in his iced tea. Luke shook his head and sighed again before his sense of humor kicked in; then he chuckled to himself.

Deana, the diner's owner, walked up just then. Setting down the chicken-fried steak he'd ordered, she peered at him closely. "You okay, Luke?"

Luke nodded. Yes. He was all right. So what if he didn't have a romance of his own going on? The Lord had blessed him in many ways. And if the Lord meant for him to have a mate, he'd just trust Him to bring a stranger here to Sweet Springs, 'cause Luke figured that was the only way he was going to find her—whoever she was.

He grinned up at Deana. "I'll be better after I eat this meal. But I could ask you the same. Seems you are a little understaffed tonight, Dee."

"You're just a master of understatement, aren't you?" she said before hurrying across the room, her order pad in hand.

Luke gave his attention to the meal sitting in front of him. He bowed his head and prayed silently before picking up his fork. He did love chicken-fried steak.

When Deana came back to take her order, Rae went with her suggestion of chicken and dumplings. She could use some comfort right now. She'd been hoping for a comforting hug from her dad, but that would have to wait until she located him—if she ever did.

Deana promised to bring her meal right out, and Rae was glad she'd ordered the day's special when it was set before her only minutes later, piping hot and smelling absolutely delicious. She ate slowly, savoring each bite, and wondered what to do next. She really didn't want to spend the evening parked in her dad's driveway waiting for him to come home. Hopefully, by the time she finished her meal, he'd be there.

She did feel a little awkward eating alone in a strange town, but she tried not to show it. She watched Deana as she moved from one table to the other, taking care of her diners. The teenagers didn't seem in any hurry to leave but hadn't ordered a lot from what she could see. The older couple got up to leave just as a young family of four came in.

The cowboy at the counter seemed lost in his thoughts as he ate his meal, and Rae, man-wary as she was, couldn't help but be surprised that her gaze kept coming back to rest on him. He was tall—she could tell that from the way his long legs wrapped around the counter stool he sat on—and he was very broad shouldered. When Deana stopped to fill his iced tea glass, he thanked her in a deep, husky voice. She watched as Deana leaned over the counter and said something that made him smile, and Rae wondered idly if they were seeing each other.

Most probably they were. It seemed everyone she knew was the other half of a couple, except for her. She didn't know what she'd done to make the Lord mad, but she was sure He must be. First her mother died while she was in high school, and she and her dad were left to take care of each other. Last year her dad decided to move here. Rae shook her head. She wasn't going to let herself go down that road again. Her dad loved her. When he'd moved away, he thought she'd be happily married in a few months. He couldn't have known that her dreams for the future would come crashing down around her.

"How was it?" Deana broke into her thoughts, filling her water glass. "How about some dessert and coffee?"

"It was wonderful. Just what I needed," Rae answered. "I don't have any room for dessert, but coffee sounds good."

"Coming right up." Deana took her plate and headed back to the counter.

Rae wondered if her dad was finally home and decided to call his house once more. She couldn't help feeling disappointed when there was no answer. She flipped the top down on her cell phone and dropped it back into her handbag just as Deana came back with her coffee.

"You just passing through or are you visiting?" Deana asked.

"Visiting, if I can ever catch up with my host. You wouldn't happen to know Dr. Michael Wellington, would you?"

"Dr. Mike? Sure. He's in here nearly every day. He's not home?"

Rae could tell Deana was curious about why she was trying to find him. Ordinarily, she'd say it wasn't any of the other woman's business, but the diner owner had been very nice, and she might have an idea of where her dad could be. "He's my dad. I guess I should have let him know I was coming. It never dawned on me that he might not be home."

Deana inclined her head. "Hmm. He's not at the hospital, either?"

Rae shook her head. "No. And of course, his office has been closed for several hours."

"Maybe I can help you locate him." Deana turned toward the counter. "Hey, Luke. We could use your help over here."

Rae got her first really good look at the man as he unwound his legs from the stool and stood up. She tried to ignore the way her heart jumped as she watched the tall, handsome cowboy arch an eyebrow at Deana and smile as he crossed the room toward them.

Luke wondered how he could have missed seeing the young lady sitting in the booth by the door. He must be slipping big-time not to have noticed the nicely dressed, dark-haired woman when she came in. She surely wasn't here when he arrived. Who was this stranger in town? *Stranger?* Luke idly wondered if the Lord had already answered his prayer, then dismissed the ridiculous thought. Most likely, she took a wrong turn and just wanted directions. He picked up his Stetson and held it close to his side as he ambled over to her table. It was a pretty sure guess that she hadn't come to find him.

"Sure thing, Dee. What can I do for you two ladies?" he asked, smiling down at her.

"Luke, this is. . ." Dee turned to Rae and grinned.

"Rae Wellington," the stranger finished for Dee, her voice light and lilting.

"Nice to meet you, Rae," Dee said and patted Luke's shoulder. "And this big, ugly cowboy is Luke Breland. He knows everyone for miles around."

"Hi." Rae smiled up at him.

As Luke smiled down at her, a delicate pink color seemed to spread up her neck and onto her cheeks, and he had a feeling she might be embarrassed that Dee called him over. "Pleased to meet you, Rae."

"She's Dr. Mike's daughter," Dee added. "And she can't find him. Do you have any idea where he might be?"

Was she kidding? Of course he had an idea where Michael might be, and she knew it. He glanced from Dee to Rae. He could see the resemblance to Michael now; only she was a much more feminine version of her father. Delightfully so, with shoulder-length, dark, curly hair, and big blue eyes. She was very pretty. But there was a vulnerability in her eyes that caught him by surprise and called to him—bringing out every protective urge he had—to come to her aid if need be, in any way he could.

"He could be at Aunt Nora's or Gram's. I'll call around and see if I can find him." He pulled out his cell phone, flipped it open, and punched in his aunt's phone number. When her answering machine came on, he ended the call without leaving a message and started to dial his grandmother's number. Before he completed the call, the bell over the diner's door jingled, and Michael and Aunt Nora walked in, laughing about something.

He snapped the phone shut and stuck it in his pocket, watching the changing expressions on Rae's face. Her countenance quickly changed from what appeared to him as excitement, then confusion, and finally happiness.

"Daddy!" Rae scooted out of the booth and hurried to her father.

"Rae!" The joy on Michael's face told anyone watching just how happy he was to see his daughter. He enveloped her in a hug. "You're here! I wasn't expecting you until Thanksgiving! What a wonderful surprise."

"Well, I guess we don't need your detective services after all, Luke." Dee nudged him on the shoulder before hurrying over to the register where the teens were lined up to pay.

Luke shrugged, but his gaze was on Rae, and he thought he saw tears in her eyes just before she turned her face into her father's chest. Feeling a little like an intruder, he stood to the side and glanced down at his aunt.

Aunt Nora had a smile on her face, but Luke thought she seemed a little apprehensive until Michael pulled her forward to introduce her to Rae. His aunt's smile grew wider then, and Luke told himself he must have been imagining things.

"Rae, honey, I'd like you to meet Nora Tanner." Michael gazed into Nora's eyes and smiled. "She's made my move to Sweet Springs a wonderful decision."

"I'm so pleased to meet you, Rae," Nora said graciously. "Your father talks about you all the time. I know he's thrilled to see you."

"I certainly hope so. I didn't give him any advance notice." Rae smiled at her father and glanced back to Nora. "But I feel at a disadvantage. . . . Daddy hasn't told me about you."

Suddenly, Luke felt uncomfortable. Both women were being very nice to each other, but something didn't seem quite right, and he wasn't sure he wanted to know what it was. He decided to take his leave and go home. But as he moved to go pay for his meal, Michael caught him by the arm.

"You leaving, Luke? Might as well stay and have some pie and coffee with us."

Before he could answer, his aunt chimed in, "Oh, yes, Luke. Please join us."

Luke's "no" was on the tip of his tongue when he glanced at his aunt and changed his mind. He knew he wasn't imagining the expression in her eyes this time. It was a call to family loyalty and support, and he couldn't ignore it.

Resigned to the fact that he wasn't going anyplace for a little while, he gave in. "Dee's apple pie is hard to resist. Guess I'll join you after all."

When his aunt and Michael took one side of the booth, Rae glanced at Luke and quickly slid to the far end of the bench. Luke slid in beside her, keeping a safe distance between them. She sure was pretty. And she smelled real good.

But the warm look she'd given her dad when she first spotted him had become cool when he'd introduced her to Aunt Nora. Luke suddenly realized Rae was anything but happy about her dad and his aunt seeing each other.

He hoped he was reading things wrong. Michael was the best thing to happen to his aunt in years. And they were happy together—anyone could see that. No one seemed to know quite what to say next, and Luke was relieved when Dee came to take their order.

Still full from the meal she'd just eaten, Rae only asked for a refill of her coffee. When she glanced across at her father, she couldn't help smiling at the grin on his face. He was as glad to see her as she was to see him; she had no doubt of that. Still, it hurt that he hadn't told her about this woman he obviously cared about. Nora Tanner was a lovely woman—in her midfifties, Rae guessed. She had softly highlighted hair and was slim and elegantly dressed. Why hadn't her father mentioned that he was dating someone, and. . .how long *had* they been seeing each other?

Rae tried to smile as they gave their orders, but she knew it was strained. She felt tense sitting there with two strangers her father seemed to know so well—not to mention how nervous she felt sitting next to the broad-shouldered, handsome cowboy.

"When did you get into town, honey?" her dad asked.

Relieved that he'd brought her out of her thoughts, Rae glanced at her watch. "A couple of hours ago. I went by your house and your office, and I even checked with the hospital. I could just picture us passing on the interstate and not knowing it. . .you to see me and me to see you."

Everyone chuckled, and the tension eased somewhat as Deana—or Dee, as Luke called her—brought back their dessert orders and refilled Rae's coffee.

"That might well have happened," he continued. "I've been telling Nora how much I've missed you and needed to get up to Albuquerque to see you, haven't I, Nora?"

"Yes, you have." Nora smiled at Rae. "He's missed you a great deal. He's been wishing you would join him here in Sweet Springs."

"Any chance of that happening, honey? Think you could give up the city life for this close-knit little community? You'd love it here. I know you would."

"Oh, wait, Dad. I'm just here on a visit." Rae smiled and shook her head. She was well aware that everyone who lived in Albuquerque thought *they* owned the mountain range that rose so magnificently over the city, but that didn't stop her from claiming it for her own. "You know how much I love my Sandia Mountains."

"I do," he agreed. "But there's much to love here. Just wait and see. I guess you are only here for the weekend?"

Rae took a sip of her coffee. How did she answer that? She hadn't told him about taking a leave of absence from work. When she left home, she'd been planning on staying for several weeks, maybe all the way through the holidays, or as long as it took to talk her father into moving back to Albuquerque, but now. . .

"I have to make rounds at the hospital in the morning, but after that I'll try to show you as much as I can so you'll know why I love it here," he added.

"I'm taking some personal time off." She watched her dad raise an eyebrow her way and study her closely, but he kept quiet. "I'll stay through the next week, if you don't mind having me underfoot. I'm not sure after that."

Rae just couldn't bring herself to commit to more than that right now. Much as she'd been looking forward to seeing her father, it was obvious that this visit wasn't going to end quite as she'd envisioned it—with her father agreeing to move back to Albuquerque.

"What do you do?" Luke asked, smiling at her.

Thankful that someone broke the silence that had suddenly fallen, Rae returned his smile. He did have *such* beautiful brown eyes. And when he smiled, they seemed to light up from somewhere deep inside.

"I teach school," Rae informed him, trying to pull her gaze away from his and feeling a little breathless.

"What grade?"

"Ninth."

"Whoa. Not an easy grade to handle, I would imagine."

"Oh, I don't know. I think the first year of high school is probably easier than junior high. I taught that for a year and nearly bailed out." Rae grinned over at her dad. "Remember that year?"

He nodded. "I remember it well. But you got a grip on everything after a few months and went on to teach some of those same kids their first year in high school."

Rae smiled. "You're right. I did."

"Well, I admire anyone who teaches," Nora said, shaking her head. "I know I wouldn't have the patience."

"What is it you do, Nora?" Rae couldn't curb her curiosity about the woman.

Nora smiled and shook her head. "Not much."

"That's not true," her father argued. "Nora does a lot of the behind-the-scenes kind of stuff. She heads the volunteer program at the hospital; she's very active at church and with her family."

"And you don't have a job?"

"No. I've been very fortunate in that I didn't have to work—and very foolish in that I didn't always use my free time wisely." Nora glanced at Dad, and he put his arm around her, drawing her close. "But I'm trying to change all of that, with the help of the Lord. . .and Michael."

Rae almost caught her breath at the expression of love that passed between her dad and Nora. It was as if you could reach out and actually touch it. If she'd wondered if this was just a fleeting romance for him, she no longer had to guess about it. He was in love with this woman. She wished she could be happy for him, but try as she might, happy was the last thing she felt. And the strain of hiding it was building.

"Michael, your daughter seems exhausted." Nora motioned in Rae's direction. "I think it's time you showed her the way to your house from here."

Her father fixed his attention on Rae. "You do seem pretty tired, honey. How about you follow me home, Rae, then you can start settling in while I take Nora home."

"No, Michael. If Luke doesn't mind, I'll ask him to take me home. There's something I'd like to talk to him about, anyway. And Rae has waited long enough to have you to herself. Luke, you don't mind, do you?"

"I'll be glad to take you home, Aunt Nora. It's on my way."

Chapter 2

Luke was relieved when they said their good-byes. He'd begun to feel a little uncomfortable again. Only this time he didn't know if it was because of the two women's reaction to each other or because he was fighting the undeniable attraction he felt for a woman who clearly had no desire to leave *her* mountains—or Albuquerque. He left Deana's Diner in the same frame of mind he'd been in when he got there. Longing for something he'd probably never have.

Luke walked Aunt Nora to his pickup and opened the door for her. He always forgot how small a woman his aunt was until he stood right beside her. At just a little over five feet, she didn't even reach his chin. Her short, highlighted hair was just beginning to show some signs of silver threads; still, she was a lovely woman. She always appeared well put together, whether she was dressed for church or riding out on the ranch. For a long time he'd thought her one of the most self-centered women he'd ever known, but she'd changed so much in the past few months. She seemed softer, more vulnerable somehow. He saw her cast a wistful glance back toward the diner before she turned to him and smiled.

"I'm sure Michael and Rae have a lot to catch up on," she said as he helped her into the truck. "They certainly don't need my company tonight."

"Oh, I think Michael would have liked for you to stay." Luke shut the passenger door and hurried around to his side, continuing the conversation when he got in the pickup. "His daughter—"

"Wouldn't," Nora finished for him. "It seemed to upset her that Michael hadn't told her anything about me."

"She seemed kind of uptight, but that was even before you and Michael showed up. I think she was just a little upset because she couldn't find him and didn't know what to do about it."

"Hmm." Nora sighed deeply.

Luke glanced over at his aunt as they headed out of town. She was chewing her bottom lip, which was totally unlike her. He'd rarely seen his aunt flustered. "Are you all right, Aunt Nora?"

"I'm fine, dear. Just a little nervous, I guess." She smiled at him. "I have a secret for you to keep, Luke."

Luke groaned inwardly. He hated when people confided in him and asked him not to say anything. But it seemed to be his lot in life. Everyone seemed to want to tell him their secrets, problems, or dreams. No sense in fighting it.

"What is it, Aunt Nora? You and Michael elope tonight?"

She burst out laughing. "No. But you're close. The subject of marriage has come up. We're thinking about it."

"That's wonderful!" Luke grinned at her. It was good news. Michael had been wonderful for Nora. That they were in love was no secret to anyone who saw them together for any length of time. "Why are you nervous?"

"I'm not sure how Rae will react to the news. I hope Michael doesn't mention it tonight. I'd like her to get to know me first." She paused and peered out the window. "I think."

Luke chuckled. "Aunt Nora, it will be fine. I'm sure she wants her dad to be happy. And you two make each other very happy."

Nora bobbed her head. "We do, don't we? Still, she's an only child, and I'm sure it's not easy to think about someone taking her mother's place. Plus she's had some heartache in her life recently. . . ."

"Oh?" Luke was aware he was being nosy, but he couldn't help wondering what kind of heartache Rae had suffered. There was something about her. . . .

"I think she just needs some attention from her father right now." Nora didn't elaborate any further. Obviously, she wasn't telling what she knew.

Luke shrugged. "Maybe. But don't you worry, Aunt Nora. I'm sure she'll come around once she sees how much Michael cares about you. Surely she wouldn't want to cause problems for her dad."

"Luke, would you make her feel at home in Sweet Springs? Show her around some when Michael is at work? Introduce her to some of the family who are her age?"

"But—"

"Luke, she isn't ready to get to know me yet. You saw her reaction at Deana's. I don't want to force myself on her. Please."

Luke always had a hard time resisting a "please" from a lady. And Nora seemed to need his support right now. "All right, Aunt Nora. I'll see what I can do. No promises, though."

"Thank you, dear."

Luke sighed and turned into the drive leading to Nora's ranch house. "You're welcome."

Rae was relieved to finally have her father to herself. She grinned at him from across the table. "You look wonderful, Dad. I've missed you so much!"

He reached over and drew her hands into his. "I've missed you, too, honey. I'm so glad to see you. Now, tell me about this personal time you're taking."

Rae didn't want to talk about it here and now. "Can we discuss it at home, Dad? I am a little tired."

"Of course we can." Her father got up immediately and waited for her to scoot out of her side of the booth. "Let me pay Dee, and we'll be on our way."

Rae pulled on the lightweight jacket she'd brought in with her and waited for her dad to join her again. Deana waved from the cash register, and Rae waved back. It'd been nice of the woman to try to help her. "Thanks, Deana!"

"Anytime. And just call me Dee. Nearly everyone else around here has ever since your dad started calling me that."

Dad grinned and shrugged. "You started calling me Dr. Mike, and now so do lots of other people."

Dee chuckled and nodded. "You're right. I did. I hope you have a nice stay here, Rae."

"Thank you." Rae hoped she did, too. But seeing how settled in her dad seemed to be, and how happy he seemed with a new woman in his life, she wasn't so sure.

Her dad walked her to her car and hurried to his own after telling her to follow him. Rae had found his house earlier, but she was glad to have him lead the way. She was impressed with his choice of homes and was anxious to see the inside. It was in a very nice subdivision, backed up to a golf course, but she was a little surprised by the style he'd chosen. Their two-story home in Albuquerque had been quite traditional, while this was a beautiful, sprawling adobe hacienda.

Almost as soon as she stopped in his driveway, her dad was there to help bring in her luggage. One glance at her bags had him turning to her with a grin. "You *are* going to stay awhile, aren't you?"

"I'm not sure, Dad. I just don't know." Rae watched him pull the two heaviest suitcases out of the trunk and move to the side. She retrieved a couple midsized cases and followed him up the walk to the front door.

He unlocked and opened the door, then picked up the luggage he'd set down beside it. "I'll bring in the rest after I see you to your room. I hope you like it. Nora helped me furnish it."

Oh, thrill, Rae thought, then immediately chastised herself. She didn't know anything about this woman, and it was way too early to form an opinion about her. Just because she didn't like the way Nora gazed at her dad was no reason to dislike her, but it sure hadn't helped Rae want to be best friends with her.

"Dad, it's beautiful!" She took in the tiled entryway and the great room just ahead. The stucco walls seemed to be washed with just a hint of yellow, giving the room a warm and inviting atmosphere. The rich brown leather couch and chairs facing the corner fireplace beckoned one to sit. Although the room had a masculine feel to it, a woman's touch was evident; there were flowers on the coffee table and several other items around the room that made it feel homey.

"Thank you, honey. I'm glad you like it. Let's get your things to your room. Then I'll make us some hot chocolate, and we can catch up."

"Sounds wonderful." Rae followed her father down a wide hall to the left of the entryway. She supposed the kitchen was to the right.

When her dad opened the door to her room, she caught her breath. Decorated in her favorite colors of butter yellow and aqua, it was lovely. She couldn't have done a better job of decorating it herself. More of a suite than a room, it was spacious enough to have a sitting area facing French doors that opened to a courtyard. It even had its own bathroom with a whirlpool and separate shower.

"It is beautiful, Dad."

He set her cases in the dressing area and grinned at her. "I'm glad you like it, honey. I want you to feel this is your home, too."

Rae blinked away the tears that suddenly threatened and hugged her dad. "Thank you."

He cleared his throat and embraced her. "I'll just go get the rest of your things. Make yourself at home and find out where everything is. I'll meet you in the kitchen. Just head back to the entryway, then straight through."

Rae did as instructed and made her way down the hall, peeking briefly into the other bedrooms. There were two more—also tastefully decorated—each facing the center courtyard. At the end of the hall, a side door led outside. A matching door across the way opened to the other wing. Rae decided to take her dad's advice and explore. Instead of making her way back down the hall, she went outside to the courtyard—which was absolutely gorgeous. It had a view of the golf course behind the house and a pool set in the center. Although it was too cool to use it now, she could just imagine taking a dip in midsummer. There was a wrought-iron table with chairs up front, close to what she assumed was the kitchen.

She crossed the flagstone walk and entered the other wing of the house. At the end was one huge suite she imagined was her father's. The room beside it was a study, warm and welcoming with its walls of filled bookshelves. The next room was indeed the kitchen, with both the great room and dining room opening off it. It was spacious, as all the rooms in this house seemed to be.

Her dad must have sensed her presence as she stood in the doorway, because he turned and motioned her into the room.

"Mmm, that smells just like Mom used to make." She took a stool at the kitchen island where her dad was stirring his mixture on the cooktop.

"Let's just hope it tastes as good." He poured the hot, aromatic mixture into mugs and handed Rae hers.

She blew on the steaming liquid before taking a sip, all the while wondering how to broach the subject that had been on her mind since she'd first seen her dad enter the diner with Nora. "It tastes just like Mom's."

Dad chuckled. "Good. 'Cause I taught Mom how to make hers."

"You taught Mom how to make hot chocolate? She was a great cook, Dad."

"Yes, she was," he agreed. "But when we first married, she made hot chocolate from those instant packet things."

"Oh."

There was a long silence as they sipped from their cups. "Dad, why didn't you tell me about Nora?"

"I didn't know how. You've been hurting over your breakup, and I wasn't sure how you would react to the fact that I'm seeing someone."

"It's hard to think about anyone taking Mom's place."

"No one could take your mother's place in my heart, Rae—"

"Oh, good." Rae sighed with relief. "I was afraid it was serious between you and Nora."

He set down his mug and reached out to cup his daughter's chin in his hand. "Honey, you didn't let me finish. It *is* serious between us. Nora is making her own place in my heart. Your mother was my first love, and she will always own a big chunk of my heart. But she didn't want me to be alone the rest of my life, Rae. She told me to find someone else. . .I just never thought I would."

"It's that serious?"

"Yes, Rae, it is. I care deeply about Nora."

Rae stared into her cup, willing away the tears that threatened. *Dear Lord, am I to lose Daddy, too?*

"Honey, you'll like Nora if you give her a chance. Please say you'll try."

Rae took a sip from her cup. She would try, but she didn't hold out much hope that she would ever like Nora. "I guess this means I don't have any chance of talking you into moving back to Albuquerque."

Her father smiled and shook his head. "Even if I hadn't found Nora, honey, I love Sweet Springs. You will, too. Just mark my words. Now tell me, how long of a break do you have?"

"I took a leave of absence until after the first of the year. And I'm not sure I can go back even then. I may have to try to get on at another school."

"What happened? I thought you were happy there."

"I was. And I thought I could handle working at the same school with Paul. I just avoided him as much as possible. I was doing pretty well until I had to deal with the fact that Laura was teaching at Zia High this year and. . .I saw them together every day." She choked back a sob. "I just couldn't handle it, Daddy."

He came around the kitchen island and gathered her into his arms. "Oh, honey. I'm sorry he hurt you so badly."

Rae sniffed. "I took the time off hoping that I'll be able to handle it by the time I go back, but I'm not sure. . . ."

"Don't worry about it right now. It might be better to get a fresh start and find a new school. You take as much time as you need to make up your mind about what to do. Maybe you'll decide to teach in a small—"

"Dad. You know I love Albuquerque. I can't see me settling in a small town."

"Well, I can hope you change your mind. In the meantime, I'll try to talk you into staying until after the holidays."

Rae wasn't sure what she was going to do. She didn't seem to fit anywhere anymore. But the thought of facing Thanksgiving and Christmas alone was almost more than she could bear. "I'll see."

Luke sat watching the news, folding the clothes in the basket at his feet. Good thing he'd thrown them in the dryer before he'd gone into town. He was out of clean socks. How that could be always amazed him—he bought new ones nearly every time he visited that new superstore on the outskirts of town. Did the washing machine really eat them? Or did the dryer blow them out the vent?

He finished folding the last pair of socks and put everything back in the laundry basket to take upstairs later. Leaning back in his chair, he took a drink from the coffee cup he'd set on the end table and watched the next day's forecast.

According to the weatherman, tomorrow was going to be a beautiful day. It might be a nice day to spend with a lovely lady. Aunt Nora had given him a good excuse to call Rae. In fact, he'd promised her he would. But for the first time he could ever remember, he was nervous about asking a woman out. He had a feeling Rae wasn't going to like him any more than she seemed to like his town or his aunt. And the last person he needed to get involved with was a city girl. But Aunt Nora had asked him, and he sure didn't want anything hurting her and Michael's relationship. And she seemed afraid Rae might do that. Maybe Nora was right. From what he'd seen tonight, Rae didn't seem to take to Nora, but maybe she had something else on her mind. After all, he didn't know a thing about her. Still, he'd made a promise. He had to keep it.

He took a long swig from his cup before picking up the phone and dialing. It rang once, twice—

"Hello?"

"Dr. Mike?" Well, of course it was Michael. He'd dialed the man's home. Who'd he expect would answer it? Rae probably wouldn't be answering her dad's phone in a town where she knew no one.

"Yes, Luke. Did you get Nora home all right? Is something wrong?"

"No, nothing's wrong. I got Aunt Nora home just fine. I was actually calling to talk to your daughter. I thought I might show her around tomorrow morning since you have to make rounds at the hospital."

"Luke! That's a great idea. Let me get her."

Although it seemed longer, Luke was certain only a few seconds passed before Rae came to the phone.

"Hello?"

"Hi, Rae. Umm, listen, I was thinking that with your dad having to work tomorrow morning, maybe I could show you around town. . .introduce you to some people. . ." Luke hoped he didn't sound as nervous as he felt. He'd never had trouble talking to anyone before. He couldn't believe how awkward he felt as he waited for her answer.

"You don't have to work?"

"Well, we just finished with the fall roundup. Things are pretty calm on the ranch right now. I can take off a few hours."

There was quiet on the line. "Rae?"

"Yes, I'm here. And thank you for the offer. That way Dad won't feel bad about working tomorrow. And I'd like to be able to find my way around while I'm here. What time would you want to get started?"

Luke was an early riser, but Rae had appeared tired this evening. It wouldn't hurt to let her sleep in. "How about ten o'clock? I could show you around for a while, and then we could grab some lunch somewhere."

"That's fine. Do you want me to meet you in town? I can find my way back there."

"No. I'll pick you up. You get some rest, you hear? I'll see you tomorrow."

"I. . .thank you. I'll see you in the morning."

A clunk indicated that she'd hung up, and Luke replaced the receiver of his phone. She didn't sound real excited about spending the day with him. . .but she'd agreed. And he'd kept his promise to his aunt. And that was that. But hard as he tried the next few hours, flipping channels on the television, putting up his neatly folded clothes, and ironing a shirt for the next day, he couldn't get Dr. Mike's daughter out of his mind.

"That was nice of Luke," her dad said when Rae joined him at the sink.

"It was." Rae picked up a dish towel and began to dry their cups, feeling both a little excited and somewhat apprehensive at the same time. The only reason she'd accepted Luke's offer for the next day was because it was obvious her dad wanted her to. The way she'd been feeling about men lately, there couldn't be any other reason—of that she was certain. No matter how nice he seemed or how handsome he was.

"He's a good man and a hard worker."

"And he's Nora's nephew?"

"Yes. It's a big family. . .the Brelands and the Tanners. You'll love them all."

Obviously, her father did. She wasn't sure she would. They were Nora's family, after all.

"His brother, Jake, and cousin, John, have a law firm in town," Michael continued. "Right now Jake is running it while John is thinking of running for the senate next year."

"For state senator?" Rae asked.

He shook his head. "United States senator."

"That's quite a goal for a man from such a small town."

"If anyone can make it, John can. He'll have my vote, that's for sure."

It seemed that Luke's brother and cousin had loftier goals than he did. But he seemed nice, and he had been willing to help her find her dad. She wondered about the ranch he'd mentioned.

"What exactly does Luke do? He's happy just being a cowboy?"

Her dad threw back his head and laughed. "There's nothing wrong with being content to be a cowboy, honey. But Luke isn't just a cowboy—his family owns a lot of land around here. . .and all over the state. Luke helps his uncle run the ranch holdings. Actually, Ben is semiretired, and Luke mostly runs things. And he's very good at it."

Her dad drained the sink and dried his hands. "I was going to ask Nora to show you around, but I think she had some kind of meeting tomorrow."

"Well, now you don't need to worry about me tomorrow. . .and you don't have to bother Nora. Luke said he'd show me around and we'd grab some lunch somewhere." Rae really didn't want to go sightseeing with Luke tomorrow, but it would be better than having Nora show her around. She sent up a quick prayer. *Thank You, Lord. I know I have to accept the fact that Dad cares about her, but I am so glad I don't have to spend my first day here out sightseeing with her.*

"Good. I'll plan to grill supper tomorrow night." He wrapped his arms around her. "It's going to be so good having you here, honey. I've missed you. And I want you to get to know Nora better. I hope you'll decide to stay until after the holidays."

"I'll think about it, Dad."

"Want to watch the news with me?"

Rae shook her head. "Not tonight. I think I'll go on to bed. It's been a long day."

Dad turned out the overhead light as they headed toward the great room. "I hope you sleep well tonight. And, Rae?"

"Yes, Dad?"

"Honey, Paul doesn't deserve you. I know you are hurting now. But he wasn't in God's plan for you. In time, you'll get over him, and you'll find the man who *is* meant for you."

Rae choked back the tears that threatened and reached up to kiss him on the cheek. "Thank you, Daddy. I needed to hear that. See you in the morning."

Rae held the tears at bay until she reached her room; then she fell across the bed and let them flow freely as she gave herself over to self-pity. Everything her dad said was true. . .but still, it hurt to have lost Paul and her best friend. Now she was losing her father, too. And she missed her mother more all the time.

How much more could she take? *Lord, You said You wouldn't give us more than we can bear, but I don't think I can bear much more.* Rae sniffed. *Do You hear me, Lord? I'm tired of losing people I love.* Sometimes she wondered if He'd stopped listening to her. She couldn't blame Him. . .she hadn't been talking to Him much lately. Not nearly as much as she used to. . .or as much as she needed to.

She cupped her hand around her mouth and shook her head. And whose fault was that? Hers. With fresh tears streaming down her face, she whispered, "Please help me, Lord, to feel close to You again. . .and to accept the changes in my life. In Jesus' name, amen."

Chapter 3

Luke had been up for several hours when the phone rang. His caller ID indicated it was from Michael's house. Somehow he wasn't surprised. He'd figured Rae would find a reason to back out of letting him show her around. But it wasn't Rae at the other end of the line; it was Michael.

"Luke?" Michael continued without waiting for him to answer. "There's no need for you to come pick Rae up. I'm going to take her to Deana's for breakfast before going to work. She'll just explore around town for an hour or two until you get there."

The deep disappointment he'd felt at Michael's first words took him by surprise—as did the relief he felt that Rae *wasn't* canceling on him. Luke released a deep breath and leaned back in his office chair. "There's no need for her to explore on her own. I was going to eat at the diner before I came to pick her up, so meeting you there will be fine with me. I was just getting ready to head out myself."

"Okay, we'll see you there. Luke, thanks for offering to show her around."

Luke chuckled. "Now, you know it's really a hardship to take a day off to show a lovely lady around town, Michael."

"Yeah. Well, still, I really appreciate it. She's had a hard time of it the past few months. Ahh—see you in town."

"See—" The sudden click on the line told Luke that Michael had hung up. Maybe Rae had come into the room, and he didn't want her to hear their conversation. Luke couldn't help wondering what kind of hard time she'd had. She did appear vulnerable to him, but he figured it was because she hadn't known Michael was seeing his aunt. Maybe that had nothing to do with it, and Aunt Nora had nothing to worry about.

He turned his computer off and took a last drink of his now-lukewarm coffee before making his way to the kitchen. He rinsed out the tall mug and switched the pot off before crossing the room to grab his Stetson and pull on a denim jacket. Pulling the back door shut, he let the screen door bang behind him and headed for his pickup.

Luke took the county road toward town. It was a cool morning, but sunny and bright. He figured it'd get into the sixties later in the day, but for now he turned on the heater to take the chill off. He loved this time of year. The crispness of the air never failed to invigorate him, but this morning he wondered if his good mood was coming from the weather or the anticipation of spending the day with Rae Wellington.

Probably the latter, he admitted to himself, although he wasn't sure why. He knew little about Rae, except that she was taking time off from teaching high school, loved her hometown, and had evidently been hurt in some way. And, of course, that his aunt was worried about Rae's reaction to Michael seeing her, but that could have been just because he hadn't told her he was seeing anyone—or any number of other possibilities.

All he was sure of was that today he was going to enjoy showing Rae around. No matter that he was also attracted to her and that he'd like to get to know her better. There wasn't much chance of that leading anywhere. She wasn't from here, didn't intend to stay, and he wasn't going to leave. Still, a few days in Rae's company might nudge him out of the mopes he'd been wallowing in lately. It couldn't hurt; that was for sure. He pressed down on the accelerator as he pulled onto the state highway.

The diner was always busy on Saturdays, and he felt fortunate to find an empty booth. He quickly slid into one of the seats just as Dee plunked a cup of black coffee in front of him and handed him a menu. His good friend appeared a little frazzled for so early in the day.

"Hi, Dee, you shorthanded again?" Luke took the menu in case Rae needed it when she got there, but as often as he ate here, he could probably recite it for her word for word.

"Seems to be a way of life lately," she answered with a deep sigh. "Pancakes, bacon, and eggs, right?"

"You got it, but there's no hurry. I'm meeting Michael and his daughter here. I'll wait for them."

"Okay. I'll be back when they get here." Dee was already on her way to another table.

Luke took a sip of the hot liquid and took in his surroundings. Usually there was another waitress out front, with one cook in the back, and Dee helping out wherever needed. Today, there was just Dee and Charlie, and Luke understood she didn't have time for the usual small talk. He just wished she didn't have to work so hard. As far as he knew, Dee didn't have a personal life. There was a time, several years ago, he'd hoped that she and John, his cousin, would get together, but it never happened. He'd always thought it was a shame. They seemed to bring out a unique side in each other.

Luke shook his head. Here he was trying to play matchmaker, like he had any experience at it. He didn't even have a love of his own. Still, he thought Dee and John would have made a great couple.

He gazed out the window just in time to see Michael and Rae pull up outside. She seemed happier this morning. . .and very pretty. Her hair curled softly around her face, and she was smiling up at Michael as she followed him into the diner.

Luke stood when Michael waved from across the room and propelled his daughter ahead of him. "Good morning, Luke! It's a beautiful day, isn't it?"

"Good morning. It is a great day." Luke found it hard to take his gaze off of Rae. She was even prettier close-up. Her cheeks were rosy from the brisk morning air, and her blue eyes seemed to sparkle. "You seem well rested today. When Michael called about meeting you this morning, I was a little afraid he'd pulled you out of bed."

"Actually, I almost had to do that when she was in school." Michael chuckled. "But she surprised me by already having the coffee going when I got up this morning."

"I do feel rested, thank you." Rae arched an eyebrow at her dad and gave Luke a smile before sliding into the corner of the booth. Michael slid in beside her, and Luke took his seat once more. Rae faced her dad. "I am an adult now, you know."

Michael kissed her on the temple. "I know. Sometimes I wish you were still a kid, though."

"Sometimes I do, too." Rae took the menu Luke pushed toward her. "What's good? I'm kind of hungry."

"Everything here is good, so just take your pick," Michael answered, glancing around the diner. "Dee seems a little short on help again today."

"I am," Dee confirmed, coming up behind him. "I haven't been able to get in touch with Nelda," she said, then glanced at Rae. "She's my regular waitress. She went out of town for a few days, but she was supposed to be back yesterday."

The door opened, and two more customers came in. Dee grinned. "Can't complain about business, though. Since you're regulars here and know me, I'll skip the small talk. Just give me your order fast as you can, and I'll get it out to you as soon as I can."

"I'll have the big breakfast special and coffee," Michael said. "With the eggs over easy."

"And I'll have the same thing, only with scrambled eggs," Rae added quickly.

Dee pointed at Luke. "I have your order, right?"

"You do."

She nodded and rushed off to another table.

"Poor thing. I hope she gets some help soon." Rae watched Dee take an order from another table.

"And I hope you can eat that breakfast you ordered, Rae," her dad teased. "It's a big one."

Luke laughed. "I was thinking the same thing."

"I just didn't want to take up her time by trying to make up my mind, Dad. What exactly did I order?"

"Three eggs, bacon and sausage, and a stack of pancakes this high." Luke grinned and motioned with his hands to show her just how high that stack was.

"Oh, no." Rae giggled and shook her head.

"With hash browns on the side," Michael added.

"Oh, well." She shrugged. "I'll share."

Dee returned with a pot of coffee and two cups. She poured their cups and set the pot down. "Hope you don't mind; I'll let you warm yours up, Luke."

Before he had a chance to answer, she spun off in another direction.

"Is it always this busy?" Rae asked.

"No. Good thing she's closed on Sundays. She's going to need the rest." Luke warmed his coffee from the pot Dee had left and took a drink.

"What is on the agenda today? Are you going to introduce Rae to Ellie and some of the rest of the family?" Michael asked.

"If she's game. I thought I'd show her around town and introduce her to Gram, and maybe to Jake and Sara, too."

"Who is Ellie?" Rae glanced from her dad to Luke.

"She's my grandmother. A real jewel, if I do say so myself."

"She is that. Ellie is the grandmother everyone wishes was theirs," Michael stated.

Dee brought their breakfast just then, and the two men watched Rae's reaction at seeing the pile of food set before her. Luke laughed when she let out a deep breath and picked up her fork as if preparing for battle.

Her dad left them at Luke's pickup, after exacting a promise from them to meet him back at the diner for lunch. They agreed, but if the truth be known, Rae didn't think she could ever eat again.

Luke opened the door for her and helped her into his truck before coming around and taking his seat behind the wheel. He glanced over at her and grinned. "If you want to walk some of that off before we come back, it's fine with me. My usual breakfast at home is a bowl of cereal."

Rae chuckled and wondered if he could read her mind. "I usually have a piece of toast. But it smelled so good when we walked in, I just had to indulge. Do you breakfast there often?"

"More than I should but not every day. And when I do, I don't usually stop for lunch."

"We can call Dad later and tell him we won't be there," Rae suggested, buckling her seat belt.

"No. He's looking forward to seeing you. And I can always just order a salad or soup."

"Good idea. That's what I'll do, too."

Luke backed out of the parking space and headed the truck down the street. "I'll drive you out to see where Aunt Nora lives and then a little later we'll head over to Gram's. Your dad is a great favorite of hers, and I know she'd love to meet you."

Rae wasn't much interested in where Nora lived, but she couldn't say that to the woman's handsome nephew. He looked even better this morning than he had last night. She liked his slow grin and the way he leaned his head to the side when he talked to her. But he was Nora's kin, and she'd best keep that in mind. Somehow she didn't think she'd be spending the morning with this cowboy if his aunt hadn't had something to do with it.

"Is your grandmother Nora's mother?"

Luke shook his head. "No. Nora was married to Gram's son. But he died in Vietnam years ago."

"And she never remarried?" Somehow that surprised Rae. Nora was a very attractive woman.

"No, she never even showed any interest in another man until. . ." He pointed to a corner store. "That's our old-fashioned ice cream parlor. They also make some really good hot drinks in the winter."

Rae was sure he'd cut his sentence short on purpose. She was certain she had an idea of what he'd been about to say. . .that Nora hadn't shown any interest in another man until her dad came along. But she chose not to press the point. "I'll have to get in there for a cappuccino or hot chocolate while I'm here."

Luke kept pointing out different businesses while they drove down the street. There was the grocery store, several clothing stores, and the drugstore.

"It's quaint, all right," she said. "But I don't see myself ever living in a place like this. I just can't understand why my dad would want to live here. He always seemed to love Albuquerque."

Luke glanced over at her. "Well, I'm not going to pretend that we can compete with your Albuquerque, but the downtown area isn't all there is to Sweet Springs. There's the mall just off the highway and all kinds of chain restaurants and motels out there. There's an eight-screen movie theater that just opened up, too. We have a really good Chinese restaurant and one of the best Mexican restaurants in the state down the road a piece. But I don't think it's what the town has to offer as far as places to go that attracted your dad."

"No? What is it then?" *Besides your aunt, that is,* Rae wanted to add, but instead, she waited for Luke's answer.

"I think it's the people and maybe the slower pace of life. Maybe he wanted to slow down and enjoy life a little."

Rae shrugged. She'd never thought about that. "Maybe. He just always seemed to thrive at home."

"Well, watch him close. I think maybe you'll find him thriving just fine here."

Rae wondered at the defensive tone in his voice. Had she insulted him? "Luke. . .I'm not putting Sweet Springs down. I'll admit it's a pretty little town. I'm just a city girl, I guess. I've never lived anywhere else. I didn't mean to upset you."

Luke shook his head. "I know you didn't. I guess I'm just a small-town guy. Let's see how you feel about wide-open spaces." He shifted gears as they headed out onto the highway.

Rae had to admit the area was pretty. Apple orchards climbed the hillside, and the sun gave the Hondo River in the valley an extra sparkle. The scenery could have been right out of a postcard. . .and that's the only place she'd ever seen anything like it. Could she help it if she felt more comfortable in city surroundings?

Luke showed her the turnoff to Nora's ranch, but the house couldn't be seen from the road. A few more miles passed before he turned off the highway. "This and Nora's land are both part of the same ranch, the T-Bar. Uncle Ben and Aunt Lydia live on down the road. The ranch is the family business, 'cept that my brother, Jake, and my cousin, John, are both lawyers. Several of the female cousins moved away and have businesses of their own. But the ranch has been in the family since Great-Great-Grandpa Tanner settled here. I live in the first ranch house built here. . .want to see it?"

"Sure, I'd love to." Rae was interested in seeing where Luke lived—and very curious now to see where this ranch and family had started here in New Mexico. She couldn't claim to be a native New Mexican. She'd been born in Oklahoma, as were her parents, but they'd moved to New Mexico when she was only two years old, and Albuquerque was the only home she'd known. She loved this state, and she would have loved to be able to claim that her family had helped settle the area. She took notice of the mountains in the distance. They might not be *her* mountain range. . .not as big and looming from here, but beautiful just the same.

The road curved, and finally she could see his house, a small two-story, standing in a grove of trees. Luke pulled up to it but didn't shut off the engine of the pickup.

"My family settled here back in the late 1800s—'bout 1881 from all accounts. The inside has been modernized, but on the outside it appears pretty much like it did back then."

Rae was surprised at how much she wanted to get out of the truck and see the inside of the house—learn a little more about the man beside her—but Luke backed out of the drive and headed toward the road again. Evidently he didn't want her seeing the inside of his home.

"Too bad you didn't get down here last month. The colors of the aspens were gorgeous."

"I wish I could have seen them," Rae said honestly. She loved the autumn colors. "Maybe next year I'll get down here. Albuquerque has its own colorful event in October too, you know."

Luke nodded. "I know. I've been there."

"To the balloon festival?"

"Yep. I've even gone up in a balloon. It sure is a sight to see. Both from the ground and from the air."

"Oh, wow. I've always wanted to do that, but I've never had the chance to go up in one."

"I have connections. Remind me next year, and I'll see what I can do about getting you a ride."

"Oh, with an offer like that, I'll be sure to."

The ride back to Sweet Springs seemed shorter than the one out to Luke's house, and Rae was almost disappointed when they pulled up at an older home in a residential section not far from the town square.

"Come on, it's time you met Gram." Luke cut off the engine.

Rae couldn't imagine why she felt so nervous about meeting Luke's grandmother, but she did. Was she a typical grandmother? Whatever that was. . . Rae wasn't sure she'd even know. She'd always longed for a large family with aunts and uncles and cousins, but both of her parents had been only children. They'd moved away from their families when she was a toddler. She could barely remember visits to see her grandparents on either side, and they'd all passed away when she was young. She and her dad were the Wellington family—what was left of it.

She walked beside Luke to the front door and was surprised when he opened it and walked in. No way would she leave her door unlocked in Albuquerque!

"Gram? You home?"

"Luke? Is that you? I'm here," a voice called. "Come on back to the kitchen."

Full as she still was, Rae's mouth began to water at the smells coming from the same direction as the voice. She followed Luke through the dining room into a large, sunny kitchen where an older woman stood at a large worktable, rolling out dough. She was of medium height and build, with short, silvery hair curling around her plump face. Her eyes were a bright blue behind her glasses, and her smile welcomed Rae.

"Well, who is this you've brought to meet me, Luke?" She brushed flour from her hands and wiped them on her apron before reaching out to shake Rae's hand.

"Gram, this is Rae Wellington, Michael's daughter. She's come for a visit, and he had to make rounds today. Rae, this is Ellie Tanner, my grandmother."

Rae was surprised when Luke's grandmother released her hand and enveloped her in a hug.

"Oh, how wonderful. We've all adopted Michael as family, so that carries over to include you, too, dear. Welcome to Sweet Springs!"

"Thank you, Mrs. Tanner." Rae was at a loss for words. The warm welcome had unshed tears stinging the back of her throat. She hadn't expected to be so touched by this woman.

"Oh, please, just call me Ellie or Gram. Everyone else does. Sit down at the table and make yourselves at home. I'm just about to take my butternut pound cake out of the oven, and these pies can wait. Would you like a cup of coffee? Or I can put on a pot of tea—"

"Oh, no, thank you, Mrs.—uh, *Gram.* I'm still full from breakfast at the diner, and we have to meet Dad for lunch in a little while, although the smell of that cake is making my stomach growl as if I were starved." Rae grinned and rubbed her stomach in an effort to quiet it as she sat down at the table in the bay window.

"Well, I could use a cup of coffee about now." Luke got up to get himself a cup from the cabinet closest to the coffeepot. "That cake sure smells good, but I guess I'll wait until tomorrow night to have a piece. What kind of pies are you making?"

"Oh, apple and cherry, I guess."

"No pecan?"

Gram chuckled. "Luke, I'll be sure to double up for Thanksgiving, but no pecan for tomorrow night."

Luke joined Rae at the table. "Not even if I shell the nuts?"

"Not even then."

As Gram and Luke teased and talked, Rae listened, enjoying the lighthearted banter between the two. It was obvious that they loved each other.

She didn't know what kind of dinner was planned for the next night, but as she watched Gram take the cake from the oven, she definitely wished she could be there. Gram immediately transferred the tall, golden cake to a plate. It smelled delicious. For a minute Rae was tempted to ask for a piece.

Luke glanced at his watch and took a final drink from his cup. "Guess we'd better be heading back downtown. Michael will have the law out, thinking I might have abducted you."

"You be sure and come to Sunday night supper with Michael tomorrow night, dear. You'll get to meet a lot more people that way."

"Oh, I'd love to!" Rae exclaimed, surprising herself. She smiled at Gram. "I'd been wondering how I could get a taste of that cake," she said, blushing at her own audacity.

"Well, I'll make sure you do," Luke assured her. He placed his hand at her back as they headed out of the kitchen. Gram followed them to the front door.

Luke's touch and his grandmother's welcome made Rae feel as if she belonged here, and for a moment she wished she did. She felt happier and more relaxed than she had in weeks. She loved the feeling of this house and was really looking forward to coming back to it. She spun back around and asked, "Is there anything I can help with, or bring, for tomorrow night?"

"You just bring yourself this time, dear. I'll find something for you to do once you get here."

"Sounds wonderful. It was so nice to meet you, Gram." It just felt natural to call her that.

"You just stop in anytime, you hear?"

"Thank you. I might just do that."

Once in the pickup, Rae and Luke waved back at Gram, who was still waving from the doorway when they drove off.

Something in Rae wanted to run right back to Ellie Tanner's house, sit down, and pour out all her troubles to the grandmother she wished was her own.

Chapter 4

After pointing out a few more businesses—the florist, the bakery, and another gift store, then passing by the hospital, Luke drove Rae back to the diner. He'd enjoyed the morning with her. He'd seen a sweetness in her at his grandmother's that he liked a lot—and would like to see more of. He didn't know exactly what she'd been through in the last year, but Rae seemed to begin to relax at Gram's, only to tense up again now, as they walked toward the booth where Michael and Nora waited for them.

It appeared Aunt Nora was right; Rae wasn't very happy about her dad and his aunt seeing each other.

Michael stood up to give his daughter a hug, and Luke waited until she'd slid to the far end of the booth before sitting down beside her. There was an expression in her eyes that had him wanting to assure her everything would be all right. At the same time, he wanted to say something similar to his aunt who seemed just as apprehensive as Rae. Maybe it was just a woman thing he didn't understand. Whatever it was made him decidedly uncomfortable.

Rae seemed to be trying as she smiled at her dad. "I met Luke's grandmother just a little while ago. She's really nice."

The tension seemed to break for a moment as Michael and Nora both grinned. "She is that. She's just. . .Gram. And I think the whole town feels that way," Michael said

"She's the glue that's held this family together in some tough times," Nora said. "And the one we all go to when we need straight talk or a hug."

"Gram asked me to come to Sunday night supper tomorrow. And she had this scrumptious cake that I can't wait to try."

"Oh, good. I was hoping you'd want to go. Ellie's suppers have become a delightful routine I would hate to miss," Michael admitted.

"Do I need to bring anything? She told me I didn't, but. . ." Rae glanced from Michael to Nora.

"Don't worry about it, Rae. Some of us bring something extra, but there is always plenty of food," Nora assured her.

Dee showed up to take their orders just then, appearing a little less frazzled than she had that morning.

"I see you have more help now, Dee. Nelda must have made it in," Rae said.

Dee shook her head. "Actually, no, and my part-time help is sick. Charlie, one of my cooks, called in his sister. She works at the Mexican restaurant but was off today. She can only help out today, so if Nelda isn't back by Monday, I guess I'll have to try to hire someone to take her place. I'm just thankful to have the help today."

"Good, because I was about to offer to help. And I know nothing about being a waitress," Rae admitted.

Dee grinned at Rae. "I probably would have taken you up on it. And on-the-job training is the very best kind. Thank you for the thought."

"You're welcome."

They each placed their orders, with both Luke and Rae ordering salads.

Dee laughed knowingly. "Breakfast was too much for you?"

"You should put a postscript on the menu, telling only the starving to order it," Rae said and laughed. "Or maybe have a petite order of the same thing."

"Now *that's* an idea." Dee hurried off to put in their order.

"So, honey, what do you think of Sweet Springs after seeing a bit of it?" Michael asked.

"It's kind of quaint, and there is more to the town than I first thought. But it's not Albuquerque, Dad."

Luke's heart sank, and he wasn't sure why. Obviously, Rae wasn't likely to fall in love with the area that was so much a part of him.

"Exactly. Life is slower here. There's time to enjoy it."

Rae raised an eyebrow at Luke.

He shrugged, remembering their earlier conversation. "Michael never told me that. It was just a feeling I had."

"What are you two talking about?" Nora asked.

"We were talking earlier about why someone would like living here." Luke shrugged. "I suggested pretty much the same thing Michael just said, but we've never discussed it."

"Well, I guess I'm not ready for a slow pace." Rae shook her head.

"Slow pace? Oh, honey, just come work here for a while," Dee teased as she brought their orders. She grinned at Rae. "There is no slow pace in this diner."

"There goes your theory." Rae gently nudged Luke on the shoulder.

"Must be the people then." He grinned down at her. Their gazes met for a moment, and Rae's smile warmed his heart.

"Might be," she agreed.

Luke's heart skipped a beat before she broke eye contact and concentrated on putting salt and pepper on her salad. He gave his attention to his own plate while Michael and Nora concentrated on the food Dee set down in front of them, commenting on how good it looked. He was pretty sure he wasn't the only one at the table who was having a problem with knowing what to say next.

Michael seemed as confused as Luke felt, but the wink he gave Nora seemed to encourage her to strike up a conversation with Rae.

"Rae, your dad says you'll be here for a little while. . .that you've taken a leave of absence. You know we have an excellent school system here, should you decide you might want to move—"

Luke's pulse jumped. Was there a chance Rae would move here?

"Thank you, Nora, but I don't think—"

"Oh, honey, don't make a decision right away," Michael said. "I know you plan on going back to Albuquerque, but keep an open mind until after the New Year, will you?"

"You're staying a few months?" Luke had thought she was only staying the weekend.

"I'm not sure exactly what I'm doing. I promised Dad I'd stay through this next week. After that, I don't know."

"Oh, Rae, you know you'd just be coming back for Thanksgiving and then again for Christmas."

"Unless I could talk you into coming up there."

"Honey—"

"I know, Dad. I'm just teasing. Even if I go back home, I'll be back for the holidays. I don't want to spend them alone."

Luke had never spent Thanksgiving or Christmas alone, and he sure didn't like the thought of it for anyone else—especially Rae.

"Sweet Springs decorates real pretty for Christmas. Be a shame to miss it."

"So does Albuquerque."

Luke nodded and chuckled. "I'm sure it does. I'll have to get up there one of these days."

"You should. Be a shame to miss it." The corners of Rae's mouth turned up in a broad grin as she teased him back. He had a feeling she enjoyed this kind of give-and-take as much as he did.

Luke glanced over to see Michael and his aunt watching them with interest. Nora cleared her throat and smiled. "I've seen the beautiful luminaries in Old Town. It is quite a treat. We have them around our town square too, but of course it's nothing like Albuquerque."

"I noticed some fall-like decorations around town. . .bales of hay, a scarecrow here and there. It is quaint. Does the town pay for that or just the businesses?"

"A little of both. This is the first year they've decorated for anything besides Christmas. The town council just approved the funds for Thanksgiving and several other holidays. . .kind of a seasonal decorating." Luke motioned to his aunt. "Aunt Nora got it started. With all the building up out on the highway, we wanted to make sure that our little *old town* stays alive."

"There's a contest at Christmastime for the best decorated business downtown. Everyone seems to get involved in that," Nora said.

Dee came back to see if they needed anything, and it seemed to be a cue for the end of the lunch break.

"Rae and I have to go to the store to pick up a few things for supper. I'm grilling steaks tonight, Luke. Nora is coming, and we'd love to have you join us if you can," Michael offered. Luke stood up to let Rae stand, noting that she seemed overly busy scooting out of the booth. She seemed to be trying to ignore him, and when she didn't echo her dad's invitation, he was left with the impression she'd seen enough of him for one day.

"Thanks, Michael, but Aunt Lydia invited me to eat supper over there. Uncle Ben and I have some business to go over."

"Maybe another time, then." Michael grabbed the ticket Deana tore off her pad. "Lunch is on me today."

"There's no need—"

"Yes, there is. Rae and I appreciate you showing her around today." Michael gazed down at Nora. "Are you leaving now, too?"

She shook her head. "I've got a beauty shop appointment in about thirty minutes; I think I'll have another cup of coffee before I go. How about keeping me company, Luke?"

He had a feeling his aunt wanted to find out how the morning went. He might as well stay. Nora wouldn't rest until he gave her a full report.

"Sure, I'll have a second cup of coffee."

Luke felt a light touch on his jacket sleeve, and he gazed down into Rae's eyes. "Thank you for showing me around and introducing me to Gram. I'm looking forward to seeing her again."

"You're welcome. Thanks for keeping me company this morning. Y'all have a good evening." Luke took his seat across from Nora once more.

Michael joined Rae back at the table. "See you about six, Nora?"

"I'll be there. Can I bring anything?"

"Just yourself. Rae and I will take care of the rest."

A glance passed between the two that was so full of love, Luke felt he was intruding. He glanced away and saw the expression on Rae's face as she watched them. No, she still wasn't happy about Nora and Michael's relationship.

Michael gave a quick wave as he and Rae left the diner. Luke took a drink from his cup, waiting for Nora to start pelting him with questions. She had a dreamy expression in her eyes, and it took a moment before she seemed to realize where she was. No doubt about it—Nora was in love.

"Luke, how did your morning go? Rae seems nice."

That was it? He'd figured on all kinds of questions from his aunt. "It went fine. And she is very nice." *And pretty, and she smells good.*

Nora sighed. "But she still doesn't like me."

"We didn't talk about you, Aunt Nora."

"Probably because I'm your aunt. It's all right, though. Michael and I talked, and he assured me things will work out."

"He thinks there's a problem?"

"Well, she was a little upset that he hadn't told her about me. And I can understand that. He should have. But he's assured me she'll come around—and that he's not giving me up even if she doesn't."

"Well, see? There's nothing to worry about, then."

"It will just be so much better if she'll accept me. Will you pray that she will, Luke? I don't want to cause a rift between father and daughter."

Luke reached over and patted his aunt's hand. "Of course I will, Aunt Nora. And I think Rae will come around, too; I really do."

Surely she would. Nora and Michael made each other happy. Rae was bound to see that. But he'd pray anyway. It could only help.

Rae and her dad stopped at the grocery store to pick up three steaks to grill that night. She tried not to show her disappointment that Nora was invited. Rae wished Luke had accepted her dad's invitation to dinner, but she hadn't wanted him to feel pressured, so she'd just kept her mouth shut. Besides, he'd probably had enough of her company for one day. She had enjoyed his company more than she'd anticipated. He was different than she thought he would be. Somehow she'd expected him to be a little cocky, but he wasn't. He didn't seem to have to try to make an impression. He was who he was and seemed very comfortable with that.

Once they got home, her dad made up a marinade for the meat while she washed potatoes and wrapped them in foil to bake. "I'll make the salad just before we eat, Dad."

"Thanks, honey. It's so good to have you here. I do hope you'll stay as long as you want."

"I'll probably stay." She sighed. "I love Albuquerque, but it doesn't feel the same now. I don't know why, exactly. It never used to have a lonely feel to it, but now it does."

He rubbed his chin. "I know. I've felt the same way."

"Is that why you moved?"

"Partly. I missed your mother, and. . .I thought you had a new life starting with Paul."

"So did I. Guess we were both wrong. Dad, how could I have misread him so badly?"

"Honey, don't blame yourself. I liked Paul. He fooled me, too."

It didn't hurt so much to talk about him tonight, and suddenly Rae realized that she hadn't thought of Paul all day. Not once that she could remember—until her dad mentioned him. She wanted to get over the breakup, but she certainly wasn't ready for another man to occupy her thoughts in Paul's place!

"I'm just glad you found out what he's like before you married him, honey. He wouldn't have been faithful. But the Lord will send someone into your life who will love you the way he should. I'm sure of it."

"I hope so, Dad. But right now there's not a man on this planet I could trust except you. I think it will be a long time before I'm ready to give my heart to anyone else."

She enjoyed the rest of the afternoon with her dad, puttering around in the kitchen and hearing about how much his medical practice was growing. She was pleased that supper with Nora went smoother than she expected it to, although she was very relieved when they shooed Rae out of the kitchen and did the dishes.

She jumped at the chance to go to her room. "I think I'll call it a night, if y'all don't mind. I haven't had a chance to unpack and get settled in."

"You go right ahead, honey. Does the 'settle in' part mean you're going to stay through the holidays?"

"I'm not sure, Dad. I'm thinking about it, okay?"

She was relieved when he didn't press the issue. "Okay. Do you want me to wake you in time for church tomorrow?"

"What time does it start?"

"Sunday school is at nine thirty, church at ten thirty. I usually go to both."

"I'll set my alarm and go with you, then." She kissed him on the cheek and smiled at Nora. "Night, Nora. I guess I'll see you at church tomorrow?"

"You will. Hope you sleep well, Rae."

"Thanks. Good night, Dad." Rae headed down the hall to her room, glad to be able to get away. The last thing she wanted to do was intercept any more of the loving gazes they'd given each other at Deana's.

Since she wasn't ready for bed, she ended up out on the patio, curled up in a deck chair and gazing up at the starlit sky. She wondered if Luke was at his aunt and uncle's. It really had been nice of him to show her around and introduce her to his grandmother. Rae was sure he could have found all kinds of things to do besides spending his morning with her. She couldn't help wondering if he was seeing someone. She'd pretty much decided it wasn't Dee. They just seemed to be very good friends. But he was so nice and so handsome; there must be *someone* he was seeing.

She heard a burst of laughter and twisted around to see her dad and Nora through the kitchen window as they cleaned up. He was laughing at something Nora said, and then he gave her a quick kiss on her nose. He was happy. And Rae wished she could be happy for him.

But she was jealous. . .and she didn't know if it was because Nora had so much of her dad's attention, or if it was because they seemed to have such a good relationship while hers and Paul's had crumbled. And she just couldn't make herself like Nora. How was she ever going to accept her?

Not wanting the couple to look out and think she was spying on them, she hurried back to her room. She didn't know if she could handle feeling like a fifth wheel around here until after the New Year.

~

Luke enjoyed having supper and visiting with his aunt and uncle. He had a wonderful family. When his and Jake's parents had been killed in wreck all those years ago, his grandparents took the boys in and raised them, but Aunt Lydia and Uncle Ben had been there, too. They'd given him and Jake their support, cheered for their baseball and football games, and advised them when needed. Their son, John, was more like a brother than a cousin. Luke loved them just as much as he loved Gram. Now, as he sat at the kitchen table with a piece of his aunt's peach cobbler and a cup of coffee in front of him, he sent up a prayer of thanksgiving that the Lord had seen fit to provide him with the love and support of this family.

"Nora told us that Michael's daughter is in town," Lydia said.

"She is. I almost brought her out here today. I was showing her around while Michael made rounds this morning."

"Oh?" His aunt joined him and Ben at the table.

"Don't read anything into that, Aunt Lydia. I was doing it for Aunt Nora. Besides, Rae is a city girl. I can't quite see her leaving Albuquerque for Sweet Springs."

"Well, stranger things have happened. What about Jake? He came back."

"Yes, but his roots were here. Rae's aren't."

"Well, what's she like?" his uncle asked.

"Real pretty. Real nice but kind of sad." It was true, Luke realized as soon as the words were out of his mouth. She was all of those things. . .and a bit irritating with her city-girl view of Sweet Springs. He'd had to pray not to lose his temper this morning as he showed her around. She didn't like his town, the area, or the fact that her father had moved here. Luke didn't think anything he showed her was likely to change her mind. Still, he hadn't wanted to add to the deep sadness he'd seen in her eyes. He couldn't help wondering why it was there, and he wished he'd asked Nora more about her. Surely she had an idea what it was Michael was talking about when he mentioned that things had been hard on Rae.

"Hmm, wonder why," Lydia mused.

"I don't know." But he intended to find out. Maybe it was that sadness that reached out to him. There was something about Rae Wellington that had him wanting to fix whatever it was that was wrong in her life. And somehow he just didn't think it was only about Aunt Nora.

"Nora is a little worried she won't accept her." Lydia took a sip from her cup.

"I'm sure she'll come around," Luke assured his aunt. "Besides, Michael and Aunt Nora are meant for each other."

Hoping to get Michael's daughter off his mind and to keep from having to answer more questions, he changed the subject. "How's John doing up in Santa Fe? Has he decided to run for senator for sure?"

"He says the backing is there. He's says he'll make up his mind in the next week or so."

The rest of the evening was spent discussing the pros and cons of his cousin's possible run for United States senator. As much as the family would miss John if he had to move to Washington, D.C., they all were convinced that he would make a wonderful senator.

At least talking about John's chances kept his mind off of Rae Wellington. . . for a little while.

~

The next morning, Rae followed Dad down the aisle of the small church he attended. She'd already met and been warmly greeted by what was surely at least half the congregation. That they loved her dad was obvious, and she could see he felt the same about them.

As welcome as everyone tried to make her feel, she was still a little uncomfortable. Probably because she hadn't been attending church at home like she should have ever since the breakup with Paul.

As they took seats on a pew behind Luke, Gram, and several others she presumed to be more family, she felt even more welcomed. There was a couple about her age with a toddler, and an older man sat by Gram. It felt good to be there, even though she didn't much like the fact that Nora sat on the other side of her dad. She tried not to show it as she greeted the other woman.

"Good morning, Nora. How are you today?"

"Just fine. You look lovely, Rae," Nora said.

"Thank you; so do you." Nora looked beautiful in the deep-rose-colored suit she wore. Rae was glad she'd packed her favorite cream-colored suit and teal blouse, because she always felt confident and at ease in the outfit.

Gram glanced over her shoulder and asked, "You are coming tonight, aren't you?"

"We wouldn't miss it," Dad answered with a smile.

Sunday school started with a prayer, and Rae bowed her head. Tears sprang to her eyes as she realized how badly she'd missed praying and talking to the Lord. She enjoyed the Bible class and the worship service that followed more than she thought she would. The minister was a fairly young man—probably in his late thirties—and his sermon about God's love and grace touched her heart. She might be a stranger in town, but by the end of the service, her soul felt as if it had come home.

She'd wanted to talk to Luke after worship services, but so many people crowded around them that when she finally located him, he was already making his way out the door.

The rest of the day sped by. Dad took her and Nora to lunch at the Italian restaurant Luke had pointed out the day before. She enjoyed the atmosphere and the meal. But hard as she told herself she was trying to graciously share him with Nora, she wished she had her dad to herself. She didn't like the way the woman seemed to be trying so hard to make friends with her. Just because her dad was seeing Nora, it didn't mean the women had to be buddies, did it?

After lunch Dad took them for a Sunday drive so that Rae would know her way around better when he had to go to work the next day.

"We could go to the ice cream parlor for dessert," he suggested.

"Oh, Rae, they make the most wonderful hot fudge sundaes," Nora added, turning to her with a smile.

"No, thanks." Rae shook her head. "None for me, but why don't you two go? I want to make some cookies to take to Gram's tonight."

"You don't have to do that, dear. There will be plenty of food there," Nora assured her.

"I'm sure there will be. But I just don't feel right going empty-handed." And she didn't want to spend the rest of the afternoon with Nora and her dad.

"All right, honey." Her dad looked at her through the rearview mirror. "I'll take you home so you can make your cookies, and Nora and I will go out for dessert so we don't snitch your delicious cookies before they can cool," he teased.

If her dad suspected that she just wanted some time to herself, he didn't give her away. Rae breathed a sigh of relief and waved to them when they dropped her off at home and headed back to town. Glad that she'd been able to cut the afternoon with Nora short, she hurried inside, preheated the oven, and went to change clothes. Rae mixed the brown sugar, eggs, flour, and flavoring, idly wondering if Luke would be at his grandmother's tonight. She'd tried to quit thinking about how handsome he was in that navy suit, crisp white shirt, and red tie that morning, but it just wasn't working very well. She'd been thinking of him off and on all afternoon, and she couldn't deny that she hoped he'd show up at his grandmother's for supper.

Immediately after church services that night, they headed over to Gram's. Rae didn't realize just how much she'd been watching for Luke until she glanced up to see him crossing the room toward her. Her heartbeat felt totally confused, coming to a stop and then going into overdrive when Luke smiled at her. She hoped no one could tell how flustered she was.

He brought his brother, Jake, sister-in-law, Sara, and their toddler, Meggie, over to meet her. They'd been the couple sitting on the pew with Luke and Gram that morning. A bond seemed to form between her and Sara once they found out they were both teachers, even though neither was actively teaching at the moment. Before long, they'd made plans to get together in the coming week, and Rae was really looking forward to it.

If she thought she'd met half the church congregation that morning, Rae was sure she met the other half that night. Luke kept her busy meeting other family members and friends. She liked the way his hand lightly touched her back, guiding her from one group of people to another. It made her feel watched over and special. He stayed at her side most of the evening, seeming to have taken it as his responsibility to introduce her to everyone.

There was William Oliver, Sara's grandpa, who'd been sitting beside Gram in church that morning. Rae found out the older couple was seeing each other and the family was hoping they would marry. She also met Luke's Aunt Lydia and Uncle Ben—a lovely couple who told her how happy they were to meet Michael's daughter. They invited her to come out and visit anytime while she was here.

Before the evening was over, Rae felt she must have met everyone there, thanks to Luke, and she had a glimpse of what a large family was like. She could almost see what her dad's attraction to Nora was—she belonged to this wonderful family.

Chapter 5

Luke woke Monday morning feeling a little grouchy. While he'd spent the evening before at Rae's side, he hadn't really had a chance to talk to her. He couldn't figure out why it bothered him so much, but it did. He was attracted to her—there was no doubt in his mind about that. Luke sighed and reminded himself he'd be better off steering clear of the city girl. Only that's not what he wanted to do.

She was sweet. She'd been so nice to everyone he'd introduced her to; he could tell his whole family had really liked her. So did he—in spite of warning himself not to.

He spent most of the morning in his office catching up on paperwork and checking in with the ranch foremen in other parts of the state. Sometimes he missed just being out on the land, but Uncle Ben had been handling things for a lot of years. He deserved a retirement before he was too old to enjoy it. Besides, if John did run for the senate, Ben and Lydia would be out on the campaign trail right along with him.

Luke made sure his cell phone had a good charge before heading into town to Jake's office to sign a contract selling off some beef. Maybe then he could check in on Rae and see how she was doing. He could offer to show her around some more, maybe offer to buy her lunch. He punched in the numbers to Michael's home phone and waited for Rae to pick up. But he got the answering machine instead.

He wondered if she'd gone back to Albuquerque, and he acknowledged to himself that he'd be disappointed if she did. In fact, deep inside he wanted to get to know her better.

He stopped at the diner, thinking Rae might have gone there for breakfast, but she hadn't. Seeing how busy Dee was, he decided she didn't need his business that badly this morning. He could get a cup of coffee at the law office.

Nancy, the law firm's secretary, smiled and waved him into Jake's office, where his brother was poring over a pile of papers on his desk. He glanced up over the reading glasses perched on his nose. Luke chuckled at the picture he made, knowing Jake wasn't happy about having to finally give in and wear glasses.

"You're a sight, you are," Luke said, crossing the room to pour a cup of coffee.

"And you are a pain, little brother."

"Got those papers ready for me to sign?"

Jake ruffled through some files on his desk until he found what he was hunting for. He glanced inside and nodded. "They're all here. I didn't expect you until this afternoon. What brings you into town early today?"

"I just thought I'd just come pester you a little while."

Jake grinned and glanced out of the window. "Right. I thought it might be Michael's daughter. I saw her going in and out of several shops earlier. Thought maybe you were going to meet her for lunch."

Luke set his cup down on Jake's desk and glanced out the window. "You did? How long ago?"

Jake shrugged his shoulders and grinned. "About a half hour or so ago. She's probably still out there somewhere."

Luke knew his brother. He was trying to find out more than Luke was ready to tell him at the moment. He eased down in the chair across from Jake and picked up his cup. "Guess she's going to stay awhile after all."

"You could probably catch her if you hurry." Jake rocked back in his chair.

Luke leaned back in his. "I came here to sign some papers, brother. Let's get at them."

Jake chuckled and opened the file. He pulled out a stack of papers and pushed them toward Luke. "Here they are. Just sign on those bottom lines. If you hurry, I'll treat you to lunch before my one o'clock appointment."

"You've got a deal." Luke started signing.

They were just about to walk out of the door of Jake's office when Nancy told him Sara was on the phone.

"Go on over and grab us a table. I'll be there in a few minutes," Jake said, then walked back to his desk and picked up the phone. "Hi, darlin'. What's up?"

Luke waved and headed out the door. Jake's tone of voice always changed when he talked to Sara. He was so glad those two had found each other again—even if he did feel like a fifth wheel around the two of them half the time.

He walked out onto the sidewalk and headed for the diner. He just hoped there was an empty table.

~

Rae woke to total quiet and glanced at the clock on her nightstand. Nine o'clock! Why hadn't her dad awakened her before he went on rounds? She threw back the covers, pulled on her robe, and hurried to the kitchen.

There she found a note propped up against the coffeepot. *Rae, I had an emergency at the hospital. Didn't want to wake you. If you can, meet me at the diner for lunch. Unless you call my office and let me know otherwise, I'll meet you there around noon.*

Rae was sure she could find her way back to the diner. Maybe she'd get ready early and explore a couple of the shops Luke had pointed out to her on Saturday. It wouldn't take long, and then she could meet her dad for lunch.

She poured a cup of coffee and made herself a piece of toast before heading for the shower.

A couple of hours later, she was downtown and finding that there was much more to see than she'd first imagined. Along the side streets there were several blocks of businesses, including several really nice gift shops, a couple of craft stores, and a jewelry store specializing in turquoise. She'd spotted the library on the other side of the square and made note to stop and pick out a few books before she went home. All in all, she had a delightful morning and was beginning to get hungry. She checked her watch and realized she'd better hurry if she was going to meet her dad on time. She rounded the corner and stepped straight into the arms of Luke Breland.

He reached out to steady her. "Whoa! Rae, I called you earlier to see if you might want to meet for a bite to eat. When I got the answering machine, I thought maybe you'd gone back to your mountains."

Rae took a minute to regain her balance and try to will her heart out of overdrive. She'd been trying *not* to think about this tall cowboy all morning. Now here she was—with his arms almost encircling her—gazing up into those beautiful brown eyes of his. Out in the sunshine they reminded her of melted chocolate, all shiny and warm.

"I'm sorry. I wasn't watching where I was going. I'm supposed to be meeting Dad for lunch, but I lost track of time."

"Found more to do than you thought you would, huh?" Luke grinned at her.

She smiled at him and conceded, "I found a few things of interest. Where are you headed?"

"Same place you are. Jake is meeting me for lunch. . .after he gets off the phone with Sara."

"They are so nice. I enjoyed meeting them last night." Rae liked the way Luke grasped her elbow as they crossed the street and entered the diner.

Luke canvassed the area from over her head. "There is only one table open. I don't see your dad here yet. Do you think he would mind sharing with Jake and me?"

"I'm sure he wouldn't. Let's grab it before we lose it," Rae suggested as the door behind them opened to three more people.

She and Luke hurried over to the table and sat down just as Dee dropped two menus on the table. "Be back in a few minutes."

Rae couldn't see anyone else waiting tables. By all appearances Dee was shorthanded again this week. She breathed a sigh of relief for Dee when two couples paid for their meals and left—only to be replaced by people waiting at the door. Her dad walked in with Jake, and she waved them over.

"I thought I saw you shopping earlier today, Rae," Jake said as he took a seat and raised an eyebrow at his brother. "Sara really enjoyed meeting you last night. She'd like to have you over for dinner while you're here."

"Oh, how nice. I'd like that." She really would like to get to know the couple better.

Dee ran back over to take their order and let out a huge sigh as she flipped her order pad to a clean page.

"I see you didn't get ahold of Nelda," Luke stated.

"Actually, her daughter called me—the poor kid sounded really frazzled. She apologized for not letting me know sooner that Nelda was in a car accident and has been in the hospital. She broke her leg and will be recuperating at her daughter's. It will be at least six weeks before she's out of the cast. And there will be physical therapy after that. Keep her in your prayers, okay? I'm going to call the paper this afternoon to place an ad for some help."

She gave them an overly bright smile before she continued. "Hope you all are having a better day than I am. What can I get you?"

At that news, it was as if everyone at the table silently agreed to make it easy on her. They all ordered the daily special.

"I don't think I've ever seen it so busy in here," Jake said as Dee rushed off to put in their order. "But I don't think she'd want us to go somewhere else."

"No, she wouldn't." Luke shook his head. "I think it just seems busier because Dee is so shorthanded and can't get to everyone as fast as usual. Thankfully, everyone seems to be taking the delay in getting their food graciously."

He was right. All of Dee's patrons did seem to be taking the slower service in stride. But watching her race from one customer to another and back and forth from the service window to give orders to her cook, Rae's sympathies were with Dee.

Charlie certainly was holding up his end, getting out orders as fast as he could, but Dee was beginning to appear a little frazzled herself. By the time Rae had finished her meal, she just couldn't take it anymore.

When Dee stopped at the table to refill her glass of iced tea, Rae stood up. "Do you have an apron and another order pad and pencil?"

"You serious?"

"If you don't mind training me on the job."

"Are you kidding? I told you that's the best kind of training." She whirled back to the service window and shouted, "Charlie, throw out a clean apron. Help is on the way!"

"You sure about this, Rae?" Dad asked.

"I just can't sit here another minute and watch Dee. I'm getting dizzy. Besides, you have to go back to work, and I need something to do—especially if I'm going to stay until after the holidays. There are presents to buy, you know."

"If it means you're staying awhile, then I'm all for it. Go to work, girl."

"It's a good thing you're doing, Rae." Luke's gaze met hers. "I was seriously thinking about volunteering, myself."

"Yeah, right." Jake shook his head and laughed. "I can see you with that apron on."

Rae ignored their chuckles as she followed Dee to the kitchen door.

"God bless you, Rae." Dee handed her a fresh order pad and the apron Charlie had given her. She helped Rae tie it in back. "I can't thank you enough."

"You may not say that in an hour or two. I really don't know what I'm doing," Rae admitted as Dee handed her a pencil.

"At this point, just getting menus and water to customers until I can get to them would be a big help."

"Well, I think I can handle that. . .maybe a little more than that. Where do you want me to start?"

"You take care of the counter here surrounding the service window. That way you can ask Charlie questions if you need to. I'll take care of the booths and tables."

"Okay. How about I see if any of these customers need anything else? Do you have their tickets?"

"Oh, you are going to work out just fine if you're concerned about me getting my money." Dee grinned at her. "I'll give them their bills. Do you know how to run a cash register?"

"I do. I worked in a bookstore while I was going to college. This doesn't seem that different."

Dee nodded. "Okay. Just ask if you have any questions. Thanks again, Rae."

"That was nice of Rae, Michael." Luke motioned in the direction of Dee and Rae as they stood in the center of the counter area. Rae had surprised him by offering to help Dee. "Has she ever done this kind of work before?"

Michael shook his head. "No, but she's always had a mind of her own, and she's not afraid of hard work." He glanced at his watch and pushed back his chair. "I'd better get back to my office."

Jake stood and took one last drink of water. "Yeah. I was thinking the same thing. You coming, Luke?"

"Huh? Oh, yeah. I need to get back to the ranch. I'll walk back to your office with you."

They all headed to the register at the same time, apparently to Rae's relief. "Oh, good. I can practice on y'all."

"And you'd better not charge us a penny too much," Michael teased.

"There's no charge for yours, Rae." Dee came up behind her. "Least I can do is feed you."

"Thanks."

Luke watched as Rae concentrated on ringing up her dad's ticket. She seemed a little nervous as Dee looked on. Her sigh was audible when Dee assured her, "You did just fine. You don't need my supervision on this."

Dee patted her on the back and went to pick up an order Charlie had just placed in the service window.

Rae rang up Jake and Luke's ticket and grinned as she gave Jake his change.

In an exaggerated drawl, she said, "Y'all come on back to see us, okay?"

Luke didn't know what to make of *this* Rae. She seemed to be coming out of her shell right before his eyes.

"You can count on it," Jake answered for Luke. They headed out the door, but Luke took one last glance back as she greeted a new customer with a smile. She sure was cute.

They parted at Jake's office. "Why don't you come over for supper tonight, Luke? You know Sara always makes plenty of food."

"I'll take a rain check, thanks."

"Ahh. Going to eat at the diner, are you?"

"I might."

Jake stopped at the door. "I thought so. Seems she's going to stay awhile. Sara wants to have her to dinner one night soon."

"Well, when you do—"

"Yeah?"

"I'll use that rain check."

Jake chuckled and slapped Luke on the back. "Somehow, I thought you would."

The afternoon flew by as Rae learned the ropes of being a good waitress. She'd just cleaned off a table and taken the dishes back to the kitchen when Dee called her out front. There were only a few people left, and Dee was just pouring two glasses of iced tea.

"There is light at the end of the tunnel. Come take a break." Rae took a seat at one end of the counter, and Dee handed her a glass.

Rae hadn't realized how thirsty she was until she drained half the glass in almost one swallow. "Oh, that's good. Thank you."

"No. Thank *you.*" Dee took a seat next to her. "I really appreciate your help today. With Nelda down, and Jen, my part-time helper, out sick with a cold, I was beginning to cave. Having you here really made a big difference."

"I'm glad. It's been fun, actually. I can help you out until after Christmas if you want. Maybe by then Nelda will be able to come back."

"Are you sure? It would be great if you really want to. I kind of hate to hire someone knowing it'd only be until Nelda comes back. It doesn't seem quite fair if they need a permanent job."

"I'm sure. I've been wondering what I was going to do all day with Dad at work."

"Well, I'm not going to turn your offer down. Just let me know what hours you want to work."

"Whatever works best for you. It seems you need help mostly during the rush times morning, noon, and night."

"I do, but no one wants to come and go. Split shifts are tough."

Rae shrugged. "I don't mind. Just work out a schedule for me, and I'll be here."

Joe, the cook who had relieved Charlie, peeked through the service window. "I think God has answered your prayers, Dee. I'd get to makin' that schedule if I was you."

Dee hopped off the counter stool. "I'm not even going to ask a second time if she's sure, Joe. I'm going to make out that schedule right now."

Rae watched her hurry to the back and smiled. Dee didn't need to worry. She wasn't going to change her mind. It felt good to be helping someone out. She rang up the last customer and brought out clean glasses and cups from the back. No wonder Dee was so slim. There was always something to do here.

The kitchen smelled wonderful. Joe was stirring a big pot of spaghetti sauce that would be part of the dinner special. Rae had been relieved to find that Dee employed two cooks, and both of them were in good health. It had to be hard to run a place like this when people called in sick. Small though it was, when full, the diner could easily keep everyone hopping to keep up.

Dee came back in from her office and handed Rae a schedule. "Will this work for you?"

Rae glanced at it and nodded. Dee had her working only three times a week and for only six-hour shifts. Rae wouldn't have minded a few more days. She was going to be a little at loose ends during the day, and she had a feeling she was going to see more of Nora in the evenings than she was comfortable with. Not to mention that she had a feeling her dad and Nora wouldn't mind having a few evenings together without worrying about her. "The only problem I see is that until your part-time help gets well, you're here by yourself too much. Let me come in every day—at least through the rush time—and help you out."

"Rae, you are here to visit with your dad, and I have you working three nights as it is. You won't be able to spend that much time—"

"In case you haven't noticed—and granted, busy as you are, you probably haven't—my dad is seeing someone," Rae teased. "I'm sure they won't mind. I'm staying through the New Year. Dad and I will have plenty of time together. I don't want to wear out my welcome, you know."

"I doubt you'd ever do that. But I can use the help, so I'll let you work as much as you want until Jen gets well—but only if you are sure."

"I'm sure." Rae was just relieved that she wouldn't have to spend every night trying to pretend that seeing her dad and Nora together didn't make her feel more alone than ever.

Chapter 6

Rae did run to her dad's to change into clothes and shoes that were more comfortable. Taking a cue from what Dee usually wore, she put on jeans and a long-sleeved, lightweight top. She was glad she'd brought her walking shoes; they had to be more comfortable than the loafers she'd worn all day.

Before heading back to the diner, she called her dad's office to let him know she'd be working at the diner that night and not to worry about her for supper. His office manager assured Rae that he would get the message. The evening rush was just beginning when she returned to help Dee.

Rae knew that the amount of on-the-job training she received in the next few hours would go a long way toward preparing her for the next few weeks. It was a bit embarrassing when she got two tables' orders mixed up and sloshed coffee over the sides of a cup as she set it on the table. But the customers were very kind—especially after Dee told them Rae had taken pity on her and offered to help out until Nelda got back.

She half expected her dad and Nora to show up and was relieved when they didn't. They were probably enjoying the evening without her.

The lull after the supper rush was a welcome one, and Rae gladly took a break. She'd just asked Joe to make her a cheeseburger when she whirled around to find Luke walking toward the counter. He had on a jeans and a plaid western shirt that made his shoulders seem even broader. Her heart hammered in her chest at the sight of him, and she realized she had been waiting for him to come in all evening.

"Hi, Rae." Luke sat on the same stool he was on the day they met. "Is Dee going to work you all night?"

"No. I'm not," Dee answered, coming up behind him. "In fact, I'm sending her home after she eats. But I sure don't know what I would have done without her help today. I was about ready to throw in the towel and lock the door to this place."

"Yeah, right."

"I was. But Rae came to my rescue, and I'm extremely grateful."

Rae felt the heat of embarrassment flood her face while Dee talked about her as if she wasn't standing right there. "Please, you tried to help me find Dad the other night. I'm certainly not doing anything you wouldn't do for me."

"Well, still—"

"Luke," Rae interrupted Dee, "did you want something to eat?"

"Matter of fact, I do. How about some breakfast?"

"Breakfast?"

"Sure. I like it best at night." He rose up off the stool and called, "Joe!"

The cook appeared at the service window and handed Rae a plate containing her burger and fries. "Yeah, Luke. What you need?"

"How about making me one of those big fat omelets with ham and cheese and green chilies?"

"Okay," Joe said. "Hash browns on the side?"

Luke thought for a minute. "Yeah. . .make 'em really crispy, please."

"Will do."

Luke sat back down, and Dee brought him a cup of coffee and a large glass of orange juice.

Rae brought her plate to the counter and took a seat beside Luke. Her heart skipped several beats when he winked at her. He really was one handsome man.

"If you stay long enough, you'll be able to read my mind like Dee just did," he said, handing her the ketchup bottle Dee set on the counter.

"You think so?" Rae chuckled. She just hoped he couldn't read hers. Butterflies seemed to take flight in her stomach when her hand brushed his. How could she possibly be having this kind of reaction to any man after what she'd gone through the past few months? She couldn't—wouldn't—let herself be attracted to Luke.

Joe brought out Luke's meal along with the BLT Dee had evidently ordered and stood talking to them for a few minutes. Rae was glad she didn't have to carry the conversation, and she finished her cheeseburger as quickly as she could without choking on it.

She took her plate into the kitchen and came back out to find the last customers, all except for Luke, just leaving. Dee followed them to the door and flipped the sign in the window from OPEN to CLOSED.

Rae was immensely glad that Dee closed at nine o'clock Monday through Thursday nights. On Fridays and Saturdays, she stayed open until midnight.

"You can go on home, Rae. I'll finish up for tonight."

"What else needs to be done?" Rae was sure there was more to do than lock the door for the night.

"I just need to fill the sugar and sweetener containers and the salt and pepper shakers. Make sure the ketchup and mustard bottles are changed out, if need be. That kind of stuff."

"I can help. That way you'll get to go home earlier." Rae took the big box of sugar and sweetener packets from under the counter and began to fill the containers at the tables, while Dee filled salt and pepper shakers.

Luke was just finishing a second cup of coffee when they got through. He stood to pay Dee and glanced over at Rae. "I saw your car down the street. I'll walk you to it."

Downtown Sweet Springs seemed to close up early during the week, and it was dark and chilly outside. Rae took him up on the offer. "Thanks."

"I forgot to tell you; you can park out back of the diner. It's well lit back there. I bet you had a hard time finding a place to park when you came back from changing."

Rae pulled on her lightweight jacket as they walked to the door. "I only had to drive around the block a couple of times. I'll park in back next time."

"Okay. Thanks again, Rae. See ya, Luke." Dee closed and locked the door behind them.

Luke placed his hand at her back as they started down the street toward her car. Rae tried to ignore the way it made her feel special and protected—and the way her heart thudded with each step she took.

"What did Michael think about you working tonight?" he asked.

"I haven't talked to him. I left a note when I went home to change, but I'm sure he is fine with it. He's not used to having me underfoot. I imagine he and your aunt had a nice evening without me."

They arrived at her car and when she pulled her keys out of her pocket, Luke took them from her. After unlocking her car, he opened the door and watched as she slid in behind the steering wheel. When Rae took the keys back, static electricity shot up her arm, and she dropped the keys on the ground.

"Whoa! That was some shock." Luke chuckled and bent to pick them up.

Rae caught her breath as he leaned into the car and put the key in the ignition for her. His gaze met hers and lingered a moment before he backed out of the car.

"It really is nice of you to help Dee out." Luke looked down at her. "Jake told me Sara wants to have you over for supper. Can I tell them what night you might be free?"

"We don't have a hard-and-fast schedule for me to work. Dee is trying not to give me too many hours, but I'm planning on helping as much as I can. Early in the week would probably work best since the diner seems especially busy on Friday and Saturday nights."

"I'll tell Sara to call you." Luke smiled down at her. "You know your way to your dad's in the dark?"

Rae nodded. "I can find my way. Thanks."

A stiff breeze blew down the street and into the car. Rae shivered, and Luke moved to shut her car door. "Okay. I'll be seeing you."

"Night." Rae started her car. Only when she pulled out of her parking space and headed down the street did she breathe easy. Those warm brown eyes could sure take a girl's breath away.

~

Luke watched the taillights of Rae's car disappear around the corner before pulling the collar of his jacket up around his neck and jogging to his pickup. It was becoming cooler, just as the weather report had predicted.

He climbed into his truck and started it up, then rubbed his hands together, waiting for the engine to warm up before switching on the heater. He hadn't meant to come into town for supper tonight, but his curiosity had gotten the best of him, and he'd found himself driving by just to see if Rae's car was at Michael's. When he saw both cars gone, he decided to check the diner.

He could tell from her comment that she still wasn't happy about her dad and his aunt seeing each other. At least she didn't seem to be holding it against him, although Luke sensed she was keeping her distance from him. And he'd do well to do the same thing. Just because she was helping Dee out didn't mean she was going to stay in Sweet Springs forever. He had no business being this interested in her. None at all.

But how could I stifle that interest? he wondered as he rounded the curve to his brother's house. It was easy to say he wasn't going to let himself be attracted to Rae and quite another to keep his pulse from racing each time he saw her. She'd been adorable tonight, blushing as he and Dee talked about her. And when he'd put her key in the ignition for her, the vulnerable expression in her eyes had him wanting to protect her and kiss her all at the same time.

He really wasn't sure what to think of her, but the fact that she'd offered to help Dee out had changed his initial opinion of her. Luke had to admit that he'd been judging her without really knowing her. And he knew better.

He pulled into Jake's driveway and turned off the engine. Maybe Sara would have a cake or some kind of pie—she almost always did. He ran up the walk and knocked on the door. He'd learned not to ring the doorbell at this time of night. They might have just put Meggie down for the night and wouldn't be too happy if he woke her.

Sara opened the door and let him in. "I told Jake that it was you. You have a knack for knowing when I make my chocolate fudge cake. I just iced it."

Luke sniffed deeply and appreciatively. "Oh, I do love that cake."

He followed his sister-in-law into the kitchen where Jake was pouring three cups of coffee. Sara cut a third piece of cake and put it on a dessert plate.

"My Meggie asleep?"

"We just put her to bed. Not as easy to do now that she's walking *and* climbing."

Luke chuckled. Last time he was over, Meggie had managed to climb out of her bed to come see him. "I should have come a little earlier."

Sitting down at the table, Luke didn't waste any time in forking into his piece of cake. He loved the moist cake with the thick chocolate icing. It was one of his favorites. "Mmm. And to think I nearly went home without stopping by."

"What are you in town this time of night for anyway?" Jake asked.

Luke shrugged and took another bite.

"Jake told me that Rae offered to help Dee out. Was she still working tonight?" Sara asked.

"Yes, she was." Luke took a drink of coffee.

"And you ate supper at the diner, right?" Luke didn't immediately answer, and Jake pressed, "Didn't you?"

"It was late when I got through working, and I was hungry."

"I asked you to come over here."

"It's not nice to just show up after you've declined an invitation, brother."

Sara chuckled and shook her head. "Luke Breland. You know you don't have to have an invitation to eat with us."

"I know. I did tell Rae you wanted to have her over."

"And?"

"She suggested early in the week. She thought Dee might need her more later in the week. I told her you'd call."

"Good. I will call and set something up with her. And I'll let you know when, okay?"

Luke tried to pretend he didn't understand what Sara was talking about. "Why?"

"Because I told her you'd use that rain check for when we had Rae over, just like you told me." Jake punched his brother's shoulder.

"Maybe that's not a good idea."

"Why not?"

"I don't have any business getting interested in her."

"She's cute. And she seems real sweet," Sara commented.

Luke sighed deeply. "And she's going back to Albuquerque after the holidays."

Jake got up to refill their coffee cups. "A lot can happen in a couple of months, little brother."

"Yeah, right." Luke took another bite of cake. His heart could be broken in that time frame.

After his second piece of cake, Sara wrapped up a third piece for him to take home. He left feeling a little forlorn. He loved being at Jake and Sara's, but at the same time, being around them always made him long for a family of his own.

He couldn't be anything but happy for them, though. It'd taken them years to finally get together. Jake and Sara had started out as high school sweethearts, but a serious misunderstanding broke them up, and Jake had married while away at college; then Sara had ended up marrying Nora's son, Wade. Several years ago, Wade had died in a car wreck, and a few months later Jake's wife died giving birth to Meggie. When Jake moved back to Sweet Springs this past spring, he and Sara had fallen in love all over again and were married on the Fourth of July.

They had something special, that was for sure. And he wanted the same thing. But he'd about given up on ever finding that special someone—in spite of the attraction he felt for Rae Wellington now. He couldn't afford to let himself begin to care about her. They were too different. She was definitely a city girl. And he was all country.

Rae drove home trying to put thoughts of Luke out of her mind. She was aware it was static electricity that had shocked them both, but it was his lingering gaze in the car that had her heart skittering in her chest. For a moment, she'd thought he was going to kiss her. And she'd wanted him to.

He was fast making thoughts of Paul disappear, and while she wanted to quit thinking about her ex-fiancé, she wasn't quite ready to be thinking so much about another man. Especially one so different from her.

While Luke seemed totally comfortable with who he was, she had a hard time picturing him being at ease around her friends in Albuquerque. But then she hadn't felt at ease around any of them since her and Paul's breakup. In fact, she hardly ever saw most of them now—funny how they'd kind of dropped her when she wasn't part of a couple anymore.

She'd found out pretty quickly how strong her friendships were, and it had become glaringly apparent they'd been much weaker than she'd thought. It all contributed to her decision to take a leave of absence.

She pulled into her dad's drive to find his car gone and entered the empty house to find a note from him. *Honey, I went to Nora's for supper. Will be home around ten. Hope Dee didn't work you too hard.*

Rae wasn't surprised—it was what she expected and the main reason she'd been glad to help Dee long-term. The way she saw it, Dee was helping her just as much as she was helping her new friend. She didn't want to be alone in Albuquerque, but she didn't want to have to endure Nora's company every night either.

Rae knew she wasn't being quite fair. Her dad had loved her mother with all of his heart, and he had every right to make a new life for himself. Just because she didn't have anyone to love didn't mean he shouldn't. Still, she couldn't make herself like Nora, but she had to try to for her dad's sake.

Trying to put it all out of her mind, she hurried to take a quick shower before her dad got home. Maybe she'd make him some hot chocolate tonight.

She wasn't fast enough, however. Dad had the chocolate mixture simmering when she entered the kitchen. He met her with a hug and a smile.

"I bet you're tired."

"A little." Rae took a seat at the kitchen island. She hadn't realized just how worn-out she was until she'd stood in the shower and let the warm water wash over her.

"You did eat, didn't you?"

"Of course, I did. A free meal is one of the perks of my new job. Did you and Nora have a nice time?"

He poured the hot chocolate into two mugs and handed her one. "We did. Missed you, though. You aren't going to be working all the time, are you?"

"No, of course not. But you don't need me underfoot every night."

"Honey, I love having you here. And Nora knows it. . . . She's glad you're here, too."

Oh, I just bet she is. Rae felt bad for the thought. She wasn't being fair to Nora, but she couldn't seem to help it. She had to try harder to accept the woman. "Thanks. But Dee needs the help right now, and I need something to do when you are at work. Besides, since I'm staying awhile, we'll have plenty of time to visit."

"All right. As long as you're okay with it. Will you mind having Thanksgiving dinner at Ellie's?"

Rae grinned. She'd been afraid they were going to have to eat at Nora's—or have her here. "That would be wonderful! I'll have to ask her what I can bring."

"I'm sure it will be a lot of fun. Nora's whole family will be there."

"Great!" Rae found she really was excited about going to Gram's for Thanksgiving. She'd get to visit more with her. And Sara and Jake and Meggie. *And. . .Luke.* Her heart skittered at the thought of him, and Rae sighed. How was she going to stop it from doing that?

Chapter 7

By Wednesday evening, Rae *almost* felt like a professional waitress. She'd even earned a few tips in the last few days. She didn't know how Dee put in the hours she did, and she was very glad to have the evening off.

She felt more comfortable at midweek church services too. Many of the members frequented the diner, and she'd even waited on a few of them. The class was beginning an in-depth study about putting one's trust in God, and Rae realized she needed to do a lot more trusting in the Lord to guide her than she had in the past year.

After class, it was good to have a chance to talk to Luke's grandmother again.

"Hello, Rae, dear. I hear you've been pretty busy helping Dee out this week."

"Yes, ma'am, I have." She wondered if it was Luke or Nora who'd told Gram about her working at the diner.

"Well, I hope you'll be able to come by and see me sometime this week. But I'd really like you to come help us stuff teddy bears this weekend, if you can find the time. We're meeting here in the fellowship hall, this Saturday morning at ten thirty. We'll have a bite to eat afterward, too."

"Oh, I'll be sure to make time! Dad has told me how the little bears you all make truly help the children who are brought into the emergency room at the hospital! I may not be able to stay for lunch; I'll probably help Dee out during the lunch rush, but I'd love to come help stuff bears."

"Wonderful!"

"I couldn't help but overhear your conversation," Nora said from behind Rae. "I'll be glad to bring Rae with me, Ellie."

Rae took a deep breath and turned to Nora with what she hoped was a smile. "Don't worry about me, Nora. I can get here on my own. I'll be helping Dee out at the diner and will probably just come from there and go back."

Gram bobbed her head. "Whatever will be best for you, dear."

"But I don't mind—"

"Nora, dear, that makes perfect sense," Gram insisted. "That way you can help me set up and clean up."

"All right, Ellie," Nora agreed. She smiled at Rae. "I'm just glad you are coming to help us. You'll get to meet a few of the young women your age, too."

Relieved that she wouldn't have to come with Nora, Rae's answering smile didn't feel quite so tight this time. "I'm looking forward to it."

Nora was called away just then by a lady about her age, and Rae turned back to Ellie. "It's been good to see you again, Gram. I've been meaning to ask for your cake recipe."

The older woman patted her on the shoulder. "I'll be sure and get it to you. And, Rae, dear. . .Nora means well, you know?"

Embarrassed that Gram seemed able to read her so well, Rae felt the color creep up her cheeks. "I'm sure she does. I guess I'm just having a hard time accepting that Dad cares about someone else besides Mom. And I—"

"That's perfectly normal, dear. And I know it can take some getting used to. I'm sure you are trying."

Rae felt her blush deepen. She wasn't trying, not really. And she had a feeling Gram saw through her excuses. She bit her bottom lip and glanced up. "I—"

The older woman looked into her eyes and smiled. "I'll say a prayer that it gets easier for you, Rae. You try to get by to see me soon as you can, all right?"

"I will. And. . .thank you."

"It will be all right, dear. Just hand it all over to the Lord."

"You ready to go, Ellie?" William Oliver asked as he walked up to them. He smiled at Rae. "Hello, Rae."

"Hello, Mr. Oliver. How are you tonight?"

"I'm just fine. But this lovely lady seems a little tired to me. I think it's about time I took her home."

"Yes, dear, I'm ready to go. I am a little tired tonight." She chuckled. "I watched Meggie for a little while today, and, oh, I just wish I had half her energy!"

Will laughed. "Don't we all!"

"Good night, dear." Gram patted Rae's shoulder. "I'll see you soon, I hope."

"Yes, ma'am." Rae watched the older couple walk off just as Sara walked up to her.

"I so wish those two would get married," Sara said, her gaze on her grandpa and Gram.

"They seem to care for one another a lot."

"Oh, they do. The whole family has been hoping they'll set a date one of these days. They spend most of their free time together anyway, and both live in houses that are way too big for one person. Besides, anyone can see they're crazy about each other."

Rae watched as Will leaned down to hear something Gram was saying to him. He nodded and grinned at her. "They do make a cute couple."

"Yeah, they do. And Michael and Nora make a beautiful one." Sara motioned in the direction of the fellowship hall where they could see the two talking and laughing with each other.

They do make a beautiful couple, Rae admitted to herself. And her dad was happier than she'd seen him in a long time. *Still. . .*

"Rae, I've been meaning to call you. I'd like to have you over for dinner one night soon. Can you tell me what night would be good for you? I don't know how often you'll be working."

"How nice of you!" Rae was glad that Sara had interrupted her thoughts. "My schedule at Dee's is pretty flexible, but she says Monday through Wednesday are her slowest nights. . .Thursday isn't too bad, but I'd hate to leave her alone for the weekend."

"How about next Monday night, then? Would that work?"

"Oh, I'm sure it will." Everyone was being so nice to her, trying to make her feel welcome. And she really liked Sara and Jake.

"About six thirty?" Sara asked.

"That's fine with me. I'm looking forward to it!"

Sara grinned. "Good! I guess I'd better go rescue Luke. It appears that Jake handed Meggie off to him."

Through the window at the back of the sanctuary, which was open to the fellowship hall, Rae could see Luke holding his niece. He seemed completely captivated by whatever she was saying to him. "He doesn't seem to mind watching her."

"Oh, he doesn't. I'm just afraid of what she might talk him into. He's a pushover for anything that child wants."

Sara knew her brother-in-law well, Rae decided as they watched him pull a sucker out of his pocket, unwrap it, and hand it to his niece.

"Uh-oh! I'd better go. I'll talk to you later." Sara hurried off toward Meggie and Luke.

Rae chuckled as she gathered her Bible and purse and started up the aisle. Her dad seemed to have disappeared, and she was pretty sure he'd walked Nora to her car. Deciding to go on to the car, she made her way to the front door where she was greeted by the minister, David Morgan, and his wife, Gina.

"Rae Wellington, it's so good to finally meet you! I tried to get to you on Sunday to welcome you, but you were gone before I could."

"Now, David, that sounds as though Rae ran out of here. You were just caught up greeting others," Gina said. "Sometimes he puts his foot in his mouth, and things come out wrong."

Rae chuckled. Gina was sweet. "That's all right. He preaches a good sermon, though."

Gina smiled up at her husband and nodded. "He does. And that's what he's here for, isn't it?"

"Why, thank you, ladies. I am sorry, Rae. I certainly didn't mean it to sound the way it might have. At any rate, we're very glad to meet you now. Michael says you are staying through New Year's Day."

"I am. I thought it was about time I saw where Dad had decided to live the rest of his life, and he's talked me into staying awhile."

"And what do you think of Sweet Springs? Do you like it?"

Rae chuckled and inclined her head. "Better than I thought I would, actually. But don't tell Dad. I want to enjoy giving him a hard time about moving away from me for a little longer."

Both David and Gina chuckled. "Just so long as you like it here. Any chance of getting you to move here?"

"Oh, no. Albuquerque is home. But Sweet Springs is—"

"A nice place to visit?" Luke asked.

Rae's heart jumped. She hadn't realized he'd walked up behind her. "I've visited worse."

David chuckled. "I would hope so!"

"Oh, now I'm sorry! I guess I don't know how to word things any better than you—" Rae clapped her hand over her mouth as David, Gina, and Luke all burst out laughing. "I am *sooo* sorry."

"Don't worry about it, Rae. It made me feel better somehow."

Gina punched David's shoulder and shook her head. "It's all right, Rae. We know you didn't mean anything by that."

"Oh, I think she did," Luke teased.

Rae ignored him. "Thank you, Gina."

"Guess I'd better go." Luke started for the door. "See you all later. Got to go wash some of the sticky from Meggie's sucker out of my hair."

Rae fixed her gaze on him and giggled. Luke's hair was sticking up in a few places, but he didn't really seem to mind.

"That Meggie is something, isn't she?" Gina asked. "I nearly lost it one Sunday when I saw her sticking a sucker in Sara's hair. It was all I could do to keep from laughing out loud."

"She's a cutie. I'll have to watch for her on Sunday," Rae said.

"She's some competition for my sermons, that's for sure." David shook his head. "Half the congregation watches that child."

Luke laughed. "And to think she's *my* niece."

"Uh-huh." David laughed. "Picked up some of your ornery, too."

"That's what makes her so much fun." Luke grinned and headed out the door. "See you later."

"Good night, Luke," Gina said and waved at him.

"Night," Rae added. *He sure is cute with his hair sticking up like that.*

She saw her dad stop and speak to him for a moment before making his way back inside. "Hi, honey. I just saw Nora off. Are you ready to go home?"

Rae chuckled. "Yes. I think I am. I need to go pull my foot out of my mouth."

"Night, Rae," David said. "When you figure out how, you let me know, okay?"

"I will." Rae giggled.

"Good night, Rae. We'll have to get together sometime soon," Gina suggested.

Rae nodded. "I'd like that. Good night."

"What was that all about?" Dad asked on the way to the car.

"Oh, nothing; just some teasing is all."

He smiled. "I'm glad you're feeling more comfortable here, honey."

So was she—except around Nora and Luke. Nora, because Rae admitted, deep down, she wasn't really giving the older woman a chance to become friends; but she was especially uncomfortable around Luke. He made her heartbeat flutter and her pulse shaky. She had to get over the attraction she felt for him. She wasn't going to put herself in a position to get hurt again. She just wasn't.

Dear Lord, please keep me from going through that again. Please. In Jesus' name, amen.

Luke stopped in at the diner before going home. He always felt a little lonely going home right after church. Seemed like everyone he knew was the other half of a couple—even Gram had Will to take her home. Luke had no one to take home. He'd have liked to have asked to see Rae home, but after overhearing her conversation with Gina and David, he realized he'd be much better off spending as little time in Rae's company as possible. He was very attracted to her. . .and it wasn't going to do him a bit of good. She would be going back to Albuquerque as soon as the holidays were over; she'd made that clear. There was no sense leaving himself wide open to being hurt when she left.

"Why so quiet, Luke?" Dee asked as she set his cup of hot chocolate in front of him. "Did you lose your best friend?"

"I don't think so, have I?" He grinned at her. She *was* one of his best friends, aside from his brother and cousin. He'd gone to high school with Dee, and she understood him well. He probably read her better than she wanted him to also. And if she and his cousin, John, ever got their heads out of the sand, she'd be part of his family.

Dee sat down beside him with her own cup of cocoa. "No, not if you mean me. But you sure seem sad tonight."

Luke grunted. "You know, it kind of makes you wonder what's wrong with you when even your grandmother is seeing someone and you aren't. Maybe I'm just too picky."

"Maybe we both are." She blew on her steaming drink before taking a sip. "Or maybe we're just too stubborn. Neither of us wants to move anywhere else, and we can't seem to fall for anyone who wants to stay."

Luke laughed. "You know, if this were a movie or a book, we'd end up with each other."

Dee laughed and spewed out the drink she'd just taken. She began coughing, and Luke patted her on the back. "I'm sorry. Didn't mean to choke you. The thought of falling for me is that funny, huh?"

Dee was still chuckling as she got up to clean up the mess she'd made on the counter. "We know each other maybe too well?"

"No. We just aren't each other's type." Luke shrugged. "But I'm beginning to wonder if I'm *anyone's* type."

"I don't even want to find out if I *am* anyone's type anymore. I'm too busy and too tired to care. It sure has helped having Rae here. I think God must have sent her here just to help me out."

"Oh? And here I was hoping He'd sent her here just for me. See how wrong I get things?" Luke chuckled and shook his head.

Dee saw through his teasing, though. "You really like her, don't you?"

"Won't do me any good. She's one of those city girls who doesn't want to move here."

"You never know. She could change her mind."

Luke shook his head. "No. She's planning on going back after the holidays. Just remind me of that every now and then, okay?"

"A lot can happen in six weeks, Luke."

A lot could happen in a week. A heart could beat faster and attraction could bloom. But that didn't mean a happy ending was always in store. If he'd learned anything in his thirty-four years, it was that. *But, Lord, I sure would like it if Rae decided she loved it here; yes, Sir, I sure would.*

"I'm kind of hungry. Want to stop at the diner and get a piece of pie and coffee?" Rae asked her dad.

"I'm always ready for pie and coffee, but aren't you kind of tired of the place?"

"No, not really." She thoroughly enjoyed the diner. It was so totally different from what she usually did that she was honestly having a good time. "Besides, it's not the same as being a customer. And if Dee is busy, I can get our order myself."

But Dee wasn't too busy to wait on them. It was only she and Luke at the counter, and a young couple at one of the booths.

"Well, hey there. Guess we all had the same idea, didn't we?" Luke asked.

Be still, my heart. Rae was almost getting accustomed to the way her heartbeat sped up each time she saw Luke—no matter how many times she told it not to. But he did look so endearing tonight, smiling at them. . .with his hair still all spiky in places. It appeared he'd tried to smooth it down, but it hadn't cooperated.

"I guess we did," Dad said. He sat down at the table closest to the counter. "Why don't you two join us over here?"

Rae quickly slid in beside her dad, while Luke unwrapped his legs from around the bar stool, grabbed his cup, and sauntered over. "Sure."

"Let me take your order." Dee pulled out her order pad. "Then I'll join you."

"We just want some of that apple pie and coffee." Rae saw the young couple head toward the cash register. "But I can get it while you ring them up."

"Nah. You ring and I'll wait."

"Okay." Rae slipped out of the booth and went to ring them up, and while Dee was dishing up their pie, she cleaned off the table the young people had left.

When she returned to the table, her pie and coffee were waiting for her. She slid into the booth and glanced up to see Luke studying her with his warm brown gaze. Feeling her face flush, she forced herself to look down at her plate and fork a bite of pie.

"Nora tells me the ranch is really flourishing under your management, Luke," Dad said. "She says you've set up a new computer bookkeeping system that has streamlined everything."

Luke grinned and nodded. "Those classes I took really helped. Uncle Ben seems happy with the changes. We're able to keep track of our livestock much better now. Not to mention our supplies and our cash flow."

Rae breathed a sigh of relief when Luke and her dad launched into a thirty-minute conversation about ranching. *Thank you, Dad.* It gave her time to get her bearings, get her heart rate back down to normal.

She and Dee were too tired to talk much. Rae asked about Nelda and found Dee hadn't heard any more from her. Dee finished her coffee and got to her feet. "You all can stay, long as you like, but I'm closing up."

"I'll help." Rae slid out of the booth.

"You don't have to do that."

"I know. But you'll get home earlier if I do."

"Thanks, Rae."

Dee went to count the cash drawer, and Rae got up to help with the closing. She filled the napkin dispensers and made sure the various containers were filled, then wiped down all the tables. During all of it, she enjoyed the murmur of her dad and Luke's conversation in the background, interspersed with their masculine laughter. It was obvious that they liked and respected one another.

By the time they were through getting everything ready for the next morning, Luke and Dad were on their feet and standing at the door.

"Guess, I'd better go on home, or Dee will lock up with me still here. See you all later." Luke headed out the door.

"We're leaving, too." Her dad waited for Rae to get her jacket on.

"Brrr—it's cold out here," Luke said, pulling the collar up on his jacket as the cold night air hit him.

Rae and her dad waited until Dee locked up behind them before they headed for his car. But as she watched Luke get into his truck and drive off with a wave, she felt a tug at her heart and wondered why it was that he was the one driving off alone. . .yet she'd never felt quite so lonely in her life.

Chapter 8

The next few days, Rae took it upon herself to help Dee during the rush hours. Dad left early to make rounds at the hospital, and Rae got in the habit of making a quick breakfast for the two of them, then leaving the house about the same time he did.

She was beginning to put names to faces, and there were a few of Dee's customers who were fast becoming her favorites. One was old Mr. Babcock. The ninety-year-old man was definitely—and justifiably—set in his ways. He liked his bacon crisp and his eggs over easy, with hash browns and toast on the side. He ate slowly and watched everything that went on in the diner, making entries into a notebook every once in a while. Dee explained that he was writing a book about life in a small town. He'd told Dee that her character's name would be Darla.

When he came to the register to pay for his breakfast Saturday morning, Rae figured she'd been accepted. He leaned over the counter and whispered, "Your name will be Marla. You and Darla will be sisters who run the local diner."

"Why, Mr. Babcock. I'm honored to have a place in your book."

He patted her hand. "You earned it by coming to Dee's aid."

Rae shook her head as she watched him shuffle out the door. He was a real sweetheart. She turned to Dee. "Guess what? You and I are sisters in Mr. Babcock's book!"

Dee chuckled. "I know. He told me. Said I'd have to share ownership of the diner."

They were still laughing when Luke and Jake entered with a man Rae had never seen. He was tall, like Luke and Jake, only his hair was lighter and his eyes were hazel. But it was Dee's sharp intake of breath that told Rae this man wasn't a stranger—at least not to her. It was curious how the usually unflappable Dee seemed to be suddenly fidgety.

She turned away quickly and gathered menus and water glasses, but Rae could see her hands slightly shaking. She peered over to where the three men had taken a seat and found that the man with them was watching Dee closely.

"Do you want me to wait on them?" Rae asked.

"No, I've got it, thanks. Besides, aren't you supposed to be at church to stuff bears pretty soon?"

"Oh, you're right!" Rae checked the clock over the jukebox. "Thanks for reminding me—I'd better get a move on. I'll be back to help with lunch."

"You don't have to do that—"

"I know, but I want to." She took off her apron and hung it on a hook just inside the kitchen, put on her jacket, and grabbed her purse. She'd stepped out front to ask Dee what time she should be back when Luke waved her over.

"Hey, lady, where you going in such a hurry?"

"I'm on my way to church. Gram asked me to help stuff teddy bears."

"Whoa! You'd better be off, then. Gram will wonder where you are. But before you go, meet our cousin, John. This is Dr. Mike's daughter, Rae, John."

"Pleased to meet you, Rae," John said, rising from his chair.

Rae waved him to sit back down. "I'm glad to meet you, too, John. I'm sorry I'm in such a rush—"

Luke shooed her away. "It's all right. We know how Gram feels about people being on time. You go on. You'll see plenty of John while he's here."

"Okay, I'll see y'all later."

Luke watched as Rae rushed out the door. Seemed like he only saw her in short spurts of time. It probably was better this way, though, because he was having a really hard time trying to get her out of his mind. Seeing more of her certainly wouldn't help that lost cause.

Dee brought water and menus to the table, and he switched his attention to watch how she and John reacted to each other.

"Well, what do we have here?" Dee asked with a smile. "It's good to see you, John."

"It's good to see you, too, Dee. How's business?"

"A little too good sometimes." Dee sighed as two more patrons came in. "Do you know what you want?"

"We'll make it easy on you, Dee. Give us the daily specials," Jake said. "That okay with you two?"

"Fine with me." Luke handed his menu back to Dee. "And coffee, please."

"Same here, Dee." John gave her his menu.

She hurried off to get water for the couple that had come in.

"She works too hard," John said.

"Yes, she does," Jake agreed.

"I'm just glad Rae offered to help out. But I hope Jen comes back soon. Rae is here more than she's at Dr. Mike's." Luke was certain he'd given himself away. He just hoped Jake didn't pick up on it.

"Oh?" Jake raised an eyebrow at him, and Luke had no one to blame but himself for the question his brother asked next. "And how would you know that?"

"I just know these things, that's all." Luke grinned. He wasn't about to tell them how many times he'd called the Wellington house only to get the answering machine.

"She seems nice," John said.

"She is. Just ask Dee." Jake motioned to his brother. "Or Luke."

"Aha." John chuckled and settled his gaze on Luke. "Two and two are beginning to add up here. Is she moving to Sweet Springs?"

Luke sighed. "No. She lives in Albuquerque and is just here until after the holidays."

"That's awhile. What does she do? Go from town to town rescuing the overworked?" John teased.

"She took a leave of absence from teaching high school," Luke said, realizing that he still didn't know why. And he didn't know how to ask without sounding really nosy. "That's all I know."

"Nora told Sara that Rae had a broken engagement several months back," Jake said and held up his hand as if he understood Luke was full of questions. "And that's all *I* know."

Well, that was more than he'd known before. A broken engagement. That *was* news and it explained a lot. He almost slapped his brother on the back to thank him for the information.

"How do she and Aunt Nora get along?" John asked.

"I think they walk softly around each other," Jake answered. "I'm pretty sure Nora would like to get to know her better, but—"

"Aunt Nora and Rae are both keeping so busy it isn't easy for them to get to know each other," Luke said.

Jake chuckled and shook his head. "No, it's not." He took a sip of tea before continuing. "And it's too bad. Aunt Nora has a big heart once you get to know her really well."

Rae felt a little nervous as she entered the fellowship hall, but she was quickly put at ease by the ladies there. Gram welcomed her with a kiss on the cheek and patted the seat beside her. Nora smiled from across the table and began to introduce her to everyone.

She'd met Gina already, and then there were about ten other ladies she recognized either from seeing them at church or the diner.

Gram explained that several of the women embroidered the faces on the bears, and several others sewed them up, making sure to add a label that told the recipient's family that they'd been *Made with Love*. Then once a month everyone got together, stuffed them, and sewed up the bottom. Sara would deliver them to the hospital for the church.

Hopefully, the bear would give comfort to any child brought to the hospital. The label also gave the church's name, phone number, and address—just in case the parent was searching for a church home or needed comfort from the minister or one of the elders. They'd had several new members begin attending for that very reason.

Rae watched the teddy bear she was working on take shape as she stuffed it. Others who were more practiced at it already had several finished. The bears were adorable.

"Dad told me how well they're received. It's got to be a good feeling knowing that you've helped a child be a little less frightened about being in the hospital."

"It is," Gram said. "We didn't know how well they would go over when we first started earlier in the year. But we've already doubled our original output. We furnish them for the local fire and police stations. Ambulances, too—just in case there's a child around that needs comforting."

Rae enjoyed the snippets of conversation around the table, letting her know these women loved each other. Sara showed up after dropping Meggie off at the church nursery where several of the teens were watching the younger children. She took a seat beside Rae.

"Hi! I'm glad you could make it, Rae."

"So am I." Rae worked a piece of stuffing down into one of the little bear's legs.

"How do you like working at the diner?" Nora asked from across the table.

"I like it a lot. It's quite a change from teaching, though."

"That's right." Gram glanced up from sewing. "It is high school you teach, right?"

"Ninth grade."

"Oh, wow." Sara shook her head. "I don't think I could handle that grade. I want to teach grade school when the children get—"

"The *children?*" Nora laid down the bear she'd been working on and peered across the table. "Sara, does this mean. . . ? Are you expecting?"

Everyone at the table stopped talking as if waiting for Sara's answer.

She blushed and smiled. "I am."

Nora jumped up and ran around to hug her. "Oh, how wonderful! I'm going to be a grandmother again!"

Sara patted Nora's back. "Yes, you are."

Rae was surprised to see tears in Nora's eyes. She seemed genuinely happy. Gram was wiping her eyes, as were many others. Rae must have looked confused, because Sara glanced at her and chuckled as she wiped away her own tears.

"Rae, you have to forgive us. I'm sure you don't know the whole story. I lost a baby when Wade and I were in the wreck that took his life." She glanced around the table, then back at Rae. "Without my family—Nora, Gram, and all the others—and this church family, I might not be here now to share my good news."

"Oh, Sara. . ." Rae swallowed around the lump in her throat at the thought of all Sara must have gone through.

"How is Jake doing?" Gram asked. "Walking on air?"

Sara sighed. "He's thrilled, of course. And a little nervous. Watches me like a hawk and treats me as if I'm made of eggshells."

"That's to be expected, you know." Nora had taken her seat again.

Sara smiled at Rae's unspoken question and explained. "Jake's first wife died giving birth to Meggie. He's a little apprehensive, too."

"I can understand that." These new friends of hers had been through a lot of heartache before they found happiness. She would pray for all to go well with Sara's pregnancy.

"Well, he'll take wonderful care of you; I know that." Nora seemed to want to assure everyone. "How do you think my Meggie is going to react to a sibling?"

Everyone at the table chuckled.

"Well, I guess we'll see in about seven months. But it's bound to be real interesting, isn't it?"

Even Rae could laugh at that.

Once all the bears were stuffed, Gram, Nora, and several others began to set up the luncheon she'd mentioned, and Rae looked at the clock. "Oh, look at the time! I guess I'd better get back to the diner and help Dee."

"Are you sure you can't stay?"

"I'd better not, Gram."

"I wish you could stay and have a bite to eat with us," Nora added. "But it's so nice that you've offered to help Dee."

Now that Rae felt so welcome and at home, she almost wished she could stay. But it was Saturday, and the diner was bound to be busy. "I wish I could, too. But I told Dee I'd be there. Thank you all for making me feel so welcome. Will you be stuffing bears again next month?"

"Oh, yes, we will."

"Maybe I can plan to stay for lunch, then." Rae put on her jacket and gave Gram a hug. Nora patted her on the back, and Sara walked her to the door.

"I'm really looking forward to Monday night," Sara said.

"So am I. Is there anything I can bring?"

"No. Just yourself. We'll see you tomorrow at church, okay?"

"Sure will." Rae waved to the other women. "See you all tomorrow!"

When she returned to the diner, Dee was swamped with customers, so Rae hurried to the back and put on her apron. It was midafternoon before they had a chance to do much more than smile at each other in passing.

"Whew! I'm glad you came back," Dee said as they took a quick coffee break about three o'clock. "But I have good news. Jen called, and she'll be back Monday evening. After she gets back, I think I can handle it with you helping just a few days a week."

"Oh, I know that's a relief for you, Dee. And I'm glad she's feeling better. Just know that I'm here and willing to help if you need me."

"I appreciate that more than I can tell you, Rae. I feel like we've become good friends in a short amount of time."

"Thanks, Dee. I feel the same way," Rae replied truthfully. It was a good feeling.

"Did you have a good time at church?"

"I did." Rae nodded. "Everyone made me feel so welcome. And the bears are so cute."

"That's good. I'm glad you went." Dee took a sip of coffee.

"Tell me again. . . . Who was that man with Luke and Jake this morning?"

"That's John, their cousin. He's Jake's law partner, but he's trying to decide whether to run for United States senator or not. I was so busy while they were here, I didn't have a chance to ask if he's made up his mind yet." She rubbed a finger around the rim of her cup and gazed out the window. "He'll make a good one."

There was a wistful sound in her voice, or so it seemed to Rae. She suspected Dee had mixed feelings about John running for office.

"Is he back for a while?"

"I don't know. Probably. He's been testing the waters, so to speak. Lining up support and everything. I imagine he's close to making up his mind, but he'll probably be here until after the holidays." Dee gave the diner a once-over. "Which reminds me—I've got to decide how I'm going to decorate for Christmas. The downtown businesses try to outdo each other every year."

"Sounds like fun. If you need me to help, just let me know."

"Thanks! Once Jen gets back, and I don't need you to help here so much, maybe I can have you shop for decorations. I don't have much time. . ."

Rae was struck by just how little free time Dee seemed to have. "Dee, when Nelda is here and Jen is well, do you ever take any time off?"

"Oh, an afternoon here and there. Once in a while I like to take Wednesday night off."

"You need more help. You are going to wear yourself out. Your business seems to be thriving. . . . It can't be a matter of not having enough money to hire more help."

Dee shook her head. "No, I can afford it. I've been doing it this way so long—but lately I have felt like I was missing out. . .like there ought to be more to my life than just running the diner."

"Is there anyone you're interested in dating?"

Dee got a faraway expression in her eyes and shook her head no, but the color creeping up her cheeks made Rae wonder.

"I just feel like life is passing me by sometimes." Dee got up to wipe a table. "Maybe I will hire someone else."

"Well, I'm here for a while." Rae took their cups to the back and cleaned off the counter. "But I think you ought to have more help."

Dee chuckled. "I'll mull it over. Thanks."

By the time Rae drove home that night, she was very glad the next day was

Sunday. And she had to admit to herself that she was glad Dee's part-time help was coming back. She wanted to continue to help Dee, but she would also like time to spend with Sara and Gram and get to know their family better.

As for Nora. . .Rae still didn't much like her, but she'd certainly seen a different side of her today. She cared a lot about Sara; that'd been obvious. And she was very excited about the new baby. But much as she liked Nora's family, she just couldn't make herself like the older woman. She just seemed so. . .so. . .stiff most of the time. Or maybe it seemed she was trying too hard to be nice, and Rae had a feeling it was just for her dad's benefit. Still, Nora wasn't going anywhere. Rae was going to have to get used to her, like it or not.

Dad had called the diner earlier to let her know he was taking Nora to a Chinese restaurant for dinner and to see if she might be able to join them, so she was surprised to find that he was already home when she got there.

"Dad! I didn't expect you to be here," she said, entering the kitchen from the garage.

"Hi, honey!" He called from the great room where he was watching the news. He came through to the kitchen and hugged her. "It's good to have you home! Nora knows we haven't spent a lot of time together since you've been here, and she suggested that it might be nice if I was here to make you a cup of hot chocolate when you got home."

Rae didn't much care whose idea it was. It was just good to have her dad there. "That was nice of her. And I'd love some, thanks."

"Want to go take a shower or bath first? I can have it ready when you get out."

"Oh, Dad, thank you! I will enjoy that chocolate a whole lot more after a shower."

"Go to it then."

Rae hurried down the hall. "Won't take me long."

And it didn't. The sweet scent greeted her as she walked back into the kitchen. "Mmm, that smells yummy, Dad."

He poured the mixture into two mugs. "It'll relax you for a good night's sleep. Want some marshmallows?"

At her nod, he plunked a handful of the miniature kind into her cup and added another handful to his before motioning her into the great room. Rae settled into a corner of the couch and gazed into the fire. She expelled a deep breath and took a sip from her cup.

"Honey, I'm afraid you are working too hard. I wanted you to have some time to relax and enjoy yourself while you are here."

"Don't worry, Dad. Dee's part-time help is coming back on Monday, and she may even hire another person. I won't have to work as much next week."

"Oh, good. I know Nora would like to take you to lunch or shopping sometime while you're here."

Rae chose not to comment on that little nugget of news. "I'm going to Sara and Jake's for dinner Monday night; did I tell you?"

"Yes, you mentioned it. You'll enjoy yourself. Sara is a great cook, and they are a nice couple. Is Luke going to be there?"

Rae's heart somersaulted at mention of the man she'd been trying so hard *not* to think about. So much for believing she had her attraction for Luke under control. "I don't know."

"Oh, I just wondered. Did he ever get in touch with you this evening?"

"No." Rae shook her head. "Was he supposed to?"

"Beats me. My caller ID just showed several calls from his house, but he didn't leave a message."

Chapter 9

Rae was still wondering what Luke had called about when she saw him sitting two pews in front of her at church. Maybe he'd let her know after church.

True to everything she'd heard, Meggie was an attention getter. She was up on the same pew as Luke and the rest of his family, and she was making faces at Luke. Rae could tell from the muffled sounds around her that she wasn't the only one fighting laughter.

It was only when Sara got up and took her stepdaughter to the nursery that Rae could concentrate on the sermon David was preaching. It was one she very much needed to hear—about growing closer to the Lord through prayer. Her prayer life had suffered recently, and she admitted it. It was spasmodic at best, and she knew she needed to pray more often. . .talk to the Lord the way she used to.

When the service was over, Rae was propelled out the door before she could talk to hardly anyone. Her dad and Nora wanted to take her to the Mexican restaurant they liked so well, and they were afraid they'd have to wait in line if they didn't hurry.

"Why, Luke. . .check you out. Showing up for Gram's Sunday night supper two weeks in a row!" Jake teased as Luke walked up the steps to join him on the front porch of their grandmother's home.

"So?" Luke was aware that he sounded defensive. He hadn't been coming to the Sunday night suppers on a regular basis—or any of the family gatherings as often in the last several months. But he wasn't about to tell his brother that it'd been getting too hard to be the only single guy there. When John was in town, it wasn't so bad. Both bachelors, they were each other's support network. But while he'd been gone, Luke found it was easier to go home and watch a little television, take in a movie—anything besides watching his whole family carry on their romances right before his eyes.

Jake seemed to sense that Luke was in no mood to be teased and slapped his brother on the back. "So, nothing. It's just good to have you around."

"Thanks. I figured John could use some support. I know how it feels to be the odd man out around here." He could have kicked himself for giving away his feelings as he saw an ornery glint in his brother's eyes.

"Support for John, huh? I thought maybe it had something to do with the fact that Rae Wellington is in the kitchen helping Gram out."

Luke shook his head and tried to hide the fact that the possibility of seeing Rae did have a whole lot to do with his being there. And Dee's comment about a lot that could happen in six weeks kept coming back to him. Was it possible that Rae could learn to care about him and Sweet Springs? Was he willing to take a chance that the outcome would be one to his liking if he tried to get her to care?

Once inside the house, he tried not to make it obvious that he was headed to the kitchen, so he stopped to talk to several people along the way. He met up with John in the dining room and on the pretext of checking in with their grandmother, they both entered the kitchen. And there Rae was, flushed and smiling at something Gram was saying to her as Rae sliced several of the pies on the worktable.

"Luke—John, you showed up just in time," Gram said. "How about helping Rae get these desserts out to the dining room table?"

"I'd be glad to. John, you met Rae at the diner, right?" Luke asked, taking the two pie pans she handed him. Gram handed John a cake plate to take out.

"Briefly," John replied. "Sara introduced us again when I got here, but I haven't had a chance to thank her for helping Dee out while she's so short-handed. She's a good friend of ours, and she works way too hard."

"Yes, she does. I've enjoyed helping out," Rae said.

"And now Gram has put you to work, too." Luke grinned.

"I put everyone in my kitchen to work." Gram chuckled. "If you don't want to help, don't come in."

"But Rae didn't know that," Luke teased, winking at Rae.

Her color seemed to deepen as she glanced at him and shook her head. "Truth is, I had to just stand here, begging, until she gave me something to do."

Rae picked up two more pies and led the way to the dining room.

"I called last night to see if you might want to take in a movie this afternoon, but no one was at home." Luke set his pies on the table.

"I helped at the diner, and Dad and Nora went to dinner. Dad thought you might be trying to get in touch with me."

Luke's stomach did a nosedive. Michael evidently had caller ID, too. Why had he not thought of that? He said a quick, silent prayer that Rae's dad hadn't told her how many times he'd called.

"Maybe you can take in a movie with us one night this week." He nudged his cousin.

If John was surprised at the invitation, he didn't say anything. "Sure would be nice to have some female company, Rae."

"Maybe I can," Rae said. "I don't think Dee is going to need me quite as much this next week. Her part-time help is supposed to be back. I am going to dinner at Sara and Jake's tomorrow night, and I'm looking forward to that."

"I'm sure they are, too." Luke made a mental note to find his brother and ask why he hadn't mentioned this little detail when he was doing all his teasing about Rae. And he'd better be invited.

"So am I," John said. "Sara invited me, too."

"And yes, Luke, you are invited. I wouldn't dare ask John and not you," Sara declared, walking up with Meggie. "I left a message on your answering machine because I didn't know if you would be here tonight or not."

"Well, it's a good thing you did. I was about to get jealous if John was invited and I wasn't!" He tweaked Meggie under her chin, and she immediately reached out to him.

"Unc' Luke, you gots a sucker?"

Luke took her in his arms and pointed to his shirt pocket. "No sucker tonight, baby. Mommy said no more. But check in here and see what you can find."

Meggie reached in and pulled out a small, colorful packet. "Gummies! Tankie, Unc' Luke. I love gummies."

She handed the packet to him to open for her and kissed him on the cheek. At least Meggie loved him. "Look, Meggie, this is Mr. Mike's daughter, Rae. Have you met her?"

Meggie shook her head and smiled shyly at Rae. "Her's pretty."

"Yes, she sure is," Luke agreed.

Rae blushed and chuckled. "Thank you, Meggie. You are very pretty yourself."

Meggie bobbed her head up and down. "Tankie. You gots any suckers?"

Luke liked the way Rae rubbed Meggie's cheek and smiled. She shook her head. "I'm sorry, sweetie, I don't."

" 'S okay. I got gummies. Unc' Luke give me." She stuffed several in her mouth just before giving Luke a great big kiss on his cheek. A moment later she rubbed his head with a handful of gummies.

"Well, Miss Meggie, I can see I'm going to have to make a visit to the candy store," John said. "Uncle Luke has apparently been making the most of my absence."

"Can'y store?" Meggie asked.

"Yeah. Maybe I'll bring you something tomorrow night."

Meggie clapped her hands on Luke's head, smashing a gummy into it, and he laughed. "Might want to rethink that, John. Senatorial candidates aren't real appealing with sticky hair."

He handed Meggie back to Sara and asked, "Rae, will you help me get this gummy out of my hair?"

Rae laughed, seeming to find it all very funny as she followed him into the kitchen.

"That niece of yours is something." Rae was still chuckling as she pulled at the candy in his hair.

"Ouch!"

"I'm sorry. Let me get a damp paper towel and see if I can get some of the sticky off without pulling out too much of your hair."

Luke's heart thudded against his ribs as Rae gently rubbed his hair with the wet towel. The better he got to know this woman, the more he liked her. . .and the more he wanted to know about her.

"There, I think I got it all."

"Thank you." His pulse began to race as he gazed into her blue eyes and saw them sparkle with merriment.

A giggle escaped, bringing his gaze to her lips. "Meggie does a good job with those sticky hands of hers."

Luke couldn't tear his gaze away. He wanted to kiss her. "Yes, she does. I may have to find some kind of candy that's not sticky."

"I don't think that's possible," Rae said, sounding a little breathless.

Luke inclined his head closer. "With Meggie. . .probably. . .not."

The kitchen door suddenly swung open, and Rae quickly spun toward the sink.

Luke turned around to see who'd entered the kitchen and glared at his brother.

Jake looked from Luke to Rae, who had her back to him. He shrugged. "I was trying to find Sara."

"She's *not* here," Luke informed him.

"So I see." Jake backed out of the kitchen, mouthing a silent "sorry."

Luke rubbed the back of his neck, trying to figure out what to say next to Rae. He was embarrassed and was sure she was, too. Had Jake not interrupted them, he would have kissed her. Now, he didn't know whether to be thankful or furious with his brother.

He turned to the woman he was beginning to care way too much for and reached out to touch her shoulder. He quickly lowered his hand as the door swung open once again.

"Oh, there you two are," Gram said. "I've worked you enough tonight, Rae. Come on out and enjoy yourself."

Somehow, Rae managed to move from the sink and get out the door without ever meeting his gaze, and Luke leaned against the counter and let out an exasperated sigh. He shook his head and rubbed his hand over his mouth. Pushing himself away from the cabinet, he headed for the dining room. He wanted to talk to Rae to see if he'd totally botched everything by nearly kissing her, and he hunted all over for her. But for the rest of the evening, she seemed to stay one step ahead of him.

Rae offered to stay and help clean up, but Gram wouldn't let her. Nora insisted that Rae and her father go on home, saying she'd stay and help since Rae seemed tired.

She was tired. . .emotionally tired. She'd spent the better part of the night trying to avoid running into Luke when what she wanted most was to do just that. What must he think of her? When he'd looked at her there in the kitchen, she thought he might kiss her, like that night in her car. And she'd wanted him to. . .even more than she had then. More than she should. And she was afraid he could tell. He'd leaned toward her. . .his lips had been only inches from hers. And then Jake had come into the kitchen right before she'd melted into Luke's arms. She should probably be grateful that he'd interrupted them. . .but she couldn't quite manage to feel that way.

Yes, she was very attracted to Luke. She couldn't deny it. She really liked being around him, and she loved the way he responded to Meggie. Oh, how she wanted to get to know him better. What was she thinking? She was just getting over one broken relationship; the last thing she needed was to lose her heart to someone else. She was just going to *have* to distance herself from Luke.

Which was going to be much easier said than done, she realized, remembering that he'd be at Sara and Jake's for dinner the next night.

"You're awfully quiet over there," her dad commented as he drove her home. "You're not coming down with anything, are you?"

"No. I'm fine, Dad." And she was going to be. She wasn't going to lose her heart to Luke. She just wasn't.

Rae kept telling herself that all the next day while helping Dee out on the day shift. She was relieved that Luke didn't come in during the day, although Jake and John came in for lunch. Dee waited on them, and as Rae watched the give-and-take between her and John, she decided that there must be something going on between the two.

She dressed with care that evening as she got ready for dinner at Jake and Sara's. She put on a long black skirt and a red and black sweater. Needing all the confidence she could muster, she'd picked one of her favorite outfits. She pulled on her black boots, grabbed her leather jacket, and hurried down the hall.

It smelled wonderful in the kitchen. Her dad was cooking for Nora tonight, and he was making his special: taco soup. "Hmm, I almost wish I hadn't accepted Sara's invitation. It smells delicious, Dad. Want me to set the table before I go?"

"No, honey. I'm fine. Nora will be here soon, and she'll do it."

"Okay." Rae pulled on her jacket. She kissed her father on the cheek and had started out to the garage when the doorbell rang. She glanced back at her dad and saw that he was in the middle of draining the potatoes. "That's probably Nora. I'll let her in."

She hurried through to the entryway and opened the door. Nora stood there with a cake in her hands and Luke peering over her shoulder.

"Surprise!" Nora hurried inside. "My car wouldn't start for some reason, and I asked Luke to give me a ride into town since he was coming in anyway."

"And since my truck is warm already, Aunt Nora suggested that you might want to ride with me. I can pick her up on the way back," Luke explained just as Michael walked up.

"That's a great idea, isn't it, honey?" he asked, glancing at Rae.

So much for keeping my distance, Rae thought as she willed her heartbeat to slow down. "Great. Thank you."

"You're welcome. You ready?"

"I was just on my way to the car."

"Well, let's go, then."

Rae kissed her dad on the cheek once again. "See you two later."

"Have fun. Kiss Meggie for me," Nora added as Luke and Rae headed down the walk.

Luke opened the passenger door for her, and Rae got into his truck, glad for its warmth. She'd have been halfway across town before her car warmed up. She buckled up as Luke went around and got in on his side.

"It's getting colder. I wouldn't be surprised to see some snow by tomorrow," he said. "That'll put the downtown association into the mood to start thinking Christmas."

Relieved that he was keeping the conversation away from what nearly happened the night before, Rae relaxed. "When do they start decorating?"

"Most start the day after Thanksgiving, but some start earlier."

"Dee mentioned that she might want me to help her. I have to admit this cool weather helps. It's beginning to feel like Christmas, even though Thanksgiving isn't here yet."

It didn't take long to get to Jake and Sara's, as they lived downtown not far from Gram's. It was a new home but was built to look as though it'd been around since the turn of the century. The bay windows and large, wraparound porch made Rae feel as if she'd stepped back in time. Once inside the house, Rae was surprised to see that it was furnished in an eclectic mixture. The living room was done in antiques; the family room, comfortable traditional. The kitchen was thoroughly modern but made to appear old—and it worked beautifully. Wooden floors and cabinets warmed up the space around tiled countertops and gleaming fixtures.

"Oh, this is lovely, Sara."

"Thank you. It's actually a floor plan that Jake and I picked out when we were young and in high school. He kept it in mind for years, and now we have our dream home."

She checked the oven and pulled out an enchilada casserole that smelled wonderful.

"Is there anything I can do to help?"

"No." Sara shook her head. "We're eating here in the breakfast area, just because it's cozy and Meggie can play while we eat. I fed her earlier, and Jake is getting her out of the tub."

The doorbell rang and Luke went to answer it.

"That's probably John." Sara was right. Luke came back into the kitchen with John about the same time Jake came down the back staircase holding a clean and sweet-smelling Meggie. John gave her a kiss on the cheek, then tickled her. She giggled and almost jumped into his arms.

"I guess it's your night, John." Sara turned to Rae and explained. "Meggie doles out her attention in a very fair way. Last night it was Luke; tonight it's John. Next time, it will probably be you."

"How sweet."

"Well, it is once you figure it out—'cause when it's not your turn, it's not your turn. But when it is, she gives you her undivided attention." Luke proved his point by trying to get Meggie to come to him. She burrowed her head into John's shoulder, making Sara laugh and shake her head.

She set the casserole on the table, along with a salad and chips. "Come on, everyone. John, just sit Meggie in her chair by you. I'll give her some chips, but she'll want down to play in a few minutes."

Once seated, they all held hands as Jake prayed, thanking the Lord for their food and many blessings.

"We figured we'd better enjoy your company as long as we can, John," Jake said, dishing up a plate for his cousin. "After you become a senator, your visits will fly by and probably won't occur very often."

John nodded. "I know. But I'll be here as often as I can; you know that. I get my strength from the Lord and this family."

"Don't we all?" Jake handed a plate to Rae.

"Especially Gram," Sara added.

"You know, she told me she'd even campaign for me," John informed them.

"This whole family will be out there." Luke took the plate Jake handed him.

"Even you, Luke?"

"Well, of course. As much as I can. I can at least do some campaigning around here. I figure Uncle Ben and Aunt Lydia will be right there with you. Someone has to hold down the fort."

The evening progressed through dessert and then cleaning up the kitchen. They went from discussing John's chance of getting elected, to the prospects of Gram and Will getting married, to the baby Sara was expecting. It was an evening of family togetherness and conversations—and Rae could have listened all night.

When the evening came to an end, and she and Luke put on their jackets, Rae expressed her gratitude. "Thank you for a wonderful time, Sara."

"Thank you for coming. Sometimes I feel outnumbered by these guys." Sara motioned to the three men. "It's nice to have another woman around. Let's get together later in the week, okay?"

"I'd love that!"

"Better pull your collar up," Luke suggested as he opened the front door. "It's not getting any warmer outside!"

"Night!" Sara called as Rae and Luke hurried to his truck. It was cold, but thankfully the pickup's heater warmed up quickly.

"That was so nice. I've always wondered what it would be like to come from a large family like yours."

"It was fun." Luke adjusted the heater and grinned at her. "But being from a big family isn't always a joy. Sometimes it's a real pain."

"Really?"

"Really. But I wouldn't have it any other way."

"No, I don't think you would," Rae said softly. And neither would she, if they were her family. She felt so comfortable around them. While she'd caught Luke watching her a lot during the evening, he hadn't brought up the near kiss of the night before—and she certainly wasn't going to. Her thoughts kept returning to that moment in time when she understood, without a doubt, that she was in danger of caring way too much about this man.

It's been a great night, Luke thought as he drove his aunt home. For the first time in a long time, he hadn't felt like a fifth wheel. Rae fit in with his family really well, and she seemed to like all of them. Well, except for Nora. Luke sighed. And possibly him.

As attracted as he was to her, he hadn't missed how she'd hugged the door of the pickup on the way to and from Jake's. And he couldn't blame her for keeping her distance. He wasn't sure exactly how she felt about him, especially after last night. He'd almost kissed her right there in his grandmother's kitchen. It was a wonder she'd even agreed to let him drive her to Jake's tonight. And he owed his aunt for that one.

"Aunt Nora, want me to come over and check out your car tomorrow?"

"If you have time. If not, I can call Ned's Auto Repair. He'll come out and tow it into town, if need be. I can drive the pickup. I just didn't much want to drive with the forecasters predicting snow if I could get a ride with you." She peered through the windshield. "I think they got it wrong, though."

"Oh, I don't know. That front may just be late in coming." He glanced over at his aunt. She seemed happy tonight. "How are things going with you and Michael?"

Her smile widened. "Very good. I'm so glad the Lord brought him into my life. You know, Luke, if we do get married and I move into town, my house will be empty. It's part of the family property. I think you should move into it."

"Me?" He loved Nora's home. Her sprawling ranch house was much nicer and more modern than his. It had a huge kitchen, four bedrooms and three baths, a separate office, and an oversized pool out back.

"Yes, you," Nora insisted. "I should have moved into town and let you have it months ago. You're running the ranch property. My place is a little closer to town than yours, and you could let the foreman move into your house."

"Aunt Nora, I don't know what to say. I—"

"No need to say anything, dear. Ben, Gram, and I have already talked about it. It's going to you."

Luke couldn't quite explain the bittersweet joy he was feeling. He'd never considered that he'd be inheriting Nora's place, although he loved it. It would be perfect to raise a family in. . .but it was awfully big for one person. Thoughts of Rae playing with Meggie came to mind. He shook his head slightly as if that would make the thought of Rae disappear. If only it were that easy.

Chapter 10

By the end of the week, Luke was pretty sure Rae was trying to avoid him. He'd looked for her at the diner on Tuesday evening but found she'd worked that morning. On Wednesday evening at church, Michael told him she was helping Dee out while she trained the new girl she'd just hired. When he stopped by the diner after church, Dee told him she'd sent Rae home minutes earlier.

Thursday morning, he was determined to track her down, but that was easier said than done. She wasn't at the diner; Dee said she was coming in later but didn't know where Rae might be until then.

Finally, Luke called Aunt Nora just to see if maybe they'd gone shopping, even though he doubted that was likely.

"No, dear," Nora replied. "I've asked Rae to go shopping several times, but she's been so busy at the diner, and well. . .truthfully, Luke, I don't think Rae wants to spend her free time with me. I think sharing the occasional meal with Michael and me is about all she can handle of my company."

"I'm sorry, Aunt Nora." And he was. He wished Rae would give her a chance. She just didn't realize how much Nora had changed since Michael had come into her life.

"Don't be. I've handed it over to the Lord. But when you think of it, you can add your prayers to mine that she'll learn to like me one day."

"I'll do that."

"Thank you, dear."

Frustrated at Rae's attitude toward his aunt and the fact that he couldn't find her, he decided to drop by his grandmother's on his way back to the ranch. And there, in the last place he'd thought to look, parked right out front, was Rae's car.

Luke pulled into the driveway and took a moment before he went inside. Releasing a deep breath, he sent up a prayer. *Father, please help me handle this right. I'm not sure why I feel the need to seek Rae out, but I do. If it's Your will that I do that, please help me to know why and what You would have me do about this attraction I feel for her. If she's not the stranger You've sent into my life, and if it's Your will that she go back home after the holidays, please just help me to get her out of my mind. And, Lord, please help her to accept Aunt Nora. In Jesus' name, amen.*

He didn't know what the Lord's plan for his life was, but he had to find out if Rae had a place in it—city girl or not. He hopped out of his truck, ran up the porch steps, and let himself in the front door. "Gram? You here?"

"Luke, we're in the kitchen; come on back."

Gram met him at the kitchen door and gave him a hug. "What are you doing here this time of day?"

"Can't I just come by and see how my favorite girl is doing?" He glanced over at the table where Rae was sitting with a pen and pad of paper and smiled. "Hi, Rae."

"Hi, Luke." The corners of her mouth turned up in a slight smile as she looked up at him.

"Dee's new waitress must be working out pretty good if you don't have to work."

Rae put the pen down and sat back in her chair. "She's working out real well. She's got a lot more experience than I do. I'm going to still help out if Dee needs me, but not as much. I'm feeling a little at loose ends now, though."

Luke didn't know what to say. He'd like to ask her to have lunch with him, but ever since the other night when he'd almost kissed her, he had no idea what to say to her. Now he settled for addressing both women. "So, what are you two ladies up to?"

"Rae is getting the butternut pound cake recipe I forgot to give her, and we're discussing the Thanksgiving menu. It's only a week away, you know." Gram motioned him over to the table. "Want some coffee?"

"Sure, but I can get it. You two get on with your planning. I'll be sure to add anything I think you leave out." He grabbed his favorite mug and filled it.

Gram chuckled. "I'm sure you will. Rest assured, pecan pie is at the top of the dessert list, along with pumpkin."

Luke took a seat at the round table in the bay window and grinned at Rae. "Well, then you've got the two most important items accounted for. You probably don't need my input after all."

"Rae is going to make my butternut cake, and Nora is making a chocolate cake. Lydia is making a couple of cream pies, and Sara is making her twenty-four-hour salad."

"I've never seen that many desserts at one meal." Rae shook her head. "And Gram has already given me the menu for the meal. How will anyone even have room for dessert? A gigantic turkey, a big ham, mashed potatoes, sweet potato casserole, green beans, dressing, gravy, rolls. . . And I know I'm missing a few more things."

"It's a big family, and we have several big eaters in it." Gram eyed Luke, who just grinned and shrugged.

"And everyone wants leftovers the next day," she continued. "Good thing we all live close. . . I'd never be able to cook it all here."

"I'll be more than happy to make something besides the cake. Just let me know what you need. I admit to being excited. I've never been to this big of a Thanksgiving dinner. After Mom passed away, Dad and I usually just made reservations at a nice restaurant and went there."

"Oh, this family would disown me if I suggested eating out! But it would be nice to dress up and—"

"Gram! Don't even think about it. We dress up a little—"

"Have someone to wait on me, for a change," Gram finished.

"I'll wait on you!" Luke exclaimed, knowing full well that the family dinner wasn't really at stake.

Gram shook her head, and both she and Rae laughed. "Calm down, Luke, we're eating here."

"Whew!" He grinned over at her. "I'm glad. We wouldn't have leftovers to take home."

"I can hardly remember having Thanksgiving leftovers."

"We'll make sure you have some to take home. After all that cooking, no one wants to spend a lot of time in the kitchen the next day."

"Is that the reason?" Luke asked. "I thought it was because leftovers taste even better than the original meal."

Luke saw the way Rae watched as he and his grandmother teased each other. Her smile seemed wistful to him. He felt a little sorry for her being an only child and not ever having had a big family Thanksgiving dinner. He couldn't even imagine what that would be like. He drained his cup and looked at the clock. It was time to get back to work. But he felt better. Rae hadn't left the country.

"Guess I'd better be going. You ladies have a good day. If I think of anything you've left out, I'll be sure to call."

"I'm sure you will," Gram came back with a grin. Luke gave her a kiss on the cheek and glanced over at Rae, but she seemed busy writing notes down. Was she remembering their near kiss of the other night?

"Bye, Rae. See you two later."

"Bye, Luke." She gave him a quick smile before giving her attention back to her list.

Luke strode out of the kitchen and to his pickup feeling relieved. Rae might be trying to avoid running into him, but it could only work so long. If nothing else, he'd be seeing her on Thanksgiving.

Rae's heartbeat slowly returned to normal. She certainly hadn't expected to see Luke at Gram's this morning. In fact, she'd been going out of her way to try *not* to run into him. Ever since Sunday night when she'd thought he was going to kiss her, and then the wonderful time she'd had with him the next night at Sara and Jake's, Rae hadn't been able to get him out of her mind—and she was striving very hard to do just that.

She already cared about Luke. But she couldn't afford to let the feelings grow. She just couldn't do that. Hurt as she'd been over the breakup with Paul, she had a feeling it would be far worse if she let herself care for Luke and things didn't work out. No. She had to keep her distance from him as best she could. It was the only way to protect her heart.

But keeping her distance was a challenge during the next week. Ben and Lydia had a party for John that Saturday evening, so that he could announce to family and friends that he was indeed running for United States senator. Lydia sat her between Luke and John, and it was a little hard to ignore him in such close proximity.

On Sunday evening there was Gram's Sunday night supper. Dad asked Luke to give Rae a ride while he drove Nora out to pick up the dessert she forgot to bring in with her. Thankfully it was a quick drive to Gram's from the church building, but there was a tension in the truck that couldn't be denied. Rae wondered if Luke was thinking about the last Sunday night supper as much as she was.

By Tuesday, when he and Jake met her and Sara for lunch at a fast-food place Meggie especially liked, Rae was beginning to wonder if the family was trying to get them together. But Sara's surprise at seeing Luke assured her that at least her new friend wasn't in on it, if that was the case. But Rae had a good time. Meggie kept them all entertained, and Luke and Jake spent most of the hour talking to the little girl.

On Wednesday, Rae helped out in the diner and was happy to find out that Dee had been invited to Gram's for Thanksgiving, too.

"Oh, I'm so glad. I was wondering what you were going to do." Rae had found out early on that Dee had no family nearby. Maybe that was one reason Rae felt close to her.

"Ellie has been asking me for years. I always look forward to going. Some years it's been a little uncomfortable with John. . ."

Dee stopped midsentence, convincing Rae that there *was* something between her friend and Luke's cousin.

Dee bit her bottom lip and shook her head. Rae waited.

"I can't believe I let that slip." She chuckled and sat back in the booth and shrugged. "John and I used to date. And once in a while we feel uncomfortable around each other. End of story."

Rae had an idea there was a lot more to the story, but obviously Dee didn't want to talk about it. And she didn't press. After all, she didn't want to go into her reasons for feeling uncomfortable around Luke. "Well, I'm glad you are going to be there. I've never been to a big family gathering, and I'm really excited about being part of it."

Dee grinned. "You are in for a treat. It's never dull when the Tanners and Brelands get together. Nor is it quiet."

No, Rae thought the next afternoon. "Quiet" and "dull" were not words that could describe Thanksgiving at Gram's. "Noisy" and "fun" were. They ate around midafternoon, to give them time to make room for dessert later, John told her.

By the time they were gathered together for a prayer, the smells coming from the kitchen had several stomachs growling.

Gram asked Will to say the prayer, and they all bowed their heads.

"Our dear Father, who art in heaven, we thank You for our many blessings. And today we especially thank You that we are able to be together to enjoy this meal and the company of these loved ones—family and friends. Please bless those who prepared it, and thank You for providing it. And thank You, Father, for Your precious Son and our Savior, Jesus Christ. In His name we pray, amen."

" 'Men," Meggie echoed, amid loving smiles and chuckles.

Everyone helped themselves to the bounty and found a place to sit. One table wouldn't hold them all, so a buffet was set up in the kitchen, and they ate wherever they could find a seat—not unlike a Sunday night supper. Rae found herself at the kitchen table with Luke, John, Dee, Jake, Sara, and Meggie in her high chair. Sitting between Dee and Sara, she was content just to listen to the family banter surrounding her.

She saw John whisper something to Dee; her friend blushed, making Rae wonder just what was up between them. They made a nice-looking couple. Luke's imperceptible nod in the couple's direction told her she wasn't the only one curious. But the wink Luke gave her when she glanced back at him had warmth stealing up her cheeks and her heart tumbling somewhere down around her stomach. She tried to avoid meeting his gaze by giving her full attention to the plate in front of her.

The meal was delicious, and Rae was thankful there would be time for it all to settle before they had dessert. The men spent the better part of the afternoon in front of the television set watching football, while the woman mostly congregated in the kitchen to clean up and talk about Christmas. Talk went from the menu for Christmas dinner, to how they planned on decorating their homes, to how the town decorated. There would be a nativity scene on the courthouse square across from the diner and lights in the trees. Each business downtown decorated, hoping to win first place in the annual contest.

"I've got to decide how I'm going to decorate the diner. I don't expect to win any kind of award, but I do want it to be pretty," Dee said. "Will you help me, Rae?"

"I'd be glad to. I love decorating for Christmas. Just let me know what you need me to do."

When the game went into halftime, Luke and Jake entered the kitchen demanding dessert. Rae could only laugh and shake her head when she saw them load up their dessert plates with several kinds of pie, cake, and Sara's famous salad.

She tried most everything herself, only in much smaller portions. By the time they'd finished having dessert and coffee, Rae was positive she wouldn't be able to eat for days. But sure enough, Gram sent leftovers home with everyone.

Dee had asked her to help out in the diner the next two days, and it didn't take long for Rae to understand why. Shoppers out to take advantage of the big holiday weekend sales kept them hopping. The diner was packed all day, but Rae enjoyed all the hustle and bustle, plus it almost kept her too busy to think about Luke. Almost. Thoughts of him managed to slip in no matter what she did.

By the time Sunday rolled around, Rae was ready for a nice, relaxing day, but she really didn't want to spend it with her dad and Nora. They seemed in a world of their own even when other people were around.

"Rae, if you don't have any plans for this afternoon, want to help me decorate the diner?" Dee asked as they headed toward the foyer.

Relieved that she had an excuse not to join her dad and Nora for lunch, Rae didn't have to think twice. "I'd love to. Just let me tell Dad I won't be joining him and Nora."

After promising them that she'd see them at evening services, she and Dee took off. They grabbed a hamburger from a fast-food place and then went to the new superstore to buy a tree with lights already on it, lighted garlands, ribbon, spare bulbs, and some ornaments. Dee had decided that she wanted to go with all-white lights after years of going with colored ones. She bought burgundy ribbons and decorations to match the color of the booths.

"Wow, that was easy," Dee said after setting the hinged tree up next to the jukebox. "I love real trees, but I feel safer having this one since I'll have it lit up for so long."

"I know what you mean. But this one looks very real." Rae helped spread the branches out. They added gold garland and the burgundy ornaments and stood back to inspect their work.

"It is pretty, isn't it?" Dee asked after plugging it in.

"It's beautiful." The glittering lights made everything sparkle even more.

They spent the rest of the afternoon putting the swag garlands in the windows, strategically arranging the power cords, and putting on the finishing touches. By the time they were through, they had to hurry to get to church in time for the evening service, and then it was on to Gram's for supper.

Rae rode over with Dee, but it was only after she spotted Luke talking to John outside that she hurried to the kitchen to help Gram. Thinking she'd safely avoided him, her breath caught in her throat when she spun around from setting a turkey casserole on the table to find him at her elbow.

"You are one hard lady to get in touch with. I tried to reach you this afternoon. John and I wanted to see if you and Dee would like to take in a movie with us."

"We were decorating the diner." But she wished she'd been at the movies with him.

"The one place I never thought to check. Michael told us you two were spending the afternoon together—just not where."

Rae sighed and shook her head. "I told him, but he seemed to have his mind on Nora." As it always seemed to be lately. She wasn't even sure they'd noticed she was at church tonight.

"Rae, they—"

Gram interrupted him when she pronounced it was time to say a prayer and asked John to lead it.

Rae didn't think she wanted to hear what Luke had been about to say anyway. Everyone began helping themselves after the prayer, and she tried to avoid Luke, but it didn't work for long. He found her leaning against the sideboard in the dining room.

"Rae, we need to talk about Aunt Nora and your—"

Once again, Luke was interrupted; only this time it was by her dad. He smiled and clapped his hands together. "Everyone, please, could I have your attention?"

He gazed down at Nora and put his arm around her. "I have some wonderful news. This lovely lady has just agreed to be my wife, and we are thinking a Christmas wedding might be nice."

Rae's heart seemed to stop before it twisted in her chest and started up again with a deep, slow thud. Everyone was gathering around her dad and Nora, congratulating them, but she couldn't seem to move.

Luke touched her elbow as if to nudge her into action. "Rae—"

"No. I won't. . ." She pulled away from his touch and rushed into the kitchen, trying to sort her thoughts, catch her breath, and keep her tears at bay.

The door swung open, and Luke walked up behind her. "Rae. They love each other. Can't you be happy for them?"

Rae could only shake her head. She didn't trust herself to speak.

"Maybe it's time you grew up, Rae," Luke continued. "I know your dad is wonderful for my aunt. She's a different person since she met him. Can't you give them a chance to have a life together?"

"It *appears* that I don't have a choice. They've already made their decision." *Without even letting me know.*

"And you aren't going to make it easy on them, are you, Rae? You're acting like a child."

She whirled to face him. "You don't know what you're talking about, Luke. You didn't lose your mother in high school. You didn't have your betrothed dump you on the eve of your wedding for your best friend, and you didn't have your dad announce his engagement to the whole world without at least letting you know first!"

"Your dad loves you with all his heart, Rae. But he and Nora deserve to be happy." Luke reached out to her.

She held her hand out and backed up, brushing at the tears sliding down her cheek with her other. "No! I am not going to congratulate them. Don't you see? I can't!"

"It's all right, it's all right." Luke pulled her into his arms. "I didn't know you were hurting so badly, Rae. I didn't know."

Rae burrowed her face into his shoulder and sobbed.

"It's okay. Cry it out." Luke rubbed her shoulders and rocked her gently for several minutes before she pulled back slightly and looked up at him.

"I'm sorry. . .I. . . ," she whispered. Her heartbeat pounded in her ears at his nearness.

"It's going to be all right, Rae." He pulled her close again and tilted his head toward her. "It will be. . . ." Luke's lips touched hers lightly at first. . .and lingered.

Rae kissed him back.

Chapter 11

Rae's fingertips rested against Luke's chest, feeling the rapid beat of his heart. When he broke the kiss and released her, Rae suddenly felt bereft. How had she let herself respond to him like that? And why did he release her so abruptly? He'd been the one to initiate the kiss.

Even after the kitchen door swung open, it took a moment for her to get her bearings and realize that he must have known someone was about to come into the room.

Her dad and Nora entered the kitchen, and she had a sudden urge to turn and run. It was only Luke's steady gaze that helped her to regain her composure and stay put.

Dad came over and gathered her into his arms. "Rae, honey, I'm so sorry I made the announcement about our engagement before I told you about it. I was just so happy Nora finally agreed to marry me that I wasn't thinking. But I should have told you first. Please forgive me."

Rae brushed at the tears on her cheeks and shook her head. "It's all right," she sniffled.

Nora reached out to touch her arm. "No, it's not. I am so very sorry, Rae. We just were not thinking right. The last thing I meant to do was start our relationship off by hurting you. We can put the wedding off for a while."

Rae looked into the eyes of the woman who apparently would be her stepmother. Those same eyes that were shining with happiness only a few minutes ago now appeared to be clouded with concern. She seemed genuinely sorry that they hadn't told her first, and Rae began to regret being so unfair to Nora. The woman wasn't an ogre. She was simply a woman in love with a wonderful man.

She switched her attention to her dad and saw the pleading expression in his eyes. "Please, forgive us, Rae."

She suddenly realized that Luke had been right. It *was* time she grew up. Fresh tears threatened, and she willed them away. "No, I'm the one who should apologize. I'm sorry for acting like a child."

"Honey—"

"It's okay, Dad, but I. . ." Rae couldn't talk anymore. Wanting to get away from everyone, she backed toward the rear door, shaking her head.

"Rae, wait," Luke said.

"Honey, please." Her dad reached out and started after her.

"No, Michael. Let me," Nora implored. "Please. Just give me your car keys."

With tears blinding her, Rae ran out the back door into the chilly night air. She heard the screen door slam behind her as she hurried down the steps. Then she heard the door bang shut again.

"Rae! Wait," Nora called, sounding a little breathless. "Please."

Rae stopped in the middle of Gram's backyard. Nora sounded out of breath, and Rae had no idea where she was going anyway. She'd ridden over with Dee, and she didn't even have her purse with her.

Nora reached out and put her arm around Rae. "Come on. Let's go get some coffee. I know just the place."

Rae looked toward the kitchen and saw that her dad and Luke were watching from the porch. She couldn't face going back inside. She sniffled and nodded as Nora led her across the yard, then out to the street and her dad's car.

Nora handed her a box of tissues and adjusted the driver's seat to her height. She started the car and took off down the street. They didn't talk. Nora turned the radio on low and just drove around downtown for a while.

"Okay now?" Nora asked after Rae stopped sniffing.

Rae blew her nose and nodded. "I'm sorry."

"So am I, Rae. Michael and I should have taken your feelings into consideration more." Nora drove back to the center of town and parked on the side street just outside the ice cream parlor. She switched the ignition off and turned to Rae. "They make a really wonderful vanilla cappuccino here. Want to try one?"

"That'll be fine." Rae got out on her side and joined Nora on the sidewalk. She was glad the shop wasn't very busy at the moment. She knew her face would be tear-streaked and her nose a bright red. She was ashamed of herself for being so unfair to her dad and Nora and for making such a scene in Gram's kitchen with Luke. And she was more than embarrassed at her response to his kiss. She felt herself flushing just thinking about it.

"Come on." Nora brought her out of reliving that kiss. "Let's get inside. It's getting cooler out."

Rae followed her into the shop, and Nora gave their order to the young woman she called Allie, who was working the counter. They waited while she fixed the cappuccinos right before their eyes. After Allie added a dollop of whipped cream, sprinkled cinnamon on the top of each mug, and handed them across the counter, they found a booth at the back of the room and sat down.

They spent the next few minutes sipping the rich, frothy drinks. Rae felt awkward and unsure of what to say to Nora, but she owed the woman the courtesy of listening to anything *she* might want to say.

"Rae, I really am so sorry we hurt you by making our announcement without talking to you first. I know that Michael feels horrible about it, and so do I. We should have—"

"Asked my permission?" Rae shook her head. "I don't think so, Nora. You both have a right to be happy. I am sorry. I have been so close-minded about how you feel about each other. I just. . . After Mom died and then the breakup with Paul. . .I guess I felt I was losing Dad to you. But Luke was right. I've been acting like a child." *And I've been blaming everyone, including the Lord, for my losses.* But deep down, she was certain that the Lord hadn't caused her mother's illness any more than He'd made Paul choose Laura over her. And she hadn't lost her dad. He might marry Nora and become her husband, but he would always be her daddy.

"Oh, Rae. Your dad is crazy about you. And I would never want to hurt his relationship with you. But I think I understand how you might be feeling. . .more than you know. Although you've handled the sorrows in your life much better than I handled mine."

Nora took a deep breath. "I'd been a widow a long time, but I had my son, Wade. And then Sara, after they married. I was about to become a grandmother. Then Wade was killed in the automobile accident, and Sara lost the baby and very nearly her life. But thank the good Lord, she came through. I felt like she was all I had left of my son."

Rae noticed the tears in Nora's eyes as she paused and took a sip from her cup. How could she have been so blind to the pain Nora had endured?

Nora put the cup back down and ran a finger around the rim, and Rae supposed she was trying to get her feelings under control before she continued. "When Jake moved back to town, and it became apparent that he and Sara were falling in love again, I thought I was losing everything. For a while I even resented my own nephew because I thought he was trying to take her away from me. I'm ashamed to say so, but I tried to break them up." She shook her head. "I handled it horribly. My attitude very nearly cost me my relationship with Sara, with Jake, and the whole family."

"Sara never mentioned—"

Nora smiled and shook her head. "No, Sara wouldn't. She and Jake are very forgiving people. Actually, it was Jake who showed me how much he loved her by offering to let me be a grandmother to Meggie if I would just accept their marriage. And Sara let me know that if we were to have a relationship, I'd better accept his offer, because she was going to marry him and become Meggie's mommy. The Lord gave me one last chance to have a wonderful relationship with my family, and Michael helped me realize that I'd better take it. Without the Lord's love, forgiveness, and grace, I would be a lonely and bitter woman. Thankfully, He gave me a way to salvage what I almost threw away."

Nora stopped and smiled, tears gathering once more. "Now, Jake and Sara are expecting a baby, and I'll have another grandchild—not by blood but by love and family ties. Rae, please believe me. I would never try to take your mother's place in your heart. But I hope that one day you and I will have a good relationship."

By the time Nora finished, tears were streaming down Rae's cheeks again, and she grabbed several napkins from the dispenser on the table. "Nora, I am so sorry. I've been wallowing in my own self-pity as if I was the only one who ever suffered a loss. Please forgive me."

"Dear, there is nothing to forgive. I only told you all of this so that you would know you aren't the only one who ever felt that way—and that I do understand. My life has changed so very much this year, and to tell you the truth, I'm very nervous about this new change. I never thought I would marry again. I was afraid to love again. But the Lord brought Michael here, and I'm going to walk out in faith that He wants us to make a life together. It doesn't mean that we can't put the wedding off for a while, though, if you'd be more comfortable with that."

Rae reached over and clasped one of Nora's manicured hands in her own. "No, Nora. There is no need to postpone the wedding. Since I'm here, I'd consider it an honor if you would allow me to help you with it."

She swallowed a lump in her throat as she watched Nora's reaction. Rae wiped at her eyes once more as Nora stifled a sob and smiled at the same time.

"Thank you. I would love that." Nora gave her hand a squeeze.

Rae squeezed back. She took a shaky breath before sipping her now lukewarm cappuccino.

They'd driven all over town trying to find Rae and Nora before Michael finally suggested checking out the ice cream parlor. They both breathed a sigh of relief when they spotted his car parked on the side street next to it.

After finding the two women in what appeared to be a serious conversation, they'd ordered coffee and waited unnoticed until Michael saw his daughter reach over to Nora, say a few words, and then smile.

Now, Luke watched as Michael approached the back booth where Rae and Nora were sitting, and he released a deep breath when Rae responded to her dad's hug. Her color seemed to heighten when Michael motioned for him to join them, and he felt a little flushed himself as he walked toward them. He couldn't get the kiss he and Rae had shared out of his mind. As he approached the table, he wondered if she was remembering it, too.

He was relieved to see that both women smiled at each other when Michael asked, "I take it the wedding is on?"

"The wedding is on. Rae has graciously offered to help us plan it." Nora smiled up at her new fiancé.

"Thank you, honey." Michael hugged Rae once more.

"I'm sorry, Daddy, I should have—"

"Shh. I'm just glad you are with us now."

Nora turned to Luke. "Can I get a ride home with you, dear? I think Michael and Rae could use some time together."

"Of course, Aunt Nora. I'll be glad to take you home."

"No, Nora. This is a special night for you and Dad. You have plans to talk about, and I've put enough of a damper on things. Dad, go ahead and take Nora home."

"I'll see Rae home, Michael," Luke offered.

"Are you sure?" Nora asked Rae.

"I'm sure. You two go on, but could you loan me your key to the house, Dad? I don't have my purse with me."

Nora handed Michael his key chain, and he removed the house key while she slipped out of the booth and stopped to embrace Rae. Michael handed his daughter the key and gave her a kiss before he and Nora headed out the door.

Feeling a little uncomfortable and not knowing quite what to say, Luke took the seat Nora had vacated and stole a glance at Rae, who was gazing down into her cup. "That was nice of you, Rae. I'm glad you and Aunt Nora came to an understanding."

"You were right." Rae finally raised her gaze to meet his.

"About what?"

"That I needed to grow up." She bit her bottom lip, bringing the kiss back to Luke's mind.

He shook his head and sighed. "Rae, I'm sorry. I shouldn't have said that. I didn't know where you were coming from, how hurt you'd been—"

"No. You were right. They deserve to be happy. And I've been acting like a spoiled brat. I'm sorry I made such a scene. . . ."

Relieved that she hadn't apologized for the kiss, Luke reached across the table and pulled one of her hands between both of his. "Rae, you could have made things much harder on them. You didn't. You just didn't. . .try to. . ."

"Accept that they love each other? No. I tried to fight it instead." Rae slipped her hand out of his clasp and leaned back against the booth.

Luke sensed she was distancing herself from him more than just physically. "Well, you have had some heartache of your own. The timing must have seemed really bad to you. I'm sorry you've been hurt, Rae."

"So have lots of other people. My selfish behavior would have deeply disappointed my mother. She'd want me to be happy for Dad, just as she would be. I know that might sound strange, but do you see what I mean?"

"I do. And I have a feeling she'd be real proud of you now. I certainly am."

"Thank you, Luke." She closed her eyes and began rubbing her temple. "I have a colossal headache. Would you mind taking me home now?"

Much as Luke wanted to talk about what had happened between the two of them in Gram's kitchen, now wasn't the time. Rae appeared emotionally exhausted, and she didn't seem to want to meet his gaze. "Of course not. Come on."

He stood and waited for her to slide out of the booth. Once outside, he helped her into his truck and turned the heater on. The silence between them was anything but comfortable, and Luke wondered if it was because they were both thinking of the kiss they'd shared. He sure couldn't get it out of his mind.

When he stopped in the drive at Michael's front door, he wanted nothing more than to pull her into his arms and tell her everything would be all right—but he didn't have the chance.

"Don't worry about seeing me to the door," Rae said, quickly opening the door. "It's cold out, and I'm just going to dash in. Thanks for the ride, Luke."

Before Luke could even say good night, she'd run to the front door, unlocked it, and hurried inside. Obviously, she didn't want to discuss what had happened between them tonight.

Luke drove toward home telling himself to be patient. Rae wasn't going anywhere just yet. She'd committed to helping Nora with the wedding. Right now he'd just be glad she seemed to be accepting Michael and Aunt Nora's engagement.

There would be time to talk about how their relationship had changed. And it had changed tonight. Of that he had no doubt.

Luke drove off, and Rae let out a huge sigh of relief as she leaned against the front door, thankful he hadn't brought up the kiss. She was mortified enough as it was and still couldn't believe she'd acted so childishly. But she'd responded *and kissed him back.* Rae shook her head. She'd been trying to block out thoughts of the kiss all evening. . .to no avail. Even during the emotional roller coaster of an evening talking to Nora, thoughts of that kiss had been hovering at the back of her mind.

From the moment he'd pulled her into his arms and his lips touched hers, she'd felt a joy she couldn't explain even now. It felt as if that was where she'd always belonged, and everything in her shouted that she was on the verge of falling in love with Luke—and that he might, just might, feel the same way about her.

Yet now, she was sure it was only wishful thinking on her part. Her feelings were deceiving her. More than likely, after her tirade, Luke had kissed her only because he felt sorry for her. And pity was the last thing she wanted from Luke Breland.

She should probably just pack up and go back to Albuquerque, but she couldn't do that now. She'd promised to help plan the wedding and she meant to keep her promise.

Rae pushed away from the door, rubbing her throbbing temple. Her headache wasn't getting any better with all these thoughts going round and round in her head. She went to the kitchen to find some aspirin before heading to her room.

After a shower, Rae got ready for bed. She was tired. It'd been a long, hard day, and she'd had to face some unpleasant truths about herself. But before she could go to sleep, there was one more thing she had to do. She got down on her knees beside the bed and prayed.

Dear Father, please forgive me for blaming You for all the heartache I've felt. I was wrong. You are the One who has held me up and kept me going through it all. I'm the one who made everything harder than it needed to be. Oh, I told myself that I was trusting You to lead me, but I wasn't.

Please forgive me. . .for not talking to You like I used to. . .for not looking to You for guidance as I should have. And for hurting Dad and Nora. I should have been happy they found each other. I realize now that bearing the heartache of losing someone doesn't mean we'll never love or be happy again. Nora will make Dad a good wife; I know she will. She loves him very much. Please help me to make it up to them.

And, Father, I promise to try to do Your will, to let You lead me from now on. Please help me to lean on You the way I was taught to do. And please, Father, help me not to fall in love with Luke. I'm not ready to risk being hurt again. It's just too soon. Thank You for my many blessings, Father. In Jesus' name, amen.

Rae crawled into bed feeling as if a weight had been lifted off her shoulders. Oh, she still had feelings for Luke that needed to be dealt with, but she felt closer to the Lord than she had in months, and she was certain He would help her. She closed her eyes and drifted off to sleep.

Chapter 12

Dad greeted her with a big smile when she walked into the kitchen the next morning. "Hi, honey! You aren't working this morning, are you?"

"No." Rae shook her head. "Dee's new waitress is working out very well. I may see if she needs any more help decorating, though."

She took a mug out of the cabinet and filled it with coffee before joining him at the kitchen island where he was eating a bowl of cereal. "I want to plan a surprise bridal shower for Nora, and I thought I'd better get an early start."

Her dad hugged her. "Thank you, Rae. That will mean so much to Nora."

"Just don't tell her. I want it to be a surprise."

"All right, I promise not to tell." He took a drink of coffee. "I know she'll love it, but I don't think there's anything she'll need to set up housekeeping, honey."

"That's not the point, Dad. I want to welcome her into our family, like we've been welcomed into hers."

"Rae, you don't know how much that means to me."

"I'm sorry it took me so long to come around. But I see how happy you are with Nora, Dad. How can I not want that for you?" Rae wished she'd come to that realization sooner rather than later.

"Your mom would be as proud of you today as I am, Rae," he said huskily.

"Thanks, Dad." She cleared the knot forming in her throat and continued. "Anyway, I'm going to stop at the diner and see Dee. After that I'm heading over to Gram's. Have you and Nora set a date yet?"

"We're thinking after Christmas. Maybe even New Year's Eve."

"Now that would be a way to start the New Year, wouldn't it? But that really doesn't give us much time to plan."

"I know. But I think Nora just wants a simple wedding. And. . .I just want to marry Nora."

"I'll be sure to call her a little later in the morning." Rae rummaged through the built-in desk in the kitchen for a pad of paper. Finding what she wanted, she stuffed everything into her purse. "The sooner we get started, the quicker this will all come together."

"Thank you, honey."

"You're welcome. I do want you to be happy, Dad."

"And I want the same for you."

"I know."

"I know there is someone out there for you, honey."

Only one person came to mind, and Rae tried to put him right back out of it. She sure hoped she didn't run into Luke today. She was still embarrassed about the night before. "Let's just get you married first, Dad."

"That's a deal."

Rae chuckled and kissed him on the cheek before heading out to her car. She left the house feeling better than she had in months. Now if she could just stay busy enough to keep thoughts of kissing Luke out of her mind, she *might* get through the holidays.

She was surprised to find that the thought of going home to Albuquerque held no appeal anymore. There was no doubt in her mind that she was over the breakup with Paul and that she could continue to work at Zia High School. She really liked Sweet Springs and the people here. But this town held another problem for her—in the form of one Luke Breland.

Dear Lord, please help me to put that kiss into perspective. Luke was feeling sorry for me and probably just trying to comfort me. I'm sure that's all it was. But I don't want his pity. And I wasn't comforting him. I responded, and I don't know how to act the next time I see him. Please help me to keep my distance from him for the next few days so that maybe I can get past this. . .growing feeling I have for him. Please help me, Lord. In Jesus' name, amen.

Rae's plan to stop at the diner changed quickly when she spotted Luke's pickup parked outside. She just couldn't face him right now. Her heart was already thudding against her ribs at just the prospect of running into him. She had to avoid that as long as she could, but it wasn't going to be possible forever. Not with her dad marrying his aunt. She was going to have to deal with it all sooner or later. Right now, she preferred later.

She passed by the front door and hoped Luke didn't decide to come out right at that moment. She turned left at the corner and headed for Gram's. Surely he wouldn't show up there this morning.

Gram welcomed her with open arms and led her back to the kitchen. "How are you this morning, dear?"

Rae was sure she was concerned about her reaction to her dad and Nora's announcement the night before, and she was glad she could reassure the older woman. "I'm fine, Gram. The Lord helped me put things into perspective, and Nora helped me see how much she loves Dad. I'm truly sorry my initial response wasn't appropriate."

"Oh, I don't think that many people noticed. I'm so glad you've accepted their engagement. They are very good for each other. Nora is a different person since she met Michael." Gram chuckled. "And we're all eternally grateful that the Lord brought him into her life."

Rae smiled. Even though she was positive Gram knew everything Nora had told her the night before, she didn't want to repeat any of Nora's confidences. "I think Dad is just as grateful. What I wanted to talk to you about—and I need to talk to Sara and Lydia, too—is that I'd like to give Nora a surprise wedding shower."

"Oh, she'd love that, Rae!" Gram walked over to the wall phone. "Pour yourself some coffee, and I'll give them both a call. We can have this planned by lunchtime!"

~

Luke took his time over his breakfast, hoping to run into Rae. At some point they were going to have to talk about that kiss. But after he'd been there for over an hour, he finally asked about her.

"I don't know where she is." Dee refilled his coffee cup. "I thought she would be in to help me put the finishing touches on the decorations this morning, but I haven't heard from her. What do you think of them so far?"

"They're great. What else could you possibly need to do?"

Dee grinned at him. "Actually, not much else. I do have something *you* can help me with, though."

"Oh, what's that?"

Dee went behind the counter and came back with thumbtacks and two sprigs of mistletoe. "I won't have to drag out a ladder if you'll put these up for me."

Luke grinned. He'd sure like to meet Rae under one of these sprigs. "Sure. Where do you want them?"

"How about one over the door and. . ." She looked around the diner and shrugged. "Where do else you think?"

Luke glanced around. "How about over the jukebox or above the cash register?"

Dee grinned at him and shook her head. "The cash register might be a tad too obvious, don't you think, Luke?"

He laughed. "You read me too well, Dee."

"I've seen the way you look at Rae. I'm just not sure she has."

"Me either." Luke sighed and took the mistletoe and tacks from Dee. "We'll go with over the jukebox."

Dee watched as he reached up and stuck the first clump in the ceiling over the jukebox and then one over the door. "That'll work. Thanks, Luke."

"You're welcome."

"What are you welcome for?" John asked as he came through the doorway.

Luke sat back down at his table and grinned at Dee. "I just did a favor for Dee, that's all."

"Oh, what was that?" John joined him at his table.

Luke pointed to the ceiling above the door his cousin had just come through.

"Oh, that should make for some interesting people watching," John said and chuckled.

"Sure should." Dee brought him his usual cup of coffee.

"Hi, Dee. The place looks real nice and Christmassy."

"Thanks. Rae helped me."

John blew on the hot liquid in his cup. "I just saw her pass by. I thought she might be coming here, but I guess not."

So much for his hope of running into Rae. Once again, he suspected she was avoiding him. Well, she couldn't steer clear of him forever. They were bound to run into each sooner or later. But, as far as he was concerned, sooner would certainly be better.

Gram was right. By lunchtime they had Nora's shower planned. It would be held at Michael's house. Sara and Lydia had brought Meggie over, and Rae was officially welcomed into the family.

"I can't tell you how happy we are about Nora and Michael," Lydia said. "We've all been praying this would happen."

"And I'm glad you are happy about it, too, Rae. . .and that you are going to be part of the family now," Sara added.

"Thank you. You've all made me feel so welcomed."

"When one marries into this family—be it Breland or Tanner—they and their family automatically become part of our family."

"I have another reason to love Nora, then—besides the fact that she loves Dad and he loves her. I've always wanted to be part of a large family."

Lydia laughed. "Your dream has come true, Rae. 'Cause this one is that. There are many you haven't even met yet. It may be larger than you wished for."

Rae shook her head. "No. I don't think that's possible."

Now they cleared the table of all shower plans and set it for lunch while Gram tossed a large salad together. Rae had called Nora earlier and issued the invitation from Gram that they all meet for lunch to start planning the wedding, just in case she came by early and saw all the cars in the drive and wondered what was going on.

But there really wasn't much chance of that, Sara told her. Nora loved keeping to a schedule, and she rarely was late for anything. Nor did she like others being late. It appeared Sara was right when, at twelve o'clock sharp, they heard the front door open.

"I'm here! I picked up the most wonderful crusty rolls to go with the salad—" Nora had barely cleared the door before she was enveloped in congratulatory hugs.

"I am so happy for you, Nora," Lydia said. "You know we've been hoping this would happen!"

"So have I!" Nora exclaimed and laughed. She hugged Rae and smiled. "I'm so glad I'm going to have you all to help me plan this wedding!"

"Well, let's have lunch and then we'll get started," Gram suggested.

After they'd all taken a seat, they joined hands and Sara said the blessing, thanking the Lord for their many blessings, and especially for bringing Michael into Nora's life. Nora asked what they thought about New Year's Eve for the wedding. They all agreed that it would be perfect.

"We want to have it before Rae goes home. It would be hard to go back and forth every week for dress fittings and everything," Nora said.

"Dress fittings?"

"Why, yes. I'd like Lydia to be my matron of honor, if she'll accept."

"You know I will." Lydia grinned from across the table.

"And I'd like you and Sara to be bridesmaids, if you would, Rae."

"I'd be honored." Rae smiled at her stepmother-to-be. After the way she'd acted, she really didn't deserve the honor Nora was bestowing on her.

"So would I. Oh, this is going to be so much fun!"

"Ellie, I hope you'll serve as mother of the bride, since my mother is no longer with us."

"You don't even have to ask, Nora."

"Thank you. Anyway, we don't want anything elaborate, hopefully making it easier to do while Rae is here."

"Rae, you know you really ought to think about moving here permanently," Sara said. "There's a job opening for a history teacher at the high school."

"Really?"

"Uh-huh. The present teacher's husband has been transferred, and they need someone fairly soon."

"Oh, Rae!" Nora exclaimed. "Do you know how happy that would make your dad? What a wonderful wedding present it would be!"

"You think so?"

"Of course it would!" Lydia agreed.

"And what better way to get to know your big, new family than to live in the same town?"

Rae chuckled and shook her head. "I don't know, Gram. I always thought I was a city girl. Never thought I'd live in a little town like Sweet Springs."

"Oh, you'd love it here. You have a built-in family, a wonderful church family, and Meggie can always use another aunt. Wouldn't hurt to check it out," Sara said, forking a piece of lettuce off of her plate.

"I. . ." What could she say? If it weren't for the fact that Luke lived here, she'd apply in a minute. And what was worse? To move back to Albuquerque, to an empty house and friends who hadn't even called to see how she was? At least here she would have people who cared. And if it got hard to be around Luke, the Lord would help her with that. Here she would have the family she'd always dreamed of having. "I'll think about it. Maybe I will apply."

"Wouldn't hurt," Gram added. "You could stay with me and try it for the next semester, until you made up your mind—"

"Ellie, she can stay with us," said Nora. "I know Michael would be pleased."

Rae shook her head. "No, I don't think so. I know Dad loves me, Nora, and you are sweet to suggest it, but the last thing newlyweds need is an adult child living with them!"

"Gram's idea is a good one, though," Sara said. "And I think the school board would be elated to have someone with your experience take the job. They called me only because they know me; I don't have any high school teaching experience."

The more Rae thought about it, the more the idea appealed to her. There was only one problem as far as she could see, and his name was Luke Breland. She hadn't been able to get him out of her mind since she'd entered the kitchen; how could she possibly ignore thoughts of him if they were living in the same town?

On Tuesday evening Luke found out that Rae had been one or two steps ahead of him the day before when he stopped by and begged a meal from Sara and Jake, hoping to find out if Rae had left town.

Sara was full of news about the plans they'd made to give Aunt Nora a surprise shower. "It was Rae's idea. I'm so glad she's taking Nora and Michael's engagement well."

That comment only served to remind Luke of the night they'd announced it and the kiss he and Rae had shared in Gram's kitchen. As if he needed reminding. It was about all he'd thought of the past few days. And evidently, from the way she seemed to be trying to avoid running into him, he'd blown his chances with her because of it. At least she hadn't left town.

"Why so glum, little brother?" Jake asked when even Meggie's stunts couldn't make him laugh. The best she could get from her uncle Luke was a smile.

"Guess it's just the gloomy winter weather."

"Luke, it's been sunny all day," Sara said as she cleared the table and brought a freshly baked apple pie to the table.

"Oh. Well, maybe it's just the time of year. You know how some people get depressed around Christmastime."

"You *love* Christmas," Jake said. "You love everything about it—especially buying us all things you know we'll have to stand in line to take back."

"Maybe I'm coming down with something," Luke said. He could have bitten his tongue when Jake leaned back in his chair and studied him for a few minutes. His brother could read him well.

"Maybe you're *lovesick*."

Sara whirled around from the cabinet where she'd been getting dessert plates and forks. "Luke?"

She came back to the table and sat down across from him. "Who?"

"Sara. You know who." Jake began to chuckle.

She clasped her hand briefly over her mouth. "Rae? Oh, Luke, that's wonderful!"

"I did not say I was lovesick. That came from your husband."

Sara cut into the pie and served them each a piece. "So you aren't attracted to Rae?"

Luke let out a deep breath and shook his head. Family. He'd said enough already. He wasn't saying any more. He took a bite of pie and watched Jake grin and wink at his wife.

He passed Nora's on the way home, wondering if he'd ever move in. He felt lonely enough in his small ranch house. He wasn't sure he could handle rambling around in one more than twice the size of his.

Wednesday morning, he went into town and found he'd missed Rae at the diner by only minutes. Dee told him that she and Nora and Sara had taken off for Roswell on the hunt for dresses for the wedding.

Frustrated that he hadn't seen Rae since Sunday night, Luke went home and spent the afternoon on horseback. It was a beautiful, sunny day, and he always found solace and peace on the wide-open range. But he didn't find it today. He didn't know what to do about his feelings for Rae, and so he rode leisurely, seeking guidance from the Lord.

Father, I don't know what to do. I'm attracted to Rae, city girl that she is. And I don't know if I should pursue her or leave her alone. It appears that's what she wants me to do, yet I can't forget the way she responded to my kiss. Please, Father, let me know if she's the one You've brought me, or if I need to keep my distance. If she is my "stranger," please help me to know. It's in Jesus' name I ask this, amen.

Luke rode for most of the afternoon before heading back to his ranch. He brushed down his horse, feeling more at peace than he had in days—although he still didn't know what to do about Rae. He'd know. . .in the Lord's time.

He took a shower and made it to the diner for supper. Rae wasn't there, but then he didn't expect her to be. That was how his week was going. She probably wouldn't even be at church tonight.

At church, it seemed everyone was talking about Nora and Michael's announcement. He was happy for them. He couldn't help wondering who in his family would marry next. It seemed even Will and Gram would be exchanging vows before he got around to it.

John walked up behind him. "All this wedding talk. Do you ever feel like we're the last two bachelors in town?"

Luke laughed. "We certainly are in *this* family, aren't we?"

But as he walked into the sanctuary, it suddenly became crystal clear to him that he wanted his bachelor status to change—and with whom he wanted to make that change. Rae was sitting beside Aunt Nora. Just the sight of her had his stomach doing a somersault and his heartbeat hammering in his ears. Oh, yeah, Jake was right. He was about as lovesick as a cowboy could get.

Chapter 13

Luke took a seat a few pews behind Rae and tried to concentrate on the Bible class that was just beginning. His life sure had been simpler before Rae came into town, but it hadn't been near as exciting. He felt more alive than he had in a long, long time. And it all was due to the blue-eyed, dark-haired woman sitting right in the middle of his family. She seemed happier than he'd ever seen her, and he was grateful that she and Nora had come to an understanding.

After the closing prayer, Luke tried to get to Rae, but with all the people coming up to congratulate Michael and Nora on their engagement, she'd gone in the other direction. He thought about taking a shortcut through the pews to get to her, but she seemed a woman on a mission as he watched her stop to talk to one lady after another. It probably had something to do with that wedding shower Sara said she was planning.

Not one to give up, he backtracked to the fellowship hall. She'd have to come through there to leave. He mingled and talked to first one person and then another, keeping his eye on Rae's progress through the window that looked into the sanctuary.

"Want to go get a cup of coffee at the diner?" John asked.

"Sure," Luke said. "Just give me a minute, and I'll see if Rae wants to go, too." But when he peered through the window once more, he couldn't find her. He'd only taken his gaze off her for a minute, and she couldn't have left without him seeing her. Letting out a frustrated breath, he headed back into the sanctuary through the other door and almost plowed right into the woman Rae was whispering to.

He reached out to steady Harriet Johnson to keep her from falling. "Oh, I'm so sorry, Mrs. Johnson. I wasn't watching where I was going."

"It's all right, Luke. You almost tripped me once before, when you were a child. We all know how clumsy you used to be. Guess you haven't completely outgrown it." With that she straightened the handbag she had slung over her shoulder, winked at Rae, and lumbered through the doors.

Luke glanced down at Rae and saw the sparkle in her eyes. He could tell she was trying to hold back a giggle. He chuckled. "Go ahead and laugh. She's right. That's what happens when people know you from the time you were born. They don't forget a thing. Nor do they let you."

Rae released the giggle and shook her head. "If you could just have seen the expression on your face. . ."

Luke didn't care how silly he might have looked. He was just glad she was talking to him. "John and I are going to the diner for coffee. Want to come?"

The smile disappeared. "Oh, thanks, but I'm taking Gram home so we can finish up some plans."

"Okay," Luke said. "How about going to a movie with John and me tomorrow night?"

"I'm sorry, Luke." Rae shook her head. "We're giving Nora a surprise shower this week. It's short notice but with the wedding to plan and Christmas coming. . . Maybe Dad would like to go, though. The shower is at his house, and he probably needs a place to hang out."

Luke didn't think she was sorry. He thought she was relieved. But here and now wasn't the time to get into it. "We'll ask him and see if he wants to go."

"Thanks. Guess I'd better get going." Rae waved and hurried over to Gram.

Luke sighed, forced himself to smile, and waved at his grandmother. He felt a tap on his shoulder and turned to find John.

"Rae has other plans?"

"Yeah, she's busy with Gram tonight. Let's go." He'd spend the evening watching John and Dee try to ignore how they felt about each other. John was right. Like it or not, it seemed they were going to remain the last two bachelors in the family.

Rae didn't know whether she was relieved or disappointed that she couldn't go to the movies with Luke, but it was probably for the best, anyway. She wasn't sure she could hide the fact that he set her pulse racing each time she saw him. And she was afraid that if she spent too much time around him—although that was exactly what she wanted to do—he'd be able to tell that she was falling in love with him. That is, if her response to his kiss hadn't already done that.

Right now, she was just glad she had plenty to do. Staying busy with shower, wedding, and Christmas plans wouldn't keep thoughts of Luke out of her mind, but it would give her an excuse to get some distance when she felt she was close to exposing how she felt about him.

But now, as she and Sara put out the cake and floral arrangement on the dining room table in preparation for Nora's surprise shower, she found herself wondering where he was and what he was doing.

"What are all the men doing tonight? Dad said he was going over to your house after he gets Nora here, but Luke mentioned asking him to go to a movie."

"Luke is out of town. He and Uncle Ben made a spur-of-the-moment trip to a livestock sale in Las Cruces. But John was going to join Grandpa and Michael over at my house and hang out with Jake. I baked a cake and made sure they had plenty of microwave popcorn and snacks on hand. They'll have a good time."

"I'm sure they will," Rae said, bringing dishes of nuts and mints to the table.

She was a little disconcerted to find out Luke had left town and she didn't know it. Then she chided herself—she'd been going in the other direction every time she saw him lately. Why should he tell her something like that?

The doorbell rang, and she opened the door for the arrival of Gram, Lydia, and Dee. They'd parked down the street, as everyone had agreed to do, and walked up to Dad's house. Before long, all the guests had arrived and were staking out a spot to hide for when Dad brought Nora to the door.

Rae turned out all the lights, except for the one in the kitchen they left on all the time. They tried to say quiet, giggling softly at Gram's occasional reminders to be quieter.

Rae heard her dad fumble his key in the lock, as they'd planned for him to do, and everyone waited for the door to open. He stood aside so that Nora could enter.

"Surprise!" everyone shouted in unison as she walked into the entryway.

"Oh!" Nora laughed and whirled around to husband-to-be. "You were in on this, weren't you?"

"Of course I was. Rae knows I can keep a secret." He looked around at all the smiling women and grinned. "But I'm going to let her take over now. Have fun, everyone."

Nora kissed him before he slipped out the door. She was drawn into the great room where she was placed in the seat of honor. She grinned at Rae and Sara. "I can't believe you had time to put this together as busy as I've been keeping you!"

"They are younger than we are, Nora," Lydia said laughingly.

The next few hours passed quickly while Nora opened beautifully wrapped packages and colorful bags. There were monogramed bath towels and linens, picture frames, scented candles, and crystal candleholders.

Lydia and Gram gave her a beautiful handmade afghan; Sara gave her two mugs, one with *Nana* engraved on it for her and the other with *Papa* for Rae's father.

"Oh, how adorable!"

"I hope Michael realizes that when he marries you, he automatically becomes Meggie and the new baby's adopted grandpa," Sara said.

Nora chuckled. "Oh, yes, he does."

Dee gave her gift certificates for free meals at the diner, amid much laughter. Most of them were fully aware that cooking wasn't Nora's favorite thing.

But the present Rae waited anxiously for Nora to open was the one from her. She hoped it would show that she truly had come to care about her future stepmother.

Nora unwrapped the present, smiling up at Rae as she did. Nora gasped when she opened the box to find a beautiful leather Bible, with *Nora Wellington* engraved on the front in gold letters.

Inside, Rae had written, *To Nora, who has made my dad a very happy man. My prayer is for God to bless your marriage and for you to have many happy years together. I'm honored to have you as my stepmother. Love, Rae*

"Oh, Rae." Nora held the Bible to her heart and looked up at Rae with tears in her eyes. "Thank you. I can't tell you how happy. . ."

Rae fought her own tears and bent down to embrace her. "You're welcome. I mean every word."

There were a few more presents to open, and then the women enjoyed the refreshments. By the end of the evening, Rae didn't just feel as though she was part of a new, big family; she felt she was part of the community.

The rest of the week sped by as she helped Nora pick out invitations, flowers, and a cake. The wedding would be at church, but the reception was going to be held at Gram's. It's what Gram wanted, and Sara, Lydia, and Rae all promised to help.

There seemed to be so much going on, and so many festivities planned for the month, Rae hardly knew what day it was. But she did know she missed seeing Luke. His absence hadn't done a thing to dispel the memory of their kiss. Rae's pulse still raced each time she thought about it. And she thought about it often.

On Saturday night, Rae talked her dad and Nora into a quiet evening at home to put up his Christmas tree. With the wedding at the end of the month, Nora had decided against putting up one at her house, but she obviously enjoyed helping decorate the house she'd be living in by the New Year.

They ordered pizza and spent several hours just getting the tree up and decorated, singing along with Christmas carols on a CD. The tree was enormous and almost reached the ceiling, and once all the lights were on it, the garland added, and the ornaments put on, it lit up the whole room.

When her dad took Nora home, Rae curled up in the big armchair facing the tree to gaze at the lights that glittered and shined, bouncing off the ornaments and garland. She made herself some hot chocolate and listened to Christmas music, wondering what it would be like to share the evening with Luke. She'd been trying not to think of him, but it was a losing battle. She'd thought of little else the past few days.

It was there that her dad found her when he got home. "You always have loved sitting in a darkened room with only the Christmas lights on. It's good to know you haven't outgrown it."

She smiled at him as he sat down in his chair. "I don't think I ever will. I do love the lights. It would be like Christmas every day if we all let our light shine in the world the way we are meant to, wouldn't it?"

Dad nodded. "It would. I know you've made the lights shine brighter for my and Nora's Christmas, Rae."

"Took me long enough to come around, didn't it?"

"It doesn't matter how long it took; it happened. Now, tell me. What do you want for Christmas, honey?"

"Just to see you and Nora happy, Dad."

"Well, you'll get that. But what else?"

What else? How about a life here in Sweet Springs, with a long, tall cowboy named Luke? She couldn't tell her dad that—she couldn't tell anyone that. But she had to be honest with herself. She was in love with Luke Breland, and a life with him was what she wanted.

Rae didn't hold out much hope that he could return her feelings. He'd seen her selfishness up close in his grandmother's kitchen, and all she'd done before that was complain and put down the land and the town he loved. How could he possibly care about her? How was she going to hide her feelings from him?

Luke and Uncle Ben didn't get back into town until late Saturday night. It'd been a good trip as far as business was concerned. But it'd been a complete failure as far as getting Rae Wellington out of his mind, and that was the primary reason he'd suggested it.

He barely made it to church on time the next day, and when he saw Rae laughing and talking to Aunt Nora right before the worship service started, he was struck by how much she seemed to have changed since his first meeting with her. She'd gone from resenting his aunt to looking forward to being her stepdaughter. She seemed completely at home here, and happy, as she talked with one of the elders of the church and Richard Shelby, the superintendent of schools.

When he watched Meggie crawl from Sara's to Nora's lap, then across to Rae, Luke couldn't deny it any longer—the city girl had his heart in her hands, and he just prayed she wouldn't crush it.

Sometime in the coming week, he was going to have to find her and talk to her. It was time they cleared the air. He had to find out where they stood. Rae had responded to his kiss. He hadn't imagined it. And he couldn't forget it.

But finding a way to be alone with her so that they could talk remained frustrating at best. That afternoon, another shower for Nora was being given by some of the civic groups she volunteered for. Naturally, Rae was invited, too.

At Gram's supper that night, Rae seemed to be avoiding the kitchen by staying in the dining room and talking to everyone except him. Tired of fighting what seemed to be a losing battle to get her alone and fatigued from his trip, Luke left early. Maybe Rae wasn't meant for him, and if that was the case, he just prayed the Lord would let him know soon so he could get off of the emotional seesaw he seemed to be stuck on.

After making himself concentrate on business until nearly noon the next day, Luke headed into town on the pretense of meeting John for lunch. He knew the real reason he'd accepted the invitation was with the hope of running into

Rae somewhere along the way. But, he'd promised himself that he would leave all of that in the Lord's hands. Only He knew where she'd be today.

Luke opened the door to go in and collided with a small woman on her way out.

"Oh, I'm sorry; are you all right?" he asked, reaching out to steady her. He gazed down at the woman whose shoulders he held, and his heart collided with his chest bone. After hunting for Rae all over town for days, here she was. At last.

"I'm fine." She sounded a little breathless. "How about you?"

"I'm good." *Now that I've found you, better than good.* Luke just stood there staring at her, blocking the door until he heard Dee clear her throat. He glanced at his friend and realized she was looking at the mistletoe above Rae's head. He grinned and tightened his hold on Rae's arm. Ducking his head quickly before she had a chance to pull away, he planted a quick kiss on her soft lips, but not so quick that she didn't have time to respond. His heart seemed to soar when she did.

Luke heard several handclaps and chuckles in the background. He raised his head.

"I. . .ah. . .what?" Rae seemed a little confused.

"Merry Christmas," Luke whispered, surprised at the huskiness in his voice.

"Look above your head," one of Dee's regulars yelled out amid more laughter.

"Oh." Rae glanced up, and color flooded her cheeks as she glanced back at him. "Merry Christmas."

Her lips turned up in a smile that didn't quite reach her eyes, and Luke had a feeling he'd messed up. Again. She'd responded; he was certain she had. Did she think he'd only kissed her because they were under the mistletoe? "Rae, we need to talk. Do you have time for a cup of coffee?"

She shook her head. "I don't have time right now."

"Where are you going in such a hurry?" he asked, guiding Rae out of the way so that one of Dee's customers could enter the diner.

"I'm on my way to pick up Nora's invitations. With the wedding right after Christmas, we really need to get them addressed and mailed out as soon as possible." She seemed to be looking anywhere but at him as she continued. "The printer called her this morning, and Nora asked me to pick them up. She and Lydia are going to Roswell to try on more dresses. Sara and I found ours, but they're still shopping."

"Do you need a ride?" Maybe they could talk if he could just get her to himself.

Rae shook her head. "No, thanks. My car is down by the printer's, and I'd better be getting down there. Sara is meeting me at Gram's so we can get started addressing them. See you later."

"Later." Luke sighed as she hurried out the door. He sat down at a table Dee was just cleaning off and shook his head.

"Sorry, Luke. I thought I was helping your cause," Dee said.

He shook his head and sighed. "I don't think anything is going to help my cause. I can't get her to stand still long enough to even talk to me about anything except that wedding. Certainly not about how I feel about her."

"And how do you feel?"

Luke ran his hand over his face. Had he really given himself away like that? He shrugged. "It doesn't matter. She's not interested in finding out."

"I wouldn't be quite so quick to jump to that conclusion, Luke. She's just very busy helping with the wedding plans. She wants to show Nora and Michael that she's happy for them. Once the wedding is over with, she won't be so busy."

"And she'll go back to Albuquerque."

"Luke. . ." Dee seemed about to say something else, but she shook her head before continuing. "Even if she goes back to Albuquerque, she'll be coming to visit her dad. It's not like you won't see her anymore. And Albuquerque isn't *that* far away. I didn't think you were one to give up so easily, cowboy."

Luke felt a glimmer of hope start to grow within him. Dee was right. Rae would be back. It *wasn't* as if he'd never see again. And it wasn't as if he hadn't felt her lips linger on his—if only for a moment—when he kissed her under the mistletoe.

There was no doubt in his mind how he felt about her. And until she told him to get lost, there *was* hope. He inclined his head and grinned at Dee. "You are right. I don't give up easily. I certainly shouldn't give up until I find out where I stand."

"Now that's the Luke I know and love," Dee said as John walked up behind her.

"Am I interrupting something here?" John asked, his left eyebrow arching almost into his hairline.

Luke chuckled at his cousin's reaction to Dee's statement but sought to put his mind at ease. "Dee's giving advice to the lovelorn."

"Ahh," John said, his eyebrow easing back to its normal position. "And you are the lovelorn one, I presume?"

Luke glanced at Dee, then back to John. Jake and Sara were aware of how he felt—now Dee. Luke grinned at his cousin. Why not tell him, too? Maybe it was time to enlist the help of his family and friends. It sure couldn't hurt.

"Why deny it? It seems everyone knows how I feel about Rae—except her."

"Well, when are you going to let her know?" John sat down across from him.

"He's having a hard time getting her alone long enough," Dee explained.

"Oh. Well, you know, if I remember right, the family had to help Jake along in his romance with Sara. You know we'd all be glad to help you out, too."

"Well, I'm not family," Dee said, "but I'll certainly do my part."

Chapter 14

Rae fought tears all the way to the printer's. When she'd gone into the diner to tell Dee what she'd done, she'd been very excited. After being approached by the superintendent of schools at church the day before—and much prayer—she'd applied for the teaching job Sara told her about. She had a feeling she just might get it. Teasing that it might just be her wedding present for her dad, as Sara had suggested, she'd asked Dee not to say anything about it just in case she didn't get the job.

Then she'd run into Luke. . .and he'd kissed her right there in Dee's diner. When her lips met his, she knew she'd made the right decision. But the elation Rae felt at Luke's kiss quickly deflated when she realized that he'd kissed her because of the mistletoe.

Now, as she picked up the invitations and headed back to her car, she told herself she had to face the truth. She really wanted the job and to live in this town. Most of all, she wanted Luke to care about her. She was pretty sure she could have the first two. But the third, and the one she wanted with all her heart, was totally out of her control. She had to give it over to the Lord. Only He knew the outcome, and He was in control.

Dear Lord, please help me here. I love Luke, but I don't know how he feels about me. I would love for us to have a life together, but after the way I've treated his aunt, he probably thinks I'm the most spoiled, selfish woman he knows. He told me that I need to grow up, and he was right. Mostly, I need to grow as Your child, Lord. Please help me to do that and to accept Your will in my life, no matter what it is. In Jesus' name, amen.

By the time Rae got to Gram's with the invitations, she was at peace for the moment and anxious to share her news about the job. They were waiting for her in the kitchen.

Rae set the box of invitations on the table and went to pour herself a cup of coffee from Gram's always-full pot, marveling at how comfortable she felt in this house and with these women. If she and Luke weren't meant to be, it wasn't going to matter if she lived in Albuquerque or here. Running back to the city wouldn't get them out of each other's lives. She might have to live with heartache again, but at least here she'd have a family and a church family to draw strength from. And most importantly, God would help her handle it all. Yes, He would.

She twisted away from the cabinet and grinned at the two women at the table.

Sara was watching her closely. "What's up, Rae? You look like you are about to burst."

Rae grinned. "I am. I've waited all morning to get over here and tell you two my news."

"And what news is that, dear?" Gram asked, setting a plate of cookies on the table.

"I found a wedding present for Dad."

"Oh? What did you get him?" Sara took a seat at the table and began to unpack the invitations.

"Well, I haven't signed the contract yet, but I'm hoping that I will very soon."

"Okay, Rae, I'm curious now! What have you found?"

"Just what you suggested, Sara. A move here—if I get that teaching job I applied for."

Gram chuckled and hugged her. "I'm so glad, Rae. It will be wonderful to have you around all the time!"

"You did it! Oh, how wonderful!" Sara laughed happily and jumped up to give her a squeeze as soon as Gram let her go. "Michael and Nora are going to be thrilled!"

"I certainly hope so. Just don't say anything to them okay? I may not get the job, but I want to surprise them, if I do."

"Mum's the word," Gram said. "Remember, you are welcome to stay with me until you find a place of your own."

"Thank you, Gram. That is so generous of you!"

"I'll be glad to have you here. It's a big house for one person."

"Why don't you and Grandpa just get married, Gram?" Sara asked. "Then neither of you would have to be alone."

She chuckled. "Well, you never know. We might just do that one of these days."

Sara laughed and shook her head. "I'll believe it when I see it."

They spent the next several hours addressing Nora's invitations and talking about the reception menu, the wedding, and anything else that came to mind. It was wonderful to sit around the table and talk, feeling that she was part of this family.

When she answered her cell phone, she expected it to be Nora checking to see if she'd picked up the invitations. Rae glanced at the phone's screen and gave Sara and Gram a nervous grin.

"Hello, this is Rae."

"Hello, Rae. This is Richard Shelby. I've just had a meeting with the board. We would like to offer you a contract if you are still interested in teaching history for us."

It was time to make a decision. "Oh, yes, Mr. Shelby, I do want the job."

"Could you be ready to start by January fifteenth?"

"Yes, I can."

She watched Sara and Gram hug each other while she concluded the conversation, thanking the superintendent and agreeing to come in later in the week to sign the contract. She'd barely ended the call when they all shared a three-way embrace.

"Now, remember, don't tell anyone. I'll tell Dad and Nora at Christmas—or right before their wedding. I'm just not sure exactly when."

"We won't tell anyone," Sara assured her, sitting back down at the table. "But this is such wonderful news—it won't be easy keeping it quiet!"

"I know. I'll probably be the one to give it away!" Rae laughed as she joined Sara and Gram at the table.

"When will you go back to pick up your things?" Gram asked.

"I don't start teaching until the fifteenth. . .so I'll probably go back right after the wedding." She grinned at the two women sitting across from her. "I do love teaching. . . . I can't wait to get back to it!"

Standing right outside the kitchen door, Luke overheard Rae say she'd probably go back right after the wedding, and his heart seemed to dive right down to the pit of his stomach. He'd been hoping she was beginning to like Sweet Springs better and that she would decide to stay. Evidently she was still determined to go back to home. He tried to hide his disappointment as he pushed the door open and stepped into the kitchen.

"Hi, ladies! Need any help?"

Sara jumped when she saw Luke standing in the doorway.

"Luke! You scared us," Gram said, chuckling and putting her hand to her chest.

"I called out, but I guess you didn't hear me." Admittedly, he hadn't called out very loud. He was half afraid Rae would run out the back door before he could get to the kitchen, even though she'd told him where she'd be. But what did it matter now? She planned on going back to Albuquerque anyway.

No. He wasn't going to think negatively. She might well leave after Christmas, but she'd be back. There was hope. And he had family to help his cause. He just might have to wait for a more opportune time to let her know how he felt and find out if she might feel the same way. For now, with all this wedding stuff going on, he figured if he ever hoped to get to talk to her, he might as well jump in and help out.

"Come on in, Luke. We won't turn down free help," Sara said.

"What do you need me to do?" He poured himself a cup of coffee and took a seat at the table.

"Here you go." Gram pushed a pile of addressed envelopes with their invitations toward him. "Just put these in the envelopes and seal them."

"Sounds easy enough." Luke took an invitation and slid it into the envelope. But when he licked the flap, the face he made had everyone laughing. He shuddered. "Eeew! Yuck! I see why you gave me this job! Gram, do you have something else I can moisten these with?"

"Oh, I'm sorry, Luke. Wait just a minute." She put a small sponge in a saucer with a little water, then set it on the table in front of Luke. "Try this."

"After I get this awful taste out of my mouth," Luke said, going to the sink for a drink of water. He drained the glass and turned around to find Rae watching him, a half smile on her face. His heart jumped in his chest. Was she thinking about the kiss they'd shared that morning? Or the one they'd shared here? His grandmother's kitchen was fast becoming his favorite room in her house. Luke smiled and couldn't resist winking at her.

Rae quickly ducked her head, but not before he saw the delicate color creeping up her neck. His heart pounded and he prayed silently. *Dear Lord, please let me be reading Rae right. I know she responds to my kisses. I think she cares, or at least could care about me. Help me to know for sure.*

Luke had to tear his gaze away from Rae, and when he did, it was to see Sara and Gram glancing from Rae to him, trying to hide their amusement. He'd been around these two long enough to know they read him very well. He hoped they didn't comment on what it was they'd decided he was thinking. He let out a sigh of relief when neither said anything and rejoined them at the table where he stuffed, sealed, and stamped envelopes for the next half hour.

He tried to act surprised when Dee called to see if Rae could come help her out at the diner for a few hours. "I thought her new waitress was working out."

"She had to leave early today, and Jen is going to be late for some reason," Rae said, stacking the envelopes she'd addressed with the others. "There aren't too many left to do, and Nora and Lydia should be here any minute to help finish up."

She grabbed her purse and hugged both Sara and Gram. "I'll talk you later. Bye, Luke."

He watched her leave before giving his attention to his grandmother and Sara.

"Okay, what's up, Luke?" Sara asked. "We know you didn't come here just to help out."

"Well. . .I have something to ask you, but if Aunt Nora and Aunt Lydia are due here, I'll wait until I have you all in one place."

"Now you really have our curiosity piqued." Gram got up to refill their coffee cups. "Wouldn't have anything to do with Rae, would it?"

"It might."

But before he had a chance to say more, Nora and Lydia arrived; they also seemed surprised to find him there in the middle of the afternoon.

"Why, Luke, I know you are happy for me, but I really didn't expect you to pitch in and help like this," Nora said, giving him a hug.

"Before you get too mushy about it, wait. I think we'd better find out what his motive is," Sara said.

"Oh?" Lydia asked.

Luke gave them all what he hoped was his most persuasive smile. "I need to ask you all a favor."

Nora and Lydia took a seat at the table. The four women gave him their undivided attention. It was time to find out if the ladies in his life were going to help him win over the woman he loved.

~

With Christmas fast approaching and the wedding the week after, Rae couldn't remember ever being busier. It was only a few days until Christmas, and she was running errands for Nora, helping her dad move things around to make room for the items Nora planned to move in—not to mention trying to get some Christmas shopping done.

Rae had signed the contract with the school board and let Zia High School know she wouldn't be coming back. She couldn't wait until the family gathering at Gram's to tell her dad and Nora. It was too hard to keep it quiet, and she didn't want to wait until the wedding. Besides, she was having second thoughts, and she needed her dad's encouragement.

She wondered what Luke would say when he found out she was going to move here. Would it even matter to him? She prayed that she wouldn't have to spend the rest of her life doing what she'd been doing for the past few weeks—trying to avoid being around him so he didn't guess how she felt about him.

Having admitted to herself that she was in love with him, she felt anyone who saw them together would know, and until she thought she could hide the effect he had on her—the shaky hands, the telltale blushing—she'd avoid him. So far, with all the errands and shopping she had to do, it hadn't been too hard.

She'd helped Dee out several afternoons so she could get some shopping done. And she'd thoroughly enjoyed the Christmas festivities in the small town. The downtown area had its Christmas decorations judging, and Rae was almost as thrilled as Dee when the diner won first place. The church held its annual Christmas caroling party for young families and children, and she helped with the younger children, including Meggie. The toddler had taken quite a liking to Rae, and the feeling was mutual.

Sara asked her over for dinner one evening, but Rae had to ask for a rain check because she and her dad were going to Roswell to do some Christmas shopping.

On the weekend before Christmas, the diner was swamped with shoppers, and Dee asked her to help out for a few hours. She'd only been there for a half hour when a customer knocked a glass off his table, and in picking it up, Rae accidentally cut herself. Charlie was going off duty, so he rushed her to the emergency room.

A few stitches and a half hour later, she was on her way home with her dad. Groggy from the pain medicine they'd given her, she thought about Nora's family gathering for the next night at Gram's and was glad she'd spent the last few nights baking the cookies and making the candy she'd promised to take. She just hoped she'd have the bandage off before the wedding—or at the very least that the bouquet she'd be carrying would hide it.

Luke was more frustrated than ever. His family had agreed to help him find an opportunity to talk to Rae alone, but nothing was working out quite the way they'd planned.

Tonight seemed be the final straw. Dee was trying to do her part by asking Rae to help her out in the diner so that Luke could catch her there. But before he arrived, Rae had cut herself on a broken glass. Dee told him Charlie had taken her to the emergency room, and she'd called Michael to let him know. But by the time Luke got to the hospital, Rae had been released and sent home with Michael. When he'd called to see how she was, Michael told him she was sleeping.

Giving up for the night and driving home, he let out a frustrated sigh. It seemed he was just going to have to cool his heels and wait on the Lord to provide him an opportunity to talk to Rae.

By the next night, when the family gathered at Gram's for supper and to decorate the fresh-cut tree she always insisted on, Luke had convinced himself that either Rae wouldn't feel like coming or she'd have some last-minute thing to do.

But when she and Michael showed up, he prayed that somehow—with all his family here—surely he would find out if there was a chance she could ever return his feelings.

While Will and Jake set the tree up, the rest of the family went through boxes of favorite decorations. It seemed everyone had a special one they remembered from years past. Once the lights were in place, everyone helped hang the ornaments. Then Gram handed each one a box of old-fashioned tinsel to put on the finishing touch.

That always took longer than anything else, because Gram insisted they do it one strand at a time. But they'd only been draping the long, silver strands on the tree for a few minutes before Nora said, "Oh, no!"

"What is it? What's wrong?" Michael asked.

"I just remembered the ornaments I made for you and Rae to put on Ellie's tree. How could I have forgotten to bring them?"

"Well, it's not like you haven't had anything on your mind, dear," Gram said. "With all the wedding planning and everything—"

"Don't worry about it, Nora. We can put them on later," Michael assured her.

"No, they need to be put on tonight. Luke, would you be a dear and go get them for me?"

"Now?" Luke was trying to maneuver himself over to stand beside Rae. The last thing he wanted to do was go out to his aunt's ranch. This was the closest he'd been to Rae in days. He frowned at Nora with a refusal on the tip of his tongue—and saw her slight nod in Rae's direction.

"Rae, would you ride with him, please? I wrapped them in that paper you helped me pick out the other day. You'll know which ones they are."

Thank you, Aunt Nora! Luke held his breath waiting for Rae to answer.

"Oh, well. . ." Rae bit her bottom lip and glanced at Luke.

"Come on. It won't take long. By the time we get back, maybe they'll have all the tinsel on."

"Okay, I'll go." Rae chuckled. "I'm not real good with tinsel. I usually end up throwing it on. Just let me get my jacket."

Luke helped her slip it on over her bandaged hand, and they hurried to his truck. He helped her get in and latch her seat belt, then hurried around to jump in and switch on the heater. Now that he had her alone, he didn't know quite what to say. They'd gone several miles in silence before either of them spoke.

"How is your hand feeling? I called last night after I heard about your accident, but Michael told me you were sleeping."

Rae rubbed her bandaged hand. "Dad told me you called. Thanks for being concerned. It doesn't hurt too much today. It was a clean cut."

"That's good. Will you have the stitches out for the wedding?"

"I certainly hope so."

Luke pulled into his aunt's driveway, aggravated at himself for not asking what he really wanted to know: Could Rae ever care for him? They hurried up to the door, and Luke unlocked it with his key. For as long as he could remember, each member of the family had keys to each other's homes. Now as he held the door open for Rae to enter, he wondered again if he could move into this house and live in it by himself.

Rae walked into the kitchen and turned to him. "This is such a nice home. I love it. Will Nora sell it now that she's marrying Dad?"

Seeing her here in the kitchen that would soon be his, Luke realized he didn't want to live in this house unless it was with Rae. He shrugged. "It's part of the family property. She and Uncle Ben have told me it's mine now. But I don't know. It's awfully big for one person."

"Nora lives here and she's just one person, but it does sort of call out for a family, doesn't it? Maybe one day you. . ." Rae cut her sentence short, leaving Luke wondering what she'd been about to say.

She walked over to the kitchen table that held a small pile of presents Nora had wrapped, and she picked out two small ones. "Got them. Guess we'd better be getting back. They are probably waiting supper for us."

She headed out the back door, and Luke wondered what made him think he'd find out how she felt about him once they *were* alone. Now that he finally had her to himself, he didn't know how to even begin. Maybe it was because he wasn't sure he would like her answer. They were halfway back to his grandmother's before he finally asked the one question that was most important to him at the moment. "I. . .guess you'll be going back to Albuquerque after the wedding?"

"Ah. . .yes. Most probably the day after."

Luke's heart twisted in his chest. It was what he expected to hear but had hoped, with all his heart, not to. He was more than disappointed. He'd wanted her to say she wasn't going, that she was staying here. But still, as Dee had pointed out, Rae would be back. He had to hold on to that.

"Will you be coming back during summer breaks?" He glanced over at Rae, but she was gazing out the side window.

"Oh, I'll be back."

Luke smiled. He could live with that answer. For now.

They arrived back at his grandmother's to find the tree finished and the staircase banister decorated. While he watched Rae hang her ornament on Gram's tree, Sara whispered in his ear. He looked up to see several clumps of mistletoe that'd been added to the décor, but after the last time he'd kissed Rae under one of those, even though she'd responded, he wasn't sure he should try it again.

After everyone helped themselves to the light supper of soup and sandwiches that'd been set out in the dining room, they all gathered back in the living room to sing Christmas carols and exchange the presents they'd drawn names for this same time last year. Most of the time they were joke presents, and Luke loved it. But tonight his heart was heavy at the thought of Rae leaving soon, and he barely paid attention to what was going on, until she handed a present to her dad and Nora.

"This is for you both. I couldn't wait any longer to give it to you. I hope you like it." She seemed a little nervous as her dad and Nora began to open the gift. It seemed to be a bundle of papers tied up into a scroll of sorts.

When Michael glanced up from reading the papers he'd unwrapped, it was obvious he was thrilled with whatever Rae had gotten them. Nora seemed exceptionally pleased, too.

"Honey, is this for real?" Michael asked.

Rae smiled and nodded. "It is. I hope you won't get tired of me."

"No way!" Michael grabbed her in a bear hug. He waved the papers in his hand. "She's going to move here. This is a signed contract to teach history at Sweet Springs High School!"

Luke's heart soared. Rae was staying. He watched her being hugged by half his family—and found her gaze on him, as if she were trying to gauge his reaction. Well, she wasn't going to have to wait long to find out just how he felt—only until he could talk to her alone so as not to have the whole family watching. Once the attention moved to Sara, who was opening a present from Jake, Luke strode purposefully over to Rae. "That's wonderful news about you moving here, Rae."

She looked at him and smiled. This time it reached her eyes. "Thank you. I'm happy about it."

"Why didn't you tell me on the way here?"

She shrugged. "I didn't know what you would think. I—"

"I'd like to tell you. Come on." Luke took her left hand in his and pulled her across the room and into the deserted kitchen. Turning her into his arms, he touched his forehead to hers. "Rae, I think it's time we talked."

"About what?" She pulled back and gazed up into his eyes, and Luke had to let her know how he felt. If she couldn't return his feelings, he'd count on the Lord to help him through it, but he had to know where they stood. Now.

"About how we feel about one another. . .how I feel about you." She didn't pull away and he continued. "I know now that you *are* the stranger I prayed the Lord would send me—on the very day we met. And I know that I love you, Rae."

Luke heard her small intake of breath and saw tears gather in her eyes. He didn't know what kind of tears they were, but he had to finish. "I know you are a city girl, but I think you've learned to love my town. . .could you. . .do you think you could ever learn to love me, Rae?"

"Oh, Luke," she breathed. "I've been in love with you almost from the moment we met. I—"

He didn't wait for her to finish. He'd heard all he needed to hear. He dipped his head, and his lips claimed hers in a kiss meant to assure her that he loved her—with all his heart. She responded in just the way he'd dreamed she would. He didn't care who came in the kitchen this time. Rae loved him. *Thank You, Lord!*

When the kiss ended, Luke whispered in her ear, "Will you marry me, Rae? If the commute into school gets too hard from Nora's. . ." He embraced her and corrected himself, "From *our* ranch, we'll move into town—"

"Shh," Rae whispered, touching his lips with her fingertips. "As long as I'm coming home to you, Luke, the commute will be just fine. And yes, I'll marry you." She stood on tiptoe and kissed him.

Luke inclined his head and pulled her close. His lips met hers, and he sent up a prayer of thanksgiving to the Lord for bringing his "stranger" to town.

Epilogue

It was the kind of Christmas Rae thought only happened in movies. But it was real. Luke bought her rings on Christmas Eve and put the engagement ring on her finger Christmas Day. Once they told the family they were getting married, nothing would do for Dad and Nora than for Rae and Luke to share their wedding day.

"After all," Nora told them, "the arrangements are all made. All you'll need to do, Rae, is find a dress and make arrangements for a bouquet. You and Luke can call any friends you might want to invite—if they haven't already been invited to our wedding. Think of the nice surprise in store for them!"

After discussing it for about five minutes, Rae and Luke happily agreed. She didn't have to start teaching until the middle of January. That would give them time for a honeymoon.

It'd been the most wonderful, hectic week in her life; she made lists, phone calls, and shopped. Sara and Lydia had run all kinds of errands for her. She'd exchanged her bridesmaid's dress for the wedding dress she'd fallen in love with at the shop where Nora had found hers. It was simple and elegant, with a dropped bodice made up of white lace and seed pearls, and a flowing white satin skirt. Another wedding cake had to be ordered, but Gram insisted on making both of the grooms' cakes.

The week passed in a blur of activity, and now as she and Luke stood beside her dad and Nora, looking out at the guests who'd witnessed their double wedding, it was hard to believe she was a married woman.

Gram sat there with Will, wiping tears from her eyes. Rae had promised Sara that she and Luke would join the family in encouraging those two lovely people to be the next to marry. Ben and Lydia had served as best man and matron of honor for her dad and Nora, while Sara and Jake had stood up as her and Luke's attendants. Dee sat with John, and they watched over Meggie. Head over heels in love, Rae couldn't help hoping that one day Dee and John might walk down this aisle themselves.

She smiled as David introduced Dad and Nora to the guests. Then it was her and Luke's turn. Rae gazed up into the eyes of her new husband, and her heart felt as if it might explode with joy when David introduced them as Mr. and Mrs. Lucas Breland.

Luke pulled her arm through the crook in his elbow and clasped her left hand tightly as they followed the older couple back down the aisle. Once in the fellowship hall, she and Luke hugged her dad and his aunt before turning back to each other.

Luke pulled her into his embrace and whispered in her ear, "I love you, Rae."

"And I love you. . .with all my heart."

Rae's arms encircled her husband's neck as he leaned forward to kiss her. Just before her lips met his, she thanked the Lord above for the family ties that brought her and this handsome cowboy into each other's lives.

Family Reunion

Dedication

To my Lord and Savior for showing me the way
and to the family He has blessed me with.
I love you all.

Chapter 1

Laci Tanner sighed as she looked over the books of her interior design business, Little Touches. She was in the black, but just barely. That's where she seemed to stay. Since opening her shop she'd struggled—first to get those books out of the red and then to keep them in the black. She wondered if it would ever get better.

She'd thought moving from her small hometown of Sweet Springs, New Mexico, to Dallas, Texas, would be the way to go in starting up a business. But the past several years of struggling to get her company up and running had left her little time to have a real life in Dallas or anywhere else. She wanted more from living than working twelve-hour days and eating takeout. And lately she'd been feeling a little lonely and a whole lot homesick.

She'd never imagined how hard it would be to compete with the larger companies in Dallas, although her family had warned her. She'd figured they were just trying to get her to change her mind about moving there, but it seemed they knew what they were talking about.

In the last few months, she'd been debating about whether or not to leave Texas and set up her business in a smaller town. . .even thinking about returning to Sweet Springs. But it was hard to admit her dream hadn't lived up to her expectations.

Lost in her memories of the grand dreams she'd woven about owning her own business, it took her a minute to realize her telephone was ringing. She picked up the receiver on the third ring. "Hello?"

"Laci, it's Mom."

As if she couldn't recognize her own mother's voice. But there was something in her tone. "Mom, what's wrong?"

"Your grandmother has had a stroke, dear, and—"

"Oh, Mom—Gram? How is she?"

"Honey, we don't know yet. But I thought you might want to come home—"

Laci swallowed a sob and pressed her fingers against her tear-filled eyes, knowing that if her mom heard her cry they'd both be bawling over the phone line. "Yes, of course I do. Are you all right?"

"I'm worried."

Those two words were all it took for Laci to know what she had to do. "I'll be there tomorrow, okay?"

"Okay. Are you going to drive or fly?"

Laci looked at the clock. It was nine o'clock at night. She couldn't get a flight out until the morning anyway, and someone would have to meet her in Las Cruces and then drive back to Sweet Springs. She wouldn't get there any faster by flying. "I'll drive."

"Please be careful, dear."

"I will, Mom. I love you. Have Daddy"—Laci's voice broke, and she paused before continuing—"give you a hug for me."

She could tell her mother was having a hard time talking, too. "I will, dear. I love you, too. And, Laci?"

"Yes, Mom?"

"Please pray."

Laci nodded even though her mother couldn't see her. "I will."

She hung up the receiver and released the sob she'd been holding back. *Gram. A stroke.* Laci shook her head and wiped at the tears that streamed out of her eyes. She didn't have time to cry—she had too much to do before she left. But that didn't stem the tears as she went about making a list of all she had to do: call Myra Branson, her assistant manager; pack for a long visit because she didn't know how long or short her visit might be; fill the car.

In between each item, she prayed the same prayer over and over. *"Oh, please, dear Lord, let Gram be all right. Please be with Mom, too."*

Laci began packing her bags while she called Myra to let her know she was going home. She tried to remember all the things that would need her immediate attention. "There's that shipment coming in on Thursday, and the Wilkinsons' drapes will be ready on Friday. And—"

"Don't worry about anything, Laci. I'll call you if there is a problem. Just get home to your family," Myra said.

"You're right. I know you'll be able to handle anything that comes up." And she would. Myra was very capable, and Laci knew she was leaving her business in good hands. Besides, she was only an e-mail or cell phone call away. None of it mattered at the moment anyway. She had to get to Gram and to her mother.

Laci had trouble sleeping that night, but it wasn't worry about her business that kept her awake. It was anger at herself for not making it to the last family reunion. Gram had wanted her to come so badly. But it had been right after she opened her business in Dallas, and at the time she felt she couldn't get away. To her way of thinking, nothing was more important than getting Little Touches up and running.

She threw her covers off and walked over to the window. How could she have thought any of that was more important than her family? She swiped at a lone tear that trailed down her cheek. What if Gram didn't make it? Laci felt the moan rise in her chest before she ever heard it escape. *Oh, please, dear Lord. Let Gram recover. Please let her be all right.*

Eric Mitchell dropped Sam, his five-year-old son, at preschool and headed toward his office on Main Street. But his rumbling stomach wouldn't be ignored. He'd fed Sam a breakfast of cereal and orange juice but had been so busy getting a rumpled shirt out of the dryer and ironing it for his son that he hadn't managed to eat anything himself. While Sam finished his breakfast, Eric had folded a load of towels he'd taken out of the dryer the night before, wondering if he would ever catch up around the house.

After he parked his car at the office, he gave in to his hunger pains and hurried down the block to Deana's Diner. He entered as John Tanner was leaving. Normally a very friendly person, John only nodded to Eric before he walked out the door. The mood inside the restaurant was more somber than Eric remembered, and he couldn't help but wonder at the cause.

He took his normal seat by the window and waited until Deana Russell, better known to everyone in town as Dee, brought him a menu and a cup of coffee. She looked about as solemn as John had.

"Dee? Is something wrong?" Normally Eric didn't pry into other people's business, but with John leaving so abruptly and Dee looking as if she were about to cry, he wanted to do something to help if he could.

She let out a huge sigh. "Ellie Breland had a stroke and is in the hospital. The family is very worried."

"Oh, no," Eric said. Ellie Breland was John's grandmother and the grandmother of two of Eric's good friends, Jake and Luke Breland. Eric had spent a lot of time at her house when he was younger, and suddenly he felt as if he'd just received news that his own grandmother was in serious condition.

"What can I get you this morning?" Dee asked.

Eric shook his head. His appetite seemed to have disappeared. "Maybe just some toast and jelly."

Dee nodded as if she understood. "Coming right up."

Eric sipped his coffee and thought about the last time he'd seen Miss Ellie, as most everyone called her. He was going over the plans to the home he'd built for Jake and Sara before they married and while Jake was still living with his grandmother. When they'd finished looking over the plans, Miss Ellie insisted he join them for pie and coffee. Eric could almost taste that pie now. No one in Sweet Springs was more hospitable than Ellie Breland. She was a very sweet woman, and he prayed she would recover completely. His heart went out to her family, to John and especially to Jake and Luke—their grandmother had raised them. He was sure they were taking it hard. He probably ought to check on them.

"Here you go," Dee said, sounding a little more like herself as she set a plate of toast and jelly in front of him. "I'm used to seeing you and Sam for supper, but you usually only eat breakfast here on the weekends. Did you have a bad morning?"

"Just a busy one," Eric said. "I did manage to feed Sam, though."

"I never doubted that for a minute," Dee said. "You take real good care of him."

"Thanks, Dee. I try." Her comment meant more to him than she knew. It wasn't easy trying to be both dad and mom to his son since his wife, Joni, had passed away when Sam was only a few months old. He worried that Sam was missing what only a mother could give him, but he did the best he could to see that his little boy knew he was loved and cared for.

"He's an adorable little boy, Eric. Tell him hi for me."

"I will," Eric assured her as she waved and stepped away to take care of a couple of customers who sat down at the table next to him.

Sam liked Dee. She always talked to him and made him feel special. Maybe Eric would bring him back for supper tonight. He slathered jelly on his toast and bit into it, wondering why his buttered toast never quite tasted like it did here. It took only about ten minutes to finish his light breakfast. After leaving the money to cover his meal and a decent tip for Dee, he headed for his office. He'd call Jake or Luke a little later to see how their grandmother was doing.

The trip home to Sweet Springs was a long, soul-searching one for Laci. She prayed her grandmother would be all right and that she would have a chance to tell her how much she loved her and how sorry she was she hadn't come home more often—especially for that reunion.

She owed her parents the same thing. They'd been the ones to visit her in Dallas, making frequent trips to make sure their "baby" was all right. Now she realized that's exactly what she'd been acting like the past few years—a baby, thinking more of herself than anyone else. She was always too busy. Too busy to call, too busy to take off a few days and make sure they were all right, and too busy to come to the last family reunion. Too selfish was what she'd been.

Now Laci was filled with remorse that she'd been so self-absorbed. Had she made the right decision to leave Sweet Springs? Looking back, Laci didn't think so. She'd been so young and full of herself—thinking that if she could just get out of her small town and into a city like Dallas she could make it big in the decorating world. Laci gave a delicate snort at the very thought of her audacity.

Well, that certainly hadn't happened. Laci sighed. *Nor was it likely to.* She managed to make a living for herself and pay Myra a decent wage, but that was about it. She could have done that in Sweet Springs. . .and been around family and friends. Instead, she was miles away from those she loved, and she wasn't getting ahead. If she were honest with herself, she would have to admit she was blessed just to be doing as well as she was.

What made her think she could compete in a city where she knew so few people? And yet Dallas was where she'd always wanted to go. Now she couldn't say why, but when she'd set off for Texas the city had seemed glamorous and exciting.

But the reality was that there was nothing glamorous or exciting about living in Dallas. Her life seemed to consist of working long hours and only going to church and the occasional movie or out to dinner with the few friends she'd managed to make. And still she'd stayed. Why? Because it was easier than admitting her family had been right and she'd been wrong.

As Laci topped Comanche Hill outside Roswell, New Mexico, excitement welled up inside her as she saw the town laid out below. She could see El Capitan Mountain off in the distance and knew she'd be home in just over an hour. Roswell was the largest town near Sweet Springs, and she and her family often shopped there. As she entered the city limits and traveled down Second Street to Main, she chuckled and shook her head at the alien displays. She might think it was silly, but the *Roswell Incident* had certainly done its part in helping the town's economy in the last few decades.

She enjoyed seeing all the changes down Second Street as she traveled straight through town and back out onto open highway. She loved the change of scenery from flat farmland around Roswell, up through the foothills of the Rocky Mountains. Apple orchards dotted the landscape around the Hondo River Valley as she neared Sweet Springs.

She passed the new mall, several motels, and restaurants on the highway before she turned off to enter the main part of town. Her mother had told her Sweet Springs was growing, and she was pleased to see how much it had.

But Laci wasn't prepared for the sense of homecoming she felt just driving down Main Street on the way to the hospital. She passed familiar tree-lined streets and the church her family attended. She spotted the law firm her brother John and cousin Jake shared, and she couldn't help but feel a spark of family pride. When she passed Deana's Diner, her mouth began to water at the thought of Dee's hamburgers and fries.

It wasn't until she pulled into the hospital parking lot that she felt sudden tears sting the back of her eyelids, and she didn't know if it was because she was home or because she was scared to go inside. She was afraid of what kind of news awaited her. She'd had a hard time getting a good signal on her cell phone on the way home. The one time she'd managed to get through to her mother, the line was filled with static. Laci wasn't sure her mom had been able to hear her when she told her she'd be going directly to the hospital to see how Gram was. Most probably that's where the whole family would be, but she wouldn't know until she got there.

She didn't bother to stop at the information desk; instead, she headed for the intensive care unit. She walked up to the nurses' station and told the nurse on duty who she was and asked if she could see her grandmother.

"She's no longer here," the nurse said, barely looking up at her.

Laci's heart seemed to stop, and she felt as if the breath had been knocked right out of her. But she forced out the words. "No longer here? I—"

"We just moved her. She's in room. . .204."

Laci couldn't contain the small sob of relief that escaped.

"Oh, dear, I'm sorry," the nurse said, finally looking at her. "I should have realized you'd think something else. She's doing much better. She's been moved to a private room and—"

"I—it's okay. She's in a room." Laci started to leave then realized she wasn't sure where the room was in relation to the nurses' station. She turned back to the nurse. "Where—"

"Come on. I'll take you to her." Her name tag read MARGE MONROE.

"Thank you, Marge," Laci said as the woman stepped out from behind the desk.

Marge led the way down the hall and around the corner before stopping next to room 204.

"I think some of your family are in there with her, but if you don't make too much noise it'll be all right." She smiled and turned to go.

Unsure of what shape her grandmother was in, Laci stood outside her room for a moment trying to gather courage to go in. She sent up a silent prayer of thanksgiving that Gram was out of intensive care. Surely that meant she was going to be all right.

But when she opened the door and peeked around it, nothing could have prepared her for what she saw. She knew others were in the room, but all she could see was the woman in the bed. The energetic woman she remembered looked frail and pale, but when she saw Laci her eyes shone bright and clear with recognition.

Laci rushed to her side.

"I'm glad. . .you made it," Gram said. Her speech was slow, and she seemed to be talking out of one side of her mouth, but Laci could only be thankful she could speak.

"I'm glad I did, too, Gram." Laci choked back a sob.

"Don't. . .you cry now. I'm. . .going to be all right." She reached out and grabbed Laci's hand.

Laci could only nod and give her grandmother's hand a gentle squeeze.

"But if I'd known. . .this would get you here, it would have been. . .worth it a long time ago."

"Mother!" Laci's mom said from behind her. But she joined the others in the room in a relieved chuckle.

Laci bent down and kissed her grandmother's cheek, happy to see she'd lost none of her feistiness. She felt her mother's hand on her shoulder, and when she turned she enveloped her in a hug.

"I hope you'll be able to stay awhile, dear. I—we all need you here."

Before she could answer her mother, her dad pulled her into a hug. "I'm so glad you came home, honey. We've sure missed you around here."

"I've missed you, too, Dad." More than she'd realized until that moment.

"It's good to see you, sis," John said as he gave her a bear hug and kissed her on the cheek. "I've really missed you."

Then her cousins Jake and Luke each took a turn welcoming her home.

"It's good to see you, Laci." Jake hugged her.

Then Luke pulled a lock of her hair as he'd loved to do when they were kids. "You're looking good, Laci. It's about time you came home for a while." He hugged her, too. "Sure wish you'd think about staying."

Laci felt bad. She hadn't made it home for a long time. Not for Jake's wedding, not for Luke's—and not for the reunion. Nor had she kept up with much of what was happening with all of them. And yet here they were, welcoming her with open arms.

She didn't deserve this kind of homecoming. But she would cherish it always.

Chapter 2

It wasn't long until Laci's grandmother told them all to go home for a while so she could get some rest.

"Let me stay awhile, Gram, please?" Laci asked.

"No. You just made. . .a long trip, and I know you are tired. You. . .can come back later for a little while."

"But—"

"No buts. Your. . .parents need to visit. . .with you."

"We'll come back later," Laci's dad said. "Your gram could use some rest."

"Okay."

"Let's go grab a bite to eat," her mother suggested. "I'm sure all you've done is fill up your car and grab a cup of coffee or a soft drink on your way here."

Her mother knew her too well. Laci grinned and nodded. "I guess I could use some food."

"Well, I'm going to take off," Jake said. "Sara tires pretty easily these days, and Meggie doesn't. I'd better go check on the two of them."

"Sara's not well?" Laci asked.

"The baby is due in a month or so, dear," her mother reminded her.

"Oh, that's right. Sara's all right, though? There aren't any problems with the baby?" Laci asked, trying not to show she'd forgotten Sara was expecting. But she wasn't even sure she ever knew. Surely she had. Her mother would have told her.

"She's fine." Jake grinned. "Or as fine as a woman can be this far along in her pregnancy, so Gram tells me." He bent to kiss Gram's forehead. "I'll stop in later, Gram."

"Stay home. Sara needs you," Gram said slowly. "I'm going. . .to be fine. 'Sides, Will is going to. . .be here soon."

"I'm surprised he isn't here now."

"He said he had. . .something he had to do," Gram said. "Said he'd be back to. . .make sure I eat."

"Well, we'll check back, but I know Will would like a little time with you," Laci's mom said.

Laci exchanged a glance with her mother. Will? Could she mean Sara's grandfather? She opened her mouth to ask, but before she could get the words out, her mother placed her hand on her shoulder and propelled her toward the door.

"We'll check back a little later, Mom. We'll let the nurse know we'll be at the diner. If you need us—"

"Go," Gram said. She lifted her hand and gave a little wave. "Eat."

"All right," John said. "But you behave while we're gone, you hear?"

That brought a smile to Gram's face. "I'll try."

They filed out of the room and rode the elevator down to the lobby where they parted company with Jake and Luke.

"I'm going home, too," Luke said. "Rae wants to come back with me this evening."

"Sara does, too. Aunt Nora said she'd watch Meggie for us. I hope Gram will be able to go home soon," Jake said.

"I certainly hope so. I don't like this hospital stuff. I'll feel better knowing she's well enough to go home. I'd like to talk her into coming out to our house, but you know how she is," Laci's mom said.

"Lydia, she's going to be all right." Laci's dad put his arm around her mother.

"I know, Ben." She reached up and patted his hand. "I'll just feel better when the doctor releases her."

"Too bad Michael isn't a heart doctor," Jake said.

"Yes, it is. He knows how much better we'll all feel to get her home."

"Michael? That's Aunt Nora's husband, right?" Laci asked. "And Will is Sara's grandpa?"

"That's right."

Laci nodded. Much had happened in her family since she'd been gone, and Laci was glad she'd guessed right. "I thought so. And I take it that Gram and Will are kind of an item?"

"You could say that," her mother answered. "They've been seeing each other for several years now. We've all been expecting them to get married, but it hasn't happened yet."

They walked outside into the waning sunlight and piled into John's new SUV for the ride to the diner. From the backseat Laci could see yard signs and posters with her brother's name on them. She'd almost forgotten his campaign for the U.S. Senate was underway. Sisterly pride in John washed over her, followed by a crashing wave of disappointment in herself as she realized she hadn't even asked how the campaign was going in the last few months. Just when had she become so selfish?

"How are things looking for November?" she asked now, wondering if her brother thought her interest was a little late in coming.

But he didn't appear to be upset with her as he maneuvered the vehicle out of the parking lot. "It's going really well. Once we know Gram is truly all right, I'll be getting out on the road again."

"We were planning to go out with him this time," Laci's mom said. "But I'll have to be sure about Mother before I leave town."

"Don't worry about it, Mom," John said. "I wouldn't want her to be here alone."

"Maybe I can help," Laci found herself saying. "I can stay awhile if you all need me to."

"Are you sure, honey?" her dad asked.

And suddenly she was. She'd put the people she loved second to herself for way too long, and it was time that changed. "I'm sure."

"We'll see. I just can't leave Mother until I know she's well on the way to recovery."

Laci could see the strain of the past few days on her mother's face. She took hold of her hand and squeezed it. "I can understand that."

Tears welled up in her mother's eyes, and she squeezed Laci's hand. "I know you can."

They pulled up at the diner, and her mother brushed away her tears as Laci's dad opened the door for her. John had opened Laci's side, and she jumped out.

"Thanks for coming, sis," he said, draping his arm around her shoulders as they walked to the diner. "It means a lot to have you here. I think Mom has really needed you."

Laci nodded, fighting back a few tears of her own. "I'm glad I'm here."

As they entered, it seemed everyone in the diner looked at John expectantly.

"She's doing better," he said. "They've moved her to a private room."

At the cheers that erupted at his words, Laci was reminded of the wonderful things about a small town. Nearly everyone at the diner seemed to know about her grandmother and had most likely been praying for her.

Dee came from behind the counter to give her a hug. "It's good to see you, girl. I've missed you."

Laci hugged her back. "I've missed you, too." Although she was a few years younger than Dee, they'd gone to school together, and Laci had been coming to the diner since back when Dee's mom ran it.

"I hope you are able to stay awhile. I think your family needs you right now," Dee whispered in her ear.

"I'm planning on it."

"Good." Dee turned to her mother and gave her a hug, too. "I'm so glad about your mother. I'll keep praying she recovers completely and quickly."

"Thank you, dear. Please do," Laci's mom said.

Dee gave them all menus and took their drink orders before punching John on the shoulder and turning away. Once, when they were younger, Laci had thought her brother and Dee would end up getting married. Obviously that hadn't happened, but still there was something about the way they looked at each other.

"I think Dee's been as worried as the rest of us," her dad said.

"From what I've heard, the whole town has been," John added. "And I think

Dee has been asking everyone who's come in to pray for Gram."

"Well, the Lord has answered those prayers."

"He certainly has, Ben," Laci's mom said.

Annie, one of the waitresses, came to take their orders. Dee must have asked Charlie, her cook, to put a rush on it because it seemed no time until Annie returned with chicken fried steaks for Laci's dad and brother and big baskets of cheeseburgers and fries for her and her mom.

By the time they finished eating, Laci could tell her mother was exhausted. "Have you had any sleep lately, Mom?"

"No," her dad answered before her mother had a chance to. "She's worn-out. But we didn't want to leave the hospital."

"Well, why don't we go check on Gram again, and then you and Mom can go get some rest. I'll stay at the hospital," John offered.

"No," Laci said, shaking her head, "I'll stay."

"Laci, you've been on the road all day. I know you're tired. Mom and Dad sent me home last night. I can stay. All I have to do is call a nurse if Gram needs anything."

"Well, let's go check on her, and then we can decide what to do," Laci's mother said, grabbing her purse.

Laci could tell she was anxious to get back to the hospital and see for herself how Gram was doing. They waved at Dee while her dad and John went to pay.

When they got back to the hospital, they found Gram looking quite perky. Laci had an idea it was because of the visitor sitting in the chair beside the bed.

William Oliver stood when they entered the room and grinned at them. "Isn't it wonderful to see Ellie on the road to recovery?"

"It certainly is, Will," Laci's mother said as she patted him on the back. "And she's looking even better than she did when we went to grab a bite to eat."

"That's because the doctor came in a. . .few minutes ago and said. . .I might get to go home in a few days."

"Oh, Mother, that is wonderful news!" Laci's mom said, giving her a hug.

"I know. And there is no need for anyone to stay with me tonight. I'll probably sleep like a baby."

"But, Mother—"

"Lydia, dear, you need to go home and sleep in a real bed."

"I'll stay, Gram. I'd like to," Laci said.

"No, I will," John said. "You've—"

"None of you will stay," Gram said firmly. "I'll only. . .worry about you not getting enough rest, and. . .that won't be good for me."

Laci's mom raised her eyebrow but only grinned at her mother.

"Nurses will call. . .if they need to," Gram said.

"Whoa, Gram. You must be feeling a lot better to order us around like that," John teased.

"She's been pretty feisty ever since the doctor showed up." Will chuckled. "But it's wonderful to see her acting that way again."

"Well, if you all. . .don't go home and. . .let me get some rest, too. . .I might be. . .a tad grouchy tomorrow."

The nurse chose that moment to stick her head around the corner and let them know visiting hours were over. After saying their good nights to Gram, the family filed out into the hall with Will following a couple of minutes later.

In the parking lot, Will looked back. "I sure hate to leave her there, but I know the Lord has answered a whole lot of prayers today. He'll watch over her tonight."

"Yes, He will," Laci's mom answered. "I know how you feel, though."

"I know you do, Lydia. You get some rest like your mama ordered," Will said. "I'll see you all tomorrow."

As he gave a wave and headed toward his pickup, Laci's heart went out to him. It was obvious he cared about her grandmother as much as they all did. She was glad he was in Gram's life.

Eric had missed connecting with any of the Brelands or Tanners all day. As he and Sam headed into Dee's for supper, he hoped she had some good news about Ellie Breland.

The diner wasn't too busy. It was a little later than usual for their supper, but he and Sam had been to a T-ball league meeting. Sam had wanted to play for over a year, and Eric had agreed to coach this year. Sam wanted to play so badly, and none of the other parents volunteered so Eric found himself raising his hand.

Now, as they took their favorite booth at the diner, Sam was very excited.

"Hey, guys," Dee said as she approached their table. "You're kind of late tonight. I bet you're hungry, huh, Sam?"

"I'm starvin', Miss Dee. Dad's meeting went on a long time." He spread his hands apart as far as he could.

"It did?"

"Uh-huh." Sam nodded. "Dad is going to be my T-ball coach!"

"He is?" Dee looked at Eric and grinned. "Do you know what you've gotten yourself into?"

"No, but I have a feeling I'm going to find out real soon."

Dee laughed. "Yes, I'm sure you will. What will you have tonight?"

Eric had to smile as Sam opened his menu and looked it over even though he couldn't read it yet.

"I'll have a grilled cheese and french fries, please," Sam said.

"Toasted just right. Do you want milk, too?" Dee asked.

"Yes, ma'am." Sam closed his menu and handed it to Dee.

"Thank you, sir."

"You're welcome," Sam said, grinning at Eric.

Eric's heart swelled with pride in his son's manners. Joni would be so proud of him.

"And you, Eric?" Dee turned to him.

"I'll have a patty melt and fries, please. And I'd like iced tea to drink."

"Coming right up," Dee said as she took his menu.

"Oh, Dee?"

She turned back. "Yes?"

"Have you heard how Miss Ellie is doing? I haven't been able to contact Jake or Luke."

Her smile was immediate. "Yes, I have. The family was in here earlier. Ellie has been moved to a private room, and they think she'll have a complete recovery."

"Oh, that is good news."

"Yes." Dee nodded and smiled. "It's the best kind of news."

Eric let out a breath of relief for his friends. He knew they were all rejoicing tonight. "Thank You, Lord," he whispered.

"What are you thanking God for, Dad?" Sam asked.

"That Jake and Luke's grandmother is going to be all right. She had a stroke."

"She did?" Sam's brow wrinkled. "What's a stroke?"

"It's when the blood supply to the brain is disturbed in some way," Eric answered, knowing it would be hard for Sam to comprehend what it was.

"Oh." Sam nodded as if he understood what his dad was saying. "Like it doesn't go where it's supposed to?"

"Something like that."

"But she'll be all right now?"

"Yes, it sounds as though she will be."

Sam smiled. "I'm glad she's going to be okay."

Eric reached over and squeezed his son's arm. "I know you are, son. So am I."

Dee brought their supper, and when she'd left the table Eric quietly said, "Let's pray."

Sam bowed his head, and Eric did the same. "Dear Lord, we thank You that Ellie Breland is recovering from her stroke, and we ask that she continues to do so and that she makes a full recovery. Please bless this food we are about to eat and help us to live this day to Your glory. And thank You for Sam, Lord. And we especially thank You for Your Son and our Savior, Jesus Christ. In His name we pray, amen."

"And thank You for Dad, dear God," Sam added his own words. "Amen."

Chapter 3

The next few days Gram continued to recover. Her speech was gradually getting better, but she was a little unsteady on her feet and would need to walk with a cane for a while. But the doctors assured them that, with therapy, she'd be back to normal soon. Everyone was looking forward to her being able to leave the hospital.

She'd already informed them she was going to her house—not to Ben and Lydia's or Nora and Michael's, not to Jake and Sara's or Luke and Rae's. Just home to her house. So Laci and her mom met Aunt Nora, Sara, and Rae at Gram's the day before she was scheduled to come home. The plan was to clean Gram's house from top to bottom so she wouldn't be tempted to get up and do more than she needed to once she was home. Her house was always clean, but they knew she'd feel she had to be up and seeing to things if they didn't take care of them for her.

Laci, Sara, and Rae took the upstairs, stripping the beds and putting on fresh sheets, cleaning the two bathrooms, and dusting and vacuuming.

As the morning wore on, Laci listened to the women teasing each other while at the same time expressing their true concern for one another. She realized how much she'd missed by being away the last few years.

She and Sara had known each other for a long time, but now she was wife to Jake and mother to his little girl, Meggie—and they had a baby due soon. Family relations got even more complicated with Aunt Nora and Rae. As Michael's daughter *and* Luke's wife, Rae was both stepdaughter and niece-in-law to Aunt Nora. The four of them—Aunt Nora and Michael, Rae and Luke—had shared a double wedding not too long ago.

What surprised Laci the most was how much her aunt Nora seemed to have changed. She didn't even seem to be the same person.

Once they got the upstairs cleaned and sparkling, Laci, Sara, and Rae decided it was time to think about lunch. After going downstairs to find out what Laci's mom and aunt wanted to eat, they called in an order and headed out the door to pick up lunch for everyone at Dee's diner.

Eric called Jake early that morning and made plans to meet at the diner for lunch. Jake was already there when Eric arrived. He slid into the opposite side of the booth Jake was occupying, but before they could start a conversation Dee was there to get their orders. She voiced what Eric was thinking. "I can tell Ellie is better just from the expression on your face, Jake. I'm so glad."

"Thanks, Dee. We all are. I know you've been praying, and I thank you for the prayers. We know the Lord has heard many prayers for Gram and answered them."

"She's a special lady. Everyone loves Ellie. I'll try to get over to visit her soon. What can I get for you guys?"

"I'll have the lunch special of meatloaf and iced tea to drink, please," Eric said.

"I'll have the same thing," Jake said with a short nod.

"I'm helping Charlie in the kitchen today. I'll have Annie bring your orders as soon as I can," Dee said, heading toward the kitchen.

"I'm sorry I never returned your call the other day," Jake said when Dee left. "We were so worried at first and then so relieved at how well Gram was doing that I forgot."

"Don't worry about that, Jake. I'm just glad your grandmother is doing so well. When is she going to come home?"

"The doctor said barring any changes she'll get to go home tomorrow. She won't come home with any of us, though. She wants to go to *her* house. But there are plenty of us to check on her." Jake shrugged. "We'll take turns or something."

"If I can do anything. . .well, I know you probably wouldn't want me to sit with her, but if I can run an errand, take her somewhere, you know. Whatever you need—"

"Thanks, Eric. I appreciate it, man. With Sara so far along I never know when I'm going to get a call, and Meggie can be such a handful that it's hard to figure out how best we can help Gram right now."

The bell over the door of the diner jingled, and they looked over to see Sara and Rae enter with another woman who looked very familiar to Eric. Was that Laci? His heart skipped a beat as she looked their way. It was.

Jake slid out of the booth as Sara spotted him and motioned to the others to follow her. "There's my lady now."

Rae waved at the two men but continued on to the cash register. "I'll get our orders while you two visit," she called.

Sara and Laci walked over to their table, and Eric quickly slid out of his side of the booth to greet them.

"Hi, honey," Jake said to his wife. "What are you all doing here?"

"Grabbing some lunch to take back to Gram's house. We've been doing some cleaning—"

"You aren't doing too much, are you?"

"No, I'm not. I promise." Sara smiled at her husband. "Meggie is at Mother's Day Out at church. We'll pick her up on the way back to Gram's, and she can eat lunch with us. Then I'll put her down for a nap. I hope."

Jake laughed. "Yes, 'hope' is the word."

Eric couldn't help but feel a pang of. . .loss? He hoped it wasn't envy as he watched Jake kiss Sara on the cheek. He missed that kind of interaction. He'd loved being married. Most of the time he was so busy he didn't give it much thought. But suddenly he felt a well of emptiness.

"Eric, you remember my cousin Laci, don't you? Laci, you remember Eric? He spent a lot of time at Gram's with us." Jake pulled the pretty brunette who had come in with Sara and Rae forward.

Was Jake crazy? How could he forget Laci? "Yes, of course I remember Laci."

And he did. In fact he'd always thought Laci was very cute and would like to have asked her out back in high school. But he'd always felt like she was somehow out of his league. She ran around with some of the wealthier kids in town, and he spent all his free hours working. Come to think of it, not much had changed—except he worked a lot more hours now, and his free time was spent with his son.

"Hi, Eric." She smiled at him.

The very fact that Laci remembered him somehow had Eric's heart hammering in his chest. She was even prettier than he remembered with her long brown hair curling softly around her face and her greenish-brown eyes that seemed to sparkle.

"It's good to see you again, Laci. I'm sure your family is glad to have you home, too."

"Oh, yeah, we are," Jake said.

"I'm glad to be here, too. I'm hoping I can help out."

Rae walked up then with two sacks of food. "Hi. I hate to break up this party, but we'd better hurry if we're going to eat this warm. We still need to pick up Meggie."

"Yes, we'd better go," Sara said. "I'll see you later, dear." She gave Jake a kiss on the cheek. "It's always good to see you, Eric. Don't be such a stranger, you hear? Drop by anytime."

"Thanks, Sara."

Laci just gave a smile and a little wave before she followed the other two women out the door.

As the three women headed for the car, Laci hoped Sara and Rae couldn't tell how flustered she'd been at seeing Eric Mitchell again. She was thankful they were talking about picking up Meggie and getting back to the house to eat, so she didn't think they knew. But Laci's pulse was still racing, and she was glad she wasn't the one driving as she sat down in the backseat of Sara's car.

Did she remember Eric? Oh, yes. She'd never forgotten him. She'd had a huge crush on him when they were in school. He was a few years older than she was, but she'd had a couple of elective classes with him and spent a lot of her high school years daydreaming about him. He looked the same, only better. His hair was still almost black and his eyes a dark chocolate color that made her think of warm homemade fudge. A few lines around the corners of his eyes only served to make him seem even more mature and attractive.

They stopped at the church Laci had gone to all her life so Sara could pick up Meggie. It was larger now. They'd added on to it in the last few years, and now it housed a nice preschool. Laci found herself looking forward to attending services while she was here.

When Sara came out of the building with Meggie, Laci was surprised at how she'd grown. She'd been a baby the last time she'd seen her. But now she was even talking—Laci chuckled as she watched Meggie's little mouth move nonstop, no doubt telling her mother all about her morning.

Rae seemed to know what she was tickled about and joined in the laughter as they watched mom and daughter make their way back to the car. "She's a talker, that one. But, oh, how she entertains us all!"

Laci didn't think Meggie could remember her, but she seemed quite happy to meet more family as Sara buckled her into her car seat beside Laci and introduced them. "Meggie, this is Cousin Laci. She's come for a visit."

"Hi, Meggie." Laci smiled down at the child. "You've grown since I saw you last."

Sara took her seat in the front, and Rae started the car while the conversation in the backseat continued.

"I'm a big girl now," Meggie said.

"Yes, you are." She seemed even smarter than she was big.

Meggie leaned her head to the side and looked at Laci. "You're very pwetty."

"Why, thank you, Meggie. So are you." She was adorable with her blue eyes and black hair just like her daddy's. She even had Jake's dimples.

"Thank you," Meggie said. "My daddy thinks so, too."

From there Meggie seemed to remember she hadn't said hi to Rae, so she greeted her and then told them about her morning until they arrived at Gram's.

They entered the kitchen to find Laci's mother and Aunt Nora still working.

"Mother can be so stubborn at times," Laci's mom was saying as they walked into the room. She was scrubbing the sink as hard as she could. "But much as I wish she'd come stay with one of us, I know she'll only feel comfortable here."

"We can all take turns staying with her." Aunt Nora took the vegetable bin out of the refrigerator and dumped its contents into a large garbage bag.

Laci couldn't believe her aunt had made the suggestion. She had never been one to put others first—at least not when Laci lived in Sweet Springs. But she'd been hearing about how much her aunt had changed. It appeared she really had.

"Aunt Nora, there's no need for that right now. I've told Mom I can stay with Gram at least for a little while."

"Oh! We didn't hear you come back in," her mother said, turning to greet the new addition to their group. "Hi, Meggie! How was your day?"

"Come on. Let's eat, and we can discuss what we're going to do about Gram over lunch," Rae suggested, setting down the sacks she'd brought in.

"Good. Hi, Nana!" Meggie greeted Aunt Nora.

Her aunt left what she was doing and came to help settle Meggie at the table. "Hi, my dearest." She dropped a kiss on the child's head. "I love you."

"I love you, too."

Sara grabbed some paper plates out of the pantry, and they found the items they'd ordered then sat down at the table.

After Laci's mother said the blessing, it was a few minutes before anyone spoke as they fed the hunger they'd worked up that morning.

"I'll move my things over tonight or first thing in the morning," Laci said, bringing up the topic of Gram again. "You all don't need to worry about taking turns staying with Gram, at least for a few weeks."

"Can you take off from work that long?" Aunt Nora wiped the corner of her mouth with a napkin.

In no hurry to return to Dallas, Laci nodded and swallowed the bite of the club sandwich she'd ordered. "I have a very good assistant manager, and I know I can trust her to take care of things for me for a while. If I need to, I can always go back for a few days, but right now I don't think it will be a problem. Besides, you all are married and have others to think about and take care of. Right now I can do this, so please let me."

"It does sound like the answer for now," Sara said. "I have to admit I'm not quite as energetic as I'd like to be these days, so I thank you for your offer, Laci. I just wish Gram and my grandpa were married. Then he'd be here, where he wants to be, and we wouldn't be quite so worried about her."

"I wish the same thing. They aren't getting any younger, and if this doesn't serve as a call to get those two married, there's no hope." Aunt Nora took a bite out of her sandwich.

"Well, we can all pray they decide to do it," Laci's mother said. "They love each other. That's been apparent for quite a while now."

"And I hate to see them apart when they would be so much happier together," Sara added.

"Do you think they are worried you two wouldn't want them to marry others?" Aunt Nora asked, looking first at Laci's mom and then at Sara.

"Oh, surely not." Laci's mother held her hamburger midway from the table to her mouth. "I'd love to see Mom and Will together."

"So would I," Sara said.

"Hmm. Maybe you'd better be sure they both know that," Aunt Nora said.

"Well, maybe we'd better," her mom said. She bit into her burger and chewed quietly.

By late afternoon Laci was left by herself. Her mother and her aunt had gone to see Gram. Rae had gone to meet Luke for supper, and then they were going to the hospital before heading out to the ranch. Sara and Meggie were going home. Aunt Nora had promised that she and Michael would come and stay with Meggie that evening so Sara could visit with Gram. Laci would go up after she unpacked her things at Gram's house. She did make time to call Myra and check in with her, letting her know how Gram was and that she would be staying for a while.

"Don't worry about Little Touches, Laci. I'll take care of your business for you. You use all the time you need."

"Thank you, Myra. I can't tell you how much it means to know you are handling everything there."

They talked for a while longer, and when Laci got off the phone she felt much better knowing she could trust Myra to handle the business in her absence. There were no problems that needed her attention, and she didn't have to feel guilty about not returning to Dallas right away.

But as she settled herself into the room that had been her mother's at one time, the quiet took hold, and Laci couldn't keep thoughts of Eric Mitchell out of her mind any longer. She'd been surprised to find she was still attracted to him after all these years. It was almost as if time had stood still and she felt exactly the same way she had the last time she'd talked to him.

It had been at a football game, and he'd been with Jake and Luke. All she really remembered was that her cousins had teased her about something, as they were prone to do back then, and Eric had come to her defense.

And the memory of him doing so had stayed with her all these years. She didn't know what he'd said or why, but she remembered feeling special, and from that day on he'd become her hero. She wondered about him now, then told herself it was only because she had no one special in her life right now while everyone else—except her brother—seemed to have someone. Did Eric? She didn't know.

She went to look out onto the backyard where she'd spent many days playing. Suddenly she wished she were a child again. Things were much simpler then. Now she was longing for home when she didn't even know what she was going to do about her business. Her life, such as it was, was in Dallas, but she wanted to be here.

And she was longing for more. . .so much more. The last thing she needed was to be weaving dreams about a high-school crush when her life was so mixed up.

Eric forced thoughts of Laci Tanner to the back of his mind as he picked up Sam and took him to T-ball practice. He spent the next hour or so trying to concentrate on teaching little boys how to stand at home base, the right way to hold a bat and try to hit the ball off the tee, and how to catch and pitch a ball. He couldn't help but be proud of Sam and sorry for some of the boys on the team. At least Sam knew the basics. Some of these little boys didn't have a clue about what they were doing, and he wasn't sure they were there because they wanted to be or because their parents wanted them to be. He figured he'd find out in the coming weeks.

Sam was wound up the rest of the evening, and it wasn't until after Eric had tucked him into bed, listened to his prayers, and turned out the light—leaving only the soft glow from his nightlight on—that thoughts of Laci began to sneak back in. Eric straightened up the kitchen and let his mind wander back over the day. He was thankful Ellie Breland was going to be all right. He knew what it was like to lose those you loved, and Luke and Jake had lost their parents at an early age. Their grandmother and grandfather Breland had raised them.

He was glad Luke and Jake had Rae and Sara in their lives, but he had to admit that sometimes seeing them together made him long for someone special in his life. As busy as he was, though, with work and Sam and trying to keep up with everything at home, being lonely wasn't likely to change anytime soon. But. . .after seeing Laci again, he sure wished it would.

Chapter 4

Gram was released the next afternoon, and the whole family gathered at her house that evening. Things seemed more normal with her at home, even though the doctor had ordered her to take it easy until he told her differently. Everyone seemed relieved just to have her out of the hospital.

Gram had more news for them. As soon as the whole family was there, she announced that Will had proposed once again that very day, and she'd *finally* accepted. But she'd made him wait to put the engagement ring on her finger until they were all together.

As Will sat down on the sofa beside Gram and slid the diamond on her ring finger, Laci felt tears of happiness well up for the two of them. She'd never been prouder of her family than at that moment—for the way they were all truly thrilled for the couple. She'd been a little concerned about her mother; but after witnessing the touching hug she gave Will and the way he hugged her back, Laci knew everything was all right.

"Well, I have to tell you we've all been praying for this," Aunt Nora said, wiping a tear from her eye. "But what made you finally decide to say yes?"

"My stroke made me realize I don't have. . .forever. We've—"

Will cleared his throat.

"*I've* wasted. . .enough time," Gram corrected, her speech still slow. "And I'm not going to waste. . .anymore. Well, only the time it takes to get my health. . .back to normal and plan the wedding. I'd really. . .like a nice one after witnessing Jake's and Luke's and Nora's. And I want *all* my loved ones. . .to be there."

Laci grinned when her grandmother looked pointedly at her. "There is no way I'd miss your wedding, Gram. I'll even help plan it if you'd like. Do you two have a date in mind?"

"Ellie thinks we ought to wait until after the election so Lydia and Ben can help John. She'd like us to do a little campaigning for him, too," Will answered.

"Gram, you don't need to put it off that long," John said.

"It takes time to plan a wedding. I. . .want a nice one. And I sure don't want to use this cane. . .to get me down the aisle. We'll see how it goes."

"Okay, but don't worry about my campaign."

"I want Lydia and Ben to help you out. I'll be fine."

"Of course you will," Laci said. "I'm going to see that you are. I'm staying to make sure you take it easy and get better. Besides, I want to help plan this wedding."

"Can you stay that long?" John asked.

"I hope so. I have a great assistant back in Dallas. If something comes up I have to take care of, I could drive back for a few days." Laci didn't tell them she was thinking of moving back to Sweet Springs.

Her mother shook her head. "Well, I don't know—"

"Mom, I can do this. It's time I helped this family some. You and Dad go help John win his election, and I'll move in with Gram for now. It's settled."

The next week was a busy but rewarding one for Laci. She felt good about staying with Gram and helping her. She wasn't happy about not being able to do things as normal, and Laci had to watch her constantly to make sure she didn't overdo it; but it was wonderful to spend time with her.

Keeping up the house was not a problem. After the cleaning they'd all done before bringing Gram home, Laci took to cleaning a couple of rooms a day and managed to keep the house looking wonderful with relative ease.

She enjoyed doing the cooking—and Gram seemed to enjoy supervising. Laci loved getting Gram's secrets to making pie dough and battering chicken fried steak. Laci felt particularly proud when Gram pronounced Laci's biscuits every bit as good as her own. Laci planned on learning to make some of her favorite dishes from her grandmother's recipe file over the next few weeks.

After a few days Laci's mother seemed to relax and even acknowledged that Laci was perfectly capable of caring for Gram while she was gone.

"At least it will be easy to keep in contact. You'll have all our cell phone numbers, and I'll check in every day," Laci's mom said.

"Lydia, I'm going to be fine," Gram said. "You need to stop worrying about me. . .and do what you can to get that grandson of mine elected. Will and Laci are going to make sure. . .I follow the doctor's orders. You can be certain of that."

Laci's mother nodded her head. "I know they will. I just hate to leave you, Mom."

Laci could tell her mother was near tears and feeling torn. It was obvious she wanted to be in two places at once—here with Gram and out on the campaign trail helping her son. But Gram understood that, too.

"Honey, it's not my time to go," she assured her daughter. "If it were, I'd already be gone."

"I know." Laci's mom sniffed and nodded.

"Well, then. He'll call me home when He calls me home. Until then we're going to live these lives. . .He's given us the way He wants us to. I'm sure the Lord wants John in the Senate. I have plenty of people here. . .to help me. John needs you and Ben."

Laci's mother took a deep breath then released it. "You're right. But I want to know all the details of the wedding plans. And it's not as if we're not going to be around. We'll be in and out of town on a regular basis."

"That's right."

"I just don't want to miss out on the fun of planning your wedding."

"We'll make sure we consult with you before making any decisions, won't we, Gram?" Laci assured her mother.

"Of course we will."

"Promise?" Laci's mom grinned at her mother.

"I promise," Gram said.

"Okay, I feel better now."

"Good. It's settled. Let's have a cup of coffee and some. . .of that vanilla wafer cake Laci made this morning. I think it may be. . .even better than mine."

~

That Sunday Gram felt well enough to attend church, and Will picked up her and Laci and drove them. Laci's heart swelled with love for the congregation she had grown up in. The members showed her grandmother how much she meant to them by coming up to talk to her, hug her, and tell her they would continue to pray for her until she was back to normal. They also welcomed Laci with open arms and offered to help out with Gram in any way they could.

They made their way up the aisle and joined the rest of the family, which was now so large they filled two whole pews. As Laci scooted in to sit beside her brother, John, she was humbled by how faithful her family had always been through the years.

But her heart ached at the realization that she hadn't been attending church in Dallas regularly the way she should have been. And she hadn't become involved in the congregation there either. Laci sent up a silent addition to the prayer being said, asking the Lord for His forgiveness and for His help to be the Christian she used to be—whether she stayed in Dallas or moved back home.

Her heart soared as she sang familiar hymns, and she let the joy of worshipping together as a family flow over her. As the minister, David Morgan, began his lesson, Laci put all else out of her mind and listened. It felt wonderful to be back in the church, and she'd never felt more at home than she did at that moment.

~

The next week Laci and Will took turns driving Gram to her speech and physical therapists over in Roswell. Will could and would have taken her to every appointment, but he seemed to sense that Laci needed time with her grandmother. He really was a very sweet man, and Laci was happy he was going to be her new grandpa once he and Gram got married.

On the days Laci drove Gram to Roswell, they had lunch if her grandmother wasn't too tired. She wasn't up to doing a lot of wedding planning yet, but they bought bridal magazines and pored over them at home.

"I'm not ready to buy a dress. But I want to get an idea of what's in style for a woman my age," Gram said as she sat at the kitchen table and turned the pages of the magazine they'd just purchased.

"That's all right, Gram. There's no hurry yet." Laci put on hot water for the tea her grandmother loved. "And I don't want you getting too tired. We want your health back first. Then we'll find a dress that's right for you."

"I don't want anything too frilly," Gram said. "I just want something simple and pretty. It's not like it's my first wedding, when your grandpa and I eloped. That's why I'd like to have a real wedding this time."

"I think you should."

"You don't think I'm being silly?"

"No, ma'am, I don't think you are silly at all. Besides, the whole family has been waiting for you two to get married. They'd feel cheated if you and Will eloped."

"That's what Will said when I asked him. I think he's looking forward to seeing me walk down the aisle."

"I'm sure he is. I know we all are."

"I should have told him yes a long time ago." She sighed. "I don't know why I didn't."

"Well, it's a big step, Gram."

Gram chuckled. "You know, we should be having this conversation in reverse."

"What do you mean?"

"I should be reassuring *you* about all these things. You're the one who should be getting married."

"That's kind of hard to do when no one has asked me, Gram."

"You aren't dating anyone in Dallas?"

Laci shook her head. "No. Not really. I have some friends I go out with from time to time, but no boyfriend." And the only man she'd seen lately that she could be attracted to wasn't in Dallas. He was right here in Sweet Springs.

"Why don't you just move home, Laci? We sure do miss you here."

The teakettle began to whistle, and Laci made them both a cup of tea. She'd always found it easy to talk to her grandmother. "I've been giving that some thought. But I don't want to get Mom and Dad's hopes up until I'm sure, so I haven't said anything to them about it."

"Oh, honey, they'd be so happy if you came back. We all would."

Laci took a sip of tea then sighed. "Being on my own in Dallas hasn't quite been what I thought it would be, Gram."

"I'm sorry to hear you've been disappointed, dear. But I sure hope you decide to come back here to live. Don't worry, though. I won't say anything to your parents until you make up your mind."

"Thank you, Gram. I know you won't. If it weren't for my business, it would be an easy decision. I don't know if I should sell out or open up a shop here or what. I'm very confused."

"Why don't you promote your assistant manager to manager to run your business from Dallas and open a shop here, too?"

"Well, I'm not sure I can afford to do both."

Gram nodded. "I understand. Maybe you could sell your inventory in the business to her. . .you know, the furnishings you've bought for the shop and the specialty items you carry and let her take over your clientele. She could change the name, and you could use that money to reopen your Little Touches here. I'm sure you would have lots of business here in Sweet Springs. There aren't many interior decorating shops around the area."

Laci felt hope grow. Relocating back here was what she wanted to do, but was it the right decision? She didn't know. "It sounds wonderful, but I'm not sure it's what I should do. I'll have to give it a lot of thought."

"And you need to. It's not something that should be decided overnight. And, Laci?"

"Yes, Gram?"

"Why don't you pray for the Lord's guidance and let *Him* show you what you should do?" Gram took a sip from her cup of tea as she waited for Laci's answer.

Suddenly Laci knew she'd been trying to make decisions without taking them to the Lord. If she'd done that before she moved to Dallas, perhaps she wouldn't be so confused now. "Thank you, Gram. You always give me the best advice. I'll do just that."

When Will came by a short time later, Laci decided to give the newly engaged couple some time to themselves. She headed downtown to her brother and cousin's law practice—or rather to the building next door to their offices, where John had set up his campaign headquarters. Her parents and John were leaving the next day, and she wanted to tell her brother good-bye.

With John running for office, her cousin Jake was taking care of most of the business at their law practice, but John liked to keep up with things when he was in town. Renting the building next door made it fairly easy to do that. Right now his campaign headquarters was filled with posters, flyers, and yard signs—and quite a few volunteers stuffing envelopes and manning phone lines. Laci was impressed.

John waved at her from across the room as he talked on the telephone. When he ended the conversation he hurried over to her and gave her a hug. "Hey, sis! I was just about to take a break. Want to go over to the diner and have some dessert and coffee with me?"

"Sure, if you have time."

"I'll make the time," he said, leading the way back outside and down the street.

"Wow! I guess I didn't realize how much was involved in running for office, John."

John laughed. "Neither did I. But I love it. I love getting out and meeting with people, finding out what they'd like from their senators and representatives. Sometimes it's a real eye-opener."

"Is there anything I can do while you're out of town?"

"Sis, you're doing plenty watching over Gram so that Mom and Dad can help me out. That means more than I can tell you."

He opened the door to the diner, and Laci had to smile as the bell jingled. Dee greeted them when they walked in and immediately came to take their order. "I didn't expect to see you again for a while, John. You're leaving tomorrow, right?"

"Bright and early. But Laci came by, and I decided to take a break. I'll have a piece of your chocolate pie and coffee, please."

"I'd like the same thing, Dee."

"Be right out with it," Dee said.

Nothing in the conversation said Dee and John were anything except friends. But something about the way she'd looked at him when she asked when he was leaving and the way John watched *her* as she left the table had Laci wondering about the two of them. There seemed to be more to it.

The bell over the doorway jingled again, and Laci turned to see Eric Mitchell walk in. He glanced around to find a table and smiled when he saw her and John.

"Hey, Eric! Come and join us," John said.

With each step the man took crossing the floor, Laci's heartbeat sped up a notch.

"Hi, John, Laci." He took a seat at the table. "What are you two up to? And how is your grandmother doing?"

"Well, Laci can answer that best because she's taking care of Gram so our parents can help me campaign."

Laci smiled. "She's doing great. When I left the house, she and Will were looking at wedding magazines."

"Who's getting married?" Eric asked.

"Gram and Will Oliver," John said.

"Are they really?" Eric looked at Laci for confirmation.

She nodded. "Yes, they really are."

"Well, I think that is fantastic!"

"What is fantastic?" Dee asked as she brought out the pie and coffee.

"That Gram and Will are finally getting married."

Dee plopped down in the empty chair at the table. "Finally?"

"Finally," John answered.

A huge grin spread across Dee's face. "I can't think of two people better suited to each other. They've been sweet on each other for a long time now. I am so happy for them. When is the wedding going to be?"

"Maybe after the election—we aren't real sure just yet. Gram wants to regain her health, and she doesn't want to have to use a cane to get down the aisle," Laci said. "I'm going to help her with the planning."

"Well, if you need anything, just let me know. Not that I know much about planning weddings, but I'll be glad to help out." Dee stood and looked down at Eric as if she just realized he was there. "I'm sorry, Eric. What can I get for you? Are you up for some pie and coffee, too?"

"Sounds good. I'll have the same thing they ordered. I skipped lunch today, and that chocolate pie looks mighty good to me."

While they enjoyed Dee's Mile-High Chocolate Pie, Laci listened to Eric and John talk about politics. But she found it hard to concentrate with her pulse racing at top speed. She hadn't expected to run into Eric, and she suddenly felt like a tongue-tied teenager all over again. She didn't know whether she was relieved or disappointed when he looked at his watch and suddenly jumped up.

"Oops! I'm running late. I have to go." He pulled some bills out of his pocket and laid them on the table. "John, have a safe trip. I don't have a doubt in my mind about the outcome of the election. You're going to be our new senator come November."

He turned to smile at Laci, and her breath caught in her throat. He had the most contagious smile.

"If you need help with your grandmother, Laci, just let me know. I'll help in any way I can."

"Thank you" was all Laci could muster as he waved and left the diner.

"Eric meant what he said, Laci," John said. "If you need anything while we're gone, he'll be glad to help."

"It was nice of him to offer, and I'll keep it in mind." She wished she would have reason to call on him, but she was pretty sure that wasn't going to happen. "Between Will and me and the rest of the family, I don't think there will be a problem. And don't look so concerned. We'll be fine. You just try to keep Mom from worrying, okay?"

"Will do, sis. Thank you for coming home. It means a lot to us all."

It couldn't mean more to anyone than it did to her. Home. There was no place like Sweet Springs.

Eric hated to leave the diner—and Laci's company—but he was almost late in picking up Sam from his afternoon sitter and getting him to T-ball practice. Sam wouldn't have liked that at all. And neither would the parents of the rest of the team.

Their first game was in a few days, and Eric had already run into several parents who wanted to coach from the sidelines. No one wanted his job, but he had a feeling they'd love to tell him how to do it.

Sam and the other little boys on his team seemed to improve with each practice, and Eric didn't know who was looking forward to the first game the most—he or his son. The only thing that seemed to be missing was someone to cheer Sam on from the bleachers like the other boys had. He had no mother, no family nearby except for Eric. A vision of Laci and a big family came to Eric's mind, and he could picture them in the stands rooting for Sam.

He shook his head. He needed to quit thinking along those lines. Attracted as he was to Laci Tanner, she was no more attainable now than she had been in the past. He'd do well to set his sights on someone closer to home. Only trouble was, no one around here set his heartbeat hammering in his chest and his pulse racing double-time as the sight of Laci Tanner did. He sure wished she lived here. But her home was in Dallas, and he needed to remember that. Still, that vision of her cheering for his son wasn't an easy one to dismiss.

Chapter 5

During the next few days Laci checked in with Myra to see how she was doing at the shop. Everything was going well, if a bit slow.

Myra again told her not to worry about how long she took. "It's not as though I work nonstop, Laci. I don't work on Saturdays unless by appointment, and we've always been closed on Sundays. If I have to work a Saturday, I'll take a little time off during the week. It's working out fine."

"I can't thank you enough for being such a loyal employee, Myra. If you need help, let me know, and we'll see what we can do about hiring someone part-time."

"Okay. But I don't think it will be necessary. I'm just glad your grandmother is all right, Laci. Don't worry about a thing here. Really."

When the call ended, Laci offered a prayer of thanksgiving that the Lord had led Myra to apply for the position of her assistant. She was a good Christian woman and had been wonderful to work with.

Laci was able to keep track of things through her laptop, and with online banking she could take care of the payroll and paying bills from Sweet Springs. While business wasn't booming, they were faring a little better than just breaking even. Myra was doing an excellent job while she was gone.

If she should decide to sell out and Myra wanted the inventory, Laci would be sure to make her a good deal. Or if she decided to open another shop here and keep the one in Dallas, she hoped Myra would stay on as manager of that shop. In the meantime it wouldn't hurt to look around and see if she could find a nice, small, older home in which to set up business in Sweet Springs. Just in case.

Will had taken Gram into Roswell for her therapy that day, and Laci was meeting her aunt Nora, Rae, and Sara for lunch. She decided to walk down to the diner instead of driving. It wasn't all that far from Gram's, and she'd be able to see if anything was for sale near the small business district of Sweet Springs. She'd noticed several businesses in older homes off Main Street, so evidently that part of town had been rezoned.

As she strolled down the familiar streets, she was struck by a sudden wave of nostalgia. Sweet Springs had been a great place to grow up in, and it would be a wonderful place to—

Before she could finish the thought, Laci saw a For Sale sign. She caught her breath as she drew closer. There, right in front of her, was a cottage that would be perfect for a shop. It had probably been built sometime in the late 1800s or early 1900s and was charming, with a front porch that wrapped around two sides of the house. The front windows were large and would make wonderful display windows. She jotted down the phone number of the Realtor on the sign, making a mental note to check on it when she got back from town.

When she arrived at the diner, Rae, Sara, and Meggie were already there, and Laci hurried over to join them. "Have you been here long? I probably should have driven, but I walked over from Gram's."

"No problem," Sara said. "We've only been here a few minutes. The doctor was running late for my appointment, so Rae brought Meggie in to meet us."

Meggie was busy with a color sheet that Dee gave her little customers. Laci bent over and planted a kiss on top of the little girl's head. "Hi, Meggie! How are you today?"

"I'm good, Laci. Wae kept me while Mommy went to doctow." She smiled up at Laci. "How awe you?"

"I'm doing good, too."

"I'm glad. I'm hungwy, too."

"Nana Nora will be here soon, and then we'll order," Sara told her daughter.

" 'Kay." Meggie went back to coloring.

"I can't believe it's Aunt Nora who'll be the last to get here," Laci said. "She's usually the one waiting for everyone else."

"She should be here any minute now. She said she'd be a bit late. She was going to run by the hospital to drop off lunch for Dad," Rae said.

Sara chuckled. "She'll be here, Laci, but I'm sure the change in Nora has been amazing to you."

"Well, yes, it has." She smiled at Rae. "I'm assuming your dad has had a lot to do with that?"

"They are very happy together," Rae said. "It took me a while to accept the fact that he'd found someone to love after Mom died. I wasn't real happy about it at first."

"You'd have been less happy if you'd known Nora before her transformation, Rae," Sara said. "She's come a very long way."

"Well, I know Dad had a lot to do with it, but actually I think the love you and Jake and Meggie have shown Nora is what turned her around," Rae said.

Sara grinned. "Jake convinced her she would always be part of our family."

Laci knew Jake and Sara had been going together back in high school, but something happened and they broke up. Jake married someone else while Sara ended up marrying Nora's son, Wade. Then Wade had been killed in an automobile accident, and Sara lost their unborn baby in the crash and had nearly died herself. All of that happened not long after Jake's wife passed away, leaving him to raise Meggie alone. About a year later he moved back to Sweet Springs to be closer to family, and he and Sara fell in love all over again.

"I guess Aunt Nora wasn't too happy about you and Jake getting together," Laci said to Sara.

"You're right. She wasn't happy at all. But with the Lord all things are possible, and He was the one who changed Nora's heart. And what a blessing it's been to see it all happen right before our eyes."

"Well, she is a wonderful stepmother," Rae said. "She helped me when I was having a hard time accepting that she and Dad were in love and when I was so confused and afraid to let myself fall in love with Luke."

"You know, this family circle of ours could sure be confusing to people, couldn't it?" Laci said with a chuckle.

"It sure could. My grandpa is engaged to my grandmother-in-law, who has been my grandmother-in-law twice. Nora, who was my mother-in-law, is now my aunt-in-law, and, Laci, I am your cousin-in-law for the second time."

They were still laughing when Aunt Nora showed up. "What's so funny? What did I miss?"

"Oh, we were just talking about our family ties, Nora," Sara said. "They are pretty—"

"Amazing," Rae said.

"Yes, they are. And yet there hasn't been a divorce in the family!" Aunt Nora said.

"And that's a blessing," Sara said.

"It certainly is—especially in this day and time."

Aunt Nora kissed Meggie, who was giggling because her mommy and the others had been, and then took a seat. "I love this family. I know I didn't always show it, but, oh, how happy I am that I'm still part of it!"

"We're glad, too, Aunt Nora," Laci said honestly. Her aunt had been a widow for a long time, and heartache had probably been part of the reason she'd been so bitter and selfish when Laci was growing up. Happiness had been a long time coming for her aunt Nora, even if a lot of it had been her own doing. Laci could only be happy for her now.

"Nana's heaw. Can we eat now?" Meggie asked.

"You sure can," Dee said, coming to take their order. "What would you like, Meggie?"

"A gwilled cheese, please. And fench fies."

"Grilled cheese and fries coming up. Want milk to drink?" Dee asked Meggie.

Meggie scrunched up her nose and looked at Sara. "Can I have chocolate milk, Mommy?"

"Yes, you can have chocolate milk."

Meggie smiled and showed her dimples. " 'Kay."

Laci couldn't help but chuckle. She was a delightful child.

Once Dee had their orders and left for the kitchen, Aunt Nora asked, "How are the wedding plans coming along? Do you need any help, Laci?"

"Well, Gram is looking at magazines and talking about it, but she hasn't been up to looking at dresses yet. Nothing has been decided about flowers or a cake and all that. Gram promised Mom we wouldn't make decisions without her input, too, so we're jotting down 'maybe' lists."

"We'd all be more than glad to help plan, too," Aunt Nora said.

For the first time Laci realized they probably would like to be in on it. "Why don't we get together with Gram once or twice a week to throw out ideas? I'm sure she'd love it."

"Oh, that would be fun!" Rae said. "Gram was in on the planning of all of our weddings."

"I'd love to help, too," Sara said.

Meggie looked up from her coloring. "Me, too."

"Wouldn't it be fun to give her a surprise shower like you gave me, Rae?" Nora said.

"Oh, I *like* that idea," Rae said.

"I love it! That would be so much fun." Laci found herself wishing she'd been here for Aunt Nora's shower and for the fun of planning all their weddings, too. But she couldn't go back and undo the past. She'd just be thankful she was here to help with Gram's now.

"Let's do it!" Aunt Nora said as Dee returned with their drink orders. "Want to help us, Dee?"

"Help with what?" Dee asked, setting Meggie's chocolate milk in front of her.

"We want to give Gram a surprise wedding shower," Sara said as Dee placed iced tea in front of her, Laci, and Rae.

"Oh, that sounds like fun. I'd love to be part of it!" Dee said, putting a glass of water and a cup of coffee in front of Nora.

"Good, then we'll count on your help," Aunt Nora said.

"Please do. And I'll be right back with your meals," Dee said.

Aunt Nora said a blessing before their food came. "Dear Lord, we thank You for this day and for this family we are part of. Please help us make Ellie and Will's wedding as special as they are. Please bless this food we are about to eat. In Jesus' name we pray, amen."

"Amen," Meggie echoed.

Dee returned with their meals and set hamburger baskets in front of Rae and Laci and a grilled cheese down for Meggie. "Have you heard from your mom and dad, Laci? Will she be able to help with the planning?"

"Oh, yes. She'd never let us forget it if we left her out. But we can do the preliminary planning—she just wants to be in on the final decisions. I think they're coming home for a few days next week."

Dee set a chicken salad sandwich in front of Nora and a BLT down for Sara. "How is the campaign going? Did they say?"

"Really well. Mom says John is drawing good crowds at all the stops."

"That's great. I know he's going to win."

"We're sure of it," Aunt Nora said.

Dee smiled and nodded, but Laci thought she noticed a wistful expression in her eyes. Evidently she wasn't the only one who thought so.

Sara shook her head as Dee left the table. "I wish that brother of yours and Dee would come to their senses and admit they love each other." She sighed.

"Oh, so do I!" Laci said. "But I wasn't sure if I was imagining the way they look at each other or not."

Aunt Nora shook her head. "You aren't imagining it. Those two have been denying how they feel for years now. I don't know what it will take to get them together."

"Well—" Sara began but then stopped midsentence when the bell over the door jingled. They all looked up to see Luke, Jake, and Eric enter the diner.

"Look who's here," Rae said.

Laci's pulse quickened at the sight of Eric and began to pick up speed as the three men waved and headed in their direction.

"Daddy!" Meggie yelled out. "Want a fench fie?"

"Sure do." Jake reached down and took one off her plate. He kissed her cheek. "Thanks, darlin'. Let's drag a table over so we can all sit together."

The men made quick work of putting the tables together, and in the process of moving around so Jake could sit between Sara and Meggie and Luke beside Rae, Laci somehow ended up sitting beside Eric. Not that she was complaining, but it did nothing to slow down her racing pulse.

Annie came to take the men's orders, and before long three different conversations were going on at the table. Laci knew the Tanner-Breland women had developed a knack for keeping track of more than one conversation at a time. She was glad she could still do it after being away for so long.

"How you feeling, hon?" Jake asked Sara.

"Real good today. The doctor says all is well with the baby."

"I'm glad."

"I thought you were working at the ranch all day," Rae said to Luke.

"I'd planned to, but without you to have lunch with, it got lonesome so I decided to come find you."

"Missed me, did you?"

"No doubt about it," Luke answered his wife.

The caring conversations between the couples left Laci longing for the same kind of relationship. . .something she hadn't given much thought to in a while.

"How are you doing, Eric? I've been telling everyone about the excellent work you do since you helped us remodel the kitchen," Aunt Nora said.

"Why, thank you, Mrs. Wellington. I appreciate all the business you throw my way."

"You do remodeling, Eric?" Laci asked. The older home she wanted to look at would probably need some work to turn it into a shop.

"He does it all," Jake said. "He built our house. You need to stop by when you have a minute and see what a great job he did."

"And he does excellent remodeling, too," Aunt Nora said. "He totally redid our kitchen, and we absolutely love it."

If Laci wasn't mistaken, Eric seemed to flush at the compliments.

"Why, thank you all. Maybe I need to put up a satisfied customer page on my Web site." Eric chuckled, and the color deepened.

Laci found his modesty about the work he did endearing.

"Anytime," Jake said. "We'll be glad to let people know what a great builder you are."

"Thank you. When I have time to update, I may take you up on the offer."

Annie brought out the men's food, and the next hour was one of the most pleasant Laci had spent in a long time. She hated for it to end, but when Meggie started yawning and Sara did the same, it seemed time to call it an afternoon.

"I guess I'd better get Meggie and myself home for a nap," Sara said with a chuckle.

"I need to be going, too. I have some errands to run," Aunt Nora said.

Annie brought their checks, but Jake grabbed them before anyone could pull out a wallet.

"My treat, ladies." He gave Annie a check card. "Put it all on there, please, Annie."

"Sure will. I'll be right back with your receipt." She walked over to the cash register.

"Why, thanks, Jake," Laci said

"Yes, thank you, dear," Aunt Nora added.

"Would you mind giving me a ride back to Gram's, Aunt Nora? I walked down, but I forgot how warm it would be by this time of the afternoon."

"I'll be glad to." Aunt Nora stood up and brushed at her skirt. She hugged Meggie. "Nana is going to come get you for a few hours tomorrow, okay?"

" 'Kay." Meggie yawned again as Jake picked her up to take her to the car.

"We'll see you all later," Rae said. She and Luke and Eric had decided to stay awhile longer.

"See you later," Laci said as she walked to the door. She glanced back to find Eric's gaze on her, and her heart did a funny little jump. When he waved and smiled, she waved back before following her aunt out the door.

Laci wondered how she could ever have thought of this town as boring. If she kept running into Eric Mitchell like this, any boredom she might have felt there at one time would certainly be a thing of the past.

Chapter 6

Later that evening Laci told Gram and Will about Sara, Nora, and Rae wanting to be in on planning their wedding, and Laci could tell they were both pleased.

"Why, that's sweet of them. Sometimes I wonder if we ought to just elope—"

Will shook his head. "Now, Ellie, that'd be fine with me. But you know you don't want to do that. You've already said so."

"Gram, you'd better *not* do that. We all want to see you two walk down the aisle. And it will be fun to put it all together." Laci chuckled. "Even Meggie wants to help."

Gram's eyes lit up. "Oh, wouldn't she make a cute flower girl?"

"That's a wonderful idea, Ellie. Meggie would make an adorable flower girl!" Will agreed.

"I suggested we all get together and throw out ideas," Laci said. "We can do that much without Mom. Then when she gets into town we can have some of it narrowed down. Unless you decide definitely that you want something. I don't think Mom would put a damper on your fun."

"No, she wouldn't. I know she wants to be in on it all, too, though. It'll be fun just to start gathering ideas for her to help with when she comes home."

"Well, we can do that. I'll call and see if they can come over on Tuesday or Thursday when you don't have therapy, or we could get together on a Saturday or Sunday afternoon."

"That will work. Most Saturdays would be okay, but not tomorrow. It's the Teddy Bear Brigade afternoon."

"Teddy Bear Brigade? What's that?"

"It's the nickname for a group of women at church who get together there once a month to stuff teddy bears. We take them to the local hospital and fire and police departments to give out to children who might need them. We used to meet on Tuesdays but found that left out the women who work outside the home, so we changed it to Saturdays. And we used to meet once a week, but now we have so much help we only need to meet once a month. We have a potluck lunch and then get to work."

"Oh, yes, I remember Mom's mentioning you all do that."

"Well, we'll be going this Saturday. When you call the girls, remind them of it, will you?"

"Of course I will, Gram. I'll go make those calls right now. I'll bring back a piece of cake and some coffee for you and Will after I'm finished calling, okay?"

"That sure sounds good to me," Will said. "Thank you, Laci."

She was coming to think of that gentle older man as her grandpa. She'd been young when her own passed away. And her dad's parents had died before she was born. It would be good to have a grandpa again.

It took several calls back and forth to settle on Tuesdays and Thursdays for their wedding-planning sessions with the others. She almost forgot to remind them about the Teddy Bear Brigade on Saturday, but they all assured her she could let Gram know they would be there.

Laci cut three pieces of butternut pound cake and filled coffee cups, loading it all on a tray to take to Gram and Will. As she left the kitchen she realized she was happier than she'd been since she'd moved to Dallas. The only thing missing was that someone special to share her life with. Thoughts of Eric's smile suddenly flashed through her mind, and she stopped short when she reached the living room. Where had they come from?

"Laci, dear, are you all right?"

She gave a little shake of her head to clear her thoughts. "I'm fine, Gram. I just talked to all the girls. They promised to meet with the Teddy Bear Brigade tomorrow."

"Oh, wonderful. It will be so good to have you all there."

Laci passed out the cake and coffee and visited with Gram and Will. But thoughts of Eric hovered in the back of her mind for the rest of the night and into her dreams.

Eric pulled the sheet up over Sam's shoulders and smoothed back the hair on his son's forehead. It had taken him only a few minutes to fall asleep. He'd practiced hard tonight then played outside while Eric mowed the yard. The fresh air and activity had him almost falling asleep at the supper table, and once he'd had a shower and lain down, he was out like a light.

Wishing he could call it a day, Eric left the nightlight on in Sam's room and went to clean up the kitchen. He was tired, too, but he needed to unload the dishwasher before he could put in the dirty ones and then fold the towels out of the dryer. He told himself that if he were ever to marry again he wouldn't take his wife for granted. A woman's work was never done, and as a man trying to fill both pairs of shoes he figured her job was harder.

All that boring day-in, day-out stuff of keeping a home and making sure the clothes and sheets were clean, deciding what to make for dinner, shopping for groceries. . . Eric shook his head. He went to the store only when they had nothing left in the house to eat. Sometimes he and Sam ate out for several days before he broke down and went. Then he bought enough to last for as long as he could. The refrigerator and freezer were packed when he got home, but other than to buy milk and bread he didn't have to go as often.

He treated their clothing much the same way. Buy a lot of what they needed—maybe then he wouldn't have to wash as often. Only that didn't work so well anymore. Sam was growing too fast, and it was hard to keep up with him.

Eric turned on the dishwasher then pulled a pile of towels and washcloths out of the dryer and brought them to the kitchen table. He sighed as he began to fold the towels—something he did often in spite of having bought so many. A woman must truly love a man to be willing to take on all those chores willingly. And if a man was blessed with having a wife who loved him that much, he shouldn't take her for granted.

He began folding the washcloths, and his thoughts drifted to that afternoon. For a moment, seeing the loving relationships Jake and Luke enjoyed with their wives had dampened his spirits. He'd had that once. And he wanted it again. But, as busy as he was, it didn't seem likely. And the only woman who'd caught his interest lately would be going back to Texas one of these days. Still. . .he sure had enjoyed sitting by Laci this afternoon. He wouldn't mind getting to know her better. He wouldn't mind that at all.

It was the next morning before Laci called about the house she'd looked at on Fourth Street. The price wasn't that bad, especially compared to what she was paying in rent for the shop in Dallas. But what made the possibility of moving back to Sweet Springs even more appealing was that it was for sale *or* lease. She wouldn't require a huge amount of money to get into it. But still she needed to give it more thought.

As she helped Gram settle in the car with her cane and a pile of little bears she'd made before her stroke, Laci found herself looking forward to the afternoon. Gram had suggested she make scalloped potatoes to take for lunch. Aunt Nora had said she'd be bringing fried chicken, and Sara and Rae were bringing salad and dessert.

When they arrived at church and went into the fellowship hall, Laci helped Gram find a place with some of the other ladies at one table then took their food into the kitchen. They'd enlarged it since she'd been away, and it was a good thing. The old kitchen barely had room for one or two ladies at a time. But this one was much larger and had plenty of room for the ten women working in it. They all seemed to be talking at once while setting out the meal on a table near the kitchen.

Gina Morgan, the minister's wife, was about Sara's age and seemed very nice. Laci also recognized Ida Connors and Susan Mead, who were close to her mother's age. And there were others she'd known for years; being here felt like home. She and her cousins-in-law pitched in with the setup, and soon they were ready to eat.

Gina asked a blessing for their work and the food. "Dear Lord, we ask You to bless the little children who will receive our teddy bears. We hope they give them comfort when they are hurting or sad. We ask You to bless this food we are about to eat, and, Father, we thank You for all our many blessings—especially for Your Son and our Savior, Jesus Christ. In His precious name we pray, amen."

Laci filled Gram's plate so she wouldn't have to navigate with her cane and took it to her; then she went back to fix her own. She brought it to the table and listened while conversations flowed around her.

"I sure hope you get better soon, Ellie," Ida said. "I'm missing your Sunday night suppers."

"I miss them, too, Ida. I'm hoping the doc will let me put away this cane when I go back to see him."

"I hope so, too. Your speech seems to be back to normal," Gina said from across the table.

Gram nodded. "It is—unless I try to talk too fast. Then I stumble some."

"We're all praying for you to get well soon."

"Thank you. I appreciate it and count on it more than you know. And I'll be having a Sunday night supper as soon as I can—I promise."

Laci remembered her mother had mentioned that Gram had started holding Sunday night suppers not long after she went to Dallas. After church on Sunday nights, anyone who wanted to come was invited. It sounded like a lot of fun, and Laci wondered if she could help her grandmother start them up again.

As lunch finished, the tables were cleared and teddy bears brought out to stuff. Made out of any kind of scrap of fabric, their faces were either painted on with fabric paint or embroidered by those with that talent. But either way they were sweet.

They became even cuter as they were stuffed. They had a tag sewn on that gave the name of the church, the address, and phone number and also said *Made with Love*. Laci was sure they would be a comfort to any child in distress or pain.

She enjoyed being part of the group and felt as if she'd done something worthwhile when the bears were all stuffed and everyone got ready to leave.

"I'm so glad you're going to be with us for a while," Gina said. "I know your family is glad you're here. And I think you've been very good for Miss Ellie. She seems almost back to normal."

Laci looked over to where her grandmother was showing her beautiful engagement ring to several ladies her age. She did look so happy. "I think she's almost there."

"We are so glad she and Will are getting married. You're never too old to fall in love."

"I sure hope not." Laci grinned at Gina. "At least that would mean there's still hope for me."

"You're young yet, Laci. But I can tell you, it will probably happen when you least expect it."

"Well, it can happen anytime then." Laci laughed. But suddenly she knew she really, truly wished it would.

Will and Gram had made plans to eat dinner in Roswell with friends, and Laci thought she would enjoy making dinner for herself. But after she had made five trips to the pantry and opened the refrigerator at least four times, she realized it wasn't that she couldn't find anything she wanted to eat—she just didn't want to spend the better part of the evening alone.

She thought about going over to Luke and Rae's or Sara and Jake's, but that didn't seem to be the answer either. Happy as she was for them, seeing them together at times made her long for something she didn't have—a loving relationship. And after her talk with Gina that afternoon, she was already feeling a little forlorn over that. So she decided to go eat at the diner. Dee was the only other woman her age who seemed to be in the same boat.

One good thing came from waiting so long to make up her mind on what to do. By the time she reached the diner, the supper crowd had thinned out some. She seated herself at the counter so she could visit with Dee if she had a lull, and ordered a patty melt and hash browns.

"Do you ever take a day off, Dee?" she asked after her order had been placed and Dee brought her iced tea to the counter.

"Sure I do. But with my apartment upstairs it's hard not to be here. Besides with Mom moved away and no family here"—Dee shrugged—"this—and church—are where I have contact with other people."

"I can understand that. I get awfully lonesome in Dallas."

"Why don't you move back here?"

Laci paused before answering. "Well, I'm not going to say I haven't thought about it a lot lately. But. . ."

"It's a big decision, I know. For what it's worth, I'd love to see you back here. If you opened a shop, I'd probably be your first customer. I've been thinking of redecorating my apartment upstairs. It could use a new look."

"I'd be glad to look at it for you, Dee. Anytime."

"Thanks, Laci. I could use the advice. But I'm trying to get you back here. So if you open a shop here, you could really help me out. And as a satisfied customer I'd tell all my customers about you."

"Now that sounds like a deal that would be hard to refuse. I could even give you a discount for that kind of word-of-mouth advertising."

"Well, think about it."

"I will." Laci nodded.

The bell over the door jingled, and Dee looked over and began to smile. "Well, look here. It's my very favorite customer. How are you, Sam?"

Laci turned around, and her breath caught in her throat. Eric Mitchell had entered the diner with a little carbon copy of himself by his side. And he was adorable as he marched across the room and climbed up on an empty counter stool beside Laci.

"Hi, Dee! We've been playin' T-ball and watchin' baseball at the park all afternoon. Our team won, and Dad said I could have a milkshake with my supper. And so that's what I want. A grilled cheese and fries and a chocolate milkshake." The little boy barely took a breath between sentences. "Didn't you say so, Dad?"

"I did. We need these to go, though, Dee. I have to get him home and calmed down, or we'll never make it to Sunday school tomorrow."

Dee nodded, acknowledging his comment while she talked to Sam. "Well, congratulations! And since you won, the shake will be on me. Think we ought to treat your dad to one, too, since he coached the team?"

"Sure! He's the best coach ever."

"Okay, what else will you have, Eric?" Dee asked.

Laci didn't hear Eric's answer. She was too busy trying to take in everything. *Dad. Eric was a dad.* Her heart sank a little further each time she thought about it. Eric Mitchell had a child. She hadn't thought Eric was married. . .but obviously he must be. Still, he didn't wear a wedding ring. Was he divorced? Either option made the dreams she'd begun to weave about Eric wither in her heart. She willed herself not to show how disappointed she was.

"Hi, Laci. How are you tonight?" Eric asked as he took a seat on the other side of Sam.

"I'm fine." She looked down at his little boy and found big black eyes looking at her. She smiled at him. "Congratulations on winning your game."

"Thank you." He kept looking at her and then asked, "Who are you?"

"Sam!"

"I'm sorry, Dad." He looked back at Laci. "Dad doesn't like me to talk to strangers," he said in explanation.

"No, I don't. But I know Miss Tanner. I was trying to get you to realize you just sounded rude."

"I'm sorry. I didn't mean to. I just don't know who she is."

Eric sighed and shook his head. "Sam, this is Laci Tanner."

"Is she relationed—I mean *related*—to Jake and Luke and Sara and Rae and Meggie?"

"She is. She is their cousin."

"Oh, hi!"

"Hi, Sam. It's nice to meet you." Laci tried hard to concentrate on the little boy and not the man beside him. She had no business thinking about Eric Mitchell.

"You're nice. Do you like T-ball?" Sam asked.

"I don't think I've ever watched T-ball."

His eyes seemed to grow larger—if that was possible. "Really? You never have?"

"No, I never have. I bet it's fun to play, though."

"Uh-huh, it is. I have a game next week if you want to watch one."

"It's on Tuesday afternoon if you'd like to come," Eric said.

Laci wasn't sure what to say, and she wasn't at all happy with Eric for putting her in the awkward position of having to disappoint his son. "I'm not sure. I may have to take Gram to Roswell for her treatment."

"If you can't make it then, there'll be another one on Saturday," Eric said.

Laci knew Will would be more than happy to take Gram to Roswell, but she had no intention of going to the game. She just didn't want to come out and say so.

But the pressure was on when Sam looked up at her and smiled. "I'd sure like you to come see a T-ball game."

"I'll see what I can do," Laci found herself saying noncommittally. "I hope you win again."

"Me, too!"

Dee came back with Eric's orders to go, and Laci felt a sense of relief that he would be leaving soon.

Eric paid Dee and turned to Sam. "Come on, son. I have to do a load of wash when we get home."

"Okay," Sam said, climbing down from the stool and following his dad to the door. But he looked back and waved. " 'Bye."

" 'Bye," Laci and Dee both said at the same time.

Sam tugged at the door to open it for his dad.

"Thank you, Sam." Eric looked back for a moment. " 'Bye, ladies. See you later."

Laci didn't realize she'd released a huge breath when they left until Dee asked, "Laci, are you all right?"

"I—I didn't know Eric had a child. I didn't think he was even married."

"He's not. His wife died when Sam was only a few months old."

"Ohh." Her first reaction was relief that she wasn't attracted to a married man, quickly followed by sadness at his loss. And then there was Sam. . .so adorable and without a mom. Just thinking about him tugged at her heart. Sudden tears formed behind her eyes. "What did she die from?"

"She had a rare form of cancer. They didn't even know about it until she got sick."

"That's awful." And it was.

"But Eric was so strong through it all. And he is such a good dad to Sam."

Laci could only nod in agreement. She was glad Dee had to hurry off to wait on new customers who entered the diner. She didn't know what to say when her heart seemed to be sinking like a rock.

Eric was a single dad with a cute son. But that was a ready-made family and completely different from a single man who'd never been married. No matter how wonderful a dad Eric was—and Laci was sure he was a great one—his son needed a mom. And Laci wasn't sure she was nurturing enough to be the kind of mother Sam would need.

She let out another deep breath and forced herself to take a bite from a cold french fry. She needed to get Eric Mitchell out of her mind and quit weaving dreams about him. And she needed to do it now. But that was easier said than done when she remembered Sam's sweet invitation to come watch him play ball.

Chapter 7

Laci's parents came in for the weekend, and Jake and Sara invited the family over for a cookout after church on Sunday. It was the first time Laci had been in their house, and she was very impressed with Eric's talent as a builder. It was a beautiful custom home.

The home looked and felt as if it had been built around the same time as Gram's, with big bay windows and a wonderful wraparound porch. It was furnished with antiques and traditional furniture, and each room was warm and homey and welcoming. But the kitchen was Laci's favorite room. It had tiled countertops and state-of-the-art fixtures and appliances. It was laid out in an easy pattern for working, but large enough for several people to work in at the same time.

The covered patio out back was spacious and shady and a great place for family gatherings. The men stood around the grill talking while Jake cooked, and the women took charge of the kitchen to prepare the side dishes.

Sara set Laci to work grating cheese for the baked potatoes at one end of the huge island while Rae and Aunt Nora put together the salad at the other end. Laci's mom watched over her baked beans that were in the oven, and Gram sat at the table supervising it all. Meggie sat beside her, coloring and watching everything.

"Do you think those potatoes should come out and go in the warmer, Sara dear?" Gram asked.

"I think they're fine, Gram."

"Nora, don't chop that lettuce too fine, please. It gets stuck between my teeth if it's too little."

Laci held her breath, waiting for Aunt Nora's response.

"All right, Ellie. I didn't think of that."

Laci saw her aunt wink at Rae and grin, and she felt herself relax. At one time Aunt Nora would have had a comeback for Gram, but she had definitely changed. And then again she might have let it pass back then—they all knew Gram and her heart very well—and loved her the way she was.

"I'll be glad when the doctor releases you from his care, Mom." Laci's mother grinned at Gram and teased, "You've become quite bossy since your stroke."

Meggie sidled up to Gram and patted her back. "Gwam not bossy, Aunt Lydy."

Gram chuckled and hugged the child. "Thank you, Meggie. But your aunt Lydia is right."

"You admit it, Mom?" Laci's mother smiled at Gram.

"I've always been a little on the bossy side, Lydia, and you know it."

"Oh, I guess you have, come to think of it." Laci's mom laughed. "And I wouldn't have you any other way. I'm glad you're feeling well enough to give orders from over there."

"No one is going to be happier than I will be to get back to normal. Laci is a wonderful cook, but I miss puttering in my kitchen. I miss my Sunday night suppers, too. I want to get back to those as soon as I can."

Aunt Nora said, "We could take over—"

"No. If I didn't know I'd be getting better, I'd say yes. But it's something I enjoy doing. One of these days, though, when I can't manage it, you will all need at least to take turns at it. I don't want the custom to die out."

"We won't let that happen, Gram," Rae said.

"I'd be glad to help you hold one now if you want," Laci offered.

"I'll see what the doctor says this week."

"Michael thinks you are making wonderful progress," Aunt Nora said.

"Well, I wish he was my doctor for this, but I'm glad he sees some improvement." Gram changed the subject. "How is John's campaign coming along, Lydia?"

"I think it's going very well. He had a rally in Farmington planned for today, and I'm sure it will go fine. He has great crowds showing up to hear him speak everywhere we've been. And the contributions to his campaign are flowing in."

"That's wonderful. He's going to make a great senator. I just know it," Laci said with sisterly pride.

"I do, too. And I'm sure he's going to win," her mother said. "I'd feel a little more confident, though, if he were married, as his opponents are."

The doorbell rang just then, and Sara wiped her hands on a dishcloth. "Jake invited a couple of more people today. They must be here now." She hurried to answer the door and was back within minutes with Eric and Sam following her.

"Hi, ladies," Eric said.

Everyone else greeted him while Laci's heartbeat did a little tumble of some kind. Then it began to beat so hard she was afraid they all could hear it. She certainly felt it. She barely managed a hello.

"Hi, Lace!" Sam said with a grin, pulling her attention away from his dad. "I didn't know you was going to be here today."

He was so engaging that Laci couldn't help but smile. "I didn't know you were going to be here either, Sam."

"You gonna come to my game on Tuesday?" He smiled up at her, waiting for her answer.

Laci's heart melted at the look in his eyes—and the hopefulness in his voice. She knew she shouldn't get his hopes up, but she couldn't tell this little boy no. "I will try to be there, okay?"

"Okay, Lace!"

"It's Laci, Sam," Eric corrected.

"It is?"

"It's all right, Sam. You can call me Lace if you want to." She liked it.

"See, Dad? It's okay. Lace says it is."

Eric grinned and shook his head at his son. "All right, son. Let's go outside and see what Jake and the other men are up to, okay?"

"Sure. Let's go outside with the other men." He looked back into the room. "See ya."

There was a moment's quiet as the women in the room watched him follow his dad outside.

"Oh, wow! He is going to be a little heartbreaker one day," Rae said.

Sara chuckled. "Is he ever! I'm going to keep Meggie away from him."

"No, Mama. I like Sam. He's nice," Meggie said.

She'd been so quiet with her coloring that everyone must have forgotten she was there.

"I'm teasing, sweetheart." Sara gave her daughter a hug before turning to Laci. "So, *Lace*, how did you meet Sam?"

"Gram and Will went out last night, so I ate at Dee's. He and Eric came in, and we sort of hit it off."

"You and Eric?" Rae asked, grinning at her.

"No. Sam and I."

"Oh, I see," Laci's mom said, sounding a little disappointed.

Gram nodded. "I do, too."

Laci could feel the color rise up her neck and onto her face for no real reason except that everyone seemed to be watching her. "What?"

"Nothing, dear." Her mom patted her on the shoulder and teased, "It's just too bad Sam's not a little older. He seems quite taken with you."

"He is adorable," Sara said. "Jake suggested inviting them over today. It must get lonesome for Eric at times, especially on a Sunday."

"I imagine he's kept busy on the weekends just trying to catch up from the past week. It can't be easy for a man to try to be both mom and dad to a child," Aunt Nora said.

Laci was sure it wasn't. But it was plain he was doing a pretty good job. Sam seemed to be a wonderful child.

"A man needs a wife," Gram said.

"And speaking of that," Laci's mother said, changing the subject, "how is the wedding planning going?"

"We've decided to meet on Tuesdays and Thursdays to do the preplanning. Then when you get to come home for a few days, you can help with the final decision making," Gram said.

Laci's mom crossed the room and hugged her mother. "Thank you for finding a way to include me."

"You're welcome, dear."

Jake opened the back door just then and stuck his head inside. "Steaks are about ready. How are things in here?"

"We're ready whenever you are."

"Good. Just bring it on out anytime now."

Sara and Laci quickly filled glasses with iced tea, and everyone helped carry them outside. Then they brought out the rest of the food. After Jake said the blessing, Sara and Eric fixed their children's plates, and then the adults helped themselves.

"Come and sit by me, Lace," Sam asked when Laci turned from filling her plate. He and Meggie were sitting at the end of the line of tables Jake had set up.

"Sit by *me*, Laci," Meggie insisted.

Laci couldn't refuse either of them. So she took her tea and her plate and sat down between Sam and Meggie. They entertained her by explaining what they liked about their meal.

"I like steak. It's kind of hard to chew, though," Sam said.

"I like the potato best," Meggie said. "It's easy to chew."

"I like the salad," Laci told them.

"It gets stuck between my teeth," Sam said with a disgusted look on his face.

Laci had to chuckle. She'd have to remember to tell Gram she wasn't the only one that happened to.

Sara and Jake joined them as did Eric. Laci tried hard to keep her attention on the children, but she couldn't ignore the man sitting directly across from her as conversation flowed around the table. It was impossible not to steal a glance at him from time to time, and when she did she invariably caught his gaze on her, sending the color rushing to her face once more. She could only hope Eric thought she was sunburned.

Eric found it hard to keep from staring at Laci as she gave most of her attention to his son and Meggie. She was very good with them. That Sam liked her so much told him a lot. Eric had never seen him take up with anyone quite so fast. But something about Laci drew Sam to her since they'd met the night before, and he'd talked about her the rest of the evening after they left the diner.

Not that Eric blamed him. His son had excellent taste. Eric had found himself thinking about Laci all evening, too. She'd been so sweet to Sam, and the give-and-take between the two had been fun to watch. He hoped she stayed around awhile.

The rest of the afternoon was one of the most pleasant Eric had spent in a long time. Sam and Meggie convinced Laci to play with them on the large swing set and in the playhouse Jake had put up for his daughter. At five, Sam felt much older than Meggie who was three, but Eric was pleased to see how well his son played with her.

The rest of the women were cleaning up and would bring out dessert after their meal had settled a little while. He and Jake, Luke, Michael, Laci's dad, Ben, and Will took turns playing horseshoes.

"Thanks for asking me and Sam over, Jake. We're both really enjoying the afternoon."

"I'm glad you could come over," Jake said as they watched Luke throw his horseshoe. "I couldn't help but notice you watching Laci. You interested in her?"

Eric was a little surprised by the blunt question, but he wasn't going to lie. "Well, yeah, I am, I guess. I could be even more interested if she lived here."

"That right?"

"Yes."

"Well, we're all trying to get her to move back."

Eric's heartbeat picked up at the thought that she might. "In that case I wouldn't mind if you and Sara could see your way to get us together a little more often. At least until I get a sense of whether or not she could be interested in me, and then I could ask her out on my own."

"Oh, I think we can handle that."

"Thanks, Jake. You're a good friend."

Jake looked over at where Sam and Meggie were playing with Laci and then back to Eric. "I know firsthand how badly a child needs a mom, and Laci would make a good one, even if she doesn't realize it yet."

"I guess I should go rescue her from Sam."

"I'll go, too. Meggie can be pretty persistent."

The two men walked over to the playhouse and knocked on the door.

Meggie opened it a tad. "Hi, Daddy! Did you come to play?"

"Well, not just now. We think you need to let Laci go visit with the ladies inside."

"Why? It's more fun out here. She'll have to work if she goes in," Sam said with the wisdom of a five-year-old.

Eric could hear Laci chuckle even if he couldn't see her. He peeked in a window at his son and at Laci who was sitting in a tiny chair playing as if she were enjoying pretend tea. "Sam, I think Laci might want to visit with the ladies a little while."

"Do you?" Sam looked to Laci for confirmation.

"Well, I think I ought to go help bring dessert out to you guys, don't you?" Laci said diplomatically.

"Oh, dessut!" Meggie began nodding her head. "Okay. Laci needs to go, Sam."

Sam was a little more hesitant. He sighed and leaned his head to the side. "I guess so."

"I'll go see what they have for us, okay?" Laci said as she inched her way out the door.

"Okay."

"C'mon, Sam. Let's go swing 'til dessut gets here."

The two children ran over to the swings.

"I'm sorry Sam has held you captive most of the afternoon," Eric said to Laci as the three adults started toward the house.

"Well, Meggie did her share, too. Don't blame it all on Sam," Jake said.

"They are both precious, and I've enjoyed myself," Laci said. "I haven't been around children in a long time. You forget how refreshing their outlook on life is."

"Jake, Eric, you two part of this game or not?" Luke shouted from the side yard.

"We're coming. Let's go show them how to throw a horseshoe, Eric," Jake said, heading across the lawn.

"Okay." Eric smiled at Laci before he turned to go back to the game. "Thanks again, Laci."

"You're welcome." Laci smiled and waved as she hurried into the house.

"Thanks for entertaining Meggie and Sam, Laci," Sara said when Laci entered the kitchen.

Laci laughed. "I'm not sure who entertained whom. Those two are something." She'd enjoyed swinging and going down the slide with them and the pretend tea party. Mostly she'd just enjoyed hearing them talk. "And they are quite ready for *dessut*, as Meggie called it."

Sara laughed as she and Rae scooped out little balls of watermelon and added them to a bowl of cantaloupe balls. "It's about ready. It's not chocolate, though, so I'm not sure Meggie will consider it real dessert. They are something, aren't they? I love the way their minds work."

"Children have a way of looking at things that reminds us all of what's important," Gram said.

"That they do," Laci's mom said. "And speaking of children. . .you know your dad and I aren't getting any younger, Laci. You and John need to start thinking about settling down and starting families of your own so we can have grandchildren while we're young enough to enjoy them."

"Mom, that's not something you can just decide on. You have to meet the right person first."

"Well, how do you know you haven't?"

For some reason Laci felt that annoying blush again as her mother continued. "Actually I think John has. Only he and Dee are too blind to see it."

That led to a discussion of what to do to get the couple to admit how they felt about each other.

The back door opened, and Luke poked his head in. "Hey, we have some hungry kids out here. When is dessert coming?"

Rae grinned at her husband. "I know who the biggest kid is—you."

Luke laughed. "You know me well, sweetheart. We're working up an appetite with all this exercising we're doing."

That brought laughter from everyone in the kitchen.

"I know that pitching must be very tiring," Rae said with a grin. "We're bringing it out now."

Laci loved hearing the loving banter going on between her cousin and his wife. She could tell from the tone of their voices and the look in their eyes that they were crazy about each other. She wondered if she'd ever have that kind of relationship. She walked outside then and saw Eric's pitch make a ringer around the pole. And she wondered who it would be with if she did.

Chapter 8

Eric had known what he was missing, but he'd never felt it so acutely until now. The day had been pure joy for him and his son, and he hated to see it come to an end. So did Sam. As they said their good-byes to the Tanners and the Brelands, he felt a loss he couldn't understand.

"Thanks for having us," he said to Sara and Jake. "We enjoyed it a lot, didn't we, Sam?"

"Uh-huh! It was fun. Thank you."

"You are very welcome. I hope you'll come back again," Sara said to Sam.

"If you ask, we will," he answered matter-of-factly.

"We'll be sure to ask then," Sara assured him.

Sam turned to Laci. "Thanks for playin' with us, Lace."

"Thanks for letting me."

"You gonna come to my game on Tuesday?" he asked once more.

Laci knelt to be at eye level with him. "I'm sure going to try, okay?"

"Okay. I'll be looking for you."

When Sam suddenly threw his arms around Laci and hugged her, Eric was surprised. He'd never seen his son hug anyone but him. He saw tears gather in Laci's eyes as she hugged Sam, and he realized she'd been touched by the show of affection, too. Eric had a hard time holding back his own tears.

He turned quickly. "Let's go, pal. We need to run by the grocery store and pick up milk for tomorrow."

"Okay, Dad." Sam slipped his hand into Eric's, and they both turned and waved good-bye.

Eric nodded at Laci and mouthed, "Thank you."

She nodded, and he hoped that meant she knew how thankful he was for her attention to Sam.

If he hadn't been pretty sure Jake would keep his word and try to get them together again, Eric would have felt much worse about leaving. Something about that woman touched his heart, and it was more than how well she treated his son. She made his heart beat in a way it hadn't in years, and he liked it. He wanted to ask her out, even though the thought of dating had him feeling like a teenager all over again. Funny how some things never changed. Some feelings were the same no matter how old a person was.

"Do you think she'll come to the game, Dad?" Sam asked as he buckled up his seat belt in the backseat of Eric's pickup.

"I don't know, Sam," Eric answered honestly. "I think she will try to, though."

"I hope so."

"So do I, son. So do I." And he did—for both their sakes.

Laci hadn't been prepared for the overwhelming feeling that flowed over her when Sam hugged her that afternoon. She didn't know what to call it—all she knew was that he'd claimed a piece of her heart that day. She'd planned on trying to get out of going to his T-ball game, but after that hug there was no way she could miss it.

She looked for them at church that evening but didn't see them. She tried to put Eric and his son out of her mind as she concentrated on the lesson David was bringing. It was about leaving things in the Lord's hands and turning one's worries and cares over to Him. With so many decisions she had to make, the lesson spoke to Laci. Should she sell her business? Should she move back here? Should she tamp down the growing attraction she felt for Eric? Those were questions she needed to take to the Lord in prayer. She needed His help with all of it.

Once the service was over and she and the rest of her family were heading up the aisle, she was surprised when she heard her name called.

"Lace, wait!"

She turned to find Sam running toward her with Eric following at a slower pace.

"I didn't know you came to our church," Sam said when he reached her. "Dad said you did, but I never saw you here 'til tonight."

"I sure do. Did you and your dad get to the grocery store?" She could see Eric making his way toward them.

"Uh-huh. We got milk and some new cereal to try. Oh, and bread. Dad makes pretty good grilled cheese sandwiches." He leaned closer and whispered, "Don't tell him, but Dee makes them a little better. But his are good."

"I won't say anything."

Sam grinned up at her. "Thanks, Lace. I hope you get to come to my game. Dad said you might not be able to make it, but I hope you can be there."

"I'm planning on it, Sam."

"Sam, are you pestering Laci again?" Eric asked as he reached them.

"I don't do that, do I, Lace?"

"No, you don't."

"See, Dad."

Eric sighed and grinned at Laci. "He does have a one-track mind right now. He can't think of anything but his next game. I've told him you might not—"

"I know. But I'm going to try to come. I don't see any reason why I can't, unless something serious comes up to prevent me from getting there."

"Oh, boy," Sam said. "I'll have someone in the bleachers to root for me!"

"You don't have any relatives in the area?" Laci looked up at Eric.

He shook his head.

Suddenly Laci realized that with no mother to come to the games Sam had no one in the stands cheering for him. Her heart twisted at the thought. "I'll be there to cheer you on, Sam. I promise."

"Thank you, Laci," Eric said softly.

"I wouldn't miss it." And if she had anything to do with it she wouldn't be the only one cheering Sam on at his next game.

"Okay! See you Tuesday," Sam said before running off to join several other children.

Laci looked up to see Eric's gaze on her. "I hope he isn't bothering you. I'm at a complete loss here. Sam has never taken to anyone the way he has you."

"Well, I've never met up with anyone quite like Sam either. He's a special little boy."

Eric cleared his throat. "I certainly think so."

"Eric, please don't worry. Sam is not bothering me. I'm honored that he seems to like me." And she spoke the truth. It wasn't Sam who bothered her. It was his dad. He kept turning up in her dreams at night. . .and in the middle of the day, too.

On Tuesday the Wedding Planners, Inc.—as they'd decided to name themselves—met at Gram's for lunch. Laci made salad and a pasta casserole and was just pulling it out of the oven when Sara and Rae arrived with Meggie. They'd stopped at a fast-food place and picked up chicken nuggets for her.

Aunt Nora arrived right behind them, and after Gram asked the blessing, they all helped themselves and proceeded to have a leisurely lunch.

"Are you going to Sam's game this evening?" Sara asked before taking a bite of casserole.

"Yes. I promised him I would. You know. . .he doesn't have anyone in the stands to cheer him on."

"That's right," Aunt Nora said. "Eric has no relatives here anymore. Oh, dear. Poor little thing."

"Well, I'm going. Any of you want to join me?" Laci took a sip of tea and waited for their response.

"I'll go," Gram said. "I'll get Will to go, too. What time is it?"

"It's at six thirty."

Gram nodded. "We'll go out to eat after it's over."

"Thank you, Gram. That will mean so much to Sam."

"I'll talk to Luke," Rae said. "Maybe we'll be there, too."

"I'm sure Jake would be glad to go," Sara added. "I'll check with him."

"Well, if you are all going, Michael and I will, too," Aunt Nora said. "I don't want to be left out."

"I love you all. You are the best family in the whole world," Laci said.

"Well, why don't you just move home for good then?" Sara asked.

"I'm thinking about it," Laci finally admitted. Everyone started talking at once about it, but she didn't say anymore. She wasn't quite ready to discuss her ideas.

Once they'd finished eating they cleared the dishes and spread bridal magazines on the table. Laci's mom and dad had left on Monday to rejoin John on the campaign trail, but they were hoping to get back to town for the weekend. The girls hoped to be able to present some ideas to Laci's mom then for her input.

"Gram has marked pages in all of these. She doesn't want the normal wedding dress—"

"Just something simple and gorgeous," Gram said. "I do want to keep it simple."

"Do you have any colors in mind?"

"Not really. I'm partial to silver or cream for a wedding dress. And I'm not talking about one like you girls wore. Maybe a suit or just something kind of. . . elegant."

"Maybe you'd be happier with something that's usually for the mother of the bride," Aunt Nora suggested. "These books have those, too."

Sara flipped through one of the magazines until she came to a page with outfits like the ones Aunt Nora was talking about. "Look, Gram. Something like this?"

Gram pulled the magazine closer and nodded. "That's more like it, yes."

"Okay! I think we have an idea of what to look for now. At least style wise," Laci said. "Now you need to think about colors. Are you going to have attendants?"

"Just your mother," Gram said. "And maybe Meggie as a flower girl."

"Me?" Meggie had been coloring again, but Laci knew her well enough now to know she was listening to every word.

"Yes, you. You'll get to walk down the aisle ahead of me and throw flower petals out on the floor."

Meggie caught her breath and grinned. "I can thwow flowaw petals?"

"Yes, you can. And you'll get to wear a very pretty dress."

Rae showed her a picture from one of the magazines. "Like this."

Meggie clapped her hands. "That's pwetty! Okay."

"Where do you want the reception to be, Gram?" Sara asked.

"Oh, I think I'd like it to be in the fellowship hall at church."

Laci began to make a list of the things Gram had made a decision on and those she needed to think about. "You'll need to settle on flowers, too. What kind and color."

After about an hour they agreed to continue on Thursday. They were getting confused on what they liked and didn't like, and Gram was tired.

"I'm going to call Will about Sam's game and then take a nap. Don't let me sleep for more than an hour. Otherwise I'll never sleep tonight."

"Okay, Gram. I'll wake you," Laci said.

Aunt Nora looked at her watch. "I have to go, too. I need to check with Michael about the game and run to the grocery store. I'll see you all later."

" 'Bye, Aunt Nora. Thanks for helping."

"You're welcome. It is fun being together like this. You need to come back home for good." She gave Meggie a kiss and headed out to her car.

"You really do, you know," Sara said as she and Rae helped Laci clean up the kitchen. "We've all missed you, and it's just good to have you around."

"I'm leaning that way. I just need to be sure." And she needed to pray and hand it over to the Lord for His help in deciding. He knew what was best.

But the more she was around her family, the more she loved being with them. Just the thought of going back to Dallas left her with an empty feeling.

Eric parked the car and walked over to the ball field to practice before the game. He hoped Laci made it to the game. If not, his son would be disappointed. But he didn't want to bring up the possibility now. Besides, she'd promised Sam, and Eric thought that if something had come up she would have let him know so he could break the news to his son.

He'd watched her closely on Sunday. Laci had been touched by his son. Eric wasn't sure what she thought of *him*, but he had a feeling Sam had gotten to her. He tried to concentrate on the practice game, but he kept watching the stands as people arrived.

It was Sam who spotted Laci while Eric gathered his little guys together in the dugout just before the game started. "Dad, she's here. Lace came!"

Sure enough, Laci was there, making her way into the bleachers. She looked lovely in her green capri pants and matching top. Her hair was caught up on top of her head, and as she took a seat she waved at Sam, who had been waving his arms in the air to get her attention.

Then Sam caught his breath and let it out with a *whoosh*. "Dad!" He began pulling at Eric's shirt. "Dad—look who all she brought with her!"

It was hard for Eric to take his eyes off Laci, but it was even harder not to notice her whole family following her. Miss Ellie and Will sat on the bottom bleacher, while Sara, Jake, and Meggie took their places next to Laci on the second one. Behind them came Luke and Rae, and even Nora and Michael. Eric grinned and waved then turned away to fight the tears forming in his eyes. He blinked several times and took a deep breath. It was hard to speak around the knot in his throat, but he finally called out, "Okay, guys—batter up!"

This was the team's third game. They wouldn't start pitching until the fifth one. Sam would be the last up to bat in the first inning, and Eric hoped he wasn't the only one to hit the ball. He'd been working hard with the kids, and they'd come a long way. But they always became more nervous when their parents coached from the sidelines.

Little Eddie Morrison was up first. The umpire put the ball on the tee, and Eric made sure Eddie was in the right position to hit it. After three tries he finally hit the ball—only it landed on the ground right in front of the tee. The ball was declared dead, and Eddie tried again—and again—with his parents calling out advice from the stands.

But he kept missing. Eric wanted to tell his parents that if they'd just let him have fun he'd do a much better job, but he knew it wouldn't do any good. Eddie struck out on his last try, and it was time for the next batter in line.

Next up was Larry Dickerson. He managed to hit the ball the second time he tried, but it went straight to first base and was caught.

And on it went with cheering in the stands for each boy. By the time Sam was up they'd made one run. It seemed strange to hear all the cheers for Sam when he took his turn at bat. Eric wished he had his camera to capture the smile on his son's face when he heard Laci and the rest of her family clap and cheer as he stepped up to the tee.

The umpire placed the ball on the tee, and Eric made sure Sam was in the correct position. "Don't be nervous just because you have a fan club, okay?"

"Okay, Dad. But isn't it great?"

Eric grinned at his son. "Yes, it is. Just do your best and have fun."

Sam nodded, and Eric stepped away.

He could tell Sam was concentrating. He glanced at the stands and had the feeling that Laci and her family were holding their breath. He looked back at his son. Sam took a swing—and missed. He tried again—and missed.

As Sam got into position once more, Eric heard Laci's sweet voice call out from the stands, "It's okay, Sam. You can do it."

And do it he did. He hit the ball into the outfield and took off at a run. The other team scrambled and tried to get the ball, but they weren't fast enough. With Laci and her whole family on their feet cheering for him, Sam made a home run.

Eric knew there would be other home runs in his son's life, but he was certain Sam would remember this one for a long time. It was the first game he'd ever played with anyone in the stands to cheer him on.

The competing team was up next, and Eric sent Sam to the outfield. He knew some of the parents wanted their boys playing the bases and the infield, partly because none of them could throw very far. The only other boy on the team who could throw a ball any distance was Larry, and he played on the opposite side of the outfield. But this time they weren't needed because the other team couldn't hit a ball that far.

Still the game was tied up by the start of the second inning. Sam's nervousness seemed to have disappeared. The rotation put him batting first this time, and they scored right away, with Larry hitting another run right behind Sam.

By the end of the game Sam's team was declared the winner. They'd managed to keep the other team from getting a run when they did make a hit. They finally won by two runs, although no score was kept in T-ball.

Sam was overjoyed that Laci and her family stayed to tell him how well he played.

"Thank you!" Sam was grinning from ear to ear. "It was so great to have someone—lots of someones—cheering for me." He looked around the circle of people congratulating him for his game. "Thank you all for coming to see me play!"

"We enjoyed it, Sam! It was fun to watch," Jake said. "You have a pretty good coach there, don't you?"

Sam grinned and nodded. "Dad's the best coach!"

"Thanks for coming, everyone. It sure meant a lot to Sam and to me, too."

"We're heading over to the Pizza Palace out on the highway for supper with Laci and Gram and Will," Jake said. "You and Sam want to join us?"

"Oh, can we, Dad?" Sam asked.

"Sure. I'd planned on stopping there anyway as a treat for Sam." He looked at Laci. "Did you drive or ride with someone?"

"I rode with Gram and Will."

Sam was a step ahead of him. "Want to ride with us, Lace?"

"We'd sure like you to," Eric added before she could answer Sam.

"Please, Lace!" Sam grinned at her.

"Yes, I'll ride with you," she said, looking at Sam.

Eric was certain it was his son who was the draw for Laci, but he wanted to get to know her better. If it took Sam to help him do that, then it was just fine by him.

Chapter 9

Jake called Eric to the side while Laci helped Sara put Meggie into their car. Gram and Will were already on their way to the pizza place. Laci wasn't sure why she'd accepted Eric and Sam's invitation to ride with them. All afternoon she'd told herself that while she wanted to support Sam she needed to be careful. She had a feeling Sam and his dad could steal her heart, and much as she wanted a family of her own she knew nothing about raising five-year-old boys.

She figured a mother learned about each age as her child grew into it—from holding him in her arms when he was born to seeing him at each stage—and that it happened over time. She told herself she was being presumptuous in even thinking about raising Sam. Eric hadn't shown that kind of interest in her. . . until now. And she was assuming a lot to think that offering to drive her to the pizza place meant he was interested in her.

Maybe it was wishful thinking on her part because try as she might she hadn't been able to keep Eric Mitchell out of her dreams. So here she was in the passenger seat of his pickup while Sam was buckled in the backseat of the extended cab.

"I can't believe you brought your whole family to see my game, Lace! That was so cool! I had more people there than anybody!"

"They all wanted to come, Sam," Laci assured him. "It was fun. And you were great. I have a feeling you're the best one on the team."

"If I am, it's just 'cause Dad plays ball with me a lot. He teaches me all kinds of stuff."

That didn't surprise Laci. She had a feeling that Eric's priorities were right where they ought to be. He seemed to be a good Christian man, and he was trying to be the best parent he could be for his son. It appeared he was doing a wonderful job, too.

After Eric parked his pickup and they started walking toward the restaurant, Sam's hunger had him skipping a few steps ahead of them.

"It was nice of your family to show up, Laci," Eric said in a low voice. "For a minute there I thought Sam was going to be too nervous to play his normal game. But then you started cheering him on, and that was all it took. Thank you again."

"You're welcome." Just hearing her presence had that kind of effect on Sam caused Laci to wonder if she'd done the right thing by going. What if she didn't go the next time? How would that affect Sam?

As if he could read her thoughts, Eric said, "I know you won't be able to come to all his games, so please don't worry about it. He might be disappointed, but he'll always remember today."

The thought of Sam being disappointed in her saddened her deeply. "I'll try to make as many of his games as I can while I'm here," Laci said. Suddenly it dawned on her that her indecision about going back to Dallas might be a good thing at the moment. She could commit only to the present.

Sam pushed open the door to the Pizza Palace, and Laci and Eric hurried to catch up with him. Gram, Will, Sara, Jake, and Meggie were waiting for them at two tables that had been pulled together.

"Hi, Sam!" Meggie said. "You played good!"

"Thanks!" Sam claimed a chair beside her, leaving the two empty ones side by side for his dad and Laci.

Eric held out the chair for her, and for a moment Laci had a glimpse of what it would be like to be a threesome with him and Sam. And she liked the feeling.

"They have a buffet tonight," Jake said. "We told them we'd have six adults and two children, but we waited until you came to get started."

"Thanks," Eric said.

Will said the blessing, and then they all headed to the pizza bar to fill their plates.

"I want cheese pizza, Dad," Sam said. "And can I have that dessert pizza, too?"

"If you eat all this, okay?"

"Okay."

It took a few minutes before everyone was back at the table with their plates piled high with pizza.

"I do thank you all for coming to Sam's game," Eric said as his son and Meggie began eating. "It meant a lot to him."

"I'd forgotten how much fun it was to watch those little ones play ball," Will said. "I'd like to go again."

"He has games on Tuesday evenings and Saturday mornings. We'd love to have a cheering section whenever any of you can make it."

"You'll be seeing us there," Gram said.

"I've told Eric I'll make as many of Sam's games as I can. . .at least until I return to Dallas." Laci knew she would delay going back as long as she could. But she still wasn't sure what she should do, especially about her business.

"You just need to move home," Jake stated. "You don't want to go back. You know you don't."

"But, Jake, I do have a business there. And while my assistant is taking care of everything while I'm gone, I have to decide what to do about it. If I move back here, it would mean giving up a clientele I worked hard to establish and starting all over again. Most of my business comes by word of mouth from one client recommending me to another." Laci shook her head. "I'm just not sure what I should be doing."

"I've told you what I think," Gram said. "I'd love for you to come home. You'd get a lot more word-of-mouth recommendations here at home than in a city like Dallas."

"Well, I did see a little house over on Fourth Street that I think would make a wonderful place to set up business in. I haven't actually looked at it, but I have been thinking about it. Maybe I need to mention it to Myra and see if she would want to take over managing the shop in Dallas or start her own business. And I could go to the bank and see what my options are."

"Maybe you could just open a consulting business here at first," Sara suggested.

"I can tell you this: Will and I have decided to keep my house and sell his once we're married. We will probably want to do some remodeling after we're married, to make the house more *ours*. We'd be more than happy to hire you and promote you, Laci. You know that."

"You lived here all your life until you moved to Dallas," Jake said. "You have a whole lot of people who would probably come to you for help. There aren't many interior decorators around here."

Laci knew she should have realized that before she moved to Dallas. Love for her family swelled. They would help her establish her business here. . .and they would have then. What had she been thinking when she moved away? But what meant the most was that they truly seemed to want her to move back. "Thank you all. I guess it wouldn't hurt to look at that house. I'm sure it would need some work to turn it into a shop."

"Well, Eric could help you with that," Sara said.

Laci turned to Eric. "Would you mind taking a look at it with me?"

"I'd be glad to. I love building new homes, but I really love working with older ones. Just let me know when."

"I'll call the Realtor tomorrow and find out when I can see it."

"Just give me a call and I'll meet you there," Eric said, pulling a card out of his wallet and handing it to her. "Most of the time it's easier to reach me on my cell phone, so you might want to try it first."

"Thanks, Eric." Laci took the card but wasn't prepared for the jolt that shot up her arm and straight to her heart at the brush of his fingertips on hers. She slipped the card into her purse with trembling fingers. What was it about this man that had her reacting like she was in high school again? Yes, she'd had a crush on him, but that was years ago and she'd gotten over it. Or had she? Was she trying to relive the past, or was this something entirely different? She didn't know. She loved being back in Sweet Springs, but she'd never been more confused about everything in her life than she was at this minute.

They were nearly through eating before Eric got up the nerve to bring up the movies as Jake had suggested out at the ballpark.

"There's a movie I've been wanting to see at the new six-screen theater," he said in a low tone, hoping only Laci heard him. "Jake says he and Sara will be glad to watch Sam tonight if you'd like to go with me." He told her the name of it. "It's supposed to be really good."

It took Laci a moment to answer as she had to swallow the bite she was chewing. Eric's heart seemed to stop beating while he waited. He would let Jake have it if she refused.

"I've heard it is. I'd love to go." She smiled at him. "What time is the next showing?"

He breathed an inward sigh of relief that she hadn't turned him down, and his heart began to beat again—hard and strong. He looked at his watch. "It starts in about forty minutes."

"Okay." She smiled and nodded. "Sounds great."

Eric looked over at Jake. "We're going to the seven-thirty showing if you and Sara are still sure you don't mind watching Sam tonight."

"Are you kidding?" Sara asked. "Meggie will love having the company!"

"I'll be by to pick him up as soon as the show is over."

"Not a problem," Jake said.

The next thirty minutes passed in a blur for Eric. Sam had been happy to go home with Jake and Sara to play with Meggie and waved good-bye with a grin. By the time Eric and Laci took their seats in the movie theater, he still couldn't believe he'd asked her out or that she'd agreed to go with him.

Something about sitting in the darkened theater had a cozy feel to him. But with Laci sitting beside him, he felt like a teenager on his first date. He wasn't quite sure how to act.

"I haven't been to the movies in a while," he whispered to her while the upcoming movies were being advertised.

"Neither have I," she said. "This is a very nice theater. I'm so glad Sweet Springs is growing the way it is. It's kept its small-town feel, though, and I'm happy about that."

"So am I." Eric was thankful she seemed at ease. Maybe his nervousness wasn't too apparent. But as the movie started he truly did feel like a teenager again. It was hard to concentrate on what was happening on the screen when all he could think about was if he should put his arm around Laci, try to hold her hand, or just sit there like they were mere acquaintances.

He certainly didn't like the latter thought. But putting his arm around her might seem a little too familiar. Finally he reached out and grasped her hand lightly in his. It was only when her fingers curved around his own that Eric relaxed and began to enjoy the movie.

When it was over and the lights came back on in the theater, he gave Laci's fingers a squeeze before letting go. "Thank you for coming with me. I really enjoyed that."

"So did I," Laci said as they made their way up the aisle. "Thank you for asking me."

He looked at his watch. He hated for the evening to end yet. Jake had told him he didn't have to hurry back right after the show. "Would you like to grab a cup of coffee or something?"

"I'd love to."

"Let's go to the ice-cream parlor downtown. They make good cappuccino."

"That sounds great."

It took only a few minutes to get back downtown, and soon they were standing at the counter in the old-fashioned ice-cream parlor. After looking at the selections they both ordered a frozen cappuccino and took them to one of the tables outside. The moon was bright, and the sky was filled with stars that looked so close he could almost reach out and touch one.

"Oh, how nice it is out here," Laci said. "This wasn't open when I left home."

"I guess it wasn't. It's a very popular spot this time of year. But it does a good business all year long. They serve hot chocolate and all kinds of specialty coffees, too."

"Mmm, that will be nice."

"Laci, your family sure would like you to move back home." He didn't add that he would like for her to do that also.

"I know."

"Do you think you will?"

"I don't know. I"—she broke off and shook her head—"I just don't know what I'm going to do."

Eric's heart sank. Attracted as he was to Laci, he needed to step back. It would do no good to fall in love with her if she was going back to Dallas to stay. No good at all.

The evening didn't end quite the way Eric would have liked it to. He would like to have known Laci was moving back. Would probably have asked her out again. But with her not knowing what she was going to do, he decided to take a wait-and-see attitude. That didn't stop him from wanting to kiss her good night when he walked her to the door, though.

But he didn't. Instead, he just thanked her again for going with him.

"I had a good time. Thank you for taking me," she said.

"Well, I guess we'll see you later. Be sure to call me about meeting you at the house if you decide to look at it." He hoped she would.

"I will."

Eric stepped off the porch. "Tell your grandmother thank you again for coming to Sam's game."

"I will."

" 'Night."

"Good night, Eric," Laci said before slipping inside the house.

He headed for his truck feeling even more like a teenager than ever.

When he picked up Sam, he didn't give Jake a chance to ask much about the evening.

"How'd it go?" his friend asked.

"Real good. It was a great movie," Eric told him as he tried to hurry out the door. "I'd better get this little guy home. Thank you both so much."

"Anytime," Sara said, standing beside Jake to see them out. "We mean that, too."

"Thank you," Eric said. "See you later."

It felt a little lonely as he and Sam took off for home.

"Was the movie good, Dad?"

"It was."

"It was fun at the pizza place, wasn't it?"

"It sure was, son." In fact, spending the evening with Laci and the others had been as enjoyable as the past Sunday afternoon had been—up to the point he'd asked her about moving back here.

"I hope we can do it again. Do you think Lace will come to the game on Saturday?"

"She said she would. You know, Sam, Laci lives in Dallas. She came home because her grandmother was so sick, and now she's staying to help her. She'll probably be going back to Texas one of these days."

"Maybe she'll move back here. I heard everyone talking about it."

Eric had no doubt his son had heard every word spoken at the table. "Well, she might decide to do that. Then again she might not."

"I'm gonna pray she moves back."

Eric didn't want to discourage his son's prayer life, but he had to prepare him for being disappointed. "You can do that. But remember—sometimes what we want isn't what God thinks is best. And He always knows what is best."

Sam nodded. "I know."

Eric let out a deep breath. He had some praying to do, too.

After Sam showered, Eric listened to his prayers, and, true to his word, Sam prayed about Laci.

"Dear God, thank You for Dad and for all my blessings. Thank You for letting me do good at T-ball today. And please let Lace decide to move back here. In Jesus' name, amen."

Eric kissed his son on the forehead. " 'Night, son. I love you."

"I love you, too, Dad."

Eric went back to the utility room, pulled out a pile of wrinkled towels and washcloths from the dryer, and took them to the kitchen table. He was sure glad it wasn't full of wrinkled clothes he'd have to iron. As he began to fold the bath towels, he thought back over the evening. He wondered if Laci felt the same shock of electricity he had when he handed her his card. He'd been totally surprised by his reaction to her.

Something about Laci drew him to her. Maybe it was the way she was so gentle and kind to Sam. She'd been sweet and pretty in high school, but she'd grown into a caring and lovely woman who had his heart thumping double-time in his chest when she smiled at him—and had him trying to figure out how to ask her out again. Even after tonight and not knowing what she was going to do, he wanted to spend more time with her. Yet, if she didn't move back here, what future could there be?

Sam wasn't the only one hoping Laci would move back home. But until then Eric needed to be careful not to lose his heart to her and especially to guard Sam against caring too much for her, as well. The last thing either of them needed was more heartache in their lives. Eric sat down at the table and bowed his head. It was his turn to pray.

"Dear Lord, I thank You for all my blessings here on this earth. . .especially for Sam. Like him, I ask that if it is Your will, Laci will move back here. But, Lord, if it's not, please guard our hearts. Please help me to know what You'd have me do where Laci is concerned. I don't know whether to pursue a relationship with her or keep my distance. So please show me, Lord. Thank You most of all for Your plan for our salvation through Your Son, Jesus Christ. In His precious name I pray, amen."

He'd come to count on the Lord more each day after his wife's death. He'd continue to leave things in His hands.

Laci found it hard to get to sleep that night with so many thoughts running through her mind fighting to be heard. She'd enjoyed going to the movie with Eric. He seemed to be having a good time, too, until he brought her home. She wasn't sure what had been going through his mind when he'd walked her to the door. He'd seemed quieter after he'd asked her if she was moving. She just hadn't known how to answer him. Deep down inside she knew she wanted to come home. But she'd wanted to move to Dallas at one time, too. She'd been wrong then. Was she right now? Was it what she *should* do? That was the big question.

There was no denying that, while being closer to family was the biggest reason for wanting to move back, the fact that Eric and his son lived here had a lot to do with it, too. Yet was that wise? She was very attracted to Eric, and Sam had already claimed a spot in her heart. But he needed a mother, and she just didn't know—and *why* was she thinking about this anyway? Eric hadn't let her know how he felt about her. Just because he'd taken her to the movie or held her hand didn't mean he truly cared. And just because her pulse raced each time she was near him didn't mean his did. She could be weaving those high school dreams all over again, with the same results—that Eric didn't feel the same way about her.

If she did move home was she just letting herself in for heartache? And yet the thought of going back to Dallas, not being able to have daily contact with her loved ones, not having the hope of running into Eric and Sam, to move through her days and nights instead of enjoying them, made Laci shudder. She wasn't sure she could go back to the boring life she had lived in Texas.

Finally, after tossing and turning, she got out of bed and went to sit on the window seat in her room. Gazing out at the multitude of stars in the sky, David's lesson on giving things over to the Lord finally came to mind.

Maybe her problems had been from lack of doing that in the past, Laci realized. Not only had she not listened to her family's advice, she couldn't remember ever going to the Lord in prayer over her decision to move to Dallas.

Nor had she gone to Him for much while she was there. She'd been so busy concentrating on what *she* wanted that she'd forgotten to ask the Lord what *He* wanted her to do. Even since she'd been home, she'd been doing much the same thing, except she was more confused than she'd ever been in her life and needed to take things to the Lord. But had she done it? No. Well, no wonder she stayed confused over everything. Somewhere along the way she'd forgotten it was the Lord's will she was to be doing and not her own.

The realization of how long and how much she'd been putting her wants first brought Laci onto her knees at the window seat, tears streaming down her face as she went to the Lord in prayer.

"Dear Father, please forgive me for blindly forging ahead with my life and leaving You out of the decision making. For not coming to You in prayer and asking Your guidance for my future. Please forgive me for drifting away from the committed Christian I once was and help me to grow as Your child. Please guide me now and help me make the right decision about coming home or staying in Dallas and about everything else in my life. Please help me seek Your will in all of this, Father. Thank You for the many blessings You've given me, especially for Your Son, Jesus. In His name I pray, amen."

Laci truly felt as if a load had been lifted off her shoulders when she finished praying. She went back to bed and drifted off to sleep in only minutes.

The next morning she was still not sure what the Lord wanted her to do, but she trusted He would let her know in due time. She called the Realtor and set up an appointment for her and Eric to look at the house. She was pleased and surprised to find the Realtor was a young woman she'd gone to school with. Her name had been Jeanette Williams in school, but her married name was Fielding.

"Laci, I'm busy with another client this morning, but I'll be glad to show it to you around two this afternoon," Jeanette said. "Will that work for you?"

"That will be fine. I'll meet you there," Laci said.

She had been nervous about calling Eric afterward, but he'd been very nice and had agreed to meet them at the house at two that afternoon.

Jeanette was there waiting when Laci arrived at the house, and Eric pulled up right behind her.

"Eric, how nice to see you," Jeanette said. "I didn't know. . .are you two looking at this for yourselves?"

"I—uh—yes—no." Laci wasn't sure how to answer her. She felt a little embarrassed at the question.

Eric came to her rescue. "I'm going to give Laci advice on anything that might need to be done to the house, should she decide to lease or buy it."

"Oh, I see." Jeanette nodded and smiled at Laci as they reached the front porch. "Eric and I have worked together some in the past. I've sold a couple of homes he's built. He'll give you great advice."

"That's what I'm counting on."

Jeanette unlocked the front door and stood to the side for them to enter the house.

"Ohh, this is wonderful," Laci said when she walked through the front door. The hardwood floors were in excellent condition, at least in the front of the house. The bay window, in what would have been the parlor, was beautiful and gave plenty of light to the room. The kitchen and dining room were also downstairs. Upstairs were two large bedrooms and a bathroom. It was just the right size for her needs.

"This area is zoned commercial, isn't it?" she asked Jeanette as they came back downstairs.

"Yes, it is. What were you thinking of using the property for?"

"I'm an interior decorator and have a business in Dallas. But I'm thinking of moving back and opening up a shop here."

"Oh, how wonderful, Laci! We could use a good decorator in this town," Jeanette said. "Sweet Springs has grown in the last few years. I'd think you'd have all the work you might want right here."

Laci hoped so, if she did move. That was still something she was waiting for the Lord to show her. She just needed to learn how to be still and listen.

Chapter 10

After they left Jeanette at the house with the promise that Laci would be in touch with her, Laci and Eric went to the diner for coffee. There was a lull in business at that time of day, and Dee was in a talkative mood when she brought the coffee and pie they'd ordered to the table. "Hey, what have you two been up to today?"

"I went to look at a piece of property. I'm thinking about buying or leasing it, if possible, to use for my business—if I decide to move back. I asked Eric if he would give me his opinion on it."

"Makes sense to me. I hope you do move back," Dee said then abruptly changed the subject. "Have you heard from John or your parents on how his campaign is going lately?"

"No. Not since they were here this past weekend." Laci noticed a light in Dee's eyes, prompting her to ask, "Have you heard from him?"

"Yeah, I did. He called here a little while ago. I'm. . .not sure why. But anyway he said the campaign is going well."

"Did he say when he was coming back home for a few days?"

Dee shook her head. "I was so surprised he'd called that I didn't think to ask. He did ask how things were going here."

"Oh?" Laci wasn't sure what to ask next. It was obvious Dee was pleased John had called her, but she seemed a little flustered by it.

The bell rang over the door, and Dee seemed somewhat relieved to be able to say, "Got to go. I'll be back with a coffee refill in a little while."

"That was odd," Laci said when Dee left their table.

"Didn't she and John date at one time?"

"Yes, they did. But as far as I know they're just friends now." She almost told him her family thought John and Dee still cared about each other but decided against it. Changing the subject, she asked, "What did you think of the house?"

"It's a jewel. The house is in wonderful shape, Laci. I'm not sure how much room you'd need for your shop or if you want to keep the kitchen intact. I'd advise you to keep a kitchen downstairs, in case you ever wanted to sell the house, but we could remodel it pretty much however you want to. The house was built to last and has been well taken care of."

"That's what I wanted to hear. I'm not sure about what I'd want to change if I do take it. I think I could use it like it is, for a while anyway."

"Just keep in mind it would be much easier to do any remodeling before you move in than after. It can be a real mess."

Laci nodded. "You're right. Do you have any suggestions?"

"Well, first I need to know how you envision using the space." Eric forked a piece of peach pie into his mouth.

"I thought at first of making an apartment upstairs. But I can see that might hurt the resale value if I did want to sell it later on. I think I could still live there, though. One of the bedrooms could be a living room, and I could still use the kitchen downstairs. The dining room could become my office space and workroom while the living area could be a reception area where I first meet with clients. I could furnish it in keeping with the time period in which the house was built." The more she talked about it, the better it sounded.

"That sounds great, Laci. You might want to think about putting in a small powder room under the stairwell so you or your clients wouldn't have to run upstairs."

"Oh, that's a wonderful idea, Eric."

"Hidden there, it wouldn't take away from the historical feel of the house. If you'd like, I can draw up a plan for the powder room for you—no charge, of course."

"Thank you, Eric. I'd like to see what you have in mind. But I'd be glad to pay you."

"Nah. I may need your advice on decorating Sam's room one of these days. He wants something to do with baseball. We can swap services."

"It's a deal. I'd love to come up with something for Sam's room."

"He'd love that. Other than the powder room it doesn't look as if you'll need to do much remodeling, so that will hold down the cost for you. I'm sure you're capable of decorating it to suit your needs." He grinned at her.

"I would hope so. Otherwise I'm in the wrong business."

"Does this mean you've decided to move here?"

"I'm still not sure—"

"You really ought to do it, Laci. Your family wants you to. Take it from me. Family is too precious to take for granted."

Suddenly Laci felt as if he were criticizing her. And who was he to tell her what to do, just because she'd asked for his advice about the house? "I'm not taking my family for granted! But I haven't made up my mind yet. It's just too important a decision to make in a hurry."

"I didn't mean to—" Eric's cell phone rang just then, and he answered it. After a quick conversation he pulled some bills out of his wallet and put them on the table. "I've got to run. There's a problem at one of the home sites I'm building. I have to check it out. Laci, I didn't mean to make you mad. I—"

"Don't worry about it." Laci knew she sounded cool, but it hurt to think he felt she didn't care about her family.

"Well. . .thanks for asking me to take a look at the house."

"Eric, you did me a favor." She handed him back the money he left on the table. "I'll get our ticket."

"Nope. I'll get it." He put the bills back on the table. "I'll talk to you later, okay?"

"Sure." Did he mean he'd call? Or just that they'd run into each other? Laci didn't know, and she hated for the afternoon to end on this note. But maybe it was best this way.

The next day was the meeting of the Wedding Planners, Inc., and this time they piled in Sara's SUV and headed for Roswell to look at wedding dresses and see if anything appealed to Gram.

"Well, even if I don't find anything, these outings with you girls are fun," Gram said. "I don't dare choose anything today. Lydia would be upset with me if I did. I'll have to wait on her. But at least this way I'll have a better idea of what I'm looking at when I see them in the magazines."

"That's true. It's hard to feel the material in a picture," Aunt Nora said. "And there are very few pictures of flower girl dresses. Maybe we can find something for Meggie."

They stopped at one of their favorite Mexican restaurants for lunch before going to look at dresses. It was then Laci told them about John calling Dee.

"He did? Hmm," Sara said. "Did Dee seem surprised?"

"Yes, she did—and a bit flustered. But she also seemed happy."

"Maybe he's doing some thinking out there on that campaign trail."

"Could be someone mentioned that Richard Tyler has been seen spending a lot of time at the diner," Rae said.

"Oh? Who would that be?" Aunt Nora asked.

"Luke might have mentioned it to him."

"Well, is it true?" Gram asked.

"Luke wouldn't lie. We've seen Richard in there. 'Course I don't know if he's making a play for Dee or not, but he's been there."

"You two aren't playing matchmaker, are you?"

"Oh, no one in this family does that, do they, Gram?" Sara asked then chuckled.

The laughter around the table had Laci looking at them curiously. "Just how much matchmaking does this family do?"

"Oh, we've been known to do a little on occasion," Aunt Nora said with a laugh.

"On several occasions, you mean," Gram said. "You'd love to have been in on it, Laci. Neither Sara nor Rae would be family now if it hadn't been for a little matchmaking."

"Is that true?" Laci looked from Sara to Rae.

"Oh, yeah, it is. And Dee got in on some of it herself. It's only fair if we do the same to her."

"I'd love to see her and John together," Laci said. "You don't think we're reading more into this than there is, though, do you?"

"Not if John called her, I don't," Rae said. "That was what Luke was hoping for. I can't wait to tell him."

Laci couldn't help but laugh. She hoped it worked out so no one was hurt. Dee looked so happy the day before.

By the time they arrived at the bridal shop they decided they should have gone there first.

"I feel stuffed," Gram said. "It was those sopaipillas and honey that did it. I don't think I want to try on anything today, but I still want to look. Just remind me next time not to eat before we come here."

They spent the better part of the afternoon oohing and aahing over dresses and colors. They saw dresses in Meggie's size, and she was ready and willing to try them on. Each one looked pretty on her, and she wanted them all.

"Well, Meggie, my love, at least we know we'll find a beautiful outfit for you. We just need to find out what colors Gram wants, and we'll know where to come," Aunt Nora said as they left the shop.

It was a delightful afternoon, and Laci prayed it would be the Lord's will for her to spend many more with this wonderful family of hers.

~

When Will came over that evening, Gram was excited to tell him about the afternoon and even had some magazines out to ask his opinion about a few things. Laci figured they could use a little time to themselves and decided to go to the diner to visit with Dee, if she had time.

She went upstairs to get her purse, and when she came back downstairs Gram was just getting off the phone. "Oh, dear, I thought you'd already left. Sara said to tell you to call her later."

"Okay. I'll call on my cell phone. I won't be late." She gave her grandmother a kiss on the cheek and gave Will a kiss, too, on the way out the door. He looked a little bewildered with all those bridal magazines spread out before him.

She stepped into her car and punched in Jake and Sara's number before she backed out of the drive. When Sara answered, she said, "Hi. Gram said I was supposed to call you?"

"Oh, yes, Laci, we need to start planning her shower. Did we decide to meet at the diner?"

"Yes, Dee wanted to help, remember?"

"Okay. Gram said you were on your way there. Ask Dee what afternoon will work best for her and let the rest of us know, okay? I hate to call her at work; she's usually so busy."

"I'll check with her and get back to you."

"Good. Oh, and see if you can find out if John has called her again. Luke and Jake have been doing a lot of calling. I think they *are* up to something."

Laci laughed. "Okay, I'll see what I can find out. Talk to you later."

Several customers were in the diner when Laci got there, but they were nearly finished eating and Annie was working, so Dee was able to chat for a few minutes.

"I talked to Sara, and we decided we need to start planning that shower for Gram. What day and time would be best for you to meet?"

"Midmornings on most days are pretty good. And on Fridays I usually have extra help, so how about ten thirty tomorrow? Is that too short a notice?"

"I don't think so. Let me check with the others, and I'll let you know."

After three quick calls they had it set for the next morning, and Laci was excited to start the planning. "Gram is going to be so surprised."

"If anyone deserves something special, it's your grandmother. She's a really fine lady," Dee said. "What kind of shower are we giving? She probably doesn't need a lot of things for her home."

"I don't know. We'll see what the others think."

The bell over the door signaled new customers, and Laci's heart fluttered in her chest at the sight of Eric and Sam coming in.

"Well, hi, guys," Dee said. "You just left here a little while ago. Did you forget something?"

"Nah. Dad just said we needed a treat and asked if I wanted a milkshake—and for no reason. Can you believe it?" Sam climbed up on the stool beside Laci. "Hi, Lace! Are you having a milkshake, too?"

"Hi, Sam. No, this is cherry limeade. But a shake sure sounds good."

"I'll have a chocolate one, please," Sam said to Dee, sounding much older than five.

"I'll have strawberry," Eric said.

"Okay," Dee said. "Coming right up."

"I still can't believe Dad is going to let me have one. He usually saves them for special occasions."

Eric shrugged. "We've been cleaning house. It just sounded good."

Laci laughed. "It's fun to be spontaneous sometimes, isn't it?"

"What's spon–tan–e–us?" Sam asked.

"It's what I did tonight. Like deciding to do something all of a sudden," Eric said.

"Oh, okay. Yeah, it is fun! Is that what you did, Lace?"

Laci shook her head. "Not really. I just decided to come visit with Dee awhile."

"And give your grandmother and Will some time to themselves?" Eric asked.

"How did you know?"

He shook his head. "I just guessed. It's something you'd do."

At least he seemed to realize she did care about her grandmother. Maybe she'd taken his words the wrong way the other day. She hoped so.

Dee came back with the milkshakes for Eric and Sam, and Laci remembered she was supposed to find out if she'd talked to John again.

"I haven't heard from Mom or Dad or John in days, and I haven't been able to get in touch with them. They must be in an area where their cell phone signals are weak. Have you heard anymore, Dee?"

Dee turned almost the color of Eric's strawberry milkshake. "As a matter of fact, John did call this afternoon. I think they may be coming in soon for a few days."

"Okay, good." Laci could tell Dee was a little flustered so she tried to sound nonchalant. "I hope so because I know Gram would like Mom's opinion on a few things."

More customers came in, and she could tell Dee was relieved not to have to talk about John anymore as she hurried to wait on them. But it appeared something was up. She just didn't have a clue as to what.

"How's practice been going?" she asked Sam.

"Good. Do you think you—"

"Sam. Remember what we talked about?"

"Yes, sir. I'm sorry, Lace. Dad said not to make you feel like you *have* to come to my games. And that you might be going back to Dallas, so I shouldn't get my hopes up." He let out a huge sigh.

Laci's heart twisted inside at Sam's words and the look in his eyes. She had to find a way to make him feel better. "Sam, what your dad said was true. I may be going back to Dallas. I'm just not sure yet. But while I am here, I intend to be at your games, okay?"

"Okay!"

Her gaze met Eric's over the top of his son's head, and he mouthed a "Thank you" to her. She nodded and smiled.

Laci didn't know who was more surprised the next morning when she and Aunt Nora and Sara and Rae got to the diner to find her brother John sitting at the counter talking to Dee.

"When did you get into town, big brother? You could have let us know you were coming. Did Mom and Dad come back in, too?"

"Hi, sis!" John stood and gave her and the others hugs. "We got in late last night. We went to a fund-raising event in Ruidoso and left when it was over. But you're right—we should have let you know. I guess we aren't used to you being here in Sweet Springs, Laci. I came in to have breakfast before I check on things at the office, and then I need to get over to campaign headquarters."

It sounded as if Jake didn't know he was there, and from Sara's reaction to seeing him, Laci was pretty sure she didn't either. She didn't think anyone knew they were coming back, but that didn't make her feel better. "Yes, well, I need to call Mom. We're starting to plan Gram's shower, and I think she might want to be in on it."

She left the others talking to John as she stepped outside to get a good signal and punched in the numbers. She felt kind of grouchy, and she didn't even know why. Maybe because she had a feeling that if she were in Dallas instead of here, she would know nothing about what was going on. She wouldn't be in on planning the wedding or the shower, she wouldn't know when her parents and John were in or out of town, and she would be missing out on the suspense with Dee and her brother. But she couldn't blame her parents and brother for having to get used to letting her know these things. Eventually they would, *if* she moved back to stay.

She took a deep breath when her mother answered the phone and tried not to sound as frustrated and confused as she felt. "Hey, Mom. I just met up with John at the diner. Aunt Nora and the rest of us are here to start planning Gram's shower. I thought you might want to meet us—"

"I'll be there in twenty minutes, dear," her mother assured her. "I tried to call you last night and let you know we were coming in, but Mom's line was busy, and I couldn't get through to you either."

Feeling slightly mollified, Laci felt herself begin to relax. "I'm glad you're here. We'll be waiting for you."

She joined the other women at the big round booth in the front corner and tried not to notice the high color in Dee's face as she brought them coffee.

"I'll be right with you," she said.

"Mom won't be here for another fifteen minutes or so, Dee. It's okay," Laci tried to reassure her. But from watching her reaction to John and the way he kept looking at Dee, she had to believe they might be on the verge of discovering how much they still cared about each other. They probably just needed a big gentle push.

Chapter 11

"Those two love each other, or I am blind as a bat," Aunt Nora said as they watched Dee and John stealing glances.

"I've thought that for a long time," Rae said. "And Dee told me they dated at one time, but that was all. She shut up like a clam after that."

"They did date," Sara said. "But something happened, and they broke up. I'm not sure anyone in the family knows why."

"Well, they might have broken up with each other, but it doesn't look to me as if they ever fell out of love," Aunt Nora said.

Laci didn't think so either. "There's something very caring in their expressions when they look at each other. How can everyone else see what Dee and John don't seem to?"

"Well, all I can tell you is that Jake and Luke are up to something, and Rae and I think they are doing some matchmaking," Sara said.

"They would," Aunt Nora said. "Those two are so happily married; they want John to have the same thing. I hope whatever they're planning works. Tell them if they need any help I'll be glad to assist."

Laci's mom arrived and slipped into the booth beside her. "Hey, darlin'. It's so good to have you here in Sweet Springs."

John walked over to tell them good-bye when he left to go to the office, and if he felt five pairs of eyes on his back, waiting to see if he talked to Dee, he didn't let on. He did say something that had Dee blushing when he paid his ticket, and even Laci's mom had to comment.

"That boy is bright, and he's going to make an excellent senator. But when it comes to his love life he doesn't seem to have a clue. Those two have been mooning over each other for years now. If he doesn't act pretty soon or she doesn't give him some encouragement, I don't see much hope for either of them ever getting married."

Dee headed over to join them, and the topic quickly turned to Gram's shower plans. By lunchtime they'd set a date, a time, and a place. Since Gram knew so many people in town, they decided to use the fellowship hall at church and send out invitations to make sure the shower stayed a secret. And they would enlist the aid of the Teddy Bear Brigade. It would be great.

The diner began to get busy, and Dee went back to work. Sara had to leave to pick up Meggie, but the rest of them decided to stay and have lunch since the smells wafting from the kitchen had stirred up their appetites. Besides, they'd only had coffee and tea, and they figured they'd give Dee their business.

"I think we'll have a huge turnout," Laci's mom said as they waited on their orders to arrive. "Everyone loves Mother. I can't wait to see her face. And after next week we'll be around awhile. Ben has some things to take care of at the ranch, and I want to help with the wedding plans. I mean, it's not every day a daughter gets to help her mother plan a wedding."

"Well, I'm glad to hear it," Aunt Nora said. "Ellie promised she'd let you in on the final decisions, and she meant it. She hasn't decided on anything. Your being here will speed up things. But we really need to get them to set a wedding date."

"I'll work on that. I know they'd like to wait until after the election, but that's not until November. Once we settle everything I'll feel better about going out and campaigning for John."

"You've been stressing, Mom?" Laci figured she had been. Her mother wanted to take care of everyone at once, and that was hard to do.

"I have been. I want to be with John. I want to spend time with you, and ever since Mother's stroke I want to spend more time with her."

Laci hugged her mother. "I know."

"I think we all want Will and Ellie married as soon as possible. They've been almost as bad as Dee and John." Aunt Nora shook her head. "Except they haven't been denying how they feel about each other."

"Well, once we have Mom and Will married, maybe we can concentrate on John and Dee," Laci's mom said.

For a moment Laci felt left out. She wouldn't mind their doing a little matchmaking on her behalf, especially because she had a feeling she'd messed up everything by being so short with Eric when he'd given her his opinion about moving home. She'd had some time to think, and she realized that maybe she was upset because Eric hadn't asked her to move back because *he* wanted her to.

~

The next morning Laci and most of her family were at Sam's game cheering for him again. The smile on his face when he spotted them in the stands was something Laci knew she'd never forget. The game was tighter this time, but Sam and his friend Larry managed to keep their team afloat. Once again they won.

"You came! I knew you would," Sam said as he ran up to her and hugged her after the game.

"I told you I would."

"I know. And I prayed you'd be here. And you are." He turned to her family. "Thanks for coming, everyone."

Laci could tell her family was touched by his appreciation of them.

"I can't think of a better way to spend a Saturday morning, young man," Will said.

"Nor I," Gram said. "And now that we're out and about, I'm going to get Will to drive me to Roswell to do some shopping and take me to lunch."

" 'Bye, Gram. See you two later," Laci said.

"We're having lunch at the diner, Lace," Sam said. "Will you come with us?"

"Oh, I don't know, Sam. I'm sure your dad has plans—"

"We'd both love to have lunch with you, Laci. I just need to do a little cleanup here and talk to some of the parents. Can we meet you there in about thirty minutes?"

"Please, Lace!"

"Sure, that sounds good to me. I'll see you there, okay, Sam?"

"Okay!"

Laci took off for downtown with a smile in her heart, looking forward to having lunch with the two Mitchell men. She was planning to go to the diner anyway, but eating alone had never been her favorite thing.

When she arrived she found her brother at a table, about half finished with what looked like a late breakfast. Somehow that didn't surprise her, but she wondered how often he visited the diner when he was in town.

"Hey, sis! Sit down and keep me company."

Laci took a seat at the table for four, and Dee came over with a cup of coffee. "What can I get you, Laci?"

"I'll just have the coffee for now and order in a little while, Dee."

"Okay, just let me know when. John, you need a refill?"

"Yes, please, Dee." He smiled at her and nodded at an empty chair. "It's not real busy right now. Why don't you join us?"

"I might grab a cup," Dee said. But the bell over the door jingled then, and two different couples came in. "Well, maybe not. Looks like things are picking up." She sighed and shook her head as she went to wait on one couple while Annie took the other.

"She works way too hard," John said.

"She does," Laci agreed.

"I wish she'd just—" John stopped midsentence. "What are you up to this morning, sis?"

"Some of the family and I went to Sam Mitchell's T-ball game, and he and Eric asked me to have lunch with them."

"Oh?" John raised his eyebrow. "Something going on I ought to know about?"

Laci wished she could say yes. But the truth was the truth. "No. Not that I know of. Sam has taken a liking to me, and when the family found out he had no one to root for him at the games we all decided to go cheer him on."

"Uh-huh. I seem to remember you had a crush on Eric when you were in high school." John had that ornery big-brother grin on his face. "He's a good man."

Laci could feel the ornery little-sister response coming. "Yeah, well, it was a crush. We never actually dated—like you and Dee did. What's up with the two of you?"

"What do you mean?" John asked a bit defensively.

"John, the only place I've seen you since you've been home is here."

"So? I eat here a lot. It's close to the office."

Laci shook her head. "I don't think that's the reason you come here so often."

"What are you talking about, sis?"

"Oh, John, anyone watching the two of you together can see you and Dee both still care about each other."

"We're good friends. Of course we care about each other."

"You know what I mean."

"No, I don't." John took a sip of his coffee and stood, pulling bills out of his wallet. "And I don't have time to find out. I'm about to be late to a meeting. See you later, sis. Love you." He bent and kissed her on the cheek before striding toward the cash register.

Trying not to be obvious, Laci watched him as he paid Dee. He smiled and leaned over and murmured something to Dee, and she nodded and smiled back. Something about the way those two looked at each other was almost tangible. Anyone watching could see they cared about each other—deeply.

Laci watched her brother leave the diner and Dee go back to waiting on customers, wondering if either of them would ever admit it. She sipped her coffee for a few minutes, almost wishing she hadn't brought it up to John. Now he would probably avoid her for a few days at least. He knew she was right. He hadn't wanted to talk about his relationship with Dee. If he felt only friendship for her, as he said, he wouldn't have been so defensive.

Of course, she'd been a little on the defensive when he'd mentioned Eric, Laci reminded herself. So who was she to be upset at her brother for doing the same?

"Lace, we're here!" Sam said as he barreled into the diner and up to the table where she was sitting.

"Hey, Sam, I bet you're starving by now."

"I *am* hungry." He climbed up in the chair John had vacated.

"So am I," Eric said, taking the chair on the other side of Laci.

When Dee came to clear John's dishes away and get their order, it took only a minute to give it. Sam wanted his usual, but Laci and Eric chose hamburgers and fries.

~

Eric let his son have Laci's full attention for a few minutes as they rehashed the game and talked about how well he had played. But once Dee came back with their orders and Sam began eating, he took his turn at claiming her attention. "I saw John on his way down to the office. Is he going to be in town long?"

Laci sighed. "I don't know. I should have asked, but I think he's a little aggravated at me at the moment."

"Oh? What happened?"

She sighed. "Big brother that he is, he started teasing me about an old crush I had when I was in high school, and I couldn't resist firing back at him."

Eric chuckled. "I seem to remember you always gave as good as you got when he or your cousins teased you. What did you say?"

"Oh, I mentioned the fact that he and Dee had actually dated in high school and it was obvious they still cared about each other."

"I bet he wasn't too happy about that. John never has liked talking much about his personal life."

"No, he wasn't happy." Laci sighed and shook her head. "He didn't want to talk about it. But I hit a nerve. I know I did. Still, I should have kept my mouth shut. If they were getting to the point of admitting how they feel, I sure hope I didn't set things back."

"I don't think it will hurt things, Laci. I've been watching them a long time, and you're right. They care. Who knows? Maybe you gave him the push he needs."

"I doubt it. But I sure hope someone will."

A nice-looking man came in and sat at the counter. From Dee's reaction to him it appeared he wasn't a favorite of hers, but the man seemed to like her a lot. "Do you know who that man is?"

Eric nodded. "His name is Richard Tyler. He's been trying to get Dee to go out with him for a while now."

"Oh, I see." Laci began to chuckle.

"What's so funny?"

"I think my cousins are using him to spur John into action."

"What? Ohh. . ." Eric nodded and grinned. "Well, maybe that's the push that will do it."

"And now I can say I saw him in here, too—maybe ask John about him."

"Well, after your conversation with him today, is it possible he might think you're trying to get a reaction out of him?"

"Oh, you're right. He probably would. I guess I'll have to be careful about what I say to him for a while."

"Probably. But—maybe I could find a way to work it into a conversation."

Laci nodded, and her smile widened. She patted him on the arm. "I like the way you think, Eric."

A jolt of electricity shot up his arm at her touch. Eric hoped that wasn't all she liked about him, because he could no longer deny he was falling deeply in love with Laci Tanner. "Dad. . .Dad!" Sam said. "Can I have the ketchup, please?"

"Oh, yes." He handed the ketchup to his son as he tried to come to grips with what he'd just admitted to himself. And he might be the only one who knew how he felt. He didn't know if he'd ever be able to tell Laci. He didn't have any idea how she felt about him, other than as a friend. Nor did he know if she was going to return to Dallas or move back to Sweet Springs. And after the way she reacted when he'd given her his opinion about that, he wasn't in any hurry to upset her again. At least she didn't seem angry with him anymore. What he did know was she had a claim on his heart, and how she felt about him or where she lived or didn't live probably wouldn't make any difference in how he felt about her.

He wondered if John was going through the same feelings about Dee, and he could suddenly sympathize with him.

"Eric? Are you all right?" Laci asked, pulling him out of his thoughts. "You looked miles away for a moment."

He chuckled. "No, I'm right here. I'm fine." Or he would be—with the Lord's help. "I'll try to figure out a way to mention old Richard over there to John. Maybe Sam and I will stop by his campaign headquarters later today."

"That might work," Laci said.

"Yes, we need a yard sign for John's campaign, don't we, Sam?"

"Sure, Dad. That would be cool. One of our neighbors had that other guy's sign in his yard. I saw it today."

"When we leave here, we'll go get one of John's signs and put it up. Can't let the neighbors have all the fun, can we?"

Sam giggled. "Nope."

Eric took a sip of iced tea and asked the question he was half dreading the answer to but had to know. "Have you made up your mind about moving back, Laci?"

"Not yet. I'm going to call Myra and see if she's interested in taking over the business in Dallas. I need to know that before I can decide about the house."

"I understand. I'm sure it's a hard decision to make."

"It is. And I want to do what the Lord wants me to do. I just haven't had a clear answer about it yet." Laci smiled and added, "I need to pray for patience while I'm waiting, too."

"I'll pray for you, Lace! I been praying you'll stay here."

"You have?"

The smile Laci gave his son squeezed at Eric's heart. He wasn't about to tell her yet, but he'd been praying the very same thing for the last few days.

Sam nodded. "Yes. Dad says I have to remember that what I want may not be God's will, and I know that. But I sure am hoping it is. And I'm praying real hard."

Eric needed the reminder, too.

"Thank you, Sam." Laci reached out and ruffled his hair. "That means a lot to me."

When they left the diner, Laci went one way and the Mitchells another. Sam was excited about seeing a real campaign office. Eric told her he'd let her know if he was able to work Richard into any conversation he had with John.

Laci went home and put in a load of wash then sat down at the kitchen table and dialed Myra's cell phone number. She picked up on the second ring.

"Myra, it's Laci. Can you talk, or are you with a client?"

"I'm at home, but I'm meeting a new client at the shop this afternoon. I was going to call you later today and see how things are. How is your grandmother doing?"

"She's steadily improving. We think she'll be able to get rid of her cane in a week or so."

"That's wonderful, Laci! And I have more good news for you."

"Oh? I'm always ready for good news."

"Well, we've gained three new clients just in the last week. I wanted to be sure about them before I called or e-mailed you. The jobs are pretty substantial. One kitchen remodel and one bedroom redecoration, and the one I'm meeting with today wants her whole upstairs redone."

"Wow, Myra! You've been working hard!"

"No, it's just time. Word gets around from some satisfied clients, and while it takes time, the business grows. I think you'll find this is going to be a very good year for Little Touches."

Was the Lord trying to tell her something? Laci didn't know. Maybe He wanted to find out if she really wanted to stay here or return to Dallas with business getting better.

But Laci didn't feel the urge to rush back just because business had picked up. She just felt she needed to get Myra to hire someone to help her. Praying that Myra's response to her question would give her the answer she needed, Laci took a deep breath.

"Myra, how would you like to own your own business?"

Chapter 12

Laci still didn't have any definitive answers about what to do after talking to Myra. She'd taken her friend by surprise, and Myra said she needed some time to think about it. She suggested Laci let things go on as they had been with her managing things in Dallas and hiring some extra help so Laci didn't feel she had to decide right away.

"It's a big decision, Laci. And it might be colored by your grandmother's close brush with death," Myra had said. "Think about it, and pray about it—and so will I. I'm sure the Lord will give us both the right answers."

Oddly enough, even though no decision had been reached, Laci felt at peace after the phone call. She had faith the Lord would guide her in making the right choice.

The next day was Sunday, and her parents invited everyone out to their ranch after church. She was glad that once again Eric and Sam were included.

"I hope you don't mind, Laci. I'm not trying to matchmake here, but I wanted to invite Eric and his son after seeing how much they enjoyed being at Sara and Jake's that day. And then I saw the way Sam came running up to you after church today." Her mother shrugged as she sliced tomatoes for the hamburgers Laci's dad was grilling. "I just had to ask them."

"It's okay, Mom," Laci said, wondering why everyone was willing to matchmake for the rest of the family but not for her. She fought off sudden tears while she sliced an onion. "Sam heard you tell me about it, and I'd have been worrying about the two of them if you hadn't asked them."

Her mother looked at her closely. "Laci, honey, are you crying?"

"I'm cutting onions, Mom," Laci said, using them as an excuse but not sure they were the whole reason.

"Oh, that's right. I didn't realize they were so strong, dear."

"It's all right." Laci didn't know why she felt so weepy today. Sam had touched her heart when he'd run up to her at church and hugged her. And just the thought of him and Eric spending the afternoon alone had made her heart twist in pain. It was then she knew without a doubt she loved the little boy and. . . was falling more and more in love with his dad each day. But Eric had given her no reason to believe he felt the same way, and maybe that was what had suddenly brought on the tears.

How could she move here and open herself up to being hurt? But, on the other hand, how could she return to Dallas and turn her back on the possibility of a lifetime of happiness here?

Laci took a deep breath and slowly let it out. Patience. She had to have patience. The Lord would guide her. He would. By the time the rest of the family and Eric and Sam arrived, Laci had her tears under control.

Sam seemed in his element around her family, and Meggie appeared to enjoy his company, too. The homemade play set she, John, Jake, and Luke had grown up using was still as sturdy as it ever had been, and the children spent the major part of the afternoon swinging, sliding, and climbing all over it.

But the peaceful afternoon suddenly came to a halt when the women were cleaning up after the meal. Her mother had used paper plates and plastic cups and utensils, but several things still needed to be washed and put away. Sara had just turned from putting the leftover onions in the refrigerator when she stopped and bent over, moaning.

"Rae, go get Jake and Michael, please," Aunt Nora said. "Sara hasn't been feeling well all morning. I think it's time."

"I'm—not sure—" Sara tried to say, but another pain hit before she could finish. Rae hurried outside.

"Well, unless you want to have that baby right here in Lydia's kitchen, we need to get Michael's opinion and let your husband know you are in labor."

In minutes the two men ran into the kitchen. After talking to Sara and watching her as another wave of pain seemed to wash over her, Michael said, "I'd get her to the hospital as soon as I could if I were you, Jake."

"We're on our way. Will you two take care of Meggie, Aunt Nora?" Jake asked as he helped Sara to the door.

"You know we will. We'll probably be right behind you."

"We're going out the front so Meggie doesn't get scared."

Laci's mom shooed at them. "Go. We'll take care of everything here. And we'll probably all be there before the baby gets here."

Excitement grew as they told everyone else a new member of the family was about to be born. Laci's dad led a prayer that Sara would deliver a healthy baby and be fine. Then everyone loaded into their vehicles and headed for town.

Laci wasn't sure how she ended up riding with Eric and Sam, but they seemed as excited as the rest of the family. By the time they all arrived at the hospital, Sara and Jake were in the delivery room.

For the next few hours they all paced back and forth in the family waiting room. Named after Sara's grandpa and Jake's favorite uncle, William Benjamin Breland was born at six o'clock that evening. He had his mother's auburn hair and blue eyes and dimples just like his dad.

Everything took a backseat to baby Ben during the next week as he was welcomed into the family. The women made plans to take turns carrying in meals to Sara and Jake and Meggie, but it was only an excuse to hold the baby while the others ate.

He truly was adorable, and Laci quickly came to love the feel of the little bundle in her arms. He made the sweetest cooing noises, and that little thumb he kept flopping in his mouth fascinated her.

Meggie was precious with her little brother, and for the moment Laci saw no sign of sibling rivalry. It seemed that Jake and Sara had prepared her well. Maybe it was because they made sure she had plenty of attention, too. Wanting to help assure the little girl she was as important to the family as always, Laci took Meggie along with her and Gram and Will to see Sam's game on Tuesday afternoon. Then they joined Eric and Sam at the diner for supper before taking Meggie home.

"How's that new baby doing?" Dee asked after she'd taken their orders and given Meggie and Sam their sheets to color. "John says he looks just like Jake. . . with Sara's hair."

"That's a pretty apt description," Gram said.

"He says he's almost as pretty as Meggie was when she was born," Dee said, smiling at the little girl. "I need to get over there soon and see him."

"He's pwetty cute," Meggie said before she began coloring.

"I wish I had a little brother," Sam said to her. "I'd teach him to play T-ball."

"You can teach Ben when he gets big like you," Meggie said.

"Okay, I will," Sam promised.

Dee grinned. "They sound like miniature adults, don't they?"

"A little bit," Laci said.

It was only after Dee left the table and the children were talking to each other that adult conversation got around to John again. "It sounds as if John is still spending a lot of time here," Gram said.

"It appears that way," Laci said. John had cancelled a few campaign appearances to stay in town and manage the law office so Jake could help Sara with the new baby.

"When I saw John the other day I had a chance to mention seeing Richard talking to Dee at the diner," Eric said. "He didn't seem to like my asking if something was going on between the two of them."

"I'm sure he didn't."

"In fact, he got a little testy about it. I have a feeling John has been spending more time in here since then—"

"It looks like you're right," Will said, as the bell over the diner door jingled and John walked in. He grinned when he saw them and headed over toward their table.

"Hi, everyone. How is that new baby brother doing, Meggie?" John ruffled her hair before pulling up a chair at the end of the table.

"He's good. 'Cept he cwies sometimes. But Mama feeds him, and then he's okay."

"Well, sometimes when I'm real hungry I feel like crying."

Meggie just nodded as if she understood. "Me, too."

That brought a chuckle from the adults.

Dee brought their orders out and asked John what he wanted. Laci tried hard not to notice the special smile John seemed to save only for Dee as he gave her his order. But it was hard to miss. Still, she wasn't going to say a word about it. Not after the other day.

But that smile of John's disappeared quickly when Richard Tyler came in and sat at the counter. Trying not to let John know there wasn't an adult at their table who wasn't watching for his reaction to the turn of events, Laci asked, "When are you going back out on the campaign trail, John?"

"Huh? Oh." John seemed to be having trouble pulling his gaze away from the sight of Dee waiting on Richard. "I'll probably be gone for a night or two next week."

"How's it going?" Will asked.

"Going? What?" Dee disappeared into the kitchen, and John seemed to relax as he turned his attention back on his family. "Oh, it seems to be going real well. I'm getting pretty good turnouts at all the rallies."

Conversation went on as usual while Dee was in the kitchen or waiting on tables, but when she was up near the counter they had to wait twice as long for John to answer a question or join in the conversation. All in all it was a pretty interesting evening. It was only after Richard left the diner that John seemed to settle down and finally enjoy his meal. But Laci was pretty sure he knew right where Dee was at any given moment.

Just as they were finishing up eating, his cell phone rang. John excused himself to take the call. "Something has come up at campaign headquarters, and I need to get over there for a while. I'll see you all later."

He went to the counter and paid for his meal, but it took him a little longer to leave the cash register than it had to leave their table.

Eric ordered ice cream for Sam and Meggie, but before it arrived at the table Gram yawned. She appeared a little drained, and Will suggested he ought to get her home.

"I am a little tired. I guess it's all the excitement of planning our wedding and now the new baby in the family. Not to mention all this business with John and Dee. Eric, would you mind seeing Laci and Meggie home?"

"Not at all," Eric assured her. "I'd be glad to see these two ladies home this evening."

Laci almost said they'd leave then so Eric didn't have to go out of his way. But Dee had just brought the ice cream to the children, and she saw no reason to ruin their fun. Besides, she wouldn't complain about spending a little more time with Eric and his son.

While Sam and Meggie enjoyed their treats, Laci and Eric talked quietly between themselves. "Sam was thrilled you all came to the game, Laci. I tried to tell him that with a new baby in the family you might be helping out and not make the game."

"I didn't want to miss it. I—Sam has become special to me." How did she tell Eric something about his son had her wanting to call him her own? Or that something about *him* had her wanting the very same thing.

"And you've become special to him. . .and to me. I can't thank you enough for being so good to him."

"Sam is easy to be nice to," Laci said. But her heart twisted in her chest, and she didn't know if it was from joy or pain. It thrilled her to hear she was special to Eric—but in what way? Was it only because of Sam? Oh, she hoped not. She truly hoped not.

When they took Meggie home, Jake and Sara insisted they come in for a while and visit. Baby Ben was asleep, but they got to see him for a few minutes, and then Meggie had to show Sam her toys. Before long they were putting puzzles together in the middle of the floor while the adults talked over coffee in the kitchen.

Laci and Eric told them about John's reaction to Richard Tyler, and Jake began to chuckle.

"Well, I sure don't think Dee is interested in Richard, but he certainly would like for that to change. It won't hurt John to know someone else is interested in Dee. In fact, it may be the *only* thing that spurs him to action."

"Does anyone know what is keeping them apart now?" Laci asked.

Jake shook his head. "Not really. I have an idea, but I don't know for sure. I think they are just afraid of being hurt."

"Well, no one wants to be hurt, but this has been going on for a while now. Do you think maybe they just like wondering how the other feels and hoping it's the same way they do?"

"How could anyone enjoy that, Sara? I mean maybe for a little while, but then—" Laci couldn't imagine wanting to play that kind of guessing game for long. At the moment she was finding it hard to deal with wondering in what way Eric "cared" about her.

"I don't know." Sara shook her head. "I just can't figure those two out."

"Well, I'm about ready to talk to that cousin of mine about it. He needs to know the whole town can see they belong together, and it's about time they admit it."

"Maybe that's the whole thing. Maybe they're afraid of making a commitment. Or maybe Dee is afraid of being a senator's wife."

Sara and Laci looked at each other. That could be it. Laci began to nod her head. "Maybe she is. That would be very daunting for a lot of women. Or maybe she doesn't want to give up her business to move to Washington, D.C., if he wins."

"She wouldn't have to give up the business. She'd just need to hire someone to run it for her."

"Ladies, we could *maybe* this to death," Jake said. "But the truth is, we don't know. It's that simple."

"You are absolutely right, Jake," Sara said. "But, if John ever found out how much fun we're having trying to figure the two of them out, he might take action."

"Maybe it's time we let him know," Jake said, looking over at Laci. "You're his sister. Why don't you see what you can find out?"

"Ha! Not me," Laci said. "I've already given it a shot. He's not going to tell me anything."

"You know. . .maybe it's about time we asked Gram to help out those two," Jake suggested.

"That might be your best idea yet, Jake," Eric said

It was getting late by the time they called it a night and headed toward Gram's. Sam was yawning in the backseat. "I sure had a good time tonight. I like your family, Lace."

"Thanks, Sam. I like yours, too." The words were out of her mouth before she could stop them.

"Mine's just me and Dad."

"I know." Laci hoped she hadn't given herself away—at least not yet. And then it dawned on her that way of thinking could lead to the same kind of game John and Dee were playing. Say a little, but not too much. Wonder and hope, but don't ask. Who was she to put her brother and Dee down when she certainly couldn't imagine just coming out and telling Eric she was in love with him? She prayed silently, *Dear Lord, please help my brother and Dee. Of course they're afraid of being hurt. Who isn't? But, Lord, I don't want to go on for years in limbo like they seem to be doing. And I hope they decide to let each other know how they feel very soon. Please guide me. . .and please guide them. Thank You for Your help.*

Sam was asleep when Eric pulled up at her grandmother's house. When Eric got out to walk her to the door, Laci said, "You don't need to see me to the door. Gram is still up, and Sam needs to be put to bed."

But Eric walked around the front of the truck anyway. "I'll at least watch you until you go inside then."

"Okay."

But as she climbed out of the truck Eric reached out and touched her on the arm, turning her toward him. "Laci, I'd like to thank you again for coming to Sam's game and for. . .making him feel as if he has family here in Sweet Springs."

"You don't need to thank—"

She was stopped by the touch of his fingertips on her lips.

"Yes, I do," Eric said as he bent his head toward hers. "Just say 'You're welcome,

Eric.' That's all," he whispered right before his lips touched hers.

His lips pressed gently against hers, and as he gathered her in his arms Laci found herself kissing him back. She wasn't sure who pulled away first, but it was Eric who said, "Thank you again, Laci."

"Th—" Laci began.

"Uh-uh." Eric's fingertips touched her lips once more, and he shook his head. "Just say—"

She could feel the corners of her mouth turn up. "You're welcome, Eric."

Eric smiled back and nodded before turning to climb into the truck.

Laci hurried up the walk but turned around and waved from the porch before opening the door. Eric waved back and drove off. Laci closed the door and leaned against it for a moment, taking a deep breath. Well, she was more confused than ever. And more in love than she thought she could be. Maybe his talk about families and moving closer wasn't all about her family, after all. Maybe he did care about her and want her to stay here for his and Sam's sake.

But even if Eric cared for her the way she cared for him—there was still Sam to consider. As much as she loved that little boy, could she be the kind of mother he needed—*if* Eric felt the same way about her? And that was a big if. That kiss didn't prove anything. He'd said, "Thank you." Maybe he was still thanking her for being sweet to Sam and not for the kiss. Laci rubbed her suddenly aching temple. How *did* one know?

Chapter 13

Laci found Gram in the kitchen, puttering around as best she could with the use of her cane. But she seemed to be feeling better than when she'd left the diner.

"Did you get a second wind, Gram?" Laci asked as she took a seat at the table.

"I must have. I took a shower, and that revived me. But I wanted a cup of tea before I went to bed. Would you like one?"

"No, thank you. But let me bring that cup to the table for you." She stood and brought her grandmother's tea to the table.

Gram followed and sat down across from Laci. "Did you and Eric and the kids have a good time?"

Oh, yes, she did. "We did. We visited with Jake and Sara for a while when we got to their house."

Gram nodded. "I know. Jake called me a little while ago. He said you all think I should talk to John."

After the events of the evening Laci took pity on her brother. "Oh, I don't know. He probably can't help it if he doesn't know what to do about Dee."

"Oh? Why do you think that?"

"Well, because. . .all this caring stuff can certainly get confusing at times."

"Yes, it can." Gram blew on the hot tea before taking a sip.

"I mean it's hard to admit you care about someone when you don't know how they feel about you." Laci knew she was talking as much about herself as she was her brother.

Gram looked at her closely then asked bluntly, "Laci, are you falling in love with Eric Mitchell?"

Laci was almost relieved to be able to tell someone. "I think I'm already there, Gram."

"Why, honey, that's nothing to sound so forlorn about. Eric is a wonderful Christian man and a great dad. I'm sure he'll make a terrific husband."

"Whoa, Gram. I said I thought I was in love with Eric. I'm not sure how he feels about me. And for the first time I have an inkling of how confused John might feel about Dee. But for me there's even more to consider. Even if Eric fell in love with me, there's Sam. The thought of a ready-made family scares me, Gram. I know absolutely nothing about being a mom."

"Oh, Laci, honey, you know more than you think you do. You've had a wonderful role model in your own mother. And I've watched you with Sam—and with Meggie and baby Ben for that matter. You're a loving, caring woman. The Lord has given you all the instincts you need, and He will guide you to be a wonderful mother."

"But I don't know how Eric feels about me." She knew how she hoped he felt but still. . .

"Laci, I haven't lived this long without learning a thing or two. I've watched the two of you together, and I've seen how Eric looks at you. For what it's worth, there's not a doubt in my mind he cares about you."

"Thanks, Gram. I hope you're right. But I guess only time will tell." She just prayed it wouldn't take forever to find out. And even if he did care as Gram believed, the thought of becoming an instant mom still had Laci worried. Sam was much too precious a child for her to mess him up.

"Well, you have some time. But I think it's running out for John and Dee. Someone needs to talk those two into getting their feelings out in the open. I guess that someone might be me. But I have to find out the right way to go about it. I'll take it to the Lord. He'll help me out."

Laci nodded. She had been trying to do that, too. She sure hoped He gave her some answers soon.

The next morning Laci still felt as confused as ever. The more she thought about it, the more she began to think the kiss had just been Eric's way of thanking her for her attention to Sam.

And Sam was the one she was concentrating on today. It was much easier to think about him than reflect on the kiss his dad had given her. Thinking about that just made Laci wish for a repeat.

Sam was another matter. He didn't need silly grown-up games in his life. He could be the one who was hurt by it all. And that was the last thing Laci wanted to do. She would continue to go to his games because she'd promised him she would. But other than that it might be time to distance herself from him and his dad a little bit.

But all of that was much easier said than done. When Sam came up to her that night after Wednesday evening Bible study and asked if he could sit with her when everyone gathered in the auditorium for the devotional and singing afterward, she couldn't tell him no. She felt a little uncomfortable when Eric came and sat down on the other side of her; but after the service he acted the same as always, and she tried to do the same. She didn't know whether to be relieved or disappointed he didn't act differently.

The kiss wasn't mentioned, but of course she didn't expect it to be—not with Sam listening to their conversation.

"Lace, we have a tournament this Saturday, and we play *three* games during the day. Can you come?" Sam asked.

There was no way she could turn him down. Not when she could tell from the expression on his face how important it was to him. "I'll be there."

"Oh, good. I told Larry you'd come to cheer us on."

"I sure will."

"Thanks, Lace!" Satisfied she'd be there, he ran off to play with some of the other children.

Eric turned to her. "Laci, that will make for a real long day for you. You don't have to come to all three games. It's mostly so the little ones feel part of the bigger league. You know we don't keep score and—"

"Eric, it's important to Sam to have someone to cheer for him whether scores are kept or not. I'll be there."

"Thank you. Again." Eric gave her a slow smile, and only then did Laci have a pretty good idea he hadn't forgotten the kiss anymore than she had.

"You're welcome." She smiled back, but she could feel color flood her face, just remembering the night before. Flustered and not knowing what to say next, she opted for running. "I guess I'd better go find Gram. She's probably ready to go home."

" 'Night then. See you Saturday."

"Okay. Good night." As she hurried off to find her grandmother, she tried to shore up her resolve to put a little distance between herself and the Mitchell men. She'd go to Sam's games as promised, but she had to draw the line there.

Laci found her resolve disappearing, though, when Eric called her later that night. Her pulse started racing the minute she heard his voice on the other end of the line.

"Laci?"

"Hello, Eric. What can I do for you?"

"Well, I've been wanting to thank you for being so sweet to Sam and—"

"Eric, you don't have to thank me or pay me back. I—" She certainly didn't want him feeling he owed her anything.

"I know that. But. . .I'd like to take you to Los Hacienda tomorrow evening. I don't know if you've been there yet, but it's a great Mexican restaurant between Sweet Springs and Ruidoso. It overlooks the Hondo River."

Against her better judgment Laci found she couldn't resist. "It sounds wonderful. I'd love to go."

"Great. I'll pick you up at seven."

"I'll see you then."

Laci hung up the receiver with a shaking hand. So much for her resolve to keep her distance.

"Who was that, dear?" her grandmother asked.

"It was Eric. He asked me to go to a Mexican restaurant called Los Hacienda." She expected her grandmother to comment about her and Eric, but she didn't.

All she said was, "Oh, you'll enjoy that. It's a very nice restaurant."

When Eric picked her up the next evening, Laci felt like a high school girl going out on her first date.

"You look lovely," he said when she let him in the door.

Laci's heartbeat took off, beating double-time at his compliment. She hoped so. She'd bought a new dress for the occasion. It was a teal green sundress with a matching jacket. Up here near the mountains it cooled down at night even in late summer.

"Thank you." Laci thought he looked pretty good himself, dressed in black slacks and a crisp white dress shirt.

They said good night to her grandmother, who was waiting for Will to pick her up for dinner, and then headed out the door.

"Who is watching Sam tonight?" Laci asked as Eric opened the truck door for her.

"My neighbor's teenage daughter, Amanda. Sam likes her a lot, and I know her mom is next door, so it should be all right."

"I'm sure it will be. Sam is a wonderful little boy. I'm sure he's easy to sit with."

Eric grinned at her. "Thanks for the assurance. I haven't left him much."

Laci hoped that meant he didn't date a lot. As they drove out onto Highway 380, in the close quarters of Eric's truck, she wasn't quite sure how to act. She didn't know if this was a date as she wished or just a thank-you as he'd implied. All she knew was there was no place she'd rather be than here with him.

It took only about fifteen minutes to get to the restaurant, and it more than lived up to her expectations. It was a large hacienda with a beautiful courtyard that overlooked the Hondo River. It was such a beautiful evening that Eric asked if they could be seated outside.

The waiter led them to a table with the view of the river below and handed them menus.

"Oh, this is so nice," Laci said, taking in the surroundings.

"I'm glad you like it. It's my favorite restaurant although I haven't been here in a while."

The night felt even more special at his words. The waiter brought them water and some chips and queso dip while they looked over the menu. Eric recommended the Santa Fe, a combination plate of enchiladas, chile rellenos, and a taco with beans and rice.

"I'm not sure I can eat all of that," Laci said.

"You don't have to. But it's a way to try some of the best in New Mexico."

"It does sound good." She smiled over at him. "I'll have it then."

Once the waiter took their order they were left alone, and it felt romantic to be watching the sunset with Eric. The sky was gorgeous with the shades of mauve, orange, pink, and yellow and a hint of blue green. "I never fail to be awed by the sunsets out here."

"No, neither do I," Eric said.

Laci was a little surprised at how easily their conversation flowed as they waited for their food. They talked about her family and how close it was, about Dee and John and John's chances of being elected in the fall.

"I think he's going to be the next United States Senator from New Mexico," Eric said.

"I certainly hope so."

"He's got my vote, that's for sure. He'll do his best for the state and keep his integrity."

"He will do that." Laci had every confidence in her brother.

The waiter brought their dinners, and the conversation turned to Sweet Springs and New Mexico and how varied its scenery was.

"I'm glad you came with me tonight, Laci. I've wanted to show you this place for a while now. I love it here."

"It is truly a beautiful restaurant."

Eric nodded. "It is, but that's not what I'm talking about. Not the restaurant, but the area. I've been thinking of building a home up here."

"Really? Where would you put it?"

Eric stood. "Come here. I'll show you."

They walked a little closer to the four-foot wall around the open part of the courtyard, and she had to stand near Eric to see where he was pointing. "Over there, across the river. I'd like to buy a piece of property like that and build a hacienda-style home on it."

It was a gorgeous setting, with the sun disappearing in the west and lights on in the distance where daylight turned to twilight in the east.

"Oh, that would be a beautiful place for a home." Laci turned to find Eric's gaze on her, and the expression in his eyes had her heart doing funny little flutters. For a minute she thought he might kiss her, and she truly wished he would. Then the waiter seated a couple at a nearby table, and the moment was lost.

"Maybe one day I'll build up here," Eric said as he led her back to the table.

As she thought of a home in that setting, Laci longed for more than returning to live in this part of the country. But she pushed it to the back of her mind as Eric pulled her chair out for her. "I can see how you would want to live here. And it's not so far away that you couldn't still work in Sweet Springs."

"That's true." He took his seat across from her. "I could work in Ruidoso, too. But for now I'll stay where I am."

Laci nodded. "Sweet Springs is a great place to live and raise a child."

"It is," Eric said, looking thoughtful.

The waiter came and lit the candle on their table. They continued to talk as they watched the evening darken and the sky fill with stars. The more they talked, the more they found they had in common. They both loved old movies and, of course, Mexican food. But they also enjoyed reading and had several books by the same authors. They liked the outdoors, and both loved to ski.

When Eric told her of his worries about raising Sam alone, Laci was more than a little pleased he felt he could confide in her.

"I never realized how much a child needed both parents until I was the only one Sam had left," he said. "After Joni died, well, it took awhile for me to get over that and realize I had to be strong for Sam's sake. I was all he had. Sometimes I feel pretty overwhelmed, though. There are days when I don't have a clue what I'm doing or if I'm doing it right."

"You've done an excellent job of raising Sam, Eric. It can't have been easy."

He shook his head. "No, it hasn't been. But the Lord blessed me with a good little boy. And He helps me every step of the way."

Her feelings for Eric soared at seeing his strong faith in the Lord. "You two are going to be fine."

"Yes, we will. And I'm ready to move on. Sam needs a mother, and I am hoping one day—"

"Well, look who's here," a familiar voice said. "We didn't see you two come in."

They looked up to see Luke and Rae standing there grinning at them. Eric invited the couple to join them, and Laci didn't know whether to be upset or relieved her cousin had interrupted their conversation. Part of her wanted to hear the rest of what Eric was going to say—another part of her was almost afraid to find out what it was.

"Thanks, but we're on our way out," Rae said. "We're going to the movies when we get back to Sweet Springs. We just wanted to stop by and say hello."

Luke and Rae left, and somehow the conversation never returned to where it had been. Was Eric going to say he was ready to find a wife? Even if he was, that "one day" sounded as if he hadn't found a prospect yet, which would mean this was the thank-you dinner Laci hadn't wanted—instead of the date she'd wished for. She sighed inwardly as Eric paid the bill and they headed outside to his truck. She'd been right yesterday. She would *have* to distance herself from the Mitchell men.

Eric didn't know what happened, but after Luke and Rae came to the table things seemed to change. The evening had been perfect until then, and he'd been on the verge of telling Laci one day he hoped she'd care about him the way he cared about her. But after the interruption he didn't know how to bring it up again.

Laci seemed a little quiet on the way back to Sweet Springs, leaving him to wonder what had changed between them. When they arrived back at her grandmother's home, he walked her to the door, hoping to recapture some of the earlier mood.

"Thank you for going with me," he said, looking into her eyes.

"Thank you for asking me. I had a very nice time," Laci said with a smile.

"I'm glad. So did I." Eric wanted to kiss her good night. And if the mood from the restaurant had still been there, he wouldn't have hesitated. But now. . .

"Good night," Laci said, opening the door and slipping inside to look at him through the screen door.

Eric sighed. He'd thought too long, and his chance was gone.

"Good night, Laci." He smiled and gave her a little salute. He headed for his truck determined to act more quickly the next time. And then he prayed there would be a next time.

Laci's plans to distance herself from Sam and Eric seemed to be disintegrating before her eyes. The love and pride she felt for the little boy grew each time he looked up into the stands to see her cheering for him after he'd made a home run on Saturday.

After Sam's team won its third game that day, she and the part of her family that had been able to make it to the game were telling him and Eric good-bye. It was then Laci knew she couldn't turn her back on Sam.

He threw his arms around her and said, "Thanks for coming, Lace." And then out of nowhere he added, "I love you."

Those three little words shot straight into Laci's heart, and she suddenly felt she knew what the Lord wanted her to do. She hugged him back and said, "I love you, too, Sam."

With those words Laci felt the decision to move back to Sweet Springs had been made for her. No matter how things turned out between her and Eric, she was moving back home. If Eric didn't feel the same about her as she did him, she'd just have to trust the Lord to help her handle her feelings for him and deal with the pain. But she wasn't going to turn her back on Sam. She was certain the Lord didn't want her to. And neither did she. She was going to be there for Eric's child as long as he needed her to be.

Chapter 14

Laci called Myra as soon as she got home from the ball field that afternoon and told her of her decision. She realized the Lord would be working in Myra's life as He was in her own. So she left the decision up to Myra as to whether she would buy out her interest in Dallas or just manage it for her.

"I was hoping you would call, Laci. And I'm not surprised at all about what you've decided. If I didn't already live around them, I'd have made the same decision to be closer to family—as my sweet husband has pointed out to me. And we've talked things over. I'd like to buy out your interest in this shop if that's the way you're leaning. And I'm very willing to change the name so you can keep Little Touches as yours."

Laci breathed a sigh of relief. That was the decision she was hoping for. She didn't want to start a chain of shops. She just wanted one, right here in her hometown. "That is wonderful news, Myra. I'll get in touch with Jared Morrison, the lawyer who helped me get the shop up and running, and let him handle the sale for us, if that's all right with you."

"It's fine."

"Okay then. I'll contact him next week and get back to you. I'll have to come back to sign the papers and move things out of my apartment, so I'm comforted we'll be seeing each other. But just know I wish you the very best, Myra."

"You know I wish the same for you, Laci. I'll talk to you soon."

Laci hung up the telephone feeling as if one chapter of her life had ended and another begun. She didn't know what the future held for her. All she knew was she would try to place it in the Lord's hands.

"Laci? Can you come downstairs, dear?" Gram called from below.

"I'll be right there." Laci felt like a kid taking the stairs two at a time.

"What can I do for you, Gram?" she asked, finding her at the kitchen table with a tablet and pen in hand.

"I've decided to have a Sunday night supper tomorrow night if you'll help, Laci," Gram said. "I know it's short notice, but I've been missing them a lot. And, besides, I've figured out that may be the way to get John and Dee together before he goes out on the campaign trail again."

"Oh? How do you think you'll manage that with everyone around?"

"Don't you worry about it." Gram grinned. "I'm not telling because I don't want anyone giving away my plans. And this isn't going to be my normal Sunday night supper for the whole church. Since the doctor hasn't released me to do things as usual, it'll be more like a trial run before the real thing. This time it's just going to be the family and David and Gina and a few others from church."

"Okay. That's probably best since you still need your cane and tire a little easier. But I'll do most of it, Gram. You only need to tell me what you want me to do."

"That's what I was hoping you'd say." Gram handed Laci a piece of paper. "I've sent Will to the store for the biggest ham he can find. If you'll help me line up the family to bring food and call the others on this list, we'll see what happens."

"What about John and Dee? Are you sure you can get them both here?"

"I've already made a point of asking Dee to be here, and she said she wouldn't miss it. And John thinks it's partly a send-off for his next round of campaigning so he'll be here."

By ten that night everyone was invited, and the food was planned. Laci was going to put the huge ham Will had brought from the grocery in the oven the next morning and bake several cakes after they returned home from church. Everyone else would bring different sides and a few more desserts.

Laci could barely wait until the next day to see what Gram had up her sleeve. Plus, Eric and Sam were on the list, and she was looking forward to seeing them somewhere besides church, the diner, or the ball field. Only when she was getting ready for bed that night did she realize she hadn't told anyone her news about staying here. But that was okay. They'd find out soon enough.

Eric couldn't help but notice something was different about Laci the next day at church. When Sam hurried up to her, she seemed more open and less guarded with him, and she looked. . .more relaxed and at ease than he'd ever seen her.

"Hi, Lace! Can I sit with you today? Dad said we're coming over to your house for supper after church tonight."

"Yes, you are! It's going to be fun." Laci hugged him. "And I'd love for you to sit with me."

His son seemed to have a way with Laci that Eric wished he could emulate. But her openness with his son didn't seem to carry over to him, and Eric wasn't quite sure how to deal with it.

At first he'd been afraid he might have damaged their relationship by kissing her the night he'd taken her home from Jake and Sara's. But then she'd agreed to go to Los Hacienda with him on Friday, and things had seemed to be going well for a while. But after Luke and Rae had stopped by their table something seemed to change.

Since then he'd been doing a lot of thinking and had come to the conclusion he and Laci weren't that much different from John and Dee. Neither one knew how the other felt except that they *cared*. But did she care about him just because he was Sam's dad? Or did she care about him as a man? And had he let her know he was in love with her? No.

Well, the next time he kissed her he wanted Laci to know without a doubt that he was telling her he loved her. But how would he ever get to that point? He didn't know. When the service was over he didn't even have a chance to start up a conversation.

"I have to hurry home to help Gram set up for tonight, but I'll see you both later, okay?" Laci said, but it was Sam she was smiling at and not Eric.

"We'll be there," Eric answered, wishing she would look at him. But she hurried off with a wave and left Eric more determined than ever to find a way to talk to her. Soon.

"I can't wait until tonight, Dad," Sam said.

"Neither can I, son. Neither can I."

~

Laci was too busy that afternoon to be nervous about seeing Eric again that night. Knowing he would be there, however, added an extra dollop of anticipation for the evening. Not that she didn't have enough already, wondering what Gram had up her sleeve concerning Dee and John.

By the time everyone started arriving at Gram's after church that evening, the whole family seemed to know something was up. Gram had evidently told Jake and Sara she might talk to John tonight, and Jake told Luke and Rae, who in turn told Aunt Nora and Michael. Laci's parents had been the last to know.

"Mom, I hope you know what you're doing," Laci's mom said when she brought her potato casserole into the kitchen through the back door. "All this could backfire and send Dee and John further apart."

"Well, Lydia, someone has to do something. And in my *condition* he's not likely to react quite as fiercely as he might with any of the rest of you." Gram chuckled. "At least I hope not."

Laci's mother shook her head. "Well, he will take interference from you easier than he will from Ben or me. But you know how private John is."

"I do. Of all my grandchildren he's the one who keeps things to himself the most. But it'll be all right, Lydia. And you don't know what I have planned anyway. Just try not to worry, okay?"

"I'll try not to." She sighed and took her dishes through to the dining room to set them on the table.

Rae came back into the kitchen from depositing her green-bean casserole and a big dish of creamed corn on the dining room table. "Gram, you might want to talk to them right here in this kitchen. It's a special one, and it's the very first place Luke kissed me."

"It is?" Laci asked.

"Yes. I'll never forget that night," Rae said, a dreamy expression on her face.

"What night?" Sara asked as she entered the kitchen with baby Ben in her arms.

"The night Luke kissed me right here in Gram's kitchen. I love this room."

Sara smiled. "I know what you mean. It's where I saw Jake for the first time when he moved back to Sweet Springs."

"I didn't know my kitchen held such romantic memories for the two of you," Gram said with a chuckle.

Neither did Laci. But after hearing Sara and Rae's stories she found herself wishing she could get Eric to come that way.

Dee showed up, and Laci could tell they were trying to act normal around her so as not to make her suspicious. But they didn't pull it off.

"You all seem. . .wound up tonight," she said. "What's up?"

"I think we're all happy to be having a Sunday night supper again," Laci's mother said. "We've missed it."

Well, that was certainly a true statement, Laci thought, even if it did avoid Dee's question. Sara and Rae quickly left the room, saying they would see if everyone was there yet.

"Well, I can tell you I'm excited," Gram said. "I haven't—"

"The girls said you wanted a head count, Ellie," Aunt Nora said, as she swept into the room. "John just drove up, and David and Gina are right behind him. Far as I can tell, everyone you invited is here."

"Good," Gram said, taking off her apron and leading the others to the dining room. "I'll have David say a blessing, and we can get started."

Gram hadn't given anyone an idea of how she planned to get John and Dee together, and Laci was almost too nervous to eat, waiting to see. She spotted Gram whispering to Will, and he grinned and nodded his head.

Then David began his prayer, and Laci and the others bowed their heads.

"Dear Lord, we thank You for this family and these friends who have gathered together tonight. We thank You that Ellie has recuperated enough to feel up to having us all here once more. We ask You to bless this food for the nourishment of our bodies, and we thank You above all for Your plan for our salvation through Your Son and our Savior, Jesus Christ. It is in His name I pray, amen."

A line formed on both sides of the table, and everyone began helping themselves. Laci found Eric and Sam and offered to help Sam fix his plate. Once he was settled beside Meggie on the bottom step of the staircase and began to eat, Laci and Eric went back to the line and ended up behind John. Laci figured that whatever Gram had planned it wouldn't happen until after they'd eaten.

But then she spotted Aunt Nora saying something to Dee, and Dee nodded and disappeared into the kitchen. A second later Gram motioned for John, and he left the line to see what she wanted. Then *he* disappeared into the kitchen. After a moment Will came out and handed Gram what looked like a key. She grinned, and after a second or two she went back into the kitchen.

It was no more than a minute before everyone heard a banging of some kind coming from the kitchen. And then a loud "Somebody come and unlock this door!"

"That's John," she said to Eric. "I'd know that yell anywhere. Let's find out what Gram's done."

When she and Eric entered the kitchen Gram was standing outside her pantry door grinning, and John was shouting at the top of his lungs, "We're locked in! Someone let us out!"

He banged on the door again while more family members made their way into the kitchen. Before long, even Meggie and Sam had come to see what was going on.

"John, I'm here, and I have the key!" Gram yelled over the noise.

"Oh, good," John said. "Somehow Dee and I got locked in."

"Yes, well, you're going to stay there for a while, too."

"I thought you said you had the key, Gram."

"I do. But I'm not unlocking that door until you and Dee do some talking. This whole family—not to mention half the town—thinks it's about time you two tell each other what we've known for years—that you love each other!"

"Oh, Gram, I can't believe you did this. It's not necessary. Unlock the door, please."

Laci was surprised John didn't sound angry—in fact, it sounded like laughter in his voice.

"Not until you two talk, and you haven't had time to do that yet."

"We've already done all of that, Gram." John chuckled then. "More times than you can imagine."

"We really have, Ellie." Dee's voice was heard through the door.

Gram looked back at the small crowd in the kitchen and raised her eyebrow. "What do you mean?"

"If you unlock this door and let us out, we'll tell you."

Gram looked at the other family members. "What do you think? Should I let them out?"

"Well, I certainly want to hear what they have to say," Laci's mom said.

"I do, too," Jake added. "Go ahead and let them out, Gram."

"Is the whole family in the kitchen, Gram?" John asked.

Gram looked around the room. "Well, yes. Most of them anyway."

"This is without a doubt the most meddling, nosy family a man could have!" John shouted. A second or two passed in silence. "But I guess we need to level with you if we're to have any peace. Please unlock the door, Gram."

"Oh, all right," Gram said, taking the key and unlocking the door.

John threw the door open and led Dee out while the group in the kitchen clapped.

Dee turned a delicate shade of pink, and John just stood there shaking his head. He handed Gram a pack of napkins, and Dee handed her some plastic cups.

"I think these are what you sent us in there for," John said.

Gram took the items and handed them to Will. "Thank you, but I don't need them after all."

"That comes as no surprise to me," John said a bit sarcastically, but he did at least have a smile on his face.

"All right," Gram said. "You've been released. Now it's time to let us in on whatever it is you and Dee have been up to."

"Us! Gram, you're the one—"

Dee placed her hand on John's arm and patted it. "John, you told your grandmother we'd level with them. And quite frankly it will be a relief to get this all out in the open. Keeping things from them has been more of a strain than I thought it would be. Please."

Laci's brother looked at Dee and then pulled her into the crook of his arm. "All right." He cleared his throat and looked out at his family. "This goes back a ways. Some of you know Dee and I dated for a while in high school, but before I went off to college Dee broke up with me, saying she didn't want me to feel tied down while I was there. I tried to convince her I didn't want to date anyone else, but she said I would once I got there."

John looked at Dee again. "But she didn't tell me the whole story. What I didn't know, until years later, was that because she couldn't afford to go to college at the time she somehow had the notion I wouldn't feel the same about her after I'd been around all those college girls. When she wouldn't date me when I came home, I thought she didn't care."

"But I did," Dee said. "I never stopped caring."

John dropped a kiss on the top of her head. "Thank the good Lord for that. But we drifted away from each other. To make a long story short—and I'm not about to tell you *all* the details—when Dee took over ownership of the diner after her mom moved away, we started seeing more of each other. Finally, in the last year—about the time Luke and Rae got together—we realized we still cared deeply about each other. But, with me running for senator and the circus that can be, I was afraid the media would drive Dee away with all their questioning."

A murmur of understanding passed around the room.

"And I didn't want her to think I was asking her to marry me just to help my chances of winning the election, as many have suggested—some even in this family. So we decided to put off announcing our plans to marry until after the election—"

A collective cheer interrupted John at his admission that they planned to get married. He just grinned and shook his head. Once things quieted down, he continued. "You've made it extremely hard on us to keep our feelings a secret because we've known you wanted us to get together for a while now. And I've wanted to shout to the rooftops that Dee and I are engaged. Not to mention how badly I've wanted to tell old Richard to quit flirting with my girl and get out of the diner—especially since some of you have been *so* willing to let me know what he was up to." He shot Jake and Luke and even Eric a look that spoke volumes. "But now you are all in on our secret, and we're expecting you to help us keep it one."

Laci was the first to speak as she stepped over to hug him and Dee. "You big lug. Of course we'll keep it a secret."

Her dad and mom congratulated the couple next, and then the rest of the family did. "I can't think of anyone I'd want for a daughter-in-law more than you, Dee. My son is a lucky man," Laci's mother said as she hugged Dee.

Both tears and laughter filled the room. Finally this couple the whole family had hoped would get together had already found their way there. . .and on their own.

"Ellie, do you think I could borrow some of those bridal magazines after you're through?" Dee asked.

"Of course you can. What fun! We can plan our weddings together! You know, Nora and Rae had a double wedding. This is just an idea I'm throwing out, but if you and John want to, Will and I would be more than glad to share our day with you—whatever day you'd like."

"Well, I'm going to leave the four of you to figure that one out," Jake said. "Now that this has had a happy ending I'm going to eat. I'm starved."

The family filed out of the kitchen, talking excitedly about how happy they were. Laci tried to figure out why she had such an ache in her heart when she was so thrilled for her brother and Dee.

But when she glanced at Eric and saw his gaze on her, she knew. Unlike John and Dee, who'd fooled them all and known where they were headed for a good while now, her love life was one great big question mark.

Later, when her mother asked if she could make it home for both weddings, Laci realized she still hadn't let them know her plans.

"It won't matter, Mom. I'll be here for both, no matter how or when they decide to have them."

"You will?" her mother asked, a hopeful look in her eyes.

Laci nodded. "Yes, I'm moving back. Myra is going to buy out my interest in Dallas, and I'm going into business right here in Sweet Springs. But I don't want to take away any excitement from Dee and John's news tonight. I'll tell the rest of the family later."

But she didn't have to. Sam had been standing behind her, evidently waiting to ask her to help him get a piece of chocolate cake, and had heard every word. He ran toward his dad, yelling, "Dad! Dad! Lace is moving back! She's gonna stay in Sweet Springs!"

Chapter 15

Eric's gaze met Laci's from across the room. She was staying. *Thank You, Lord.* He took a step toward her, but her family surrounded her. So he shared the joy with his son instead.

"Isn't that great news, Dad?"

"It sure is, Sam." Eric picked up his son and hugged him close. He didn't know which of them was happier at that moment, Sam or him. But Eric's heart seemed to beat a tune to the thought that went over and over in his mind. *Laci is staying. Laci is staying.*

And he was going to have a chance to tell her he loved her. If she didn't return his feelings, he'd just trust in the Lord to help him deal with it. With John and Dee's admission that they'd finally gotten together after years of loving each other, Eric was determined he wasn't waiting that long to let Laci know how deeply he loved her. So many years those two had wasted when they could have been together.

He wouldn't let that happen to him and Laci. Besides he had Sam to consider, too. His son loved Laci. If the two grown-ups he looked up to couldn't figure out how they felt and let each other know, what kind of example was that for Sam?

Tonight was not the time. But soon, very soon, he and Laci would have to talk.

~

But the next few weeks didn't provide the opportunity he'd hoped for. Oh, Laci came to Sam's last few T-ball games, but she always had to hurry off afterward to run some errand in connection with wedding or shower plans.

The few times he saw her at the diner, she seemed to be just leaving. Or she was only there to pick up Dee so they could go to Roswell or Ruidoso to look for something to do with the weddings.

Eric kept telling himself he didn't need to rush since Laci wouldn't be going back to Dallas to live, but then he would think of all the years that had passed for John and Dee. He couldn't let that be the case with him and Laci. At the moment, though, he had no choice but to bide his time. She was moving back. He'd have his chance.

Even Sam was moping around the house, and Eric knew it was because he missed seeing Laci, too. Finally, early one evening the week after Sam's T-ball games had ended, he called Laci at her grandmother's only to find she was over at Jake and Sara's.

On the pretense of taking Sam to see Meggie and the new baby, Eric decided to pay Jake and Sara—and Laci, he hoped—a visit. But when he arrived he learned she'd just left.

The frustration must have shown on his face because Sara and Jake insisted he stay for supper. He gratefully accepted the invitation. But it wasn't until afterward, while Meggie and Sam were playing in the den, that he confided his true feelings to his two good friends over a cup of coffee. Weeks ago he'd told Jake he was interested, so it didn't come as a surprise to either of them that he'd fallen in love with Laci.

"This family can spot the lovelorn a mile away, Eric, and you've had that look," Jake said with a chuckle. "Sara and I had a feeling you were a goner and have been thinking about ways to get you two together for weeks."

"Well, I hope you have better luck than I have. I can't seem to get two minutes alone with Laci lately. In fact, I'm beginning to wonder if she's avoiding me."

"She could be," Sara said. "But I don't think it's because she doesn't care. I think she's fallen in love with you, too."

"What makes you say that?"

"As Jake says, this family has a knack for that kind of thing." Sara smiled. "And we share our concerns about each other with each other."

"Then what's the problem? Why is she avoiding me?"

"Well. . .I'm pretty certain she loves you and Sam. But I think she's afraid of becoming an instant mom—that she'll mess up somehow. She loves Sam, but I think she's worried she won't be what he needs as a mother. . .and that would mean she wouldn't be what you need in a wife."

"Oh, that's—crazy. We need *her*." But Eric's heart melted. He knew full well the fears and doubts he had when Sam was born and even more after his wife passed away. It wasn't as if they gave out manuals when a child was born. He'd never had any experience in how to be a dad either, but with the Lord's help he felt as if he'd become a fairly good one. He had no doubt about the kind of mom Laci would be to Sam. None at all. For the first time in days Eric began to hope.

"Well, you know as a group this family is good about getting people together. Do you want us to have Gram lock the two of you in her pantry?" Jake asked, smiling.

"No, but if I don't run into her on my own soon, I may change my mind."

"Just let us know. We can swing into action at a moment's notice." Sara chuckled.

"I'll keep that in mind." And he would. It felt good to think he had at least part of Laci's family on his side.

After John and Dee decided they'd share Gram and Will's wedding day, the next few weeks were among the busiest Laci could remember. She was thankful, though, that the wedding and shower plans took up so many hours of the day. It gave her less time to dwell on Eric and wonder if she'd ever know how he felt about her.

Sam had only a few more games to play, and she managed to make every one. But then she became sad when the twice-weekly chances to spend time with him and his dad disappeared. With John's campaign in full swing and making plans for the weddings, her family hadn't gotten together since Gram's Sunday night supper. Laci was finding that seeing Eric and Sam only for a little while on Sundays or Wednesdays at church wasn't enough.

They seemed to be going in opposite directions each time they saw one another anywhere else. She told herself that if Eric wanted to see her he'd pick up the phone and call or come by. But then she was rarely at home and hadn't encouraged him. She had no doubts, though, about how she felt about him. Absence from him and Sam was definitely making her heart grow fonder.

She continued to pray for guidance in what to do about her feelings for the two Mitchell men and figured the Lord was giving her a lesson in patience. He'd let her know in His time.

Meanwhile she was growing closer to her family. They had all promised to hold John and Dee's engagement a secret and had kept their word. The wedding date had been set for the weekend after the election in November. That would give both couples a chance to enjoy a wedding trip and return home in time to celebrate Thanksgiving with the family.

Laci was glad when Dee promoted Annie to assistant manager so Dee would have free time from the diner to plan her wedding. Deciding to have a double wedding with Gram and Will gave her the opportunity to plan her own without raising suspicions about her and John.

The trips Laci and Dee made to Roswell and Ruidoso looking for dresses enabled Dee to try them on "just for fun." When she found the one she wanted, she'd know what size to order and have it shipped to her instead of bringing it home with her.

Laci was thankful for the busyness during each day, but then at night she wondered what Eric and Sam had done that day. Did they go to the diner for supper or eat at home? Did either one of them miss her half as much as she missed them? She didn't think it was possible. Then she'd take her confusion, doubts, and hopes to the Lord in prayer, trusting that someday she'd have the answers she sought.

Eric was beginning to think he would have to ask Jake and Sara for help if he was ever going to tell Laci how he felt. He kept missing her everywhere he went. But he worried he wouldn't know how to tell her how much he loved her and assure her she was the woman he and Sam both wanted and needed.

Then one day a few weeks before the start of school Sam came in from playing. He had missed the cut-off date for turning six since his birthday wasn't until

November, so he'd be starting kindergarten this year instead of first grade. And school and its activities were clearly on his mind.

"Dad, who's gonna make cupcakes for me when I need to take them for a party this year?"

"Well, son, I guess I can manage it. I made a cake once."

"It was kind of burnt, Dad."

He remembered it well. "Okay, how about we buy some from the bakery?"

"Do you think Lace might make them for me? She'll be living here then."

"Well, she probably would, son, but—"

"Dad." Sam let out a big sigh. "Why don't you just ask Lace to marry us? You love her, don't you?"

"Yes, son, I do. It's just not that easy."

"Why not?"

"Well. . ." *Why not?* "Sam, you just gave me an idea. Hang on." He punched in Jake's number. "I need that favor. Can you find out where Laci is going to be for the next thirty minutes?"

Jake chuckled. "I'll do my best."

"Okay. Call me back on my cell phone."

"Will do."

"Come on, son. Get in the truck." Eric grabbed his keys from the counter and led the way outside to his pickup.

"Where are we goin', Dad?" Sam asked as he climbed in and buckled up.

"To find Laci."

Laci and her grandmother were in the kitchen poring over recipes, trying to decide on the best chocolate cake recipe for the groom's cake for Will. John didn't like chocolate so they'd already decided his would be lemon.

"Why don't we make both of these, Gram, and let Will decide which one he likes better? I'm sure it's going to be your chewy chocolate one, though."

"That's probably the best idea. I'm sure Will won't mind the decision-making process one bit."

"No, I don't think so, either." Laci chuckled, knowing how much Will loved cake.

The phone rang, and Gram went to answer it while Laci was in the pantry gathering the ingredients they'd need. She heard a knock on the back door. "I'll get the door, Gram."

She deposited a box of cocoa, two cake pans, and cooking oil on the counter by the canisters and went to open the door.

Her heart did a nosedive into her stomach when she saw Eric standing there.

"Hi, Eric. Where's Sam? Is something wrong?"

"No. Well, at least I don't think so. Sam just needs to talk to you. Says he needs you. He's in the truck out front."

"Why didn't you bring him in?" Laci asked as she hurried around the corner of the house.

"He wanted me to get you." Eric followed at a slower pace.

True enough, Sam was in the truck. Laci opened the door and asked, "What is it, Sam? What do you need, honey?"

"Oh, Lace! I've been missin' you! I need you to be my mom. *Please* say you'll marry Dad!"

"But I—"

"*Please* say yes, Laci," Eric said from behind her.

Laci looked at Eric and then at Sam. "What? I—"

Eric grinned. "I figured Sam might have a better chance of convincing you to marry me than I would." He turned her to face him and took her hands in his. His gaze caught hers, and she couldn't look away. "I love you, Laci Tanner. We love you. With all of our hearts. And we want nothing more than for you to marry me and become my wife and Sam's mom. . .if you'll have the two of us."

"Oh, Eric. I love you both so much. But I know nothing about being a mother, and I—"

Eric pulled her into his arms and claimed her lips with his, silencing her words. He kissed her fully then, after a long moment, stepped back. "Please just say, 'I'll marry you, Eric.' That's all we want to hear."

Before she could say anything he kissed her again. She knew now. He loved her.

Laci pulled back then. She gazed into Eric's eyes, her lips turning up into a smile. "Yes, I'll marry you, Eric."

"Woo-hoo!" Sam yelled. "Lace is gonna marry us and be my mom!"

Epilogue

Mid-November

If Laci thought she was busy before, she found the pace nearly impossible to keep up with after she and Eric announced their engagement. Gram and Will and John and Dee had quickly insisted they share their wedding day with them.

"I've never seen a triple wedding before, but just think how much our guests will love us if they get three weddings out of one outfit," Gram had said, chuckling. "We'll have all our relatives and friends in one spot. We might as well kill three birds with one stone."

It made sense to everyone. The doctor released Gram to resume her normal activities without a cane, and from then on there was a whirlwind of activity in and out of Sweet Springs. After all their trips to Roswell and Ruidoso, Laci and the other women found the wedding outfits they wanted while accompanying Laci to Dallas to sign the papers to her business and pack up her apartment.

Their three dresses were beautiful. Gram's was a gorgeous silver taffeta gown that brought out her silver curls. Dee's gown was an ivory charmeuse slip dress with a lace overlay, and Laci chose a champagne-colored lace and organza gown with a dropped waist. Meggie's dress was ivory organza with tiny rosebuds scattered randomly around the skirt.

They'd had parties to address and stamp invitations and one surprise shower after another. Gram was especially touched by the shower the Teddy Bear Brigade helped with. She'd thought she was planning one for Dee and Laci but found hers had been in the works much longer.

True to everyone's expectations, John was elected the new United States Senator from New Mexico, and he and Dee would be taking up residence in Washington, D.C., in the coming year.

Laci still couldn't believe their wedding day had finally arrived. Gram and Will would go first, then John and Dee, with Laci and Eric's wedding last. They would all walk down the aisle, with Meggie as flower girl and Sam as ring bearer leading the way. Then David, the minister who had married the rest of the family, would perform each ceremony. He'd laughingly accused them of trying to get a group rate.

Laci blinked back tears as she watched her sweet grandmother and Will, and then her brother and Dee, become man and wife. Then finally it was time for her and Eric.

Her heart felt as if it would burst with love while she and Eric said their vows in front of their loved ones. As they shared their first kiss as a married couple, she felt a tug on her wedding gown. Laci looked down to see Sam grinning up at her and his dad. "Now you really are my mom," he said.

"Yes, I really am," Laci assured him.

Eric reached down and lifted Sam up between the two of them, and they turned to the room full of family and friends. Then David announced, "I now present to you, Mr. and Mrs. Eric Mitchell—and son."

Amid laughter and applause Laci and Eric each kissed Sam on the cheek and then, behind his back, shared one more kiss of their very own. Her heart overflowing with love, Laci thanked the Lord for the family He had given her in birth—and now for the family He had given her in marriage.